'*Incidents in the Life of Ma[rkus Paul]* [shows] Richards at the top of his g[ame] [...] the weight and significan[ce] [...] anchored by a narrative [...] and detached, rooted in a st[...] . . . It is not a subtle approa[ch] [...] one, and tremendously effective. The novel sparks with an immediacy and power that is rare to find in contemporary fiction: these are old questions and timeless concerns given face and voice by one of Canada's finest writers.'
— Robert J. Wiersema, *Victoria Times-Colonist*

'David Adams Richards' 14th novel brilliantly scours the conscience of a community . . . [He] moves deftly between the multiple voices and points of view . . . [and] never fails to capture the right details to a scene. . . . That Richards can consistently bring such potentially mawkish figures to vivid life is just one reason to keep reading him.'
— *Quill & Quire* (starred review)

'In a stark, stunning and profound new novel, New Brunswick's David Adams Richards (*Mercy Among the Children, Nights Below Station Street*) exposes Canada's rawest nerve . . . the construction of this novel is brilliantly conceived, and flawlessly executed. This is Richards at the height of his powers, which is very high indeed. The word masterpiece is not too strong.'
— *National Post* (Donna Bailey Nurse)

'In his masterful new novel, David Adams Richards shows why it matters who explains the complicated relationships between whites and Natives in his beloved Miramichi. . . . *Incidents in the Life of Markus Paul* is remarkable for a tightly woven, multi-layered plot and the minute detailing of a way of life that is disappearing in New Brunswick.'
— *National Post* (John Racovali)

'*Incidents in the Life of Markus Paul* is a solid offering with timely insight from one of Canada's most acclaimed storytellers.'

'. . . the searing emotion and stirring probity we have come to expect of an author fighting to stave off anachronism's claim to right and wrong, good and evil . . . the characters themselves, who could have been frozen into moral archetypes . . . attain a welcome level of complexity. . . . Richards's larger picture includes a moral lesson at once topical and timeless.'

'Delving into race, politics, corruption, police work, media and the power of public opinion, the novel is a superb rendering of our propensity to confuse charisma with wisdom and judgment with justice.'

'David Adams Richards' latest thrills with small-town suspense and mystery. . . . *Incidents in the Life of Markus Paul* is a page-turning thriller delivered by Richards in his finest form yet. The who, why and hows surrounding Hector's death, and the deaths that follow, pile up like pulp logs that drop on the reader's head in a series of stunning surprises.'

David Adams Richards is a Canadian author located in New Brunswick. His recent novel, *The Lost Highway*, was shortlisted for the Governor General's Literary Award for Fiction, and longlisted for the Scotiabank Giller Prize. *The Friends of Meager Fortune* won the Commonwealth Writers' Prize for Best Book, while *Mercy Among the Children*, also a novel, won the 2000 Giller Prize and was shortlisted for the Governor General's Literary Award and the Trillium Book Award. Richards is also the author of the celebrated Miramichi Trilogy (*Nights Below Station Street*, winner of the Governor General's Literary Award; *Evening Snow Will Bring Such Peace*, winner of the Canadian Authors Association Award; and *For Those Who Hunt the Wounded Down*), as well as the bestselling nonfiction book, *God Is*.

Incidents in the Life of

MARKUS PAUL

David Adams Richards

SANDSTONEPRESS
HIGHLAND | SCOTLAND

First published in Great Britain in 2012 by
Sandstone Press Ltd
PO Box 5725
One High Street
Dingwall
Ross-shire
IV15 9WJ
Scotland.

www.sandstonepress.com

First published by Doubleday, Canada, 2011
www.randomhouse.ca

The publisher acknowledges subsidy from Creative Scotland
towards publication of this volume.

ISBN: 978-1-905207-96-1
ISBN e: 978-1-905207-97-8

Original cover design adapted by Raspberryhmac, Edinburgh.
Typeset by Iolaire Typesetting, Newtonmore.
Printed and bound by TOTEM, Poland

For you, once my friend, long ago.

1985

I asked for quarter
In contempt –
You said it was I who should repent
Someday you all will see
The quarter I asked
Was not for me

– Poem written on scribbler paper,
found by Amos Paul in the ruins of
Roger Savage's house, October 17, 1985

The day Hector Penniac died in the fourth hold of the cargo ship *Lutheran* he woke at 6:20 in the morning. It would be a fine hot June day. He could hear the bay from his window – it was just starting to make high tide – and far offshore he could see lobster boats moving out to their traps.

Hector hadn't worked a hold before. He had bought new work boots and new work gloves, and a new work shirt that he had laid out on his chair the night before, and he had checked his jeans pocket ten times for his union card, five times last night and five times that morning.

He was far too excited to eat, though his mother had made him a breakfast of bacon and eggs.

"I do not know if I will get on," he said in Micmac, drinking a cup of tea. "They might think other men need the job more." He stared at a robin outside on the pole, and then across the yard at Roger Savage's house. Roger, the white man living just on the other side of the reserve's line.

"You go on up and try," his mother said. "Amos said you would get on. You tell them you are on your way to university to someday be a doctor."

"Oh, I won't say that," he answered. But he felt pleased by this.

Hector was not at all a labourer. He had rather delicate hands, and a quiet, refined face. But loading the hold with pulpwood was the best work he could do at this time to get some money, and he knew if the men would help him learn he would be a good worker.

His mother had put a lunch into a brown paper bag, but couldn't find the thermos for his tea.

"Don't worry, they have a water boy at every hold – that's all I need."

He asked about his half-brother, Joel Ginnish, just as his chief, Amos Paul, pulled into the yard, in his old half-ton truck. Joel once again was in jail.

"He'll be back out soon," his mother said.

Hector smiled. "I don't know if he'll ever forgive me for being born. I think in all honesty that's where his trouble started."

"You have a good day working," his mother answered.

Then Hector remembered the cigarettes and gum he was going to take to the hold, to treat all the other men, and ran upstairs to get them.

Amos Paul, his chief, the one responsible for helping him get this job, and helping him many times besides, had promised him a drive to the boat, and he ran down and got in the cab. Amos's fifteen-year-old grandson Markus Paul was in the truck with him, on his way to fish mackerel off the lobster wharf at the end of the shore road. Hector would be working the *Lutheran* at the pulp wharf in Millbank some seventeen miles away. Amos would go to early Mass to celebrate the anniversary of his wife's death.

It was because of old Amos that Hector was being allowed a union card.

When Amos's truck had turned in the Penniacs' yard, its throttling woke up Roger Savage, the white man who lived next door. Savage, planning to work the *Lutheran* as well, knew he would be too late to get into a hold if he didn't hurry, but missed waving down Amos for a ride.

"Everything on you looks so very shiny and new," Markus said in Micmac to Hector.

"You think I am too shiny?" Hector asked, worried.

4

"No, no – but you wouldn't want to be one bit more shiny, Hector, I'll tell you that!"

Those would be the last words they ever spoke together.

Roger Savage was one of those men who without realizing it would become cast in a brutal light. He was the kind of man other men call "a hard worker," which means he always did a variety of jobs that required his strength to get them done. He had not graduated high school. But he had worked on and was about to receive his GED later that summer. That is not to say he was stupid, but it stipulated a kind of attitudinal demeanour, which others not so bright could use to construe the type of man they were dealing with: that harsh labour meant a harsh man. But it was more than that. It was from everything, from television to books, that Roger got the idea that he was the man who must change, that he was the man who must break out of the sod of anger and mistrust into the blossoming world that other men had supposedly gone into.

He worked from the time he was thirteen, carrying buckets of water to the ships that came in. He cut wood with his father – sometimes 120 cord a year. He was a carpenter in the winter and helped maintain the rink for those boys and girls to play a game he himself never did.

He stayed on the ice flats for smelt, with the great nets mended by his own hand, and the chainsaw blade sharpened by himself alone. He worked as a spare on lobster boats when he was needed. He'd been in storms and rough seas enough, which those who hadn't been would at various times use for Maritime culture and grand performance onstage. The house he lived in was ninety years old, blackened by soot up one wall, and having tarred and speckled shingles that were put up by his father. It was sunken to one side, and so near the reserve as to have some say it overlapped its border. No one seemed to mind this, for he was not a bother to anyone. He was not at all odd, as others called him, just a loner.

Starting at seventeen he got on in the hold of pulp boats,

though he never sided with the union. Still, he worked boats reverently, taking the cuts and spills from the loads all in stride.

One day, the year he turned twenty-two, he was put out of the hold because he came too late to the yard. This was a union decision made because of who he was. However, it was bad luck for the other lad who worked in his place.

An accident caused the death of Hector Penniac – a First Nations man from Amos Paul's reserve. But within a short amount of time the death came to be viewed as suspicious. And once it was, it came to be viewed as criminal. There were two possible motives for Roger to have caused this death, one bigoted and the other union related – a retaliation for not being allowed to work that day by a man the union had problems with.

"He had not wanted to be put out of the hold," people said, "and made sure Hector and the two union boys inside paid the price!"

The two other men in this hold were Bill and Trevor "Tanker" Monk, president and secretary of the Stevedores Local 837.

You were supposed to stand along the edge of the hold when the pulpwood came down on the hoist. But Hector didn't. Why, no one knew, but Hector did not stay there. Some believed he had walked over to the side to take a piss. This is what Tanker Monk said the boy must have been doing. As he walked to the centre, the hoist operator lost the steel tether to the load.

What was special was this: Hector was "different" in a way in which most Micmac boys – or any boys – wanted little to do with. To the young men he was "a queer." They left him on his own. Some said he had propositioned them in the gully where they used to drink, put his hand on their knees, or even farther up their legs. Yet after his death many who knew him said this was false. They wanted to rectify their feelings against him, because of what they now considered a valiant death, and so he became, in a matter of days, a heroic figure to the boys on the reserve.

Roger Savage lived close to this reserve, and a certain number did not like him either. Or such was the thinking applied after this incident.

At any rate there was a good deal of excitement around this "death," as there always is around any death in a small community where everyone knows each other. People could partake in this excitement, and even feel a kind of kindred remorse and love, without suffering greatly. But from the first, this death was special. It would in fact over this summer become an event that would encapsulate undercurrents that had been troubling the reserve for over thirty years: land reform rights, logging and fishing rights and activism from the left in the guise of university pronouncements and paper editorials, etc. It would put this Roger Savage in the media glare, like a man coming out of a whorehouse might hold up his hands against the flash.

They brought the body up from the hold, an old coat wrapped about the head and face, but the arms dangled. Someone on the ship had been sent down by the captain and had tried to wash away the blood.

"Who was killed?" went up along the highway.

"An Indian."

The news entered the reserve like that. That is, it entered the reserve as "An Indian was killed loadin' the boats."

That is how Markus Paul first heard of it while he was fishing mackerel on the lobster wharf. It had been a quiet, uneventful morning. He had got a drive up with Amos and Hector as far as the turnoff. He lived with his grandfather and his older sister in a small house on the bank side of the bay – beyond the first fields of the reserve. His life at fifteen was almost identical to that of Roger Savage's at the same age. Markus's grandfather Amos had been elected chief a year or so before – and until that moment nothing spectacular at all had happened.

They had had three marches during the year – one against prejudice and two to hopefully bring notice to the climb in suicides on their reserve, of which four had happened, six in total attempted.

"An Indian was killed today up in Millbank loadin' pulp," one white youngster said to another as they fished off the far side of the wharf.

At first it didn't register with Markus that it could be anyone he knew or that it was anyone from his reserve. But he knew saying "an Indian" meant for those whites it was not so grave or even noteworthy. It gave them a certain feeling of remoteness. So Markus stared at the green water, as the waves undulated under the tar timber. Then suddenly he thought it might be Hector. Shaken, he picked up the four dried-out mackerel he had caught using his red devil lure, laced a string through the gills and carried them along the sunny and dusty shore road, walking in his bare feet.

Roger Savage himself did not know that the boy who had replaced him had died. He had run up to the ship minutes late, and was informed that his place had been taken. But he sat on a pulp line and waited, thinking he might get on after lunch, because the workers would shift holds. About ten in the morning he had had a drink from a pint of rum, to wait out the boredom. He said little to the other men, about things he thought weren't worthy to speak about. In fact he was almost always that way.

"Lucky the whole hold wasn't done for, and all of us dead," one of the men in the hold with Penniac said when he climbed the ladder. Tanker Monk had not known Roger was in the yard, and was doubly surprised to hear that he had been hanging around where the loads were hooked for his hold. The hold he, Roger, was supposed to be in. So this looked like mischief from the start.

This was the story that came from the incident:

About the time Markus heard of the death while fishing

mackerel, three Micmac men were sent by Isaac Snow, perhaps the most forceful of the First Nation men, to guard the body of the boy, he being up there alone dead in the pulp yard, lying on a flat bit of grass among a group of uncaring white men. (In fact many of the white men did care, and Roger Savage, who had known Hector for years, was one of them.) But this was an instinctive move by Snow to grab attention for a reserve that had other, hard-pressing needs; it was an opportunity to remind people of them. That is, he was sickened by the death of a member of his band, but it was also a political move.

Savage had not awakened until he heard Amos's truck turn in Penniac's yard. The two union leaders were in the hold with Hector, who was given, by the yard boss, the job Savage had been late for. This would prove bad for Roger later on. Because there was something else unknown for at least a few days, though rumoured from the start.

It was this: Roger had hooked.

That is, after lying about for three hours nursing a horrible hangover, wondering why he just didn't go home, and taking a drink from a pint of rum being passed about by two men called the leaners – because they did nothing but lean against the pit props and watch the work – he was asked to hook the cable together as the load of pulp was raised. They had laid the eight-foot pulp on the cable and brought it together above the last log; This particular cable was joined at the lifting point by a steel clamp.

This clamp had given way. Roger was not hired to hook on – the one who was hooking on that morning, George Morrissey, had left the yard for ten minutes. Just by chance all of this had happened without the least notice. Roger had wanted something to do. He shouldn't have done the load, but he did. Now he felt responsible for hooking a bad load. It could have been his fault, but he felt he had hooked sound.

When people inspected the clamp later, it seemed someone

9

had pried it open. That was either criminal negligence or malicious forethought. No one said this at first, however. It would all take time.

Roger had wanted to use his money to finish building a room he had started on his old house and get staging up and new shingles in the summer. His little house was dropping, and he wanted to raise it up on a hydraulic jack and mend the back end. And he hoped he would use what he had from working lumber boats to buy out Cullen Savoy's lobster licence the next year. What was more intriguing was this – something that would haunt everything else: the dicey fact of riparian rights to three salmon pools on the North River that Roger Savage had inherited and which many Micmac, especially Isaac Snow, said belonged to them. The riparian rights were water rights to the salmon pools that bordered Roger's land. He said he owned them, the band said they owned them, and as yet, they had come to no meeting of minds.

Hector had been the only First Nations boy to graduate the year before. Two First Nations girls graduated, but boys from this particular reserve were usually less successful. But Hector had been determined. This would become an important point when discussing the discrepancy between the two: one a white boy living a rather traditional, and to some a pointless, existence – as Barack Obama might say, "clinging to guns and religion" – and the other a native boy, wanting to do something out of the ordinary for others, in fact a humanitarian.

Roger went home and sat at the table, saying nothing and listening to nothing. He looked numb, and on occasion he moved his hand up to his forehead and took it away. He put supper on – a pot for boiling potatoes, and some fried pork chops. But when it was ready he did not eat. He put some salt on the potatoes and stared at them a long time. Then he stared out at his gravel drive, and the damp yellow stalk weeds in the yard. He blinked impassively at passing cars. He

10

did not answer the phone. And then others started to appear in the evening yard. It was a cool June night, but one that suggested great warm weather would come.

He sat at the table and drank his tea, moving the tea bag back and forth in his cup as he always did, and looking at the old crooked table as if he was mesmerized.

"An Indian was killed loadin' a boat today!" Kellie Matchett yelled into him.

"It was Hector," one of the men whispered.

"I know it – I was there. Now please go."

"What?"

"Go!"

He did not like Kellie Matchett – and within ten minutes of his telling her to leave the yard, Kellie was phoning upriver to Roger's girlfriend, May, explaining to her that something really terrible had happened on the wharf, and it involved Roger. Kellie Matchett was of course only relaying information to her sweet friend May. She was, however, quite happy the news was "terrible."

Later, before dark, the police came, and Constable Drew asked Roger out to the car. The officer was shorter than Roger and had a small bone structure, yet his disposition was pleasant enough. He had heard many things about this Roger Savage already – not of any substantive criminal nature, but of a man who kept to himself and did not like others, and who had threatened men to stay off his land.

Roger sat in the front seat, the window rolled down halfway.

"Did you hook, or did George Morrissey?" Constable Drew asked, looking down at his notebook.

"George hooked – I was just wasting time," Roger said. His voice was unusually quiet and powerful. Drew told him nothing was being suggested but not to leave the area until the matter was cleared up, because the leaners, the two brothers who were drunk, had said he had hooked. And there had been some confusion in the hold when the load dropped, and no one was sure at the moment if the load was hooked wrong or had hit the side – which meant the crane operator had made a mistake, or the man who hooked on did. The Monk brothers did not want to blame anyone. But they themselves had been close to death, and Roger, some said, had been hanging around suspiciously.

"What do they mean, suspicious?" Roger asked.

"Well, do you think it was suspicious that you were hanging around?" Constable Drew asked.

Roger shook his head. "No, not at all," he said. "I work there. The leaners are there every day drinking, and picking up what they can, and no one calls them suspicious."

He should not have said that and he knew it. But the very word *suspicious* allowed him a glimpse into what was in store. That is, he knew in his heart it was really not at all suspicious, yet suddenly his answer had made it so.

He went back into the house, went to the attic and began to shake, violently. He was in a bad spot. He had always felt people did not like him. Now they would have reason not to.

Also, he had told them George had hooked, because it was George's union card that was at stake, not his. But to say George had hooked, even to keep George's union card secure, put Roger in a terrible light if George recanted and those two leaners told on him. So he realized what was now too late to take back. He could not now tell the truth, saying he was lying only to protect someone else.

Roger's shaking lasted well into the first night. Then he became aware that he must pull himself together. At some point he decided to offer money he had saved for the house and the siding for Hector's funeral.

On the second night of the wake, Roger walked into the funeral parlour. Young Markus Paul was standing near the front and saw the change in attitude when Roger entered. It was one of suspicion and dislike. No one this disliked could be unaware of it. The air was filled with the scent of oak and flowers, and people were lined up at both doors. The coffin was closed, and would remain so.

"Penniac's dead and you're alive," one boy said when he and his friends noticed Roger at the side door. He said it in Micmac, not thinking Roger would understand. Roger did. He knew Micmac well enough. The youngster was hushed by the chief, Amos Paul, and told to show respect.

Later that night, after he went home, Roger drank a pint of rum himself and fell into a twitching slumber, which he woke from periodically. He drank often, and always on his own.

It was all a terrible thing to have happen. And that Indian boy was right – he, Roger, was alive and Hector was not. So he felt he had to do something, and one was to offer money for the funeral.

Isaac Snow and Joel Ginnish held a meeting that night also. Joel was not supposed to be on the reserve, because of the trouble he caused. But his half-brother's death signalled a change in attitude toward him. Not only was he once again accepted, his presence seemed valuable and desired, and his mother was comforted by him.

Both Isaac Snow and Joel Ginnish were certain they had to do something. The fact that both were seen together – one a politician, one an outlaw, both of them unquestionably brave – did not go unnoticed. Isaac had already been to the chief's house twice to ask him how the band council was going to handle this crisis, and went away disappointed with the old man's answer, that there was no crisis that he could see to handle.

Isaac, who had last year come back to the reserve too late to run for chief, felt he was obligated to show he could lead. To Joel, just released from jail for theft, not to do something would be cowardice.

"There is no crisis," old Amos Paul had said in his slow Micmac, giving his innocent, almost toothless, smile. "So let's not make one."

Over the next week this became the crux of the secondary argument. That is, the first argument about what really happened had a secondary amendment, which stated that those who were telling people what must have happened did not have their own motives examined, out of fear of being called, if white, prejudiced, and if native, a traitor.

Markus Paul sensed this, because he was the chief's grandson. But he too said nothing.

So Roger went to the Penniac family with the money from his last cashed paycheque.

By this time many believed Roger had hooked the load that killed the Micmac who took his job, and he had done it because Bill Monk was in the hold. Then Roger did something unfortunate to lend credence to this idea – he offered money to the family, as if to buy them off.

The money became a sore point with certain powerful people on the reserve. And with Joel Ginnish in particular.

"There will be no money for Hector from him," he said.

Roger now posed a predicament to the Micmac band itself; in fact he became the focus of the dispute between the old chief Amos Paul and the younger more dynamic Isaac Snow. This in fact was the true crisis, and what everything else revolved around. At first the crisis was nebulous, detached from specifics. Isaac Snow had wanted the reserve to run one way, Amos Paul another. Now something specific had been placed within the border of the reserve itself: Savage's claim to riparian rights, and his ramshackle house. Both pools and house overlapped Micmac land, and everyone on the reserve knew this.

So Amos Paul had to decide what was more honourable – doing nothing or doing something. The younger men felt they had to act – make a case if they thought there was anything suspicious in the death of Hector. So already they were pressing the old chief, asking him what he would do, and as always, both slowly and deliberately, he was trying to come to some conclusion about what should be done. And as always, to some of them, he was procrastinating. Worse, this involved Roger, the grandson of his friend Lawrence Savage whom he had guided for at the camp along the back Tabusintac, whom he had worked for on the waters and was paid to do so. So he was in a conflict of interest.

It was also the very worst timing. Just before the accident, the band council had decided to approach Roger about these things, his house overlapping their land and the fact they believed his pools belonged to them. But when they realized it was a year he was trying to get his house repaired, in order to get married, they decided to let it go. They would give him another year before speaking to him about it. And they had signed off on that just three nights before the accident.

Now it put everyone in difficulty and it was not the band's fault. They had not gone to the wharf and they had not hooked on the loose pulp. They had not tampered with the clamp as many said Roger Savage had. But the idea was even more subtle. It was as if he was wilfully flaunting their decision to be magnanimous.

Amos Paul had to deal with this his very first term as chief and at the twilight of his life. His primary concern was to satisfy men and women who wanted justice. But it had to be just, and he had an obligation to keep Roger Savage safe. That is, Roger Savage was his responsibility now.

The Penniacs, of course, did not take the money.

Roger, money still in hand, went along the shore and stared out at the islands in the bay draped in evening mist.

He walked back along the bleak shore road, with clouds overhead. He looked like a common labourer, his pants and his boots dusty, his forehead broad, his eyes dark brown. He was a very good carpenter and a good mason. He was exceptionally strong and very quiet. Bad luck had plagued his family most of his life, and he had decided that the one thing he could not do was become embittered by it. His mother had left him as a child. His father had fallen from a scaffold when working on the bridge. He had taken care of himself from fifteen on. He had no training from a father to be a man, and so came to manhood on his own. He had lived in his father's house, rumoured to be part of the native settlement of 1815.

It did look in hindsight as if offering his money was not a spontaneous act of generosity, but calculated to assuage the guilt of privilege. This was the crux of the problem, and Chief Amos Paul sensed it. He also sensed something more – that the white papers would soon get hold of the story. And a lot would depend on who they sent to cover it.

He hoped this would not happen, but told his grandson Markus that night while sitting on the back porch, "This will work against Roger, I know. The papers might jump on him."

Over the next few days, as the old chief went along the streets of his shabby little reserve, people asked him what he was going to do about this man Roger Savage.

"What do you mean?" he would say.

"I mean, we make an appeal for his land now, is what I mean!" Joel Ginnish, obviously upset, said. "We need a chief who will take our side – he should be off our land. There is no doubt this is a racist act against our people!"

"Do you understand," Amos answered, "this has nothing to do with him claiming the land. One case does not involve the other. So we must see what happens."

Before, Amos sounded wise and reasonable; now he only sounded old. So Joel Ginnish turned away and went over to Isaac's house.

After he offered the money, Roger went home and drank a large glass of water sitting at the kitchen table. Still in his own mind he might have thought that nothing was wrong – or that everything would be alright. But then he became very uncertain. He had said a few months ago that the First nations men weren't welcome anymore along his back fields if they insisted his pools were theirs.

But saying that they were not welcome was a very stupid thing, and he realized it now.

His hand was trembling, for he had told a lie and he would be seen in a bad light because of it. He had told people he hadn't hooked on, because George Morrissey, who was supposed to, might lose his union card. But now George didn't want any part of it; was saying he had no idea Roger was going to hook that particular load. Roger had phoned George and asked him to back him, but George said, "Who told you to hook? I was just going to take a piss."

Others had already told George not to get involved – that this was a dispute between Roger and a bunch on the reserve. But these words were like a thunderclap over Roger's head. How was the clamp left opened? He was sure he had hooked right. So now he had to continue with his story, that he did not hook, for if he admitted to the lie, he was by proxy admitting to something more treacherous.

He looked out the back window, across the flat, dry field, across the small pit props that rested black against the sky on this humid day, dead like soldiers, and at the back door of Hector's, where there was some wash on the line, and an old wash pot overturned, and upstairs a dry curtain and a broken window. He saw Hector's older sister open the door and enter so quickly it was hard to believe he had just seen her. Silence again. Then the sound of a fly buzzing against the window.

He stood and took the skill saw and began to cut the two-by-four for the last section of the back room he was redoing. When he stopped cutting, with the fine sawdust on his arms, he sat and thought: "They are already thinking – I mean some – that it was set up. How could I ever do that to anyone?"

"Why did I hook on," he said bitterly. "Everything was all right before."

From his youth he had prosecuted the world only on his own terms, and had learned no talent to solve problems when the world turned against him. He was a loner, and most often those who turned against him were not alone.

He washed his arms and face, with turpentine and water, of the paint and sawdust and went along the back road, with the high pines, to the grave. The gate seemed to swing on its arc too fast when he opened it, and Roger stopped for a moment and tightened the hinge with his powerful fingers. Then he went down and stood before the mound of dirt. He was in the little Micmac graveyard, with old graves crumbling from the 1840s.

He had never been off the river in his life, and probably never thought that he would have a crisis placed before him, like the mound of dirt. Like many boys he thought that his life would be very exciting by being like everyone else's. And what in the world was wrong with that? Many people who labelled him old-fashioned ended up doing what he had done to begin with.

He went back home and the night was sweet but the trees blew in the wind, and the smell of cold sand came up from the bay, and the twizzle-shaped seeds fell from those trees in front of his yard – the one they had been so proud of in the years gone by.

Perhaps Roger loaded it there and then. That is, his rifle.

Part I

September 1, 2006

Markus Paul had never forgotten the case, had never solved it.

He had been a policeman since 1992. And people told him he surmised too much. Certainly he drank too much. In the late August, wherever he was, he would begin to think of things that had happened that summer and he would long to go back to his reserve.

He remembered that the day he and Little Joe Barnaby went fishing, he had put the biggest worm on the smallest boy's hook. And set the line down in the best rip, and Little Joe took his shoes off and wiggled the line up and down, waiting for the trout to strike. Markus went up on a limb of the spruce above him and watched the shadows of the pool.

"There there there," Markus would whisper, "it's coming it's coming – now!"

But the trout would pass by, or skim away, and the water would become still. There was a smell of spruce gum in the trees, and the pulpy smell of warm air travelling in the branches. Little birds hopped on small dead twigs a few feet away.

"Will I ever never ever be able to catch a trout?" Little Joe said later.

"Sure you will," Markus said as they walked back up the road in the white twilight with bugs flitting over their heads. "Here, do you want to carry mine for a while?"

"I don't want to kill them," Little Joe said, holding the trout, his socks sticking out of his pockets. "I want to catch them and eat them."

"That's the best policy," Markus said. He still remembered the warm air, and the scent of warm spruce gum, and the birds hopping.

Behind them Markus's girlfriend, Sky Barnaby, was listening to the older girls talking – they whispered about Much Fun. It was a fine and dreamy night. The waves washed on the shore when they got down to the bay, and someone saw a shooting star.

Once, when Markus was in South America, as part of the bodyguard for the governor general and her entourage, he found himself visiting the adobe villages of the natives in the hills outside of Santiago, and crying. He did not know why, and would never be able to tell you why. But he sat on a stump in a yard filled with children and broke into tears. A strange thing to see, this man, six foot three, who was a native man like they were – and yet all those children simply made him cry. A little girl with a big hat and huge earrings came over to him and took his hand gently, smiling.

Some nights he had to stay up, for the governor general and her entourage were celebrating something, and he would look up at the Chilean sky and count the stars.

"Amos, they aren't the same stars anymore," he would say.

He had his black belts in two disciplines. And you could insult him and he would laugh. Or shrug. Or like his ex-wife and ex-girlfriend you could call him a big baby and he would nod and say yes.

He had married young, a white woman – young Samantha Dulse – but that did not last, even though they were still friendly and she probably still loved him, and then he had a native girlfriend, whom he did not love enough. In fact, he did not love either of them enough. He had loved Sky Barnaby. He had always loved Sky Barnaby, from the time he was fifteen. But she was wild too, and had knifed a man in a fight downriver in 2000. It didn't kill him. However, Markus had lost touch with her. It all seemed so long ago.

His own people disliked him. The whites distrusted him too, and like his grandfather Amos he was morally on his own. So Markus often thought of Amos. On the trip to Chile a man, drunk on too much champagne, tried to intercept Her Excellency – and Markus reached his hand out and grabbed him by the collarbone and quietly caused him some pain for a second. Her Excellency did not notice. It wasn't much – but it ruined the evening for him. He had been invited to dine with some Chilean native men, but now he felt he could not leave Her Excellency at that time, and so declined.

"I will not leave the building until Her Excellency does," he said.

He stood near her for three more hours, and got back to his room without having eaten a thing. He took off his shirt and looked at the reflection of the tattoo on his upper chest. It read: *Sky*.

It was the anniversary of Little Joe's death. He had not thought of it until he looked at the reflection of the tattoo. He blessed himself and said a prayer, and thought of the grave-yard in Canada, in the Maritimes, on the Miramichi, so far away.

"I didn't mean to get Little Joe killed," he called to Sky one night in 1992, when she was far up the road. "I didn't – mean to – " It was in the winter and he stood by the trees, snow coming down over him almost all night long.

"You should have joined the military," a Canadian sergeant, also part of the bodyguard, had said to him that night in Santiago.

"Yes, well, it is something, isn't it, sir," he said.

"What is something?"

"That people like you and I will never be liked and almost always be needed."

23

After that they did what Canadian men everywhere do. They didn't speak of racism or the global war – they spoke of hockey. For what in hell else was there really except the precarious balance and the fire dance on ice.

1985

1

Markus's grandfather Amos Paul had been a small, wiry, happy-go-lucky man who travelled all over the province to powwows, had the respect of everyone. He played bingo, and tried to get businesses to donate money and commodities to his reserve. He had started a toys-for-tots program at the supermarkets in both Chatham and Newcastle, and made sure three or four native children were sent to camp each summer from the Tim Hortons sponsor. Being chief and wearing the bright vest of the chief was a grand thing. Until now.

He was very bothered by the case of Hector Penniac. Something might happen, and he could foresee it. He must take his reserve's side. Yet he believed that he must protect Roger Savage if he had done nothing wrong. But little by little the idea that he *had* done something wrong began to infiltrate the thoughts of his friends and colleagues and make it seem as if the ingrained hatreds of the past were again haunting them.

"However," Amos would answer them, as he walked home from church with his missal tucked up under his arm, "no one is sure, are they?"

Markus realized now, years later, that he himself had felt shame when he heard this, and a deep feeling of betrayal. The betrayal came because most of the reserve wanted Roger Savage's confession, and most wanted his old house torn down and a lodge put up, to perhaps bring in sports fishers. Roger's place hampered this because it sat directly in front of the pools of which Roger claimed riparian rights. Now no one wanted to blame Roger in order to get this house and these pools, but no one was foolish enough not to know that if he was blamed, this house and these pools would be easier to access.

Everyone wanted this, and Markus's grandfather himself became an inhibitor of this. Markus knew he should have trusted his grandfather more then, and years later, in 2006, he was spurred on because of how his grandfather was treated.

For many felt a real chief, someone like Isaac Snow, could get Roger's pools for them and confiscate his house. Not for the little recreation centre that old Amos wanted, but for a big lodge for rich white men to come and pay money to fish. When asked by some of Markus's young friends what he would do about all of this, Amos only said: "The rec centre is what I am concentrating on now. To get that done – the rest will blow over. The school is built here – and we have two Micmac instructors. Why, we are the first nation in the province to have this happen." He smiled, delighted, and then frowned. "But this other stuff – well, who can say it was more than an accident? Do you remember Roger Savage doing anything that was even close to this? I know he had trouble and got in fights at dances – but, well, that was different. Besides, the police have taken him in three times now, and have brought him back. If they wanted to charge him they would have. We will have to let the police decide." And he smiled once more.

"But they don't want to charge him because he is white," some said.

Amos did not choose to answer this. He simply shrugged. He knew this was not true. If not because of Hector, then because of where the load itself dropped. No, it was danger-ous to all concerned in the hold, the white men as well as Hector, so they would charge him if they had to.

But to Joel Ginnish, who had tried to be patient, it seemed Amos was afraid that if he made a ruckus he would not get the recreation centre built – and that was the reason for his silence. Some also believed he was afraid to call people racist.

Markus pondering the case for years, would remember how he himself had acted.

"But there are racists," Markus told his grandfather – somewhat condescendingly.

"Oh son, yes, I know," Amos said. But he said he was not thinking of Roger Savage when he thought this, nor was he only thinking of white men.

Markus remembered, because everyone was saying how deliberately Roger had set Hector up, that he felt his grandfather was a fool. And everyone said that Isaac Snow would take care of it for them. And Joel Ginnish would do what he had to do. That to spite the old man, no one wanted the recreation centre now.

The idea of the old chief vacillating put more pressure upon Hector's family – his father, his mother and his mother's elderly wheelchair-bound uncle – to accept the condolences of some of the men who now wanted their attention, or at least wanted to use the death of Habisha's son for attention. (That this could not be stated shows how sensitive the subject was.) What was unfortunate was that Habisha knew that some of the very men offering condolences had teased Hector the most, and that on more than one occasion she had to tell them to leave him alone. That he was different. Once some of the boys had painted Hector's ears blue as a joke.

She also knew her first-born, Joel Ginnish, was a terrifying presence in her house, but Isaac was invited by Joel to visit them often during those days, and he saw the scale of their pain and their gratitude to him.

As for Joel, he had never gotten along with Hector's father, his stepfather, and they often came to a tussle, and he had been put out of the house many times in the dead of winter. Joel never forgot this, or anything else. But if it was not for Hector's death, he wouldn't have been allowed back on the reserve, for the band had tried to expel him. His new status, his revised status, his rehabilitation all came because of the death of Hector. This was also something subtle and unspoken.

Habisha felt guilty about this whenever she looked at her first-born, with his toss of wild hair and glittering eyes, and believed that she in some way had undermined his life by remarrying too soon after his own father's death. When she tried her best to apologize now, he looked at her and shrugged.

"I'm here to help you, Mom, that's the only reason I am back" was all he said to her. But he never glanced at his stepfather – and the strange feeling in him now, akin to giddiness, was that he would prove himself to his mother come what may. That he would do what he had to do. That this was his one chance to take on the world.

Many young men were often at the house, saying they would do what they had to. Isaac wished their condolences to have a sincerity that matched their wishes to comfort. He himself had been very harsh with Hector once or twice in the past. This is something Isaac regretted very much. So now he became very harsh to Roger Savage, as they sat about the table drinking, and speaking of him.

"That Roger, why would he do something like that?" Joel said, looking at him for advice. "It means war with me – it means I won't stop," Joel said.

Isaac did not know exactly what to say about it, but he did know this – even if it was untrue, the momentum had started, and they were going downhill and could not stop, so they would quite likely proceed as if it was true, until the end. Did that make them different from other men? No, it made them the same.

This is why the situation was so delicate. It was a strange word, *delicate*, used like this. The situation was delicate meant that violence might happen and blood might flow. That as always was the problem with the world, as Amos Paul tried to tell his grandson.

Situations that caused things to be called delicate were very often the worst situations, but you began by explaining them like little flowers that bloomed somewhere in small forgotten summer fields.

"It is strange to call things delicate, which means they might explode. I suppose in that way we are like sappers."

"Granddad, they treated you terrible, and Momma, and my aunts and uncles too," Markus said. "They used to drive through the reserves on summer nights before the Second World War and take pictures of our reserve as if we were in a zoo!"

"Yes, it is right, they treated us very poorly."

"*Poorly*! They treated us worse than dogs – you especially know that."

"I treat my old dog pretty good," Amos said, as a joke. But he knew his grandson was not joking.

Markus said, "Do you know that apartheid in South Africa was modelled after the reserves in Canada!"

The old man fumbled about and nodded and patted the old dog's head. He had not known that, and tried to think of what to say, and suddenly his face brightened a bit.

"Well yes – but we can't blame apartheid on Roger Savage, can we? In fact we shouldn't even be blaming him for painting Hector's ears – it was Joel Ginnish himself who did that!" Saying this, he smiled in victory.

So although Markus did not agree with his grandfather, some small part of him resisted joining in with those who wanted to protest by blocking the long drive to Roger's house or by netting his pools that they wanted to claim. Markus was fifteen at the time – and many of his friends wanted him, as the grandson of the chief, to join them.

The trouble was this. His grandfather was losing cred-ibility, and if he did not join, he might jeopardize not only his own standing but by extension that of his grandfather.

29

2

Roger couldn't sleep. The old lace drapes hugged the window when the breeze blew off the bay. There was a smell of crab from the long pebbled shore. The smell of herring too, for they used herring in the lobster traps, and the smell of salt on the small rock garden in the yard. He would lay in bed, thinking of nothing, or suddenly his whole body would jerk up and he would remember the lie he had told about not hooking.

He sat up in this room looking out over the still water and remembered many of the winter storms, and how snow would come up over the white houses and circle the white driveways and enclose the dark barns, and how all of this seemed to keep him safe. How there were no books in his house, and very few conversations about anything that wasn't immediate, that there was no talk of politics that wasn't local, and no history, except that of D-Day.

His long, cold winter days were spent in school in much the same way. That is, people expected certain things of him. They expected him not to graduate. They expected him to take shop class and become a carpenter. And they would expect those sorts of things until he died, and there was now no way to change them. He was a labourer and they expected him to be one, a jack of all trades and they expected that too, and what was more telling was that he had expected the same things, and relied on them to expect what they did. But last year, he went onto the reserve and was tutored by Mrs. Francis, and got his GED. That was going to prove something to them all. Then he took his GED and went to town and applied for jobs. But it didn't even matter to them that he had his GED. So he went back to being what they expected. And now somehow this unspoken pact was broken, and he had no idea what in the world to do or to expect. But he realized that the newspapers were beginning to assess him and to believe in a certain way that he had done what was expected as well.

He was sorry for that boy. Hector had told Roger one day he was going to be a doctor. No First Nations friend of his paid any attention to that, until now. Now it seemed as if this was the main problem. The papers had mentioned not only who Roger was – "a journeyman labourer," they said – and what he did – but what Hector had planned to do. He thought of this, as he folded his arms and looked out the window, taking a drag off his cigarette once in a while, and calmly moving the curtain back just an inch or so when he wanted to see if anyone had come into his yard. But what did the papers say?

"Hector Penniac was planning to go into medicine at Dalhousie. He would have been the first doctor ever from the Micmac Reserve here."

At first Roger thought nothing of this, but now it seemed to be an instrument in deciding the very qualities of the two – and the guilt or innocence of him. He dragged on his smoke and thought of this too, and looked at the cigarette paper as it burned, as if telling him in the vast quietude of the moment that his trouble was once particular and universal. He was building the room for his girlfriend May, yet she herself was now scared because she had read what was in the papers as well.

So though he tried not to give in to worry, there was much indictment in how one said what was to be said in the paper. And he was beginning to see that papers were deceitful in how they said what they did. And this deceit was pervasive, and what was worse, it was believed by the vast majority of

31

those who wanted to believe it. So in some respects he was already convicted. He was too smart not to know, though he could not articulate it well. Like always with those who were expected to be only one way, he often pretended he didn't know what he actually did.

That night, after the heat relented, and the wind off the bay made you think of lost Irish ghosts, of little girls who died on the crossing, and lepers from Sheldrake Island in 1847, as wind here always did, and would always do, he fell into a light sleep, and dreamed Hector was standing before him making him laugh.

"Yes, I knew you were alive," he said. "Can you wait until I wake up and get Isaac and Amos? They want to see you too!"

When Roger woke it was daylight, and a fine rain fell, and he heard a tractor, which Mr. Cyr had donated to the band, travelling along the shore road going toward the rec centre.

Roger worked in the heat all day, cutting wood on his back woodlot, and came home in the evening with welts on his neck from the flies, his socks soaked through with sweat and dried blood. No one had said a thing to him when he went down to the corner to check his mail. There was little mail. Only an advertisement for golf courses in P.E.I. and a bill from hydro.

But what was more telling was this: he had often gone over to the site to help with the mortaring, for Amos Paul and his men were hard pressed to get this done. Since the accident he had not gone down the shore road to the reserve. He sat in the back room and tried to read one of the romance novels that his mother had read at a rate of one dozen a week and had left around the house when she went back home to a life of other men and questionable pleasures. But very often he would put the book down and stare into nothing at all.

3

The rain started to fall, and the ship – the *Lutheran*, which those who loaded called simply "a boat" – had to sit where it was, for over two weeks, with the generator going, a feeling of profound silence on the deck, with porthole windows looking out at the sawdust-strewn lumber wharf, while the investigation into the death continued. The Monks went aboard to show where they had been, and how they had seen the load fall in time, and had tried to grab Hector but it had happened too fast. The clamp was examined. It wasn't twisted or bent; so if the load fell it had to have been left opened. The Monks brought the water boy with them, to show where he had been standing, and he said he had yelled at Hector to get out of the way, as well. Then Roger had to stand where he had been, and show what he had done, which he lied about. This very physical act of having him recreate a scene he said had not happened made it seem very suspicious.

"It was not me who leaned over an' put the clamp to 'er," he said. He said this again and again. Standing in the harsh sunlight with the smell of rinsed water running from the ship's sewer flukes made it all seem base and suspect.

The inner bulwark was examined. Then, too, the entire yard. There were still three and a half rows of yarded pulp – each stretching back an acre or more. And the boat could not go until the investigation was over. Or at least this was the consensus. The Dutch wanted to go home, wanted all of this to be over with. They were not saying anything here – they stared at everyone with mild, impassive faces. They were polite and even timid.

However, to the papers back home in Rotterdam, they complained and even bragged about everything, about how stupid the people were here, how backward, saying that Roger Savage's name fit him very well. They did this until their captain told them not to open their mouths again to any papers home or here. The ship needed to offload in England take on new cargo for Rotterdam and he had to get going. He decided by the third day that whoever was needed at an inquest could be flown back at Canadian expense. This was his decision, and he cancelled all shore leave and moved toward slipping port.

The investigation continued very slowly. The coroner had little to go on. He was a retired local police officer and had relied on the reports about the load.

"The load fell and killed him," he sniffed, "which is pretty obvious."

Everyone had been co-operative, but the place had been cleaned by the able-bodied seaman sent into the hold. Things were washed away when the body was moved. This caused a delay in his final pronouncement. And there was no expert on hand to testify to the skill of the hook-on, or where Hector was exactly when the load came down. The Monks said the clamp was not hooked, and that the load started to tumble at fifteen feet above their heads. The rumour was that this was done in a thoughtless moment as an energetic and malevolent joke, and that Roger couldn't be charged for there was no proof, but that he would never work another boat.

Except it was done by a man not used to playing pranks or jokes – he had no form for that – which under the flat, grey sky seemed almost more deft and subtle reasoning to call him what people were calling him, a killer. Malicious or malevolent. The action seemed to have been the result of a spur-of-the-moment decision. One could think of thick, gleeful

34

hands suddenly doing this as soon as poor George Morrissey's back was turned.

"He waited his chance," Kellie Matchett said to young May, Roger's girlfriend he was hoping to marry. "I mean, that's what they say."

"What do they say, Kellie? You tell me now."

"Oh, I don't want to."

"You must. You can't keep it from me!"

"Well, if you must know, they just say he waited his chance!"

Looking at his hands, and his broad back, and his blunt nose seemed to signal that kind of sudden resolution. And no one felt more sorry or concerned than Kellie – and one could certainly see that – for she would always tell you if she didn't like you, especially if others didn't either.

"I just hope the police solve it for your sake dear!"

But everyone had to wait for the longshoremen from Saint John who were part of the safety board to take a look at what had happened. Three men arrived, a father and his son and another man. The father had a blunt, impassive face, and his son's face was just as so, with large, unwavering eyes. The third man was small, with the habit of blinking and chain-smoking.

They milled about the yard and interviewed for almost two days.

They interviewed the leaners, and the leaners – both at one time good men, but spendthrift out into solemn mooching and tattling – said Roger hooked. And what was more, delighting in their faces was the idea that for once they were telling the truth.

"Don't want to admit it, do he, though?" one of them said.

"Yeah. Big-feelinged that Roger always was," the other said.

Then both of them stood there looking sheepish and important.

They did not say it was not an accident, but many were hinting at Roger Savage's known temper after his mother left back to her house and disowned him and his father died. He threw a temper tantrum at school and there had been one fist fight with Joel Ginnish, and a good one too, down by his pools last spring runoff.

Each person in the yard that day gave a statement – the same as they had given to the police.

Roger Savage denied doing anything.

"But you did hook?"

He said nothing.

In his younger years he had been a fighter at school, because he did not learn how to read or write well, and people remembered this now. This proved he was still the same. All of this had been proved, all of it was true.

The fact that George Morrissey did not want to say he had left the yard was suddenly challenged by George Morrissey himself, who said he had left the yard – and that Roger Savage, who hadn't been hired that day, simply took it into his "big fat head" to hook on. This was anathema to the safety board men, who had arrived to deal with one of their brothers. When they learned that it was someone who had not been hired for this specific job, they retreated and said as far as Roger Savage was concerned, he was on his own. He would not be their brother that day. They would protect Mr. Morrissey from being accused. In fact they had to act for the union, and in doing so, strangely acted on behalf of the company hiring them, who also did not want a lawsuit, and so could point to the fault of one man. And this is what the ship the *Lutheran* wanted too. A longshoreman culpable meant that they weren't. This would free them to leave.

This left Roger, unwavering, and unbending, to himself.

"This is not right at all," the man with the chronic blink said on a rain-washed afternoon, looking out over the dreary water from the watchman's shed on the property and drinking a cup of tea. "He knew that boy was there – he had a beef with the union bosses in the hold, and then the boy is hired on. This just don't smell right at all."

"Don't smell right," the father said.

"Don't pass the smell test," the boy said, "for sure."

Further to this, the *Lutheran*'s company had claims on the wood, and now that it was mostly loaded, had put in a request to leave – this came from the Dutch company's head office in Amsterdam. So, as the captain hoped, the ship would be allowed to slip port before the final inquest.

For the *Lutheran* had other worries. It had to be finished because another ship, the *Liverpool Star*, was to berth. This was a contentious subject between the safety board and the Dutch company. And it involved Markus's grandfather as well. For Amos did not want the *Lutheran* to be allowed such a luxury – to slip port while the death of one of his own people was under investigation. Yet from the whaling days until now, no company wanted to spend money on sailors sitting in dock. Besides, they could easily put pressure on the owners of the wharf itself, who needed their business, and the woodlot owners who needed to sell their wood to the ships coming in. It was a depressed market – if things got bogged, it would only cause hardship for those trying to make a living, for there were other ships riding high outside the bay, waiting to come in.

Markus's grandfather tried to keep a positive outlook and keep everyone calm. He ran from one company spokesman to another and one police officer to another and one safety board expert to another, hoping to be influential for the Penniac family and for the band, and to keep Joel Ginnish, who was becoming an awful bigmouth, quiet. Hoping to get the funeral paid for and a stone placed in memory, and a written declaration of what exactly happened. He was assured he would get the safety board's statement as well as the police and autopsy reports, for the band and the family. In these he hoped, for his old friend's grandson, that it would be called an accident.

"Everything will get done," he said. "They are treating us with the utmost respect."

This is what he wanted. But he knew the shipping company was not treating them with the utmost respect. In fact the shipping company was not treating them with respect at all. The men from the company were simple Dutchmen who wanted to go home. They had to offload in England and pick up cargo for Rotterdam. Then if everything went well, after hurricane season they were to head south to Jamaica. This is what they all hoped for and spoke about in the galley at night. And this is why they hated this place now, and hated the man who had spilled the logs.

But knowing this, Amos had to say they were treating him with respect. Like a girl on a date whose boyfriend leaves to dance with some other girl, he had to pretend that this in itself was attendant to the fun.

So Amos paraded about saying everyone was helping him and all things would turn out well, and one must give these things time. Yes, he knew he was lying, but he did not want to cause pain.

During this time Isaac Snow went to ask Amos: had he heard the rumour that the ship was leaving? Isaac had walked into the house while the old man was sitting down to lunch. The old man looked puzzled and surprised, and said simply, pointing to the table: "There is enough here for both of us."

Markus said nothing. Except he was aware of Isaac looking his way every now and again.

"If the ship leaves, there will be hell to pay," Isaac said. "Joel is home," he said. "Joel is home" was a statement not only of fact but of concern. Of course Amos, like everyone else, knew Joel was home. No one could help knowing Joel was home.

"The ship won't leave. They told me in writing."

"They told you in writing?"

"Yes – they did – they told me in writing."

"If the ship leaves without Roger being charged or the Dutch giving their statements at an inquest, then I will have to do something. I will have to – you know this. So now is your chance to get it straightened out."

"Straightened out – that's interesting. Why is that interesting?"

But Isaac only looked at him mystified.

"Straighten it out!" Isaac repeated. "We will regret it if we don't!"

He said this sternly and looked down at the frail old man, whose white hair was cut short and whose shirt was buttoned up to his Adam's apple and whose cheerful face was a mass of wrinkles so that it seemed as if tears would form a myriad of streams in his cheeks.

"Well, we might regret something if we do," old Amos said, the entire face of wrinkles brightening up.

What was it that they wanted? Amos asked Markus later.

His face looked very serious, and not at all puzzled, but wise and definite in what he had to say. He put some tobacco on a paper but he did not roll it, he only held it in his hand.

They wanted to protest – but what?

Against Roger, whom they'd known since he was born, and his flimsy little house at the edge of nowhere? Why, his house wasn't half as nice as Isaac's. And more importantly, his education was revamped by Mrs. Francis. So why would he do this!

And if they received from this protest what they wanted – everything in the world they wanted – would they give up their protest? No. He had long ago learned that they would not. If they got the three small pools from Roger (not even holding pools except in high water) that had been in Roger's family three generations, they would not give up – because they could not get what they wanted. They wanted justice for crimes of the past. For something they could not get even for. And they had suffered terrible crimes, yes. But they could not get even. They wanted to live in the past the way they had once been, and could not be again. And no protest would ever change that fact.

"You mean we should let what happened to us go?"

"I am an old man. I don't know what to tell you about letting things go – but how could we ever get revenge without burning the entire roof off the world? The only people who can make peace now are us. No white can do it – it is only in our power, and so we have to, in order to live. And the only person they will burn the roof off is Roger. Once you betray someone, you hold it against them – that is what they do – so we have to forgive them. But Roger is not one of them."

Markus did not believe him, and could not believe that his grandfather would speak such words. But old Amos only shook his head and went on rolling his cigarette, and then took the old dog outside, closing the screen door behind him.

The next night Amos wanted to find out about Hector's life and he invited those of Hector's age to the band council, and he sat in his chief's chair, which was far too large for him, its wood pressing against his old bones, while the other council members sat near him. Here was Mrs. Francis who organized the weekly bingo. Here too was Mr. Billy Ward, and Mr. Jack Sonny. Few of them ever had spent one day in the comfort an average child in Newcastle had. In front of them, boys and girls, dressed like American children, their coal-black hair and eyes giving them away, stood up and began to talk, as Amos looked down at a spring from a ballpoint pen that he kept squeezing, as if he wasn't at all interested.

Two or three youngsters took to grandstanding about how they had stood up for Hector when he was in the gully. How this guy or that said something to him, and how this native or that stood up for him. Markus was slightly amazed. Why did they now say this with such conviction? Why was it important for them now to be the friend of this man most of them had teased or ignored?

40

"Hector couldn't even go up the road unless he was with someone – all the whites liked to torment him," one boy said.

"Who did?" Amos said, suddenly looking up.

"Just look right and left and you'll know," the boy answered, which meant, look to the white houses either French or English.

"Oh, I see," Amos said.

Old Amos looked down again, and having put the ball-point pen together made a mark on a piece of paper, as if he was drawing a boat, and mumbled something. Then he looked up with his small, bright eyes, sighed and thanked the boy for speaking. Then he put his head down again. The next to speak were two youngsters, a boy and girl who came together holding hands and giggling. They wanted the recreation centre named after Hector. And they also wanted a holiday to mark his passing every year.

"A what?" Mrs. Francis asked.

"A holiday – we could have a native holiday – "

That in fact seemed like a good idea to everyone.

After they all had spoken, Amos thanked them in Micmac and then in English for coming to the meeting and shuffled a few papers in front of himself.

"Well, what are you going to do?" Joel Ginnish asked, looking about at everyone, for he thought the meeting was called to coordinate some action against Roger. Yes, he was back home. And at certain moments he still felt the heaviness of Roger's left hook. Suddenly the man they had all wanted gone was here. He was a curious mixture of charisma, charm and bitterness. Amos stared at him a long second. Amos in fact had always liked him.

"Yes, well, it's a terrible thing," he said, "a terrible thing."

4

There was one white man at the meeting. He was a thin faced man, his red cheeks whiskerless, young, with a straw hat back on his head – as if planted there by some idea that was not his own. He had a pony tail down his back. A pony tail showed, a kind of empathy, or as in Isaac's case, strength and freedom. Two pony tails, two reasons to wear it.

The man was tall and wore a leather tie.

His name was Max Doran, and he was from the paper down south. His face registered that kind of determination. He was the face of white concern.

Just as Roger had been told he should be resolved to be a labourer, so Max Doran had been told if he was resolved he would get the real story.

This story was thrust into his lap, because another young journalist, whose name was Gordon Young, could not do it. (Young had recused himself because he was a cousin of Roger Savage, something no one at the paper knew.).

Max wanted the story – but like many people in the province, he believed he already had it. Everyone knew what had happened here.

So at the end of the meeting he looked here and there, trying to find the family of Hector Penniac. He rolled his sleeves up to show his freckled arms, so white on the bottom. Then, taking his gum and carefully folding it away, he walked out with the band members and disappeared, with Amos staring cautiously after him.

"Who is that skinny white boy?" Mrs. Francis asked.

"That is Max Doran – the famous journalist," Amos whispered to Mrs. Francis. "And I am now afraid."

That night after he got home, Amos silently put on the kettle and put bread in the toaster and sat at the table, and watched the toaster and listened to the kettle simmer into life.

Markus stood at the counter with his arms folded, not saying anything, hoping his granddad would say that yes it was terrible and he would take action.

But his grandfather said this: "I am thinking, how would this be murder, done like this? What do you think? It wouldn't be much more than a fluke – at best a fluke," he said, nibbling his toast.

"So a fluke is still a fluke," Markus said. "Some people are saying now . . . well, you know – Hector was, you know, and so might Roger have been, you know. And, well, maybe it was a quarrel, you know?"

"Yes . . . well, you might be right, of course." Amos had heard these rumours from Mrs. Francis. "But then again, if I wanted to murder someone, I would not rely upon a fluke."

"Then why won't he say he hooked?"

"Because – I don't know. Maybe because he lied at first for Mr. Morrissey's benefit and can't now take it back."

But that lie did loom very large against the large blue bay outside.

Early the next morning Amos and Markus went along to the ship the *Lutheran*. Amos told Markus to stay in the truck while he asked to go in, to check out the hold. But Markus came and stood beside him.

There amid the scent of peeled pulp was the pungent scent of Hector's death. The smell, and traces of blood that had not been washed away entirely by the ordinary seaman Vanderhoof, who had dutifully tried. They could tell that Hector had been closer to the centre of the hold when the pulp hit him. The pulpwood that had crushed the young man's skull was still lying in the

43

centre of the hold. That is, it had not been placed away and no regard to where it would go had been decided upon.

The other loads had been placed, however, and were snug, and the other holds were also full. This hold was not yet filled, and no more loads would come to it. It was small, and had a cubby section just below it, where two men would work. One man was working the cubby that day, three men in the upper part of the hold. The ship took about 110 tons of wood. It had been refitted below with new engine parts and a new generator; it was an old ship, actually launched sometime in the late forties. It carried a crew of twenty-seven men and women, nineteen of whom were ordinary seamen.

Some Dutch men looked down upon Amos and Markus quizzically, not used to seeing First Nations people. The Dutch men – and two women – had an innocent aloofness. It was as if what had happened had been a story told to them, and now they believed it fully. With Amos, they were mute and dumbfounded. But at night, alone, the men howled at the idea that this little fellow was chief. This was something Amos knew, and took in stride.

Without looking at them, Amos yelled up, "How did the load come down?" and he jerked his arms to show the way he thought it might have happened.

But no one answered, because they had been warned by their captain not to say another thing. The papers in Rotterdam were calling Roger Savage a murderer, or close to it – that is, stories had circulated wildly, and everyone was interested in what had happened. The captain forbade them to speak, or they'd be fired, because any suggestion that the sailors themselves knew something would keep them in dock longer, and perhaps they'd be made to testify. This was the last thing the captain, Jon De Berg, wanted, and so he forbade them to speak.

"You will walk the fuckin ocean like our Lord if I hear another word," he said. Testifying would mean an unending delay in a court none were familiar with. He had made a

44

petition to slip port and leave by weekend, but had no answer as of yet. The shipping company, too, feared a lawsuit and had instructed the captain, who had not left the wheelhouse all week, not to speak, and not to let his men speak.

"Where was the Micmac boy?" Old Amos called up, in his singsong way. He sounded like a little gnome far, far beneath the Dutch, below deck and below water. In fact, he could hear the water along the bulwark. The seamen stared at him, and then over at Markus trying to make them out. Amos took off his hat and waved it at them.

But they did not answer. There were no more leaves where any of them could get drunk. All they could do was stare at this godawful pulpyard and a line of broken spruce trees cut by an old asphalt road. Yes, it was terrible. But they were in a foreign land, and this calamity had nothing to do with them. They talked of the barbarity of the people among themselves, but the truculent captain reminded them that they too had been pillagers for centuries and that some of their own ancestors had been part of terrorizing many indigenous peoples in the Dutch East Indies, until the Japanese took over the islands in 1940. But the men did not believe this history was comparable to the present calamity.

"Believe it or not," the captain said, in his strong Rotterdam accent, born of poverty not unlike that of Roger Savage, "and howl all you will, but say nothing outside your berth. For it is a lesson in Dutch history what the Canadians did for us in war – and many back home are already reminding the papers of that fact. So be quiet all of you. If the boy did something wrong they will decide it among themselves. If any of you did see it – step forward now and I will phone the Royal Canadian Mounted Police."

He waited.

Not a soul stepped forward.

So as far as the captain was concerned, the sooner they were out of the strait and at sea the better. Besides, the men were aware that the *Liverpool Star*, which they were holding up, might if it came to it make sure the *Lutheran* was held up when unloading in England. One call at the right time and place might make them have to wait in channel an extra four or five days. They stared at the bulwark of their own ship, and thought longingly of their own families.

Old Amos put some tobacco in his mouth and chewed it while he inspected the walls. Two steel girders jutted out about a foot from the smooth wall of the hold and ran parallel to each other on both sides, about fifteen feet above them. There were two chains hanging halfway below that, to a foot above the wood that was holed. On either side of the hold, the water buckets sat, one on its top and the other on its side, with both ladles lying in the same place. Above the heads of the sailors, the sky, murky with blue-grey clouds, and far above them an osprey looking for some flatfish or perch. Amos was standing on the pulp that had been placed in the hold the morning of Hector's death and he looked at it quizzically. He wondered how many loads came down that day – then looked up at the girders again.

When the men above him turned away, and he was sure he was not being looked at, he hauled out his small Instamatic and took five pictures. Then he looked over at Markus and smiled and winked.

Then he straightened up his sore back and brushed off his pants and climbed back up the ladder, letting Markus go before him.

When Amos got to the deck he looked down at the hold, and then at the pulp still in the yard. Then he tried to rub his back with his right hand. Then he nodded at all the men looking at him, aware that he seemed most foreign to these foreigners.

"Old back on me – just about had it." He smiled.

Then, with his grandson leading the way, he walked down the gangplank with his shadow off to the side, cast into the green and beautiful Miramichi water.

He walked toward the crane and looked at it, and at the date of the last inspection, three years before the accident. Amos was very troubled. Craig and Co., which owned the crane and the yard, would not want to be seen as negligent. But they had an out. Roger Savage had hooked on without being hired to hook on. The company had already issued a statement to the paper that Roger had been asked to leave the yard. No one could determine at the moment if this was in fact true. Most of the time it wouldn't be. That is, he was often there, and had been hired to work before. He was known and a very good worker. So letting him wander the yard wouldn't be considered anything out of the ordinary – until scrutiny and cover-up said it was.

So Amos scratched at the side of his face, and looked up at the pulleys, and then walked over to the last stretch of pulpwood in the long lot and looked back at the ship, humming lonely in the clear day, and said to himself:

"Dear, dear."

And looked at Markus and sighed.

Isaac waited for Amos to make a report, some report about what he intended. But nothing happened. Old Amos came back from the ship and went in and ate his supper of fish cakes and pickled beets. Isaac went back to the house and again, just like the last time, Amos was feeding his face. He waited at the door because he'd been told by Amos that he would be the first to receive any new information. But old Amos simply ate his supper, with the radio turned on to the French country music station. "J'aime Cherie" was playing.

Amos, with the five pictures he had taken but not yet examined, had no information that Isaac would want. For if he said, "It is nothing to worry our noodles about," Isaac would not believe him. If he said, "It was an accident," Isaac would not want to hear him. He knew Isaac wanted him to say: "It is a murder and I am taking action – I will block the road to his house until Savage is charged with murder, and we will take over the riparian rights to those pools! And build our lodge, and you will be in charge of them!"

This Isaac now wanted because it was needed by those who surrounded him, and he needed to please them.

But then Amos considered all of this slightly further and decided that Isaac did not want him to say he would take action either, for it would make Isaac less important if Amos mounted his own protest. In fact the one thing he could do to quash Isaac's power at this moment was to usurp Isaac's part in it. But he did not. He had to solve something first.

"Roger is not a bad man," he said.

"Go tell that to Hector," Isaac said.

"Oh yes, well, dear me."

So Isaac stayed outside, and Amos lay the photos out on the table and strained to see what they said. He sat eating fish cakes as his grandson Markus watched him, as he picked up a photo, shook his head, tapped a photo with his finger, shook his head, then ate another fish cake. Now and again he would look over at his grandson, and Markus would edge forward in his chair, with his feet wrapped about the legs, hoping the old man would speak. So the old man said:

"Markus."

"Yes?" Markus asked hurriedly. "What?"

"Snare me a piece of bread, will you?"

Isaac went away without Amos speaking further to him.

This was the day of the first newspaper report by Max Doran. The article was not specific, but gave a needling sense that things had been botched from the start – and not only by the wharf, but by the band counsel. This was what Amos expected, and again he was troubled.

"But you might be judging him all wrong," Mrs. Francis said. "He probably wants to say nice things about Hector – won't that be nice for the family if he does?."

"Yes, he might want to say nice things," Amos admitted, "but I wish we had all said nice things about Hector before."

The next morning, Amos went to Isaac's house, and standing in the small foyer with his hat in hand, asked the man if he would like to go up to the ship.

"Yes, I would like that," Isaac said. He looked at his wife, and nodded as if to say, *Now things will get done.*

Amos nodded too, happy to please this fellow finally.

So both got into Amos's old truck and travelled up the highway. Amos had only first and third gear on the truck, so the engine was either lugging along or whining. And every once in a while he would look over at Isaac apologetically.

"Roger probably hooked more than one load – trying to do Hector in – that's how I think and that's what many of our men are thinking too," Isaac said when Amos looked at him again. "I mean he could have jammed it opened with a rock or taken that supporting pin away. What do you think?"

"The captain has treated me with the utmost respect," Amos said, "and he is very concerned about all of this."

But as they drove down the old lane they saw something, little by little, emerge through the dark spruce trees, saw it as if a conjurer had played a trick – that was the feeling Amos had when he first realized that the ship's berth at the wharf was empty. He and Isaac stared at nothing – space and nothing else. It struck them almost as perverse, to stare at this empty wharf, while farther out in the water, as if to add insult to injury, the *Liverpool Star* was turning its engine over.

"My god – it's gone!" Amos said at last, in astonishment. He said this in astonishment because the fourth hold had not been filled, and he felt that the workers would have done this before they left. But they had left it the way it was, and took what they had in the other larger holds. What would that do

49

out in the sea, where these holds had to be balanced? This fact is what Amos had been relying on.

Finally he looked at Isaac and shrugged, and smiled. "They all ran away, Isaac. Look at that!"

Isaac looked at Amos and said nothing. But his face was filled with a compressed rage. The incriminating load of logs was left on the wharf, as if perhaps the sailors thought it was bad luck to take.

"Do you think I should take the logs?" Amos said.

"How in hell should I know."

"Well, maybe I will take the logs, then," Amos said. "What do you think? I mean, will they think I am stealing?"

"We once owned a hundred billion tons of wood, and you worry about a few logs."

"I suppose you're right. They might have thought they gave the ship bad luck. What do you think?"

"How the hell should I know? All they ended up doing is running away!"

Amos got out of the truck, and painfully and slowly loaded the eight-foot logs into his box and got into the cab again. He looked at Isaac and smiled as if confused.

"Yes, they left us," he said, "but does that matter? We do not need them to figure this out. We are both very clever, you and I – and if we work together we can come to solve it ourselves."

But the compressed rage on Isaac's face remained. He wanted nothing to do with this small fellow beside him.

"Call the Coast Guard and have the ship pulled up," Isaac said. "Do it now – they are still in Canadian waters. They haven't even reached the last bell buoy yet."

Amos simply shrugged again. "What power do we have over the Coast Guard?" he asked quietly.

Amos, who had finally got his chance to be chief, now realized the position he was in: although he had thought he would be having powwows and ceremonial meets, and exhibition hockey games against triple-A teams from around

New Brunswick, a crisis was developing and he was in over his head. He remembered how many people had said Isaac should have run for chief when he came back from out west the year before. And now Joel Ginnish was out of jail and back on the reserve, his half-brother dead, and both Isaac and Joel were walking up and down.

5

Isaac was a far, far grander-looking man than tired little Amos Paul. Isaac wore his hair long, in a ponytail down his back; he wore a deer shirt with symbols. In winter he stood out against gale-force winds to protect a stretch of land for Micmac hunters – a photo of him in the local paper attested to his courage.

Markus had dreamed that Isaac and Amos would join together and do wonderful things. But now little Amos Paul seemed outclassed and alone, hobbling around trying to keep things safe.

On the night after Amos and Isaac had been to the wharf, Markus made his way to Isaac's house just after dark, with the smell of gas in the cool air, and thin clouds beginning to form far away, and the early croaking of frogs. The road stretched down between dilapidated houses and past unpaved streets running up against the hills into black shrubs and twisted windfalls.

He was bothered by the thought of Hector, because of what he knew in his heart. No one had cared for Hector the way they should have. Not even Markus. They had all teased him for being skinny and tiny like a girl. And this is the one thing he had told Amos after the meeting of the band council. No one had spoken to Hector, no one cared about him, and he was mostly alone. That is why he went up to work the boat that day. He was lucky to get on, because of Amos. Because who ever bothered with him?

Sometimes Hector would sit on the big rock down on the

shore and skip stones for an hour or two, without saying a thing. The only one who was kind enough to skip stones with him was Little Joe Barnaby, who was eight.

Markus had always felt sorry for Hector. But what good did that do now? he had asked Amos. For he hadn't been much of a friend himself.

Amos had only nodded his head and patted his grandson's hand.

Rumour stated that the load was rigged, that the ship had been paid off to leave, to take the evidence out to sea. Just as the clouds swirled over Markus' head, so did rumour. Not only was what had happened to Hector a terrible tragedy but it was romantic, especially to the girls, who Markus himself wanted to impress.

"But," Markus ventured after arriving at Isaac's house and seeing all the youngsters sitting about and drinking beer in the yard, calling out to old adversaries as if they all were bonded together forever, "my granddad says if he did hook on, he would still have to hook on right or the load wouldn't have lifted and maybe even would have dropped before it got to the boat. Or as it swung over it."

"There's a hundred ways to do it," Joel Ginnish said, coming to the door and looking down at the boy as he made the motion of a knot. And everyone looked at Markus as if he was making things needlessly complicated because he was old Amos's grandson. Joel's words came from Joel, and that is why they were taken seriously. At that moment, Joel could have said anything and it would work to his advantage. So he stood there solemn and dignified while he spoke.

Yet Markus knew that Joel Ginnish was no expert. He had never worked at anything. When Markus thought about it, the statement "There's a hundred ways to do it" was not true at all. In fact, others there who had worked a boat or two would know that it wasn't. But none were bold enough to contradict the statement. And what they were saying about Roger Savage was that he was a criminal. Not just stupid or blundering, but a real criminal who wanted to kill people.

"We've got to get even," someone said, "for Hec," and people began to nod. And many began to call the boy Hec instead of Hector then and there.

Markus, with his very limited experience, still knew Hector's death would have had to involve prior knowledge and premeditation if it was more than an accident. Besides that – and it was a big besides – as long as Hector had stayed on his side of the hold, away from the drop, he would have been fine. And who in the yard would have known that Hector would step out as the load was coming down?

"No," Isaac said to Markus, putting his hand on his shoulder, "the load ricocheted and killed him. Let's not destroy his memory by saying it was his fault."

"I don't want to do that," Markus said, knowing that idea that he wanted to be negative about Hector's memory seemed more plausible than the fact that he might be telling the truth.

The year before, Isaac and Markus and Amos had all been part of a big, happy family. They had done things together, riding about in Isaac's Mercury, for Isaac had wanted to be known as a friend of the chief and a friend of the chief's grandson. They had gone to the gravel pit and Isaac had let them shoot his .30-30 rifle at Custer – meaning, bottles. Last winter they had even shot a moose – well, *they* didn't, but Isaac had – and Isaac had showed Markus how to hunt.

Isaac had been over to Amos's house for a beer or two to talk about the recreation centre and the skill saws there. Then Joel had come along. Joel suddenly acted as if he was instrumental in everything. He told people who Isaac was going to see and who he wasn't. He carried Little Joe Barnaby around on his shoulder. Joel had boxed in the Golden Gloves in 1979, so Markus was a little shy around him.

"Have you ever been in trouble?" Markus had asked.

"Oh, I been accused of lots of stuff," Joel would say, and kids liked him all the more.

That night, Markus went to bed thinking his grandfather was not in the best position and not the most favourite on the reserve anymore. Isaac was no man to fool with; he would do what he had to do in a crisis. And it certainly seemed like a crisis now. Markus did not know what to do. He could pray like his mother had, but he was too embarrassed to do that too.

Markus had read C. S. Lewis's "The Inner Ring" in a course he had taken that past year, from one of the teachers who still felt it wise to teach classics, from Cicero to Burke, and had suddenly realized what it was that was bothering him. This very essay C.S. Lewis had written, about the willingness to forgo a certain integrity in order to belong to a group, was dangerously close to describing exactly what was happening with him and the other boys. And he had found this out one afternoon.

Joel had set up a ring out back of his house so they could learn to box. He was teaching the boys to feint and jab, and teaching them to move laterally, and for the shorter boxers to come inside, to utilize their upper bodies and throw the uppercut. The men stood around watching this, the broad heat of midday on their backs and shoulders; the women watched too, yelling at times to their sons or boyfriends. Joel himself smiled at Markus and waved him over, and all the men and women turned towards him.

"No, I won't do it today," Markus said with a shrug.

Joel smiled. "Chicken – just like yer old man."

"You mean my grandfather?" Markus said.

"No, I mean David, yer old man – chicken."

Markus felt this was the meanest thing he had heard about his family. He had heard other mean things, but this was perhaps the meanest so far. He stood at the side of the lane and watched, and the men turned their backs on him. Markus hated what was said about his father, but he did not want to go over there. He felt it was because he was the grandson of Amos that some of the other boys said they wanted to get him into the ring. Even his great friends Andy and Tommie Francis, who were each older than he was by a year or two.

He was not frightened – it was worse than that. He was embarrassed that these friends, whom he had once laughed and played baseball with, now said they wanted to get him into the ring because Joel Ginnish was walking about the reserve, as Amos joked, as the big sheriff.

So Markus knew he would have to fight his friends or stay away. He chose to stay away – for now – hoping that this would allow him to save face.

Old Amos, hardly able to read or write, had said that this was what would happen. That is, that men would form this alliance and rely upon each other to tell each other what was right or wrong. So old Amos, without having read C.S. Lewis, was worried about the same thing as Markus.

But, Markus thought, Isaac had proven himself in a hundred battles with authority, with the RCMP, with crass and obnoxious legislation. And now everyone wanted justice, so what was wrong with that? Was Isaac fair? He was as fair as the white people were. Was he kind? He was as kind as they had been to his own father, who had been falsely accused and hanged in 1955. Did Isaac's father's death inflame the idea of injustice in Isaac? Of course it did. Had he sought revenge? Most certainly! Would he use other whites to call down to nothing people like Roger Savage? Sure. Much of what was said about Roger was probably true. Did it matter if it was proven? So much was unproven against the Micmac band, and what recourse had they had? So to start a war against Roger and use psychology that the whites would fear was fine by Isaac. That is, from now on, no one was allowed to say that Roger was innocent. And Joel Ginnish, acting as Isaac's right-hand man, let Markus know this himself.

"We cannot call him innocent," Joel said. "The white man is not innocent."

"But what if Roger *was* innocent?" was the question Markus continually asked, because it is what Amos had told him to ask.

"Ask it as you would for any Indian friend of yours," Amos said.

But the answer came: So what if, in this one instance, truth was not cut and dried? Why did it ever have to be? If Roger Savage was singled out, that was okay, for how many First Nations men had been singled out? And to belong, to be inserted into the inner circle, to be loved by those who believed they were sweeping their broad wings toward ideological change – beside that, what did a Roger Savage matter? That Roger was beginning to be called a racist after the funeral, what did it matter? Roger had visited the grave of Hector Penniac – everyone knew about this. For everything he did was now seen.

Joel went about saying that those who wanted to join Isaac were fine. Those who did not want to join were then against him. And if you were against him, then you were against the First Nations themselves. And the First Nations would then stand against you.

This was all whispered, and yet there was such wonderful power and truth and sincerity in the whispers that Markus trembled.

Who, then, could go against Isaac's new group, to halt this presumption? Or to even dare to call it presumption? Perhaps there was only one man on the six-hundred-person reserve brave enough to do so.

And that man was seventy-five-year-old Amos Paul, who had been given an honorary elders' dinner just last year. This was the only man, old and arthritic, who had hunted moose from the time he was a child, who had chased moose down in the winter air, who had fished on the sea and had laboured against discrimination and injustice, who had known both, who had fought in the battles of the Second World War, who had been decorated and then not allowed to enter the Legion with his regiment to have a beer with those his rifle had helped save – this man was the one who now looked across the withered fields and small houses, where every window told of tragedy and broken promises, and stared into the faces of Isaac and especially Joel and saw aggrandizement, not at the expense of Roger Savage – no, that was not the point – but at the expense of the band itself.

When Markus had come home that night from Isaac's, the old man was sitting at the kitchen table, doing a jigsaw puzzle, and as always searching everywhere for the small piece he already held in his hand.

"He will have a right-hand man," Amos said, not looking his way, but mulling over the puzzle.

"Who?"

"Who would Isaac want? Well?"

"I don't know! Maybe Joel."

Amos said nothing for a moment. Then, "No, he won't *want* Joel, but he will need him."

He hemmed and hawed over the puzzle. "Joel. Do you know he steals out of our own nets and sells the fish?"

"Everyone says that," Markus said.

Old Amos hemmed and hawed once more, and held the piece out and dragged it across the puzzle trying to find a place where it would fit.

"It's true. He stole from Francis's net and Ward's, and he stole from mine – four big fish last week. And do you know who he sells them to?"

"No," Markus said.

"He sells them to the Monk brothers, who sell them again up the road. That's my fish he stole, and Mrs. Francis's, who has all those kids, and Denny Ward's. And yet" – here he inserted the piece – "Joel is now chief appointment maker. So what am I to say?"

Then he added: "You remember that I have taken some

pictures of the boat, and it is a very strange accident. Very strange all the way around."

Two days after Isaac had invited those boys to his house and spoken of Hector's death, Joel woke early and went to the corner store to buy the paper. There was nothing in it about Hector that day – yet there was a Canadian Press report about the United Nations. Then he looked to see if his letter about his brother's murder had been printed. It had not been.

Very upset with the lack of action, Joel took the ceremonial hunting-lodge spear right from the hunting lodge and threw it into a tree that Roger was standing beside, near the edge of a secondary pool where the river followed the bend, close to Micmac ground. Roger came out there each day to see if the salmon had made their way up after the Micmac nets were lifted. The grilse run would of course be bigger later on. The fish did not stay in these pools very long, but Roger could tell the strength of the run by seeing them, and decide on the number the band was catching. He did not mind the band catching them – his dispute was with Joel, who he believed took far too many. Roger took the spear out of the tree and was going to break it, but realizing how old it was he set it on the bar and walked away.

Hector had had nothing to do with Roger's pools, but this was now seen by some as the reason for his death.

So by evening everyone on the reserve had heard of this act of defiance against the white man Roger Savage who had taken their pools.

Markus wanted to think that his grandfather had somehow sanctioned all this action. But he soon knew that this was not the case. His grandfather only seemed old and bewildered.

In fact, the next evening the old man walked to the band council meeting that came after the spear throwing. Joel stood among them, accepting the congratulations of some boys, while the night smelled of sea salt and tar, one side door having been left open. Amos walked through the crowd and up to him.

"You should not have thrown that spear," he said mildly, his right hand trembling slightly. "You might have hurt someone. And for what – a salmon pool that will come back to us for good in a year or two more. No, my boy, you should not have done that." He fumbled about, looking from one face to the other. But there were no friendly faces.

Joel shrugged. "My brother's dead," he said, "and you're worried about a spear thrown at a fuckin tree!" He was the first to leave, as if he did not want to disrespect himself by staying.

Other people turned away, and soon the old man was alone with Markus, who was waiting silently outside to drive him home.

"What happened, Granddad?" Markus asked.

"I do not know what I am supposed to do," Amos said.

After the band meeting, back in Isaac's smoky kitchen, some of the young men told him that he was their chief.

Isaac held up his hand. "Give me time now," he said, "to find a reasonable explanation."

But the reasonable explanation was already there. More importantly, Isaac was already legendary. Not to use him in this crisis, not to exploit him, would be senseless. And each of the young men knew this would be part of the reasonable explanation that Isaac would discover.

So this was when the warrior group around Isaac was formed. It was only six or seven men, those who were the most trusted by him, those who were the more secretive and brave.

But the painful fact for Markus, who was not allowed in the group, for he was not trusted, was that this group was formed as a rebellion against Amos Paul and included many of his friends, who no longer included him. Dates and treaties that had gone back almost two hundred years were spoken about as being dissolved. "It is all dissolved," Joel said, shaking his head, "all dissolved. There is no more reserve, no more Canada. We will do what we want."

No one said this, but most knew that sooner or later a crime would have to be committed.

Each morning Markus saw Roger Savage walk along the demarcation line toward his woodlot and come out later in the day, after cutting wood or checking his pools and the beaver lodges farther upriver toward Tabusintac.

Roger was not a coward. He had walked into a meeting two nights before. And with men standing beside the door, he had excused himself as he passed them. There in their midst, with Amos in his seat as chief, Roger said, "I have nothing against anyone here, and have never had. I will tell you, if you come upriver to net my pools, I will hay yours." That is, he meant he'd put hay in the water, which would carry down-river and sweep the Indian gillnets.

The silence was unbearable. Old Amos nodded but said nothing. Isaac, taller than Roger but probably no stronger, simply looked at him and did not speak.

This was not out of fear, of course, but out of respect for the band meeting. From 1755, from the time of the first band meeting held here with people from other races, everyone was allowed to have their say.

Later, Roger continued working on his house after dark using two propane lanterns, for he had a large propane tank, so that he himself appeared only in shadow and the saw-cuts of dust fell like warm grace.

But soon after that, Max Doran, with his shiny eyes and straw hat and terrible earnestness to get at the truth, which he believed he had already arrived at, started to attract notice. And then the papers started their stories.

Suddenly. Like a hailstorm.

Part II

September 6, 2006

Markus liked John Wayne movies and often walked to the store late at night to get them, coming back through side lanes to his apartment. Yet he could never get used to his VCR and always seemed to push the wrong buttons. He heard that now VCRs were almost obsolete.

So if he had never learned to use what was obsolete, how could he learn to use what was coming? He had a cell phone, but it was almost never charged. He no longer drove a squad car, but his old red Honda. He was an insomniac and would wake at night and walk, sometimes for miles, along the road. He had pain now and again in his chest. He'd been in London and sat near the fountain in Trafalgar Square, where Nelson had viewed the sky. He'd flown someone back across the ocean – he'd been the bodyguard of a famous author who had come to Canada and was very distressed that people would want him killed. The RCMP had given him Markus.

"What will happen if the assassins get through the door?" the author asked.

"I am sure they never will."

"But if they do – if and when they do?"

"If they do, you will not be here, and I will face them alone."

Markus had wanted to get the author's autograph, but never did.

He had watched John Wayne's last movie, *The Shootist*, four times. Each time tears came to his eyes. Lauren Bacall was still beautiful in that movie.

Then he would write in his notebooks, which were piled helter-skelter in the corner of the room.

"Where is Roger Savage's rifle?" he wrote in 1998, after that trip to England.

Now, in the early fall of 2006, he would come home from work and stare at his bookshelf. He had a good two thousand books stashed everywhere, packed in boxes and on shelves. He was looking for the book that would define that summer long ago when Hector Penniac had died. For himself and Max Doran. He believed he might find it. That one book.

When the time was right.

1985

1

Late one afternoon in early July of 1985, as Amos sat out on his old couch behind the shed and looked down over the small lot to the great bay and his few crabapple trees that never seemed to have a reasonable crabapple, a newspaperman, Max Doran, came to see him. The reporter was about twenty-five with reddish blonde hair tied in a ponytail. He had done a good job on several labour disputes and a case about pollution in the last year. It was his dogged determination to hold others accountable that had made him a hero. He gave up on nothing, and intimated some terrible things about those he wrote of. He had his own slogan: "Viewer discretion is advised."

Like many who believed in sedition, he'd had, from youth, a deep puritanical strain.

The whole nature of investigative reporting was to expose – and to say Doran was impartial was absurd. He had never been impartial. But he had a very strong sense that his facts were the legitimate ones, that his posture was moral, that the purity of his notions were liberal and therefore inviolate. He would not lose a story; he would continue until the end. He had been threatened before, and was hard to scare. He believed he must try to change the fabric of government. And someday, Max knew, he would write his blockbuster.

Amos had heard of Max Doran. Amos had read him. This is why Amos feared him.

A veteran journalist had taken Doran under his wing two years before, a man who had never written anything too memorable but had once drank with Louis Robichaud and once with Dalton Camp. He told everyone he was Doran's mentor, and now lived vicariously through the work the boy did. So this veteran told Doran to take this story, and to look at the strain of overt bigotry in the province, as he sat in his faded grey suit drinking his fifth gin of the day.

"You know this has been Canada's festering sore!" the man pontificated. "You need to get those arrogant lying bastards – make our government wake up."

Max could not detect the envy in the old socialist's voice. He listened to this advice while his mentor cupped his hands over Max's hands, leaned close and rasped, "Festering, festering, festering fucking sore! The arrogant bastards, all of them! For once in his fucking life he was kept from a job by an Indian, and the prick kills him – kills him! If that load had dropped from the very top, it might have killed them all."

"Don't worry," Max said, gently. "I intend to take this all the way!"

"Yes, yes," his mentor said, sitting up and finishing off his gin, "I pray you will, for an old man who has been in the fight too long – take it all the fucking way!"

It made Doran feel good to be considered working class, to go to the press club and drink scotch with older, haggard, alcoholic reporters from the Louis Robichaud years who now looked forward to their pensions, and who spoke of great stories they themselves had never done.

This story, about a "deeply disturbing" death in the north of the province – a place that had more than thirty-two percent unemployment at any given time, a place given to bad roads, disputes and violence that you always heard about – would be the catalyst to change his life.

So in some ways, Doran already believed the allegations against Roger and was simply finalizing a report that he had been waiting to file most of his life.

"I had no idea that this plum would be handed to me," he told a colleague. The younger journalist, Gordon Young, wished him good luck and quietly offered him a piece of advice that his mentor had not: "All kinds of people will say all kinds of things. I would not go on the reserve at the invitation of any one person or group. I would interview only those involved or having some knowledge of what happened in the pulp yard on that day – anything else will lead to a conundrum."

Max humbly nodded his thanks.

He got directions to find Chief Amos Paul, and went to the house and knocked, but no answer came. So he looked in the living-room window and saw right through to the backyard – for the living-room had a window at the front and the back. And there Amos was, a little old man on a lawn chair, whittling on a piece of poplar.

"Well, once again you've had an awful time here," Max said, holding out his hand.

"Oh, what an awful time," Amos said taking the hand limply and letting go.

"I'm talking about the killing of Hector Penniac," Doran said more loudly, as if the old man was deaf.

"Hector – did you know him?"

"No, I never had that privilege."

"The what?"

"Privilege."

"Ahhh," old Amos said, holding his whittled stick and looking at the ground. "So many people have not have that."

"What do you think happened?" Doran asked.

"He was killed in the hold up there . . ."

"Well, I know – that's why I'm here. So do you, sir, think this is a criminal case?"

"My soul," Amos said, and grinned and scratched his cheek.

Then Amos spoke in his mild mannered way, and looked up at the young man looking down at him. "Perhaps, in a way, we do not know yet," he said. The old man knew that many people, no matter who they were, said they wanted the truth, and then wanted certain answers to fit what their idea of truth was.

Max continued: "Some say it was another crime against the people here – that the dispute is really over fishing? That Hector paid the price because of this dispute between his brother and that man . . . his name . . . his name . . ." (here he looked at his notes) ". . . Roger Savage, who was at the scene?"

"I do not know," old Amos said truthfully. He began tapping his stick and looking out toward the trees. This man had already made the connection between Joel and Hector, and Joel and Roger – and therefore Roger and Hector. That was a pretty good start, the old fellow thought, to get Roger in trouble. So after a time Amos simply did not answer Doran anymore. Doran would speak and Amos would blink.

Doran sat down on a rock, and looked over toward the wood where Amos was looking. He spoke about the over-cutting of trees and the great pollution up at Little River, the ducks that had died. One hundred and thirty-two ducks. What did a First Nations man think of that? One hundred and thirty-two ducks.

"A bunch of ducks, for sure. I don't know," Amos said.

Doran spoke about the ship, the *Lutheran*, having left port, and the case now seeming stalled.

Amos puzzled over this a moment but said nothing.

Max opened his notebook again, looked at his five pages of notes, and asked how old Amos was. Amos told him. Doran asked if he'd fought in the war.

"Many," Amos said, smiling and still tapping his stick on the ground.

"And what is the one thing your people need?"

"For all time?"

"Yes, for all time."

"To be left alone," Amos said. And he set about rolling a cigarette. He took his tobacco out and put the rolling paper on his knees and spread the tobacco. Then he rolled it carefully, with his tongue stuck in his cheek, and licked the paper. Then he snapped a match, and lighted it. Then he rubbed his ankle, which he had broken the year before falling from his roof, and which still pained him. He was rubbing his ankle as Doran made his next comment.

"I want to help you," Doran said.

"You do?"

"Yes. You need to realize that. I am here to help – so what is it you need?"

"I need a cold pack for my ankle," old Amos said.

Once last year, after Doran's most famous article, about a mayor he had secretly taped, had been published a young woman – a hairdresser – came up to him in the mall, and asked: "How can you do that to people?"

But Doran had pressed on; he'd been certain of that story. And he needed no hairdresser to tell him what to do. Once, Max saw the mayor on the street and couldn't help but tell him he had no hard feelings. He stuck out his hand for the mayor to take. Part of what he did was for himself, and part of it was to please his mentor, who egged him on, but part of it was to help pay his mother's rent and the night nurse she now needed. He had never had a date, and except for a few older alcoholic journalists, he had never had a friend. His father had deserted him and then had died in New York ten years ago.

"Come here," Amos said now, and the young man walked with him to the edge of the field. When they were standing side by side, looking out over the dark edges of black spruce, Doran squinting expectantly, Amos said, "If I could, I would like to move my hunting camp from there into the boggin above the highway – beyond the Tabusintac and into the region where I went as a boy with my mom and dad. That is all gone now. Can you help me move my camp? If we do it one board at a time it will take most of the summer." Then he laughed and patted Doran on the back, hard enough to drive the younger man forward so that he almost fell.

71

Amos grabbed him to steady him. "Don't worry, it will all turn out," he said. "I am sure if you knew Roger you would like him – at least a little."

"Oh, I think I know him fairly well," Max answered. He was angry now, and he smiled slightly.

For a moment they were silent. Amos dragged in smoke through his mouth and let it out through his nose and looked at the young man mildly. "Mr. Doran, have you hunted?"

"I don't like guns – "

"Fished?"

"No . . ."

"Been in a storm at sea?"

"No."

"Lived in the woods and hunted for food, and killed moose on your own?"

"No."

"Excuse me – but do you even know one rifle from another?"

"No, I know I cannot match you there." Doran laughed. "I know you know far more about it then I do – "

Amos interrupted him, mildly: "I am not at all talking about me, son. I am talking of Roger Savage, who you just said you know – yet you have done nothing he has, lived nothing like him. So please. you should not judge."

Doran shrugged. "I am not judging anyone, Mr. Paul"

"Then I am happier with you than I was," Amos answered, winking.

All Amos talked about on the way back to the house was the recreation centre and the new school, and how the reserve was really coming along. But when they arrived, Doran spied the pulp in the truck, and looked at it peculiarly. He put his hands in his pockets – and Amos decided this might be his way of trying to look grown up.

"What is this?" Doran asked.

"The wood that was dropped," Amos said. "What is strange about it?"

"I don't know. What do you mean?"

Amos shrugged and said nothing more.

"*Is* there something strange about it?" Doran asked.

"Yes, it is peculiar – I think. I am about to make myself lunch. Would you like some smoked salmon?"

Doran left the old chief and continued on, muttering to himself about the old fool. He walked here and there, along the patched road, with crabgrass and broken bottles in the ditches, the smell of old cinder block in the weeds, now and then bending over to brush off his shoes. And as he walked he saw the small spindrift houses, the broken porch steps, old sheds, and older dogs. That is, he did not see what old Amos did when he looked at the same scene – that with a Rec Center and school, things were better.

He tried not to be angry at the old fellow. But no one made a fool of Max. He jutted his chin out, thinking this. Mr. Cyr, sixty-eight years old, who owned the paper Doran worked for and many more like it, was waiting to see how this reporter would do his job, for he could have put other reporters on the story. The managing editor had vouched for Max, and Cyr had sent Doran a telegram which Doran cherished more than anything: "Awaiting your report with much anticipation, for this is the place I grew up." It was almost as if a gauntlet had been thrown down, and he, Max, must prove himself. He remembered too what his mentor said about bigotry being a festering sore.

Doran sat down on the side of the breakwater and ate his lunch – two egg sandwiches his mom had made. He looked out toward a far-off island, shimmering in haze, and some of the lobster boats that were making it over the soft swell toward the wharf. He was lonely. He was also afraid – he did not know of what. The First Nations people who saw him slowed down, waved, and said hello.

"What a strange place this is," Doran thought. He had

wanted the chief to be more upset and now he nibbled at his second sandwich wondering what to do.

As he was walking back toward his car he came upon young men pitching horseshoes in a field by one of the houses. So he went to ask about Hector. They stared at him a long time, wondering if they should answer. But these men, Andy and Tommie Francis and two others, finally did respond.

"Of course he was murdered," one of the men said. "Who wouldn't know that – or be able to figure it out? We're Indian aren't we?"

"Well – I went to the chief – "

"Whose chief? Not my chief anymore," Andy Francis said, laughing bitterly. "Look what he did – he took the logs from the ship himself so no one would see what happened."

So Max asked about Roger Savage, and took out his notebook. He learned Roger Savage was after Hector because Hector had taken his job on the boat, and Roger had fought with Hector's older brother.

"He couldn't handle Joel, no white man can," one of the young men said, "so he went after the weaker guy – that's what happened. He went after someone littler and weaker, and we weren't there to protect Hector. Roger thought he was going to work in the hold, and when he wasn't allowed, he tried his trick."

"Hector," another young man said, and he believed this truthfully, just like most of the boys gathered about, "was going to be a doctor and come back to our reserve and work."

Max Doran was said nothing. His face was inscrutable, as it often was when he interviewed people. But he was thinking, how could such a life not be honoured? And in that regard he was right. "There have been too many Rogers," he whispered to himself. "Too many old Amos Pauls. who just simply go along to get along." He thanked the boys and continued on his way.

He went to Roger's house and knocked. There was no answer. He knocked again and walked around to the new room the man was building. No one was home, the place so silent it was unnerving.

Before Doran left the reserve, he walked back to the chief's house and took a picture of those logs, to publish with his article.

The article was printed four days later. Doran had been asked about his sources, about the dispute between Roger and Hector's family. But all of these things did pan out – in fact, the fight between Joel and Roger was in the public record.

The editor who had vouched for Doran let the article go to print after a few changes. "It is pretty hard hitting against that boy Roger, and the chief – who is that? Amos whatever? Why don't you take the accusations against the chief out. They aren't needed," the editor said, and so Max took them out. Still he had decided the chief was the real problem toward progress.

"The man Isaac Snow is the real hero in all of this any-way," he told his managing editor. "Not that comical little old man who simply wants to be called chief, and takes me down the street to show me a damn fire hydrant."

But Max did tone down the article. He took out any flat accusations. And though he wrote the article, he included a paragraph from the Canadian Press to make it seem broader based, and not so personal. So the article was fairly non-specific. It recounted the event, spoke also of how depressed the region was, how little the Micmac had and how they were kept from fishing lobster though it was their only livelihood in the region. It mentioned how Hector had wanted to take a job at the wharf, and how his was one of two union cards given to First Nations that year. But then, at the end of the article, Max added something. He quoted one man as saying: "We've always had trouble with him."

"This *him* they talk about is the person who has denied he hooked the last load, the load that fell on Hector Penniac – Mr. Roger Savage."

This was the last line in the two-column article. The line everyone worried about.

And the paper printed a picture of the derelict and murderous logs.

2

Early in the morning, Roger Savage's girlfriend, May, phoned him, and told him to buy the newspaper – for he was now on the front page. Her voice was shaking, and for a few moments Roger did not know it was her.

"The first page," she said. "The first page!"

May was more concerned now that the report was on the front page, and wanted to know what he had to say.

"Let me read it first," he said. He tried to sound light-hearted, but he wasn't.

He walked to the store, and knew people were watching him. When he bought the paper, the clerk, a man he knew, didn't look at him as he rang his twenty-five cents in.

Roger walked home as if he was carrying his own death sentence.

He read the story, and for the first time he knew something he had not foreseen was to be made of the accident. That is, who he was and what he represented in the Canadian consciousness was going to come into play – though he did not know how to say this – and was going to be used against him as a rebuke. The byline – "Max Doran, with files from the Canadian Press" – gave it all a very formal and frightening air.

"What did I do," Roger said, even questioning himself now. "Maybe I was always a bully – that's what they say!"

No one wanted to be accused of supporting a man who would do this – yet by not supporting him he suddenly became not a single individual who might do this but "that kind of man." What was absurd is that Roger wouldn't have supported any man who would deliberately do this – but perhaps because of his own sense of honour, he would still have said hello to him.

More to the point, the union, which would have, or might have, supported Morrissey accidentally doing the exact same thing, could never support Roger, because he wasn't supposed to have hooked. The company backed the union because they feared a lawsuit.

"It don't matter what they say about me – I didn't do nothing," Roger told his girlfriend later. It worried him that his girlfriend, for the first time, did not completely exonerate him but was silent as he tried to explain himself.

"But I didn't do nothing!" he yelled. "You have to believe that or I will lose my mind!

"Well, I know that," May said at last. "And don't yell at me – I'm not the newspaper man."

"I know you aren't," he said.

"But people said you hooked and the paper implied you did, even if you says you didn't! And that you fought with people down there. I know you were upset all last summer with that Joel man, and he is Hector Penniac's brother. What is the newspaper to say if everyone tells them that? I mean, they is only human – aren't they now?"

"Damn the paper, I did not hook! And the man who wrote this would not know a hook or a pin – and wants everyone all riled up over nothing." And Roger hung up. The possibility that he would have to lie like this had never before entered his head. But now he had to hold to his lie no matter what. What was worse, he had thought of a lawyer he'd once guided for moose, and had phoned this man, and the lawyer had suggested he take a lie detector test since that would strip away all the rumours.

"I'll think it over," Roger said.

But with that statement the lawyer knew Roger was hiding something. And Roger could not face phoning him again. He pondered whether he should admit that he'd hooked; but he felt that if he did so this late, he would never overcome the suspicion of murder. And the Natives would burn him out for sure. So he did not phone the lawyer back, and the lawyer was free to tell people this, and it became known that Roger Savage would not take a lie detector test.

Roger's hair was short and his nose blunt, his arms and shoulders strong, his neck thick. His legs too were thick and strong, and he most often wore leather shoes rather than sneakers, and had his jean cuffs rolled up. He had not seen his mother in two years, and his father was dead. He had earned his own way entirely since he was sixteen. He had fought the people who wanted to help him and had sent social workers away. And now he was worried about this paper man, and how sending the social workers away and fighting at school would work against him. But he was worried too about the lie that he had invented at first to protect Morrissey and now could not take back.

The article was not like a punch in the head – he had taken enough of those – or a bad cut with an axe – he had taken one of those too. It was not like anything he had felt before – cold on the ice flats or the bump of waves out on the bay at night when it came up to swell. No, this article was much different. It made him ill. It was as if voltage crept through him. As if, worse, he who had never felt he had to explain himself to anyone must now explain himself to the whole province and tell them he had not done anything wrong. And worse, the surge of this strange electricity that came from the paper told him that the more he spoke, the less he would be believed.

He sat in the house and smoked, and it got dark, and then darker. It was like fighting a giant shadow. Each time you swung your fist, your arm went through, the shadow disappeared, only to reappear in another part of the room.

The article deeply worried others too. And one was a little fellow named Chief Amos Paul.

Amos was very bright. He was annoyed that this death would now play into Isaac's hands. He was not saying Isaac wanted this, but he knew Isaac would be told he wanted it, and be forced in the end to act as if he believed it. The newspaperman would act as if he believed it too. He would have to. For if the newspaperman now said there was no miscarriage of justice and it was all nonsense, he would be looked upon as being criminal. So this newspaperman had to continue; he had no choice. And that was bad for him. And it meant that others would spur the newspaperman on, by telling him not to be cautious but to be resolute, and he would do so in order to keep his story on the front page.

This did not mean a miscarriage of justice had not taken place, however. Nor did it mean a crime had not taken place either. But it did mean that this crime had made opportunities that those who sought opportunity could not ignore. Amos was not quoted in the article – and that placed him outside the concern of those who were quoted. And their concerns suddenly seemed to be exactly the right concerns to have, while Amos's little concerns seemed pedestrian and old-fashioned.

If Amos did not see this as an insult toward him, fifteen-year-old Markus did. He became disheartened that the man he loved, and whose people up until this moment had loved, was now not even acknowledged as chief. This would plague Markus Paul for years.

Amos did not take a phone call from Roger late in the day. It was not that he did not want to take it, just that at this moment he couldn't tell Roger anything to give him hope. And there were so many phone calls of support for the band.

"Yes, yes, yes – something will be done – yes yes, yes!' Amos continued to deflect the enthusiasm.

Then, three days later, Amos got another phone call. "Here is what I will do," Doran's managing editor offered. "The police are stalling – I think they are frightened. But I have a reporter here who is not. I will send Max to the river again and he will write about the progress of the case. He will be fair to all – and he will be fair to Mr. Savage as well. The paper has a policy and we adhere to it pretty ethically. What do you say to that?"

All of it made Amos feel uncomfortable. Especially how this man said the word "progress." For Amos was one of those old fashioned men seen in every race, who do not believe in progress when it concerns the hearts of men. He saw that every generation believed they would be the generation to set things straight, and no generation did.

Amos asked to speak to Doran, but was told Doran was finishing up another story. Doran was actually standing by the desk, making hand signals, and mouthing: "Tell him I respect him very much."

His boss waved his hand at Doran to be quiet. Then he said: "What could be the harm? I mean: the truth! The absolute Truth for a change – no dilly-dallying – and you find out if it was an accident or a murder of one of your own people?"

But the secret was, Doran did not need old Amos Paul's permission because he had been on the phone to Isaac now for two days. And Isaac wanted Doran, and no one else, to file the stories. The idea that this was because Doran was a white man they could trust was taken as implicit – but for Isaac it was about control. He had to at least try and control the information coming from the reserve, and the primary reason for this need was Joel Ginnish. Isaac had to keep the most unpredictable member of the reserve satisfied. This was his most pressing problem.

Isaac had already been at a meeting with the Minister of Fisheries. At this meeting Isaac was offered eleven commercial lobster licences if he would assure the government there would be no problems that summer. The Fisheries said it was an initial offer, but Isaac said it was far too limited – and it also amounted to blackmail. Also, there was no discussion of

81

the home fishery, because the natives refused to consider giving up any part of their treaty right to fish for food for themselves, and certainly not in exchange for the eleven lobster licences.

So it was Isaac who told Doran to come up.

"Should I get Amos's permission?" Doran asked. "I mean, I won't stay on the reserve but I'll be there a lot, so I should – "

"Phone him," Isaac said. There was a long pause. "But then phone me back and let me know what you decide." And he hung up.

Doran, used to boys and young men, had never heard such power in a voice. He was a little in awe. So he had the editor phone Amos.

"Some say Amos is complicit in a cover-up," Doran said, though no one actually had said this. But at this moment he was almost as angry with Amos as he was with Roger. And he told all of this to his mother before he went.

So even if Max Doran did not want it, sooner or later he would be in the cauldron too. And Max seemed to sense this as he left for the Miramichi. He knew in his heart and soul that being a good journalist was always and only what he wanted to be, but already something about this wasn't right.

3

Amos Paul had an old Ford truck and a dory, a small fishing boat that was up in the yard, with a hole just below the starboard gunnels. He was trying to get a recreation centre built, and was working on a program for young native children from his reserve to visit other reserves across the country. There were some new houses being built and two shapely new fire hydrants. He had thought he was doing very well, until this moment. Now, he was thrust into something he did not know how to respond to. To not let Doran on the reserve would be best, but it would look like collusion, especially when Isaac wanted him to come. Still, Amos did not want him, and wished he would go away.

But who would Amos be in collusion with? The priests who had once beaten him at the French school? The English cottagers who never looked his way? The police who had put his wife in jail and had hit him in the face? Where would this collusion be, and who would it be with? But so many already thought this of Amos – to say Doran could not come into the reserve would reinforce what was already being said.

Now Amos himself was baffled and tormented, because nothing at all had been proven against this Roger Savage. Still, it looked very bad for Roger now – and as always, people were now saying that they'd always known Roger was this way. People – whites as well as natives – were telling stories of how they themselves had had to deal with Roger.

"I had to backhand him myself a few times," one white

man had told Amos at Sobeys two days before. Amos said nothing to all of this. Sometimes he would say, "My, my," and sometimes he would say, "Dear, dear," and sometimes he would be silent altogether.

It was like picking a person out of a group of people and saying he must be guilty for all the others and then tying him to a post and shooting him. Roger's father was dead, his mother had deserted him; he was alone in a house he had a deed to that his own mother had tried to take from him because she had had an offer from the band to buy it for twice what it was worth. That is, she had tried to cheat her own child.

So Amos, in protecting Roger, had a far, far harder task than Isaac, who people were saying was both brave and noble.

Amos could get himself out of this predicament easily, by siding with them. It was tempting enough, for other sentiments on the reserve were like a giant magnet pulling him. But he did not.

The only thing Amos could say was: "Roger Savage has not done anything wrong – as far as I can see – so he is under the band's protection."

The reserve's interconnected politics were not lost on Max Doran. But to him, this was not at all the issue. He did not blame Roger Savage, a man brought up where he was, but also he could not see how Roger was in the least innocent. This is what he told his mother before he left Saint John. He did try, on the way up in the car, to fathom how it might be that a man such as this was innocent. Perhaps the death was an accident. He knew he did not like people like Roger, so in his own way he really tried to think positive things about him, but he found it hard to do so. Men like Roger did not just bully and beat men like Hector Penniac; they bullied men like Max Doran – and always had. People like Roger were exactly the kind who would destroy people like Hector. And the lie Roger had told about hooking was everything. In fact, it is what put Doran in such a shaky spot.

The one conversation by phone he'd had with Roger had come the day before. His mother, who was worried, and sat knitting with a great deal of nervousness, asked him to call. So he had. But Roger had become upset almost immediately.

"Tell me you hooked," Max said finally, "and I will resolve to find out how it happened the way you say it did."

"Well . . . but I did not hook," Roger said. "And I have been talking to a lawyer."

"Talking to a lawyer!" Max said, bemused. He could do nothing else. The man was a liar.

There was another reason for Doran's constant deliberation, as he told his mom. It was this: Did those who ran the paper gave one fig for him? No, and he knew they did not. Some of them, he knew, hated him. "Do you think, Mom, if I don't do a good job, I will get another chance? There are five other reporters who want this!"

So if Doran did not use this one story to advance himself, he was as doomed as Hector Penniac.

"But do you need such a spotlight?" his mother asked.

"I want to report!" was all he could answer.

"Would you give up this story to bring Hector back?" his mother asked, almost kindly, looking up at him and trying to smile. And his heart went out to her, because she was ill.

So this thought came over him too as he got to Rogersville, and it bothered him more than once. Would he give up this story to bring Hector back? He knew he could say yes in a second, but he was unsure whether it was true. Also, would he give up a story if it provoked a death?

The road to the Miramichi was long and crooked enough to think of these disturbing things.

After Doran's first article was published, he was silent, wondering what his mother had said about it. Yet everyone at the paper was impatient with him. And he'd had to ask himself if he was determined enough to see things through, come what may, or should he really be doing something else?

So a week after the *Lutheran* drifted away, there came an article, suddenly and explosively, which showed Max Doran could not take Roger's explanation seriously, and believed his reticence bespoke proof of a guilty conscience. Max needed to link a fascinating story in the national media with his own story, so his own story might tag on to the one already in the national press. It was Isaac Snow who had brought this up with him, who asked him why his story wasn't getting more recognition. It was Isaac who was disheartened by how small-potatoes the local story was, and so he had spurred young Doran on.

And this is what Doran wrote:

"The murder of a First Nations man, Nathan Blacksnake, in Saskatoon last month brings home our rather blasé attitude toward the death of Mr. Hector Penniac, a young Micmac man who went to work a boat up on the Miramichi, and was found dead in the hold at quarter past eleven that morning. He lasted at this job – a job that he needed – just two hours. That in itself is a tragedy. What is more so is the attitude of those in authority who must deal with this. How much are they willing to divulge to us? The ship has already sailed, the case seems closed; it is being called an accident. Hector Penniac graduated with honours, and wanted to be a doctor and come back to a reserve sorely in need of gifted men. Some people on the reserve are hesitant to talk – and who can blame them? For years we, as white men, told them what they could and could not do. If we are to respect ourselves as human beings, that must change now, and the guilty, whoever they are, must be held responsible."

Although Doran never stated it, when he mentioned Mr. Blacksnake, who was sickeningly beaten to death by three white men, he implied that Hector Penniac had been murdered too. No one wanted a bad story or a wrong story – but a story, like anything else, has its own life, and Max Doran, in trying to be fair, was in fact following the life of the very story he had created. So far the paper had been spared embarrassment by their connection to the land claim case on the river, and to the Dutch shipping company of which they themselves owned a percentage. But in receiving compliments from certain friends and people in positions of authority, especially at the university, Doran again felt shallow – for he believed he had written in the main what Isaac Snow had wanted, and this sat very heavy on him. In fact he couldn't look at this article he had written, even though he was receiving accolades for it.

Roger was twice more taken in by the police to be questioned. He sat in the office and said what he had said before – he'd had nothing to do with Hector's death. He had not hooked, and he was sorry for the death of the man. The police became as insistent as temper allowed, calling him a coward and a bully, saying that he would not get away with it. "Would you know how to hook to have the clamp jam open – I mean, if you did it?"

"Yes, I would jam it open. The weight would shift and might make the logs fall – I suppose . . . but it wouldn't be for certain."

"But you could do it?"

"Yes."

"It's damn funny that you know what happened. I mean, that's what people say you did, as a prank. You didn't really want to kill him, did you – just have fun and scare him so he would quit and you'd get the job?" a policeman named Hanover asked. "Why don't you just admit how surprised you were that Indian fella got a job? And now you are sorry about it – we know that."

"Sure – except I didn't hook."

They kept Roger in the office more than four hours. But finally they had to let him go home.

Both times, First Nations men went to the police station

and waited in the dry, listless parking lot to hear what would happen. And both times Roger came out, walked past them and went home. Both times, he reiterated he had not hooked. And there was no proof he had hooked, except for the leaners, who were both drunk and said so.

Both times, Joel Ginnish shrugged and put his hands out as if all this was beyond him, and then they all turned and followed Roger back to his house.

"You hay our nets, you'll be in for it," one of the men said.

"Yeah – or step over our line, too, when you're in your yard."

"Or speak to our women," someone else said.

Then they all broke out laughing, even Roger. And all of them would laugh, and then stop laughing, and then Joel would say something, and that would strike them all as funny, and all of them, even Roger, would laugh again.

Doran went back to Saint John and had a meeting with the Fisheries officers about the lobster. While there his mother asked him to stop, to turn that story over. To think that maybe another story about something else might interest him. He sat with his mother during supper hour, putting a blanket around her because of the breeze from the Bay of Fundy bringing in fog.

"Isn't this my destiny?" he asked. "Isn't this my one chance?" He shrugged at the night falling, and shivered slightly, lighting a cigarillo, his face tragically certain in the match's flare. "I have learned about Roger Savage, Mom – he is the worst of all. And you, Mom, are the best of the best – and human beings should never be allowed to forget the difference!"

It would be Doran's tragic certainty that Markus would notice within the next few months, and think about in the years and years to come. And the blockbuster Doran wanted to write when the world gave him enough experience would be because of this tragic certainty, too.

There *were* a few grim reminders of the unfair play in Max Doran's approach – reminders that came from a few solitary and somehow unacceptable complaints to the paper about bias. (These complaints would come more frequently over the summer.) They came to the paper by way of scant letters to the editor, letters saying nothing had been proven. At times there was also a halting statement from one of the youngest reporters, Gordon Young, who had lived long in that forbidding area near the reserve, and who did not trust Isaac Snow or Joel Ginnish, for as he said, Isaac Snow was a born politician and Joel Ginnish was a born thief, and he knew them both, better than Mr. Doran ever would. And he said this without the least worry that those who measured themselves by conventional wisdom would think his statements insensitive. Why he did not care what in hell people thought, him with his soft hands and his hushpuppies, no one knew – but perhaps, some reflected in a pejorative way, he was a throwback to another time, when discrimination against the First Nations was openly accepted. Or perhaps, in a real way he cared very much for the reserve, and could not allow an untrue sentiment to pass as true, even if others thought it true.

"After all they have been through," Max said to Gordon Young one Tuesday afternoon when the argument began again in the office. "And you are questioning my few reports?" Everyone laughed nervously at the old-fashioned, deeply conservative young journalist Gordon, who was in many ways an outcast among them. And Gordon Young, who had come from a place even more remote than the reserve, wore silly clothes, and who had been foolish enough, or perhaps not, to believe in integrity above anything else, even above Irony, said that this is not what he was questioning. "No sir, Mr. Doran," (for he always called Max "Mr. Doran") "I am not questioning the suffering of the first peoples. I have First Nations nieces and nephews, and will not question that. No, I am questioning others using this

89

suffering to exploit a story, and go in a wrong direction because of it." He mentioned the crane, the stevedores, and other details from that day Hector Penniac died. And he decried in the most gentle way he could the idea of some people using an uneducated and solitary man like Roger Savage to satiate the already insatiable dislike of that kind of man, a dislike that many, many academics and some students applauding Mr. Doran seemed to feel – people who were writing to the paper with their "unending" support of the band.

Max looked at Gordon Young for a bit, and wondered about him a little. Then he replied, with the same bemusement he had felt with Amos Paul, "Ah, I know all of that, Gordon. All of it. I've paid my dues, lad. I've been on twenty stories like this. And I have come to this conclusion painfully. These guys are always the first to cry foul. And I do not want to blame. No, I don't. But what keeps hounding me is this: one little Indian goes to the wharf and gets a job, and the poor little bastard is killed outright. And Roger is a liar and a killer. One, he had an ongoing dispute with that family. Two, he fought with the brother over this dispute. Three, he expects to be hired. Four, he arrives late and is surprised that his seniority has been rebuffed. Five, he is angry and starts to drink. Six, he hooked as soon as he got a chance – I went to the wharf and watched how it could be done. You know how long it took? Twenty-five extra seconds!

"So what am I going to say – that he didn't have an ongoing dispute with that family? That he is a good guy? These guys are always good guys! He's a good guy who won't take a lie detector test – a good guy who took a swing at his principal. He won't admit that he hooked, that he deliberately waited his chance. If he was so brave as to hook, why wouldn't he admit that? I'll tell you why. Because he thought he would be applauded by all the rednecks up there for doing this – and now it has blown up on him! He did not think people would be so incensed. And he can't imagine how

90

wrong he was, and he is weaselling about, trying to get out of it. And you are blaming students at the university – kids who still have some ideals."

"I'm only saying that some students, who have written the paper, in support of you, have never stepped foot on a reserve or ever saw a pulp boat," said Gordon Young. "I worry whether you can stop helping them try to prove their case."

Max Doran was embarrassed by this impromptu lecture, and said nothing else. But this was the one real rebuke he had had. There was silence for some time. But then Gordon Young, who was not a household name like Max was at the time – and would not be a household name until nineteen years later, when he would become known for many great stories, seemingly in another time and dimension – this young journalist asked Max if he had ever heard of Winston Churchill. It seemed a very strange question and people laughed at the general bend and tone of it.

"Know all about him," Max said, sitting up now and angry, his hair suddenly damp with sweat.

"Then you know what he said to an empty house of commons after Chamberlain signed the Munich Pact – "

"Sure, but you tell me."

"Mr. Churchill said, "You had a choice between war and dishonour, you chose dishonour and you will have war!"

"And what does that mean to me?" Doran said, looking over some notes, propping these notes against his knees and looking up.

"It means that lots of people are at war with their own honour, and often chose dishonour – because certain of those they want to impress do not know or value honour. I think you have to have more time with this story – you and you alone can get it right."

There was silence again – and bitter silence, too. Then Max Doran said, "I have no worries about my honour, lad, or getting anything right."

"Well, it keeps materializing in front of us – the word

racist – because you have already implied that about Roger, and he is an easy target. That's what worries me about honour." Gordon paused and then said calmly: "Could you call Joel Ginnish a racist? Because if ever Roger was a racist then Joel is too – "

Most of the people listening did not yet know who Joel was; Doran had never mentioned him by name.

"We are talking about a murder here!" Doran said, just as calmly "A murder – not racism. That's the difference – "

"Churchill was a British imperialist, I think!" a young journalist named Katie Houtte said, her eyes shifting from one to the other. That's what she had heard, and she knew war was bad – so she said what she thought she must.

Gordon Young glanced at her without comment, then looked back at Doran, and said very quietly: "I do not believe you are charging Roger with murder. The murder cannot be proven, and won't ever be proven as much as racism itself, which has been implied in the last the weeks. It is hard to stop playing Grey Owl, if the act brings national attention. It bothers me – pandering in this regard – and always has."

Katie asked who Grey Owl was, and again Gordon looked around as if troubled by something immeasurable he could not overcome – the way Canadians believed truth was democratic and objective and already arrived at.

Doran waited a moment, lighted a cigarillo. "Don't worry, it won't go on much longer – Roger will confess, and everything will be over in a week or two at most, and I'll see to it," Doran answered. "For I am not backing down from this. And if it was your story you wouldn't either. Maybe you should have taken it – I guarantee there is not a reporter who wouldn't come to the same conclusion."

Gordon reflected that Doran's mother was sick, and that he had a bottle of medicine he was taking home to her. Doran kept the number of the doctor in front of him on the desk. And Doran pretending he was not worried made it obvious that he was. Gordon felt ashamed of himself when he saw this doctor's number on a yellow pad by the phone. "Leave him alone," he thought. "He is probably right – don't yourself get involved, simply because Roger is your cousin." And he remembered his own family, and how they always maintained that Roger would do something terrible sooner or later. And if Gordon's family, who worried about Roger, thought this, then perhaps it was the case. Perhaps Roger had pushed the clamp on only partway simply because he was angry – not intending that what did happen should happen.

So Young shelved the discussion. And people spoke of the fire downtown two nights before and whether it had been deliberately set. They moved away from Doran's desk, and the heat came through the broad windows and landed upon the typewriters and the filing cabinets and the picture of Mr. Cyr, who looked out over his employees with a kind of Rotarian disinterest, and everyone went back to work.

The journalist Gordon Young was upset about this second story and then the third, which came shortly after, and even thought of resigning. And no one understood why for a while. Then they discovered that Gordon was Roger's cousin, and that seemed to explain it. They also believed he was jealous.

Max Doran, meanwhile, believed Roger deserved his scrutiny. But as Markus Paul reflected years later, Doran must have found himself in a terrible bind. He could not admit Gordon Young was right about these articles, for then he would have had to change tactics. And he would lose the support of those he counted upon. For someone would say, "I knew he didn't know what he was talking about."

And someone else would get the crème of the story and the national attention Doran craved. And this is what he feared more than anything else. This and the idea that the young journalist in some way might want him to suppress this story. So as Doran told his mother, he believed others were trying to suppress this story – and he was priggishly determined not to. And the longer Roger went without being charged, the more determined Max Doran became to show how valuable his reporting, his scrutiny and his exposé were.

But it was not Max Doran alone who felt this. It was most people, as Markus remembered, during that time. All of them, himself included, thought that what Max Doran was doing was justified.

So, prodded by all these thoughts, Doran had to keep going.

That is, as Markus Paul now knew, Max was much like a lobster in a trap. He would come in through a large door to find a small one, and then a smaller one still, always looking forward, always finding himself able to fit in, not knowing he would never be able to back out.

4

Doran went back to the reserve and interviewed the people who should have known the most about what happened: the Monks, the two brothers in the hold.

"So, you work the holds?"

"Yes, sir – "

"Work hard?"

"Yes, sir – work some hard. Well, we all do up here at this end of 'er. It ain't like workin on a big newspaper, not that there is nothing wrong with that – but one slip and yer dead in there. And we was working hard that day too, and most days, up in the morning before dawn most days."

"And you don't mind the hard work?"

"Ya gotta do it – so no – I don't mind."

"And you were in the hold on that day – "

"Yes sir, I was – I mean, we both was in the hold on that day that young Indian boy Hector Penniac died."

"And what happened?"

"A load shouldn't be hooked like that. I don't know – I thought, now Morrissey knows some better than that. That's Georgie Morrissey, our friend there, George. And then when we brought the boy's broke body up – well, we heard it was Savage hanging around the fourth hold all morning long. Savage, who was a problem on the wharf and always fought with Hector's brother there – Joel, you know."

"What was wrong with the hook?"

"Jammed partway open. So the swing like a pendulum would make her scatter, let me tell you – "

95

"How was it left opened?"

"It just was – that's all I know. I don't want to cast blame on him or no one else. I just want to work the boats."

"Could it have been an accident?"

"Could have been, but who wouldn't clamp it down? It's a poor hook on anyways. We were treated like we was hookin on in the '50s – so it only takes a little to make it all go bad. Still you have to want to make it go bad to do so."

"Can you tell me about Mr. Savage?"

"No, boy, I'd rather not say nothing about him. Our lawyer there, Mr. Reynolds our lawyer, told us not to."

"You have a lawyer?"

"Of course – Mr. Reynolds, all the way from Fredericton. The union insisted we do. You know, something happens like that – who is safe when that happens?"

"Why – have you been threatened or anything?"

"Won't say," Tanker sniffed.

And Billy Monk added: "The Indians say they're gonna burn Roger out for what he done, but if he did do it – what is they supposed to do? No, there is a lot a fair Indians – don't you think there ain't. I know Joel Ginnish a long time, and you'd go a hard walk to find a better man."

Roger made up his mind, sitting alone that night in his house after the interview with the Monks came out. He would stay. Hell or high water, he would stay – he would hay the pools downriver from his land (that is, put hay in the water which would carry down river and sweep the Indian Gill nets) and burn out those who burned him (since everyone was saying he was going to be burned out). That is, all his life they had expected this from him, and in some way, in some inscrutable way, the gods planned and wanted it too. For if they did not, why put him here, on this scrape of earth? If they had not wanted Sisyphus to roll the boulder up the hill, why condemn him to it? Camus said Sisyphus was free on the walk back down the hill. Roger was free the moment he realized he had lost everything, perhaps even his fiancée, whom he ached for and loved.

And now he had no choice. They had told him to take shop in school and he had, they had told him to work and he had. They had even told him not to hope for anything beyond the few square feet he owned, and he hadn't. So now this would be the one thing – the one thing he would not allow them to take away.

"Anyone who comes close, I will shoot," he wrote in a scribbler that was found by Amos Paul after the events of the summer. "I won't let no one rob this house from me!"

He wouldn't say squat to the reporter either, and he wouldn't back down. He would by this act become essentially what the press said he was, and he would do what they believed he would do, in order to retain his sense of self, even though this sense of self was almost directly contrary to what the papers believed he was. So if there was a choice between war and dishonour, he would choose war. They had forced his hand to choose war, and he instinctively knew he must. He also knew this: the press was hoping he would not come out of his house, and hoping too to have this go on, and for it to blow up, to sell papers and to prove he was what they had already implied. By taking this course of action, he showed them exactly what they wanted. And he realized that Max Doran would get the story that would propel him into the national spotlight, with both arrogance and sanctimony.

But in the end, Roger Savage had no choice.

This is what he told his girl. And she was a nice girl too, May, a pleasant, kind girl who had always done what was expected of her. Just as her mother had married and had a nice wedding, so she too wanted to marry and have a nice wedding, and just as she had gone to the dances and said the same things everyone said, so she expected all the same things to happen to her. She had great aptitude in small things and wanted others to recognize them. So she pooh-poohed great aptitude in great things. She didn't want to look at the big picture, because the picture her mother and father had always focused on was small, and the picture most of her friends focused on was small. So the big picture had nothing to do with her. And this is what Roger, without knowing it, was forcing her to get involved in – the big picture – and she did not like that. So a week or two after the story came out, people were hedging their bets for her. Her mother and her father and her best friends, like Kellie Matchett, were wondering about Roger because everyone was saying he had deliberately tried to kill men in a hold. Now, one person could say that, and that would be fine – and two could as well – but when you had seventy thousand papers saying it every day, that was the big picture, and May did not like big pictures.

She did not know what to do – and Roger sensed her confusion. When she came to visit, she was nervous and jumped at noise, and had eyes as big as saucers. And he knew he frightened her when he spoke of his rifle. Once when he came to the kitchen, she was backed up near the counter staring at him as if she wanted to run away.

5

Markus Paul, now that he was older, knew more about how Max Doran was caught in a trap, and felt more sympathy for him. And he also believed that Isaac had not wanted to use the newspaperman for his own advantage in the deepening crisis.

But in another way, perhaps Isaac *had* wanted it. Or like any other politician, he did not worry over what he wanted or did not want. He existed on what might happen that he could then use. To say he had planned this was silly. He was the proof positive that mankind planned almost nothing. That is, he did not hope for Hector to die, or in his wildest dreams ever thought that he would, but it was now suddenly best that he had. He knew, strangely, that anyone else would not have moved so many whites to concern. It was because of Hector's tiny frame and his eloquent talk – the very things some boys, including Joel, used to mock. So Isaac had been forced to act more concerned than he was, and he could not help it either, for he saw how Doran was even more upset at the gruesome pictures of the death than he was, and he could use this as well.

Isaac did not start out to be opportunistic, but no politician alive can give up opportunity. The boy's death meant little to him for a while. That is, politically. Then two things happened. Joel Ginnish came home and wondered why things were not being done about such obvious contempt toward his brother, and Isaac was compelled to play the part he had trained himself from adolescence to play.

Part of it – perhaps much of it – was sincere, but from the moment Doran came to visit him, something secretive began to happen. He realized he did not want things to go well for the band, for the investigation or for Roger – for any one of these things could hamper the power struggle he was now in against Amos Paul. And most of all, he did not want Max Doran to have sympathy for Roger.

He knew this, and his wife knew this, but both knew they could never mention it. So both of them were depressed when anything positive happened and both of them exalted when anything bad did. And neither of them could help feeling this. For like anyone in opposition, Isaac must hope the ruling party failed.

To his way of thinking, the death of Nathan Blacksnake would be avenged. So this death must be too. He could not allow Nathan Blacksnake's case to take precedent over the case of Hector Penniac in the broadening public consciousness.

Max Doran did not want this either – for he wanted to make his own story the one urban Canadians gravitated to. So although he tried to rein himself in one moment, he pushed forward with his incriminating articles the next.

All this did not give Roger Savage much hope.

Isaac, with his grade seven education, knew all about Max Doran in a second. But he also knew this: if you pushed Max Doran too far and he truly felt he was compromising himself, he would never trust you again. Isaac was a born politician. At seventeen his whole reserve, on his instruction, had mounted a protest over the collection of seaweed. It was a government experiment, collecting seaweed to be used as fertilizer. But not one native had been employed. No one had been able to get a protest started – and Amos Paul, who at that time was forty-seven, had helped Isaac organize one. Their friendship had started then, soon after the death of Isaac's father, and had not been strained until now.

"What do you plan to do?" Joel asked in Micmac. He was

sitting back in the kitchen chair, on two legs, with his arms folded, chewing gum and watching his mentor.

Isaac knew much about Joel, and had followed him from afar. Joel had been a grade-school plotter. If you wanted a chair, he would bring you a couch. If you wanted a bicycle, he would bring you a car. Once he told some white cottagers he could get them a nice new door, and then he took the front door off his stepfather's house and sold it.

"Can't you get another?" he asked his outraged stepfather. "From Indian Affairs?"

He had robbed his old uncle's pension money and forged a will. Or two wills. Isaac couldn't remember. Joel stored his marijuana bales in the old cement store on the other side of the reserve, and sold it to boats coming in off P.E.I. He made thousands a year from this and complained he was poor. He sold fish to the Monk brothers, who constantly demanded more fish. The RCMP were well aware of this, and had planned a raid. Joel knew this, and Isaac knew that Joel would press for a barricade to claim sovereignty. This is what he had been trying to promote since the first band meeting about the crisis. If they put up roadblocks, the roadblocks themselves would protect the marijuana until he could get it moved away. This was as much of a concern as anything.

Joel was handsome and a bane to women. He had been kicked out of school in grade nine for impregnating a teacher. He would sit on the school steps and try to explain to her that he had no money to take care of the child. He once took a Sunday school group into the woods and forgot about them when something more important attracted him – a bobcat he chased for four miles. Late that night he realized their picnic must be over.

"Oh, come now, it won't be hard to find them in the dark," he told their worried parents. "They're white."

But Joel was a necessary part of the reserve. A man who would and could take action whenever you needed him, fearless, bold and a great fighter.

So after being let out of jail for smuggling cigarettes across the border – "Only two and a half truckloads – what's the problem?" he said – and stealing from his own people's fish traps, Joel was now always appearing at the door with a grave concern that his brother's memory be treated with proper solemnity.

"You're quite the captain," Isaac had said to him for the last four years, as a warning. "Look at you, you're always up to no good," he'd joked all last winter, as a warning. "Haven't they locked you up yet?" Isaac would always say this jokingly, but as an indication as to where they morally parted company.

"Not yet," Joel would say, smiling, "so let's blow something up."

Isaac well knew the band would have problems with anyone so volatile, that Joel would continue to do very reckless things unless he could be held in check. Yet a division between them now would make one or the other a liar, and both were in this position where they must rely on each other.

They both lied about unity in order not to be considered liars. Isaac, for his part, realized the only way not to have Joel do something erratic was to include him, and try then to handle him.

That evening, sitting in the soft, darkening room in Isaac's house, they devised a plan. It was a warm night, and the window at the front was opened. They heard children on the beach, and saw the lights twinkling off the wharf, and far away a buoy light too. Joel had his audience with the man he admired. But in reality Joel admired men only so long. He had no friends, only contacts. This is what Joel wanted: First a work stoppage at the recreation centre. Then if need be, the one thing the whites could not stand, a blockade, disrupting all traffic needing to use their roads, and essentially isolating Roger Savage's house.

Both of them felt gratified to have each other's support in this, but Isaac knew in his heart as a shrewd politician that it probably wouldn't be enough, and to keep himself in power, in the spotlight and in the political arena, he would have to order more action, even if his better nature told him not to. Not only his own warriors but others from other reserves would want him to also. He was in contact with many other reserves by now.

Then the only thing to keep them out of shoal water was more accusations against the one easiest to accuse – Roger Savage. Isaac as a decent man was beginning to feel uneasy about this. Yet he must keep it going – for would they keep it going against him if they had a chance? Yes, they would. So he must now keep it going too. He had started with a handful of seaweed when he was seventeen and it had never stopped. This was the direction progress must take.

The one thing in their favour was that young reporter, Max Doran. Doran was convinced of Roger's guilt. They had to promote this, simply by reinforcing it. The rest would take care of itself. Besides, Isaac did think Roger was guilty, so what was the harm? As an astute politician, Isaac was using Doran as a way not so much to create publicity as to gauge public opinion, and to register any changes that might be coming. In so doing Max Doran was acting as a sounding board without being aware of it. And the articles that he wrote generated much support.

As for Joel himself, in his animated way he pressed for the blockade not only because it would disrupt traffic and bring attention to what had happened, but also because it would keep the RCMP away from the reserve and allow him a free hand with the bales of marijuana in the old store.

And though he would have been astonished if anyone had told him this is why he really wanted the blockade, and he would have been morally outraged at this terrible assumption and lack of sensitivity, this in fact is what he did want.

Later that night – and it had turned into a wild night – Joel left and walked down the shore road, past where the last reserve light was flickering and into the dark. If you were a man like Joel, you would have seen much violence and hatred against you already, and you would know intrinsically how you were dismissed, how your family was and your people were. Why would you not want a blockade to bring attention to this? In fact the one thing a person sought was and should be freedom. And this is what Joel wanted too, because if your land was taken, what did it matter if it was a century or even two centuries before?

But he also had a criminal mind, and this hampered his search for freedom and turned it into something it was not, and at the same time promoted his criminal acts as acts of freedom and defiance, giving these acts a sanctity they did not possess.

The night had turned cold too, and he buttoned up his jean jacket as he walked. He knew he must get rid of his stash of marijuana before the police came in – but the waves were high, it had come up big sea, and the small drifters rocked in the swells out in the dark. The boat wouldn't make it across, and poor Joel knew something else – he suspected the man he was selling to had been compromised and had made a deal with the RCMP to catch him. So even if the boat did come across, it was sure to have undercover officers.

He went to the old store and sat in the dark wondering what to do. He could sell the bales to the Monk brothers, but perhaps not at the moment, and for less money – but then he would have to start making inquiries to them if they wanted to buy it. Then he would have to move it. And he tried to think of where – just in case the police did raid. And he could think of only one place – the old shed on Isaac Snow's back lot. Isaac never went there and neither did anyone else. But it would have to be moved at night, within the next day or two, and he would need some help. He thought of the Francis boys, Andy and Tommie, who wanted to be warriors. Yes, they would do it for him, without question. As for Isaac knowing – well, it was best not to tell him. He had too much to worry about.

"Besides, he told me to get it out of here," Joel said out loud, in exasperation. "So I'm only doing what he wants."

He would have been mystified, and hurt, if anyone mentioned it might be wrong to do this to Isaac Snow.

"Who's more of a friend than me?" he would have said incredulously.

He heard the waves crash down on the beach, and far away one small light from somewhere flickered against the storm.

6

It was July 1985, and the reserve was as yet quiet. It might remain so if Amos could keep things settled. If not, things might happen that would cause enormous difficulty not only for his people but for other people as well. And each day the old man woke to this realization.

Amos was not a great politician because he was not, as is said about so many politicians, from René Lévesque to Richard Hatfield, cunning. He had helped Isaac for years until Isaac went away, and then he had become chief. Now Isaac was back, and he looked upon all that Amos had done with derision, as if it was not enough.

That he got a chance to build a recreation centre was the greatest moment in Amos's life. He was so happy he invited the whole river to a moose barbecue. He had a famous native hockey player break the sod. Their picture was in the paper. He still had a copy of it on his fridge, along with a picture of Markus in his baseball uniform, and all Mrs. Francis's grandchildren – twelve of them, all lined up, and the five youngsters she had adopted. That is, if they truly gave Nobel prizes for humanity, Mrs. Francis would and should have had one.

Amos did not hire only certain families for the work, as other chiefs might have done, he hired everyone he could. It was a way for Amos to say, "This is going to be a new council. Things are going to be done in a new way."

Now Isaac and his lieutenant, Joel Ginnish, had organized a work stoppage. Isaac did this supposedly as a protest over Hector. But in reality he did this because everyone expected it and he could do nothing less. And even the newspaper had expected it and hinted at it a week before – hinted that although Isaac was patient, this patience might not last. In reality he was doing what the paper suggested.

It came down to one thing for Amos – why had Hector not been at the side of the hold, as he should have been? This is what puzzled Amos more and more as time passed. Amos had been on the ship, but he found out very little. The only thing he could come up with is what he reported to the council later. That is, that as far as he could tell no one could see down into the hold from the ground, so that would suggest that Roger had done nothing intentionally at all.

"Then why is the paper suggesting it?" Mrs. Francis asked.

She believed the paper had the answers, because the paper believed it did and the public supposed the paper was right and for the most part supported what she said.

"I don't know what Mr. Doran got right or wrong," the old man said. "I am not at all sure where he gets his information – but there are a lot of loose tongues."

But all of this was only making them more anxious. For the little reserve was isolated, and surrounded by white villages. Once again their own slights toward Hector plagued them, and made their own decision making cathartic.

Amos sat there wondering why he thought so differently at this moment. Why he thought so differently from all the people angry at Roger.

Then he took the papers back to his house, and spread them out in the attic where he had his little desk and the life of his parents and even his grandparents still lingered, and began to read Doran's articles, one by one.

Something was wrong with each article, but he did not quite know what. The interview with Tanker and Bill Monk told him nothing about Hector or what was going on, or what they had been talking about. This is what he mentioned later to his grandson Markus.

"The one thing they do not mention is why Hector was standing where he was, or if they told him to come back to the wall and protect himself if the load fell. That is what anyone should do!"

It was very strange for old Amos to sit in the attic or the kitchen of his little house and think that something was wrong with someone who said they were supporting his band of people. It made him happy one moment and sad the next.

"It is a puzzle," old Amos thought.

So this is what he told the council the next night. No matter who you put the blame on collectively, you could not do so singularly, for nothing had been proved. It was not fair to do so. It was not fair to Roger to blame the death of Nathan Blacksnake on him.

"Who the hell is Nathan Blacksnake?" someone said.

"He is the boy who was murdered out West."

"By who – Roger?"

"No. I am only saying, he did not have anything to do with that, so why make the connection to that – unless – well, unless you want to imply more than you say." Here he raised his voice, and tried to sound stern. "So let us not bother about Roger anymore," he said. "Let us wait until it is cleared up or brought to trial. Let's get back to work and finish the centre and let the kids go off to Tim Hortons camp. People are saying with the new bill passed we will be able to do what we want with the lumber and the rivers – but that is no better than not being able to do anything. There is more than one way to put dirt in your eye!" Here he smiled childlike. And he sat and waited for the response. The poor old man thought he would get applause. But no one moved, so he continued.

"Let this go," he said, "and live to fight another day."

But no one except Mrs. Francis took his side. In many

respects it was as if Hector had never really existed. For the Hector they now spoke about none would recognize. He was a much greater and braver man than skinny, shy little Hector whose ears they had painted blue as a joke.

Joel Ginnish suddenly stood on top of an auditorium chair, and looking down at Amos, said he lived to do one thing – remember Hector.

"He went there knowing he would be killed, and yet he climbed down into that hold and did his work like a man," Joel said, looking about furiously as if wanting someone to disagree with him.

"I know he did," Andy Francis said, now standing on his chair as well. "I know he did, for a fact I know! I am living for one reason only, to remember Hector the right way!"

"You are?" Amos said, astonished.

"Yes, I am – living the whole entire rest of my life to remember Hector!"

"Oh my," Amos said.

What would happen if Amos went against them now?

Ever since the ship had gone, Isaac had been polite to but dismissive of the "little half-pint chief."

That is because people were simply telling him he was chief now. Besides, the government officials were phoning him before they spoke to Amos. And Joel was saying things to impress this chief, Isaac Snow, and to impress the boys who were young enough to be impressed by him, like Andy and Tom Francis. Joel was saying that they would take over, and take over soon, and the reserve would be run more efficiently and in a new way.

"What about Amos?" Andy asked.

"Like father, like son. And I knew his son," Joel said.

Amos had stayed awake half the night one winter to keep his son David alive. He walked to his house each morning and stayed with him until late at night, trying to feed him soup and keep him sober. He took his rifle from him and gave it to

Roger Savage's dad to keep, for he did not want David to injure himself or anyone else.

In the end Amos took the boy Markus in with him. Later that spring, he sent Markus away to school in Rogersville – and three times Markus escaped and came home, once through the woods so he would not be detected, and ended up on Amos's doorstep. So Amos thought to himself: "Markus is very brave – already as brave as most men. Someday I will start a school here, and teach my children Micmac."

And that is what he was now trying to do. But he wanted to do it for the future, not the past. And though he was old, he believed this crisis showed that the difference between him and Isaac was a fundamental one.

The past was gone – yet in so many ways they were told by their elders and leaders that in order to embrace the future and heal, they must re-establish the past that was gone. In this, they had been on a hamster wheel for a hundred years. To leave the hamster wheel was to leave the reserve. To leave the reserve was to leave the land. To leave the land was to leave the past. To leave the past was to leave who they were as a people. That would change them forever. Yet in some way, some how, they must leave it. This is what Amos knew. And he knew this is why Isaac, young as he was, would fail. Not because he was not noble – he certainly was – and not because he wasn't just – he was just – but because his nobility and justice were directed toward something that was impossible to hold, that would slip through his fingers like starlight. And Amos knew all starlight – even that of the great sun – as soon as it reached them had already passed by.

A "half-pint," Isaac had called him.

But still and all, half-pints were sometimes knowledgeable about what heroics really were. And what they were not.

7

Two nights later, five youngsters met. Markus and the two Francis brothers, Tommie and Andy, and Little Joe Barnaby and his sister, Sky. Tommie and Andy were older and both had quit school and showed impatience that Markus had not.

Markus and Little Joe and Sky were inseparable. Sky and Little Joe lived at the edge of Stone Street, which ran down beside a narrow gully toward the road, and where one day a few years ago Little Joe saw the body of a man lying in the snow with his eyes glazed over. He ran and told Markus to come and look at the dead man, not knowing in his excited state that it was Markus's father.

Markus would see Sky, who herself had just turned sixteen, every evening now. He would wait all day to see her. (He had at one time written her a poem that he had hidden.) In fact he could not think of life without her. To him, Sky would always be part of his life. At this time in his life he believed that they would be married, and he would someday be chief. Then he would daydream about doing many great and important things, and dying for her too. He knew he would die for her in a second. As long as he lived, he believed that would never change.

Some days they would go swimming together – just the two of them. And once she jumped into the water quickly, just in her bra and panties, and swam under the drifter and out to the buoy. Her beauty was so captivating at that moment that he grew weak – a secret all women know, even the kindest of them, to sap men's strength away.

Most days were spent waiting for her after supper hour.

And then around seven o'clock she and Little Joe would come across the old softball field, hand in hand, and he would walk over to meet them. They would stand in the dry dust near the pitcher's mound talking and then move off toward the row of dilapidated trailers, and sit in behind them, near the woods, where the blackflies never seemed to go home. There, their position in the world was established. They did not have to talk to the elders and they did not have to obey orders.

There was talk now of an insurgency and of the Mounties stopping it and raiding the reserve and breaking the warriors up.

"I will do something if it comes to it," Markus said. He knew Sky was looking at him, and didn't want to look her way for fear of losing her attention. Sky's first duty was to take care of her brother, Little Joe, and then remain loyal to those she loved. That is, if there was going to be something happening, Little Joe would come first in her mind.

Tommie and Andy, though they were grandchildren of Mrs. Francis, thought they were much more in tune with the times than their grandmother. Often at night her poor tired body would be seen going along the streets looking for them, because she did not want them to get into trouble. Often now they were drunk.

In the last few days they had been running errands for Joel Ginnish, and spoke as if they were his confidants, as boys do when older men suddenly become aware of their usefulness and take them under their wing.

"What will you do if Amos can't make up his mind?" Tommie Francis asked Markus now. "Isaac will have to." Though his grandmother was on the band council, Tommie was making his own statements now.

But this question assumed that Amos had not made up his mind, and that there was only one way for that mind to be made up. And this more than anything showed how trying

112

the times were, this belief that there was only one way to make up your mind, and you had to be as radical as Joel Ginnish or your mind wasn't made up.

So Tom simply continued: "I might just go up and burn a white lobster boat if that's what they are going to treat us like – if Amos is so wishy-washy."

Markus was furious about this remark, stated in front of him with obvious disrespect.

"Yes, you go ahead," he said, "and let me know all about it. For you have always let me know about things you thought you would do, and as yet have not done."

He said this very deftly, and picked up a stick and tossed it into the corner wood. When he did, a squirrel began to scold, and a dog at one of the old trailers barked. Though the Francis boys were both older, they were not as tough as Markus, and so did not answer him. But still he was prodded on the back of their cant.

"I am going," he said, "for a walk to the wharf. Who wants to come?"

Both said no, that they had to meet with Isaac – they were warriors, and they would do whatever they had to do.

Markus said nothing.

"I'll go if you go," Little Joe said.

Little Joe, with his feet half as long as his sister's, and his legs stretched out to their knees, sat beside them. When Markus stretched out, Little Joe did too. When he sat up, so did Little Joe. People knew who Sky's father was, though no one said. But no one knew who Little Joe's father was. Or very few did. Their mother had died in a car accident just the year before, so Sky was the mother in many ways to Little Joe.

"Maybe you should talk to Isaac too, Markus," Andy said.

"Why?" Markus said hesitantly. "Why don't we talk to my grandfather?"

"Well, Isaac would know what to do – and Amos might not," Tommie said. "It's time to decide. That's what Joel says – it's time to decide!"

113

Yes, it was time to decide, and this was the terrible problem.

The three native constables on the reserve – everyone called them Huey, Louie and Dewey – had not been seen outside the small jail. They had practically disappeared, because they had a role to play. If they did not have a role to play they would be out in the car, patrolling the streets, but since they knew if they were out in the streets they would have to arrest someone, or join someone, they did nothing. So the streets were bare and broken and tired and no one patrolled them. They were supposed to patrol them or have the RCMP come on the reserve, and Amos was trying to get them to do this. The day before, the three of them had walked up the street and walked right past Joel Ginnish holding Isaac's rifle, and nodded and said, "Oh hi, Joel," and turned and walked back to the jail. In many ways Markus did not blame them.

But now he thought of something. "It was the last load before noon – so maybe it *was* an accident. You know, people just getting careless."

But no one answered. Andy Francis took a drag off his cigarette and let the smoke speak for him as it came slowly from his nose. Markus lit a cigarette too and took a quick, almost cryptic drag, and held it in his hand, looking at the burning ash, and then flicked the ash twice with his finger. Markus inspected the scar on his left wrist that he had gotten some years before snaring rabbits. He could still feel Sky's leg pressed against his, and that was worth everything. He had once asked her if she had ever done it with a boy, and she had said, "No – but sometime I will."

"And who would you – with?" he asked shyly.

"With you," she said so softly he almost did not hear.

Markus said he was going to the wharf to see where the RCMP were.

He stood quickly and walked up the shore road, toward the lights, Little Joe between him and Sky. Like a man who must breach rifle fire in order to prove what side he is on, he was walking into the dark, knowing that Tom and Andy would not do it unless they had lots of boys with them. He disliked how Joel made them run errands and took their little bit of money, but he did not tell them. The secret was people wanted Joel off the reserve because he was always causing trouble of one sort or another, but they were frightened to say so – and anyone who said so would be called a traitor.

But no one could just put him off the reserve. Not now, after his brother had been killed. In the past his own family had had him arrested. Once he had bound them with duct tape, and was rifling through the drawers of the house. People phoned and could hear little muffled sounds in the background: "Help us! Help us!"

Then the Ward family came to Sunday dinner and saw the Ginnish family tied and gagged in the kitchen, the youngest girl gagged, and in pigtails, and Joel in the living room watching TV and drinking a rum and Coke.

"Oh, I would have untied them. I forgot all about them! You'd think they would have figured out how to untie themselves!"

But now, all of a sudden he was "the right-hand man." Why? Because no one else on the reserve would dare ducttape their family up in the kitchen and then go watch television in the living room, that was why. He was righthand man not in spite of his volatile nature but because of it.

Surely it would not come to rifle fire, but whatever it came to, Markus Paul, as the fifteen-year-old grandson of the chief, must participate.

"It's getting some dark," Little Joe said.

"Maybe if I pull out my pants pockets you'll be able to follow me," Markus said, and Little Joe began to giggle.

When they got to the wharf road they saw the abandoned lighthouse, with its windows busted almost a generation

115

before, and wild grass covering the steps, and the widow's walk above. But there were no RCMP officers at all, with rifles pointing at the reserve as they were told.

"It's all a big joke," Markus said.

"Yes," Little Joe said, relieved.

"Isaac just wants us to have our own fishery and have someone speak for us," Sky whispered, as they half stumbled in the dark. "That's what Andy says."

But Markus was very perceptive, and everyone knew this. They never liked to argue with him for long. He knew he must defend his grandfather. And he felt there were two errors in what she said. The first was that the band did have its own fishery – it did not have a commercial one, but it had a home one, which people like Isaac Snow wanted to fold within the envelope of a commercial fishery. This is what was being opposed by the white fishermen, and was now in the courts and might go the natives" way. But Markus knew that it was Amos who was trying to work out a deal and not only Isaac. And Markus wanted this to be understood. Some of the whites were poaching and stealing, yes. But so, too, some of the Micmac were stealing salmon and selling them to white buyers, which didn't do any of them any good until they all had a share.

Amos was trying to resolve that as well.

Markus also knew that the only thing Hector might have had to do with these issues was if he was killed because of them, or if Roger was so angry about them that he became murderous. But this was extremely unlikely. Everyone knew this, and nobody said a thing, for to say anything was to say they were using Hector's memory for their own purpose, and no one wanted to. So Hector, whose ears Andy's and Tommie's new hero Joel had painted blue as a joke, became their martyr. And this, Markus knew, would someday be known – that is, not that Hector was a martyr for them, but that he was one in spite of Joel's painting his ears blue.

116

Markus told Sky all of this very succinctly, and she never answered, and as always, with most people when they win an argument, there was a feeling of having done someone injury, and Markus tried to make it up by telling jokes.

The group came up on the shore road again, leaving the breakwater behind. Little Joe Barnaby was cold, so Markus took off his jacket and held it out to him. Little Joe kept smiling, thinking he was surrounded by his friends, who would protect him, and he would protect them as well.

"No," Little Joe said, refusing the jacket, but Markus pretended he didn't hear him. "I don't want it," Little Joe said, but Markus again pretended he didn't hear him. So Little Joe put the jacket on, over his thin T-shirt with a little donkey on the front, and buttoned it up, so he looked as if he was walking in a trench coat. Then Markus gave him some bubble gum. The wind came from the north and was like a winter gale suddenly.

Then some more people showed up, walking toward them. Tom and Andy.

"What's going on? What are you doing – did you see the RCMP? Where are they? Joel wants to know."

"There's no one anywhere," Markus said.

They waited awhile, and then some talked about going onto the wharf and demanding some of the lobster traps. But they didn't do that. They waited another while. It was pitch black now, and they smelled the salt from the bay, and they turned for home, the only place that seemed left to them. Behind them the faraway lights reflected a bit on the night sky. Suddenly the boys began to yell at the empty cottages that sat on huge manicured lots. When they got to the long turn in the road, called dead man's turn, just before the reserve proper, they passed Roger's house. Only one light was on. Everyone was silent.

Things would either be true or false. He was either a murderer or not. There could not be a middle ground. They were all silently thinking of this.

117

"Markus, I can't get this gum to blow bubbles, it keeps stumbling about in my cheeks," Little Joe whispered.

It was pitch black, and Markus took Little Joe's hand.

At the decline into the reserve at a time of night when they were usually in bed, Amos watched the little troop of kids as they came lumbering home. Yes, they had made it safely back, without any trouble, which he had been worrying over for an hour. For Amos knew that if any of them were hurt, he would be responsible. Of course most people, no matter who they were, would never hurt children. Yet Amos knew that just as a few men on the reserve would sooner or later proceed from one level of harm to another, so would certain white men.

He knew, too, there was probably no longer a way not to blame Roger Savage for what had happened to Hector.

Amos had gone to see Savage that night. He just walked in the back door of Savage's house and sat at the kitchen table. He was pleasant and happy, as if nothing was amiss.

"What's happening?" Roger asked.

"Oh nothing, boy, nothing. Well, you know, not much."

"What have they been saying about me?"

"About you? Oh nothing. I mean, I haven't heard them saying nothing."

"Amos, I don't think that's true."

"True – yes, no one is saying anything. Mrs. Francis thinks it's all an accident. And I think if we can get our heads around it, most people will say within a day or two – I'd say a day or two – that it was an accident. Mrs. Francis has sent away to the place there to get your graduation ring, so that is good!"

Roger nodded, and made Amos a cup of tea. The summer wind blew across the lawn in a sweet, sad way, as if this breeze had just come from a fairy tale and found its way here.

"I was thinking, though," Amos said, "that if you could put the new room you intended to build on the other side . . . I was thinking that might help."

"But there's no room," Roger said. "It belongs to Mary Cyr's family."

"Oh well – that's right, there is no room over there. Well. All things will get straightened up," Amos said. "But then I was thinking, if you could just admit you hooked, it might go a long way – you know?"

"But I can't say nothing now one way or the other – for whatever I say now is a lie."

And so Amos left Roger and told him not to worry, for he was chief, and the little sad trumpets of wind blew down the lane as he walked.

Amos's father had once told him about people willing to join something. He said this: "There is always a big hidden giant in the room, and this giant attaches itself to people in a crowd, and moves them in one direction or another. Those who do not join this giant are outcast, and sometimes will get stepped on by great big feet. Those who join the giant have the benefit of puffing themselves up and acting like one, and sometimes do the stepping – until their friends leave and then they just get smaller and smaller. And sometimes after it is all over, they simply disappear!"

"Joel is a big giant," Amos thought, "for now. But someday he will be the smallest man on the reserve. And so will Doran. Doran someday will be the smallest man on the paper – and maybe someday he won't have a paper anymore."

So Amos must solve this himself before it got out of hand. The Micmac police officers on the reserve had gone into hiding – they were like seamen who left a listing ship to the passengers. Someone had stolen a purse, and one of them came out to investigate, asked four people four questions and, realizing it might have been Joel or his friends, scolded the woman for leaving her purse lying about, went back to the jail and closed the door.

Now the wind blew and sad old Amos watched the road,

and Roger's house. Roger's house already looked as if it was under siege. Yes, but weren't they all?

At night Roger would sneak away and keep an eye on his pools or walk the hills near where his mother lived in the small pink and rouge house up near the highway, with its old twisted metal door, bent from kicks, and its porch sunken. He could not leave for long, for he was worried his house would be taken over by the group around Joel Ginnish, so most often he left only for an hour. In fact he went to visit his mother for the first time in two years the night Amos visited him. And he was like a little boy with her, nervous and scared, and hoping for her approval, which he had never in his life had.

Then there was this: To keep his hopes alive, his mother – who had abandoned him years before for friends whom she drank with and fucked, playing bingo, going to dances and quarrelling – crossed the line into a bigotry Roger never had, pretending solace, and Roger had to endure the very narrow-mindedness that had once informed his youth, about people he had generally said nothing against. He remembered, too, what he had escaped from, the screaming and hatred in his house.

His mother sat in her soft chair looking him up and down and said "Tch-tch" with her tongue. "Tch-tch, you got yerself into a fine old mess, haven't you. I knew you shouldn't have taken that old house – that only got it all started."

"Mom, be quiet."

"Living right next to them – didn't I tell you that – sooner or later you're bound to upset a few. Niggers of the north is what they are. I always said."

"Momma, be quiet – go to bed if you're going to talk that way, I don't need to hear it."

His mother's civil bigotry was horrible to listen to. But she was the only mother he had. Her words came and went with the wind in the grass, and the smell of manure across the highway in Tanker Monk's cherished little field. Tanker and Bill Monk, who were in the hold with Penniac, and who shied away from looking at him now – when he knew they did see him. He knew they had been under the load and could have been killed themselves. Despite this, he hoped they could tell him something about what actually happened, so he'd gone to their door. But they had nothing more to say.

"Roger, you were the one who dug the hole, get out of it yerself," Bill said. "I don't know if you was drunk or just bitter over a loss of pay. I woulda made it up to you, but I've had no contact with anyone over this, and I am doing it for you – even if you don't think so."

"No one is gonna help me outta this mess," Roger said to his mother now, staring up at the stars, in the doorway, with the wind smelling of pine and spruce.

His mother lit a cigarette in quick affirmation of what he said, and her match flared in the dark by the metallic stove. It was as if she was casting blame with that match.

And he decided not to visit her again.

That night he went down the back road under the sweet moon and lingered in the pines near the river. He was thinking of leaving, just going away, giving up the old house and all he had lived for. But he couldn't think of himself being anywhere else. He stood out on the shore, a man contemplating his small, winding pools, and the rocks jutting up, like a painting by some fine local artist.

Later, he telephoned his girlfriend. And the phone rang and rang. He telephoned his girlfriend again, and the phone rang and rang again, and at last her father answered and asked him pointedly what was true and not true about what he was hearing.

"I don't know what you have been hearing – nor do I care," Roger said.

And so his girlfriend'sH father told him May was fast asleep, and would have a busy day tomorrow too.

8

The First Nations dispute with the Department of Fisheries went on and on. And it seemed that the progress of the case with the fisheries paralleled the accusations levelled against Roger.

Twice more Isaac was called to meet with officials, and people outside the dispute were involved in the negotiations. The premier wished everyone could meet halfway. Each time Isaac was offered more, and each time his conditions were met, to the point where he could or should accept. But each time Joel, as his advisor, spoke to Isaac in private, and both times, on the verge of an agreement, Joel managed to wrest this agreement away. And his logic came down to this: "We can get more because of what has happened. If Hector's death means anything, we can get more – much more."

Isaac knew that to balk at Joel was to make himself a target among those who were insisting he finally do something. These meetings were in reality the most important meetings between Joel and Isaac. They sat together in a small room off the main fisheries office in the legislature, drinking coffee from a silver coffee pot. Both of them were exhausted and spoke quietly together in Micmac. And Isaac lost both of these important meetings – because both times Joel told him there was no consensus among his supporters, and he was ready to go back home. He looked sad and disappointed: "I have my own people to think of now," Joel said with a pinch of sanctimony.

"Aren't they *our* people there, Joel," Isaac smiled.

But Joel only stared ahead.

"He thinks he's Jesus Christ!" Isaac thought one day.

So Isaac was unable to sign because if Joel, with his charisma and charm, walked away he would take all the warriors with him, and there would be no unity. So the position Isaac found himself in was not unlike Amos' position with Isaac, and saying no to the fisheries did not reveal his strength but his weakness.

It soon became clear to the Department of Fisheries that it did not matter how many licenses they offered this year. And the deputy minister of fisheries was extremely astute. He told his boss after the first meeting that the men were bent on something else that the Government had no control over. He sent a memo to his minister stating that every moment that the crisis did not end only meant that it would be harder and harder to have it ended. After the second meeting, he suggested the fisheries cut off all negotiations, and put pressure on the Micmac leaders to bargain in good faith.

Joel saw this as a moment to raise the temper of the conflict. "Another broken promise" was the headline in the *Telegraph*; and this was the first time a quote from Joel was used.

The deputy minister could see clearly that a power shift was coming, and he telephoned a friend, a well-known reporter from the CBC, asking him to get in touch with Isaac. "Isaac is the one who we should speak to," the deputy minister said as diplomatically as he could, calling on every past favour.

Isaac himself knew that he must prevent Joel from becoming spokesman, so he gave the first interview on TV the next night. But in doing so he had to reiterate Joel's position: that is, that no deal could be arrived at now.

The deputy minister wanted to isolate Joel Ginnish. But he also wanted to do something else. He wanted to start negotiations with other reserves in the area, and come to a separate agreement with them. This would be done to show

how Isaac and Joel were negotiating in bad faith. So the feelers were sent to other reserves along the bay waters on July 7, and the deals eventually would be signed on August 22, striking a great blow at Isaac's prestige.

The Deputy Minister could not handle his own Minister however. In over her head, she felt she must show resolute toughness. That is, she attacked the biggest target, for she knew no other way. "Damn it," the Minister was quoted as saying, "who should care what happens to Roger Savage. Half the white men up there are bigots as far as I'm concerned!"

This caused a late night meeting in the department with the Minister, Deputy Minister, Premier and two advisors from Indian Affairs. The statement was firmly retracted the next day, and the Deputy Minister was quoted as saying his Minister had been misquoted the day before. Then the Deputy Minister, a quiet unassuming man with twenty-three years's experience, tried to save the reputation of his inexperienced Minister and resigned.

But there was something else going on that remained hidden. Isaac's Acadian wife, Colette, had a white father who was a fish-buyer off the wharf in Nequac. And as this man sat in his truck on the wharf staring out at the white caps, he realized something important. If Isaac could hold out and get an agreement that would allow him to fold the band's home fishery into the commercial fishery they were after, it would allow for commercial native fishing at times of the year when white fishermen could not fish – and this would make both Isaac and his father in law quite rich.

At this same moment, Joel was angry, and it was for the simple fact that no matter how relevant he was to the negotiations, Isaac was still getting the attention. It was at this moment he began to dislike Isaac Snow very much. So it didn't matter to him if he heard that the Minister of Fisheries was in negotiations with other reserves, and his own reserve was being isolated, he would not negotiate. "Isaac's always been a big thorn in my side," he began to tell his followers. But when someone else said something about Isaac, Joel reacted very quickly and slapped his face.

Two days after Isaac appeared on TV, Max Doran wrote another report.

Doran had received a call from the men in the yard, authenticated what they said, and then reported on the fact that the hold Roger had hooked to was out of succession. That is, Roger had been supposed to hook to the third hold. The backhoes were always two or three loads ahead along the wharf, but Roger had simply picked the load to the fourth hold, and waved to the crane operator to send it there. This, of course, was done at certain times and there was probably nothing suspicious about it – except that thinking made it so. Yet when this fact was published in the paper on the third week of hot July, on the front page, everyone took notice more than they would have at any other time. This report hit both Amos and Mrs. Francis hard – for they had spent much time trying to make people realize that the dropped load was only an accident, and you could not charge Roger for the terrible suffering the First Nations had endured. But few of the young men wanted to listen to this now. What men like Tom and Andy Francis wanted to do was break into Roger's house and hold him down.

It seemed that Roger had deliberately sent the load that he had tampered with to the hold where poor Hector Penniac was.

The paper's editors had no real knowledge of how men worked, had never themselves once walked up a gangplank, so they did not know the subtleties of what had happened and could easily imply to the public that there had been a giant crime.

Once again, the small, tidy, well-dressed young reporter Gordon Young brought this up with Max, saying that although it may have been planned, perhaps it wasn't

125

planned maliciously, for he had had uncles once in the yard who worked themselves until their fingers bled. So perhaps there was nothing at all suspicious about this work within the pungent moil of wood and heat. That is, if you wanted the small hold to finish, so that the workers with seniority would move forward to the bigger holds, and you were a worker with seniority sitting on the dock, wouldn't you send an extra load or two to the smallest hold, knowing you would be hired in the afternoon?

But even Gordon Young knew it looked abysmal for Roger now, and so did Markus Paul when he read this in the paper. And so did Max Doran, who actually seemed shaken to have to report this.

"Do you think I want to condemn him?" Doran said to Gordon. "At first, yes – maybe I did think he was to blame. But I have tried everything to get him to speak in the last two weeks! And now I am convinced he is to blame."

Gordon nodded, and was silent a moment. Then he said, "The real problem is, no one is telling the truth there. The union is protecting itself, and the head of the union controls a good many of them – the company is fine with that, for it is Savage who is out of line. But then there are the First Nation men themselves. Did you talk to any of them about how they had treated that Hector? Well, you should not be so credulous – it's bad for business. I will tell you, some are using this just to milk all they can from it! That sounds bad – but they are no different than other politicians."

"I am not at all that credulous," Doran said. "I know everything you said, I thought of it all. I am, however, certain Roger is lying – and that is where the story is."

"Yes, I am aware of that – he might be lying. But others might be lying as well. There is a certain silence about those Monk brothers too. Those in the hold that day."

But Doran argued that the only one who did not seem to be telling the truth, the only one who was out of place, was Mr. Savage. Here at five in the afternoon the whirr of fans occupied the room, and the solemn late-day shadows began to appear, tenuously as they did in summer, and the smell of brick heated by the sun came in from a slightly opened window. There was a sudden energy at five, as if office romance was in the air, with a man and woman who always drove home together, or the humming of electric typewriters that had suddenly stopped. That is, all but one.

Doran, his left knee held up with his hands, said: "Why is Roger not speaking, and why has he lied? Why was he hanging about and hooked to that hold? These are not just questions, they are facts. And why did Hector need the job? Because no one on the reserve had a lobster licence! What have we done to them!"

"Yes, you are right," Gordon said. "But what I am saying is, if they could arrive at the truth – a truth which would exonerate Savage at this moment – do you think Isaac or Joel would do so?"

"Of course they would – I am sure of it," Doran said. He was angered this was mentioned because it was a question all of them had to think about, and no one could answer for someone else. He knew Isaac was a brave and good man, but he could not answer for him either. Nor could he answer for himself. For the story had gained much attention, and his copy was on the wire, even as far away as New York. So he tapped a pencil and looked at it a moment. Both he and Gordon Young suddenly looked at his pencil tapping and knew that Joel and maybe even Isaac would not use a sudden truth to exonerate Roger Savage now. And perhaps Doran would not either. And perhaps even the public would be disappointed – so certain were they that things were the way they had been reported.

But there was something Markus Paul was able to find out some years later. Even though he was getting the notoriety he had craved, twice Doran had asked to be taken from the story; yet the paper told him he must continue. Isaac had asked him to include something about the treaties and the fishery dispute in his next story, and the natives' demands for licences, and Doran felt he had no choice. For that powerful man Isaac Snow could stop him in a second from getting a story and then give it to someone else. He had brooded about this, and then he had rashly asked to be taken from the story. But the paper did not take him from it. "We have no one else who has as many connections – you are the one! So stand tall and you will be as known across the country as you are here!" The managing editor had squeezed his shoulder and smiled.

Doran did not tell Gordon Young this, and they said nothing more. But Doran knew that unless this story ended quickly, it would scatter out of control.

So he decided. "I have to continue now – I have no other choice. If I leave this story without finishing it, there will never be another story for me. So I will do – I will do what I have to do. And if Roger pays – well, he pays!"

"No one will believe anything I say from now on," Roger joked to Joel himself after he read the latest report about him intentionally sending the load to the wrong hold, "so I will not be saying anything else."

"Well then, can I say things on your behalf?" Joel joked. "Like how you've decided to give your pools to me?"

"Not yet."

"Well, we'll get them one way or the other."

Then Joel said: "You know my cousin the dope fiend there, well he has everyone calling you The Bigot of Bartibog, so if you hear that, I wasn't the one who started it. Just to let you know." And he even patted Roger on the shoulder, for old time's sake.

Part III

September 11, 2006

Markus Paul surmised many things. One was how smart Amos was, but more importantly, how great the forces against his grandfather were during those days in 1985. It was not that Amos hadn't minded what was said about him – no, he minded greatly. He couldn't help it. It had made the last of his life sorrow-filled. But he kept his own belief that Roger Savage had done nothing except hook on.

"The Bigot of Bartibog!" That, at times, meant them all – English, French, Indians too.

A few years after it was over, in the fall of 1989, at the library on a university campus, Markus was reading about Amos Paul – though the writer wouldn't have known it. Markus was reading a stanza from the poem "Self-Dependence," by Matthew Arnold, and suddenly, looking into the October sun high in the sky that fresh afternoon, he thought about his grandfather, and was filled with terrible emotion in this half-cool place of racks and almost forgotten books.

"Bounded by themselves, and unregardful
In what state God's other works may be,
In their own tasks all their powers pouring,
These attain the mighty life you see."

"Where is Roger's rifle?" he had written when watching television on September 11, 2001.

And now, five years later, he asked himself this question again.

1985

1

Amos Paul had lived seventy-five years (in fact he had had his birthday just before this trouble with Roger Savage started) and by now believed a terrible crime had been committed. Yet he did not know who to turn to, to say it. He might turn to Max Doran, but he felt that Doran would not believe him. So he stayed in his garden and looked after his vegetables and patted his dog and walked about Sobeys looking for bargains and stood in the mall and spoke to old men who remembered him from the war years. But he did not know who to say anything to.

The crime, he believed, had taken place inside the hold, involving one or two men who had told the other to be quiet. In the small hold at the rear there were only four people, Hector and three white men. So that made him question things. It was hot and miserable in the hold, and tempers might have flared inside instead of outside on the dock.

"How can you be so sure?" Markus asked.

Amos shrugged.

"If we give it time, we will see that something happened. I don't know what, but someone will help somehow. Someone will come forward to say what they saw."

"Mr. Doran is pretty certain in the paper."

"Yes, he is – he is very certain. But still, he is only human and wants to blame the right person. I've discovered the papers do this just like anyone else. And that's exactly how Isaac's father died – someone certain wanted to blame the right person, and that was in the paper too, and Isaac's father was hanged. Nothing can be as strange."

But Markus knew that this kind of thing was not strange at all, and in fact was the more ordinary circumstance.

Amos's five little pictures didn't seem to prove anything either, Markus thought. But Amos insisted that something had happened to Hector that might have had nothing to do with the load.

"Roger is cantankerous and bullheaded, and dead wrong about the stupid pools that are really ours – but he is no murderer," Amos said. "But you see, because he is dead wrong about the pools, it is easy to ascribe to him traits that are dead wrong as well."

So he went over what the police and safety inspectors had told him about the case.

The small under-section of the fourth hold had been almost filled, and two men were reassigned the night before to go to other holds. Hector came on that morning with three men to do the last of the small hold. He would be employed for about a day and a half, until the job was finished. Then, those with seniority would be placed in one of the two larger middle holds. That is, Tanker and Bill Monk. When Roger came he was told that all the holds were hired, and that in all likelihood was why he sent the extra load to the fourth – in order to help facilitate its finish.

Hector had just gotten his union card the week before. This was his first boat. Roger responded to this in disappointment because he had not counted the card-carriers right and believed he would get on. And then he had to sit it out.

But looking at the pictures did not tell Amos very much – and his eyes, though still as bright as a hawk's, were not as good anymore. There was something he was not seeing. There was something else he had to know in order to solve this.

But he said this: if Tanker and Bill Monk had seniority and

would be moved forward, then they were in the upper portion of the hold, while the other man, Angus Peel, was in the under-cubby. Then he said, speculatively, "That man Angus is our key – because he wouldn't have been near Hector and the Monk brothers or Angus Peel's son, the water boy – yes, the water boy is the key, maybe! What I am saying is – well, here is what I am saying. The surprise Roger felt at having not been picked to work even the fourth hold was not as great as the surprise Bill and Tanker Monk must have had when Hector, with his new union card, came down the ladder. "

It was Amos who had gotten little Hector Penniac his union card. Now of course he regretted it desperately.

Amos sat out in the back by the shed and looked out over the islands. Out there was where the real braves were years ago – the great warriors who ran large canoes from here to Chaleur. They would not have bothered with this, until they found the truth from their chief.

"Never you mind," old Amos said to the blind old dog, patting it roughly. "We will have to figure this out – won't we, though!"

And then he would go down and weed his garden in the heat, or drink from a pitcher of lemonade.

The day after the report came out about what hold Roger had skipped and what hold he'd hooked to, old Amos got up very early, dressed very carefully and walked very calmly to the RCMP station. There he sat for over an hour, silently with his hands on his knees, watching the many people come and go. He wanted to talk to them about the pictures, and the way the logs were, and if anything could be garnered by how the logs lay on the body.

"I am no expert," he kept saying, looking around and smiling. "No, I am no expert, but my theory is – "

The people in the office would look at him and walk away. He held the pictures in his hand, and would wait for someone

134

else to come by. But some of the people he spoke to weren't even police officers, but secretaries and clerks.

"Look here, please. I am no expert but – see how the logs are all in just this spot – and the walls – I thought it was strange – not a bit of bark scraped along the walls – after such agitation! But there are marks from other loads swinging."

"How do you know it is not from that load that fell?" a secretary asked him.

Amos's face brightened, and he said: "Well, the marks from other loads are between two and five feet off the ground, which shows they hit the walls when the men grabbed them. But if the other load fell from fifteen feet, then it should have hit further up on the wall – for it wouldn't have missed the walls altogether."

He continued to speak to whoever would listen, but they nodded or politely ignored him and walked on. So he sat in the seat, and as he was prone to do he said, "They are treating me with the utmost respect."

At about ten in the morning Amos had his meeting with Sergeant Hanover of the local RCMP, but found that his inquiry about the hold was not answered. The man dismissed it, as a person in power is certain of having the answers a common man would be too much of a novice to understand. Amos, in his new spangled shirt he had decided to wear, and his old cowboy hat with the pin-sized hole at the tip, and with his whitish grey hair drooping down under it, looked ridiculous in the sergeant's eyes. The sergeant wanted to know the situation on the reserve, and wanted to know about a person or two. He also wanted to know about a certain woman claiming a band card, given by a boyfriend from his reserve – and did he know about this.

"No, I do not," he said, seemingly amazed that anyone from his reserve would do this. Of course he knew all about it. The woman was alone and poor and they had given her a moose quarter last winter. But now he said no, and stuck to it.

Then he took out a cigarette and lit it and looked at the sunshine coming in on the small plastic flowers in a dish on the desk.

"Do you know there is no recreation centre along the North Shore that is as nice as yours will be?" Hanover said, intimating a kind of official enmity. "Even the whites don't have one as good."

"Of course I know."

"Well then. Every one of you have to remain calm – don't go for the war paint, eh?" the sergeant said. "You haven't lost anything yet. We'll figure this out. If he did this intentionally, he will go to jail. We're going to offer him a deal – he might plead guilty to a lesser charge." And here he stacked some papers, and looked to the side of the desk to find a paper clip.

Amos stared at the man saying this with a good deal of patience. He took another drag of his cigarette. They had lost five hundred thousand acres of land, two river systems and two major bays. Had the whites forgotten that? he wondered. Had they forgotten the band had lost Hector Penniac? No, to be fair, he knew many whites had not forgotten that.

"Everything will be taken care of," a constable told him, more politely, at the door. "Don't fret – it will all turn out." What they really wanted to know was if Isaac could keep the men under control. It was as if they had resigned themselves to the fact that he, old Amos, could not.

"Oh yes, he does a good job, that one," Amos said in his singsong way.

"Well, he's doing better than you, isn't he," Hanover said.

Amos only smiled. But he felt outmanoeuvred, outdistanced and ashamed.

They did not know that as chief he once would have been able to put them to death with a nod of his head. And yet Amos Paul never would have done so.

Amos walked down the dusty lane, his old legs crooked and the sun in his face. Twice he turned to look back at the

136

little station with its glass door and evergreen shrubs. Twice he thought he should go back to explain to them why he came there and show them the pictures, and tell them there was something wrong, with where the logs had lain and where the water buckets were. One of the water buckets was broken, but it lay far from where the logs had landed.

But no, he didn't think he needed to do that anymore. He stopped to take a small rock from his shoe, and kept going.

That night Amos went to bed and lay on his back and tried to think of all the things he had discovered in his life about white men. It was not that they themselves were different, but they considered others to be and then tried to control who was. And it did not matter if they worked for the paper or the university or somewhere in between. And some were certainly brave, and some were certainly foolish. So therefore they were just like other men. Now and again, here and there, was a sound like thunder. He thought of his recreation centre. His mind was filled with mortar and bricks, and offices and basketball courts. He certainly was proud of it. He thought of his wife, dead now seven years, and what she would think of his being chief – well, it wasn't that important, but still, not every man became one. Then he thought of his retirement and what he wanted to do. He wanted to get on a bus and go all across North America, and Mrs. Francis whose husband had died said she would go with him. So he had asked about tickets and had taken a map and plotted their journey. But was she only fooling? Maybe when the time came she wouldn't go. He wanted to see the land of the Apaches and Sitting Bull. The land of the Lakota Sioux. Not that he felt they were any greater than his tribe, but certainly more had been said about them. They said they hunted by horseback, and many called them the finest light cavalry in the world. His own people had run caribou and moose to ground without the need of horse, and had run thirty miles on snowshoes without the need to rest, and fought both Inuit and Huron for a thousand years. So then to go to Wounded Knee, maybe for a day. Yes, perhaps he would get to do that.

He lay in the dark, his hands behind his head, thinking. Something was not right. That was a bad thing. But so many things against the natives had been let go, and now it seemed a crushing force for instant justice had taken over. And the big, blustery, do-good-all-the-time heapin' big reporter had come in to make it right. (This is what Amos called Doran privately.) And once it started it could not be stopped. It must run its course like a fever. Just like the little boys who died of the flu all those years ago. The fever had come, and the reporter had caught it – and it was spreading, faster and faster, and he did not think he could stop it.

The real truth was, he was picked as chief because Isaac wasn't here at the time. Isaac came home a month after the election. He knew he was just an old man they wanted to make feel good. Now Isaac was home, and no one listened to Amos anymore.

It nagged at him, and he wondered what would happen. Years ago, he himself had been at a hanging of an Indian friend. At that time no one, except the poet Alden Nowlan, had taken up his cause – and Amos was driven down to the hanging by Roger's father, for no one else would take him.

How strangely fate worked. For now it seemed the same was happening to Roger, and there was nothing he could do, and he felt as bad as he had the first time.

He had asked Markus at supper if he would help him discover the truth. It was a harsh thing to be a boy living with an old man.

Markus had said, "Yeah, okay, Granddad," but the old man felt lousy having to ask a boy for help.

"We will figure this out, Markus – you and me. Something happened in that hold. Something to do with a water bucket – I am not sure what . . ."

"Yes, Granddad – you and me."

2

Men did not go back to work at the rec centre site, and the boys who had been hired to pick up bricks, like Little Joe and Markus, had no one to supply bricks to – unless Amos Paul did the mortar all by himself. He was too old to do that. He was too tired to even try. Andy and Tom decided that Amos was wrong and Joel, who bought them smokes and talked about his connections and girls, was right. So when Markus asked them to help, they looked at him with suspicious disregard, and gave him the kind of blunt silence given to friends on the outs. Then they came back to warn him not to go to work there himself.

"Joel is going to do something," they told Markus. "He told us pretty soon Isaac is going to put him in charge. He is already Isaac's bodyguard – Isaac won't go anywhere without him now. You're either for us or against us!"

"Well, tell me this – why would Isaac need a bodyguard?"

"All important people do," Tommie said.

It was the spotter plane that made Joel Ginnish famous about the reserve, and proved that he would do dangerous things.

As they milled about one day, keeping an eye on who was coming and who was going, some boys saw the RCMP spotter plane in the sky. They ran and told Joel Ginnish. Joel had been lying on the grass, was looking up at the blue sky, thinking of what he could do next, and how he might do it, and what might be said about him if he did. As he lay there staring up at the sky, some boys came to him and told him what was happening.

So he stood up and watched the spotter plane going back and forth above them, a small Cessna with a white under-carriage. And it was close enough over his marijuana store. He shrugged, looked up at it, and spit.

Some boys went to Amos to ask him what he was going to do, for really it was up to him whether or not RCMP came onto the reserve. There was a delicately worded policy that allowed the three native constables to be the principal law enforcement here unless a true crisis loomed. So the young-sters sought Amos's advice. But Amos, sitting in his backyard watching the starlings fly about the birdhouse, had watched the plane a long time. He smiled and said that as far as he could tell they were not on the reserve – they were above it – and he could think of little to do to them if they were above it.

Then some of the little boys surrounded him again and asked him what they should do – they were supposed to have jobs where they would take bricks to the men who were making up mortar, and haul away the old gravel to the truck. (None of the children were actually needed, it was just to give them something to do.) Amos told them the men did not come because they were protesting. He told them to go home and wait. Or ask Joel Ginnish what to do.

"What are they protesting?"

"The death of Hector."

"But why would they stop work on our rec centre?"

Amos told them he himself wasn't sure.

Later he went to find some of the men who a few weeks ago were complaining they had no work and were now all of a sudden on strike because of something that Amos had not done. All that afternoon, almost until supper hour, he trod along the old asphalt roadway filled with heaves and ruts from the winter, trying to find those men who had so eagerly anticipated work. But not one of them he spoke to would go back to the centre.

"You couldn't pay me enough," one man said.

"Me neither," said his friend.

Amos did his best to talk them out of this reaction, did his best to tell them that things must come about through the courts, but all the men old enough to vote turned their backs on him, and he was alone on the windswept roadway toward evening. The windswept road and high waves crashing up over the breakwater meant a storm was looming. As he walked down the lanes he came to the spot where his son had died. He tried not to look at it. In fact he walked around it as if he was walking around a giant puddle.

When he turned to go back home, he saw Little Joe, wearing the floppy hat he always wore, trying to wheel his load of brick up a scaffold toward the recreation centre's main wall, his little arm muscles taut, and stumbling under the weight, with only Markus there to help him, their pant legs flapping in the wind.

"I will build it myself," Markus said, "so don't fear, Grandpa."

This made the old man lonely enough to cry.

So Joel watched the plane for a while. The plane no longer skirted the road where the old store sat vacant and sad, and he was not thinking too much about it now, until the boys came back and said Amos said to let it go, that there was not much you could do to a plane in the sky.

Joel declared: "That's not what I say."

They cheered when he said this, so he went to Isaac's house and complained to him.

But Isaac told him to let it go as well.

Joel shook his head, and listened to the plane as it came over the house, and went back out over the bay. "But what about the sound – do you like the sound of it?"

Isaac looked at him and shrugged, and said: "I don't like the sound of people constantly nattering in my ear, either. Leave it go. There are more important things."

Isaac had heard that morning from the Wissard boys that Joel had taken salmon from the nets. Yet Joel had come to him the evening before and said Roger or someone up river had hayed those nets in high water, and bogged them down. But if Isaac mentioned this to Joel himself, Joel would be astonished and hurt, and go away brooding that people so insulted him. Still Isaac mentioned it – that is, the rumor that Joel had stolen fish.

"Me do that?" Joel said, hurt at the suggestion. "I'd rather light my nose on fire."

"You'd rather light your nose afire?"

"Give me a lighter. You know that whites have hayed our nets a dozen times."

"Yes, I know that, I know that – but I do not think Roger ever did."

"Then you should join Amos," said Joel, "for Amos is the one who doesn't think Roger did nothing either!"

So Isaac went off to find Amos and talk to him. He did not come back for a long while, and Joel saw Isaac's 30:30 sitting on the shelf. He drummed his fingers and looked at it. Then he went outside with it cradled under his arm.

"What are you going to do?" Tommie Francis asked him.

Joel walked to the shore and without aiming fired from his hip at the plane as it made its sweep down toward the old broken store once more. The plane banked, seemed to twist in the air, and every one of the boys ran and hid. Joel couldn't shoot straight, so he was lucky he hadn't actually hit something.

Everyone now called Joel a crazy son of a bitch.

And everyone wanted to touch him, pat him on the back.

Later that day, Markus walked back along the shoulder of the road, with Little Joe behind him. Little Joe now seemed to be his only pal, the only one who had remained faithful. They were talking about going fishing for trout, and how they would dig the worms later that day.

142

As they came to a narrow part in the turn of the road they met Joel Ginnish, with Andy Francis, coming back from the shore with a group of boys. All were exhilarated, all were defiant, all were trying to prove their outlandishness.

All were filled with welters of insults toward those they met whom they didn't deem worthy.

Ginnish's shoulder connected with Markus's and sent him back a foot as they passed.

"Oh sorry, Markus! Hey, are you still working at the rec centre? What a fool," he said, and kept walking.

What hurt Markus was not that he had done this, but that Andy and the others broke out laughing.

Little Joe looked at them as they passed, and then turned to watch as they disappeared. He smelled the salt water in the evening air and it made him lonely suddenly.

"What did Joel say, Markus?" he yelled, trying to catch up.

"Nothing at all," Markus answered.

"Are they coming fishing with us?"

"No, I don't think so."

That night, Amos lay on his back in the bed nearest the window in his upstairs room. He could hear the wondrous waves of the great Miramichi that his ancestors had heard three thousand years before. Now and again he sneezed, and sometimes he sighed. The other bed had belonged to his wife. Over her bed was a cross. On the night table between their beds was the Virgin and Child. Amos thought about how that man who had hanged – his friend – had not been guilty either. Seven years later they found out the truth, but what could they do then? The courts gave his friend's wife some money. So, what if Savage was not guilty? Would they kill him and then give his mother money? Certainly she would take the money. That was the big sticking point for Amos.

They said a hanging was over quickly, but Amos knew that for thirty seconds this man whom he had known since childhood struggled and gasped for air, and must have wondered why they were so stern and hateful to him, who had done nothing but get drunk in the wrong place, as he had most of his life. But this time it had happened next to a taxi driver who had been killed.

"The Indian did it," people said in court. "The Indian did it."

The man had smiled like a child and trembled and tried to be brave, and looked about nodding to everyone before they put the hood over his head. "I didn't do it." The man had shrugged.

Who could stand to do that? That is, put the hood over someone else's head?

Amos knew Isaac never forgave anyone involved. And he had become more famous because of his father's death than if it had not happened. For it was talked about as an unjust death. So Isaac, many felt, was destined to do something to prove how unjust his father's death was. And when, a few weeks ago, it had looked to be an ordinary summer, with ordinary church picnics, and ordinary lazy afternoons, this idea had been thrust at Isaac. And unexpectedly a sociology professor at the university had invited Isaac to speak; and the auditorium was packed. The audience had given him a standing ovation, and there was prolonged applause when he said that this summer would be the summer of a powerful restitution, and Amos had felt about to disappear. That was because he could do nothing as bravely as Isaac, and everyone, especially Isaac, knew this.

Now Amos lay completely still, staring at the stars outside. Markus was on the other side of the door, too worried to knock on it. But Amos knew he was there. Markus's sister, on the other hand, had joined the protest against her grandfather.

For a long time the little house was dead silent. Finally Amos spoke. "You told me they say there are about two billion stars in our galaxy," he said cheerfully to his grandson.

"Yes, I did."

"Well, so far I can only count about thirty-seven. Where are all the rest?"

"They are there, Papa," Markus said.

"I am not so sure." Amos sighed and lit a cigarette. "Thirty-eight . . . thirty-nine . . . forty," he said.

"You are doing good," Markus said.

"Counting or being chief?"

"Both," Markus answered.

They were silent.

"I am not so sure, son," Amos said. "And I am sorry for us all."

He believed in miracles, Amos did. That is why the mother and child were on the night table. That is why it was so important to him. He believed that the truth was always revealed, for no matter how much men wanted to hide something, they could not. How was that? There was not a thing in the world that was hidden irrevocably, so this mystery too would be solved, if only they gave it time. That is, when they said nothing was hidden, everyone meant that the big crimes would be solved. But Amos was thinking of the multitude of little things – the betrayals of one another that maybe caused even worse things than big crimes – the unending small things that finally killed love in the soul.

3

The next morning at dawn, Isaac woke and went into the woods at the back of his house. From here he walked to the river, then up along the shoreline, his feet sinking in muck, plagued by the thousands of blackflies alive at this time of day, until he came to the sandbar, where the reserve line met Roger's land. All along the shore he looked for traces of hay and saw none. This disturbed him greatly. For it meant that the hay was not put in the river this far up, for some of it surely would have bottled. That meant that Roger did not spill his carts of hay into the water to sweep away the native nets – someone else did. He was plagued by this as much as he was by the blackflies. He too, like so many, had grown up without a father, and at times you could tell that even in his strength and determination there was the look of vulnerability in his quiet face. But not one trace of hay, and the nets swept away, meant that the haying had taken place close to his reserve. Yet he knew that to blame Joel publicly would cause the entire campaign to collapse. An internal dispute is what their enemies would want, and they had enough of those. They had enough people just waiting to call them liars and thieves. He knew a few people had different ideas about him – not the great man, the image projected, but a manipulating politician. He too had to fight against many things.

He was more than angered by this act of Joel's. He was hurt deeply by such a trivial kind of betrayal, and exasperated that what he feared would happen had. The problem was, he had given up discussions on licences this summer –

and he had done so to gain more attention and a more favourable bargaining position for next year. But if this was found out – this childish stunt – what favourable position would they have? Just as he had to make sure Roger was considered guilty (which he believed), he now had to assume Joel innocent (which he did not believe). That was the price that came with power. And now he had much power.

He sat on a rock for an hour watching as some grilse made their way up into the dark pool above, now and again flipping their silver bellies in the sun.

That evening, a great grey sky hung over the reserve and the bay looked like turquoise. The waves were listless, and the First Nations boats were moored beyond the breakwater, their bows thrust out of the water and their anchor ropes covered in seaweed.

Doran was out for a walk with his camera to collect pictures for his scrapbook. He was now a solemn character, thin and seeming out of place, but still welcome as he put his camera up to his eye here and there. Two girls hugged each other as he snapped them. Little Joe managed a big wide grin. Farther along the dusty street near the old store that sat at the crossroads with its windows broken, he saw a big eagle in the scarred tree. The sun came out on the patches of white-washed brick of the old store. He walked farther along and came to the back of the reserve where an old asphalt road led out to the village and he decided he would go there to take some pictures too. There he took pictures of signs and traffic lights all with a measure of impulsiveness, and then went in for a drink at Bunny's. He ordered a beer and was surprised to see Roger's mother playing the game machine in the corner. She was chain-smoking and running in her quarters. He took his beer and went over to see her.

"Oh," she said, her voice husky from being awake all night, "you're the reporter everyone is talking about. Even on the national news."

"So, what do you think of all of this?"

"What do I think about all of this? I think the little bastard finally went and killed someone. That's what I think about all of this. You have a few quarters?"

Doran took some out of his pocket, and she grabbed at them all, finished her rye and looked at him while clinking the ice and holding the glass against her cheek.

"Why do you say that?"

"If a mother can't tell the truth about her children, what else is there?" she said. She turned to him and smiled, tossing her head, and her eyes cast on him were knowledgeable in the art of seduction she had performed most of her life. "Buy me one?" she asked.

So he bought her a rye and then walked back toward the reserve by the same road, his thoughts troubled by this woman, and by so much else. Yes, he was becoming famous. And the only way to continue to be famous was to prove what he had suggested in his writing. To back down now – after being interviewed on two CBC programs – would ruin him. He knew this. In fact, if any other scenario was proved, he might be sued for libel. That is how far out on the branch he had crawled. Therefore, as much as he might find it personally distasteful, he was glad the mother had condemned her own son.

The evening was quiet and rain had started just lightly as he came to the old cement store, and he walked toward it, peered through its dark and broken windows. He wanted to get a picture of it at twilight – but first he must get the best angle. He thought of publishing this picture with a story concerning the mother – it might work. But as he was setting his camera to take the photo, Joel Ginnish came out from behind the store and called out to him.

"What the hell are you doing?"

"Nothing – I just wanted a picture."

"Get out of here, spy," Ginnish said, and came forward, and grabbed the camera from him.

"Give me my camera back," Doran said.

"Spy," Ginnish said. "You're not allowed here – do you understand? You stay back at the front end of our homeland. Don't you dare come up again, or Isaac or no Isaac," he said, pushing at Doran's chest with a finger.

"Give me my damn camera back!" Doran said.

"You're a spy – you're with the RCMP and Isaac don't know that but I do. Don't take no pictures of this place."

And he turned away, tossing the camera behind him. Doran just managed to grab it.

Doran, shaken, went to speak to Isaac about this. He said he had to be sure who was in charge, for he did not want to deal with Joel again.

"Don't worry," Isaac said, "he is no trouble – no trouble at all."

Two days went by. And Isaac was still debating what he should do with Joel when more news came.

Isaac was told to go to the police station. There, Hanover told him the police would not recommend the charge against Roger Savage. There was simply no way they could prove at all what had happened. No, the case could not go to court as an indictable offence. However, he still could be charged with mischief – and no one liked or believed him anymore. Everyone knew he had done something. Why, he wasn't even spoken to when he went out anywhere.

Charging Roger is what Isaac had been waiting for, what he had been on the phone about, and how he had kept Joel civil. It was his promise to the young men, that Roger would be charged, and they wouldn't have to see his face again, and the pools would be theirs.

But, just as when the *Lutheran* went and left them, so now this struck him as another complete betrayal. He had the same repressed rage on his face all day. He could not get Hanover's look of unconcern out of his mind.

"We can't say he hooked, deliberately or not," Hanover

said. Then he shrugged and smiled. "I doubt if he'll be working many boats again."

This last statement's trivial nature infuriated Isaac Snow even more.

"Don't go out of whack," Hanover said, "or it will be a long, long summer for everyone. You want to know something? Roger's mother's in jail – been in since yesterday. Want to see her?"

"No, I don't want to see her."

But Isaac was too astute not to realize what Amos had realized some time before – that really Joel and his men did not want Roger charged, for that would defuse a situation they were relying upon to continue. And it was in Isaac's best interest too to prolong it, for the gain it could assure him. For him to want Roger charged would mean he wanted this to end. But it could not end without a confrontation.

He knew this, and Joel knew this, and the young journalist Gordon Young who had grown up close to them all knew this too. Only Doran seemed to miss this essential point.

Hanover phoned Amos as well, and later that afternoon Isaac went to see Amos.

"Well, that is good," Amos said, a little chagrined. "Doesn't it prove that an accident or maybe someone else might have done something? Maybe we can get twelve licences – and fish lobster on the Point Sapan side this year. Next we can go for a bit more of them – you see, I was talking to some fishery men and they all said the same thing."

Isaac was in a difficult position now. He knew he had to act against the white authorities, or have the others act. Even if Hector's death was an accident. And in his heart of hearts he was no longer sure. But although he had known Roger for twenty years, he had to say that it was no accident, and although Roger had come into his house, he had to say that he did not know him, and although Roger had helped him

150

drop an engine into his car, he had to say the man had not done one good thing.

He had to, not because he was leader, but because it was expected of him. And if he did not do so, Joel would. And it was better for everyone involved if Isaac rather than Joel handled things. There would be less violence and perhaps no violence at all.

Isaac went back to his house, slammed the door, and took a small dish and flung it into the air. His wife was lucky enough to catch it before it smashed into the dining-room cabinet. Then he sat down and looked at Joel and those around him.

"Take him out now," Joel said, "and try him, just like they tried your father."

"Hmm?" Isaac said, as if he hadn't heard.

"We will try him," Andy Francis said, his hair tied back in a tiny pony tail, and his huge steal toed boots making his big feet look like a clowns.

"Hmm?"

"Try him ourselves!" Andy said, more loudly – with the first blemish of disrespect, which pricked Isaac suddenly.

"No, we can't do that," he said calmly.

"Why not?"

"Because I have thought of this all day. We do not have the manpower to do so. It would take a life to get him, and then all hell would break loose, so we cannot do so. We would have to hold him in the little cell here, and the RCMP would come and get him, so there would be a gun battle with them, or we would kill him."

"We *should* kill him," Andy said. "I didn't know you'd be scared."

"You want to kill him?" Isaac said calmly, without looking at the boy, and he took out his buck knife and stuck it into the table. "There – take this. You go kill him. See how long you last against Roger Savage." He yawned after he said this.

"What do you propose then?" Joel asked, unfazed. "Because right now we either do something or do nothing. And doing something is always better than doing nothing. That's my motto."

Isaac mashed his hands together, and thought of the hay.

His wife Collette lifted the knife from the table and wiped the spot where it had stuck in with a cloth. Then she poured her husband tea.

"What if we do something else – something that will draw more attention?" Isaac said. "Our main concern is for our children not to have to live like we have had to. We must make people realize this is what we want." He looked at Andy Francis now, and Andy smiled timidly. "Never mind, boy," he said, "very few men here could take Roger Savage in a fight."

"Could you?" Tom Francis asked.

Isaac sniffed, nodded but said no more. That is because he had never bragged about his physical strength and was not about to now. And unlike Joel Ginnish he was by nature not a violent man but a brave one. Not that Joel was so violent; he just had no wherewithal to be anything but what he was. Isaac, angry at Joel about the hay and the spotter plane, smiled in spite of himself, for he remembered him at fourteen, only his head visible in the back seat, being driven up to town for a paternity test.

"I didn't mean to do it – it just got the best of me" was all he could say.

So Isaac patted Joel's arm, and reached a compromise with the man who was now considered the head of the warriors.

They would build a large barricade and protest Roger's house being on their land. Roger would not be able to come and go, and they would keep him where he was until the prosecuting attorney reopened the investigation. In fact the barricade would force them to arrest him, or at least remove him, and then the land would be theirs.

Barring an all-out assault on Roger, the barricade seemed

the best possible way to accomplish this. And doing it for the rights of the band seemed the best policy as well. "But no violence against him!" Isaac warned, pretending this decision was political in nature, and not, as it was, because he could not dislike Roger the way some did.

The next evening, as they walked back from the trout pond on the Church River, Markus, Sky, Little Joe and two of little Joe's friends stopped to watch as the barricade was put up, with lumber and brick that was supposed to be for the recreation centre.

Men hot-wired the cement truck and took it right from the yard, and parked it across the road, along with a half-ton. It seemed everyone wanted to do something more than the other fellow. And the little kids Markus was with ran to help. Some couldn't even pick up the poles, but they still tried. Markus stood there with his four trout that he had caught just at dusk with a tiny butt bug. He had been very proud of his fish and he had let Little Joe carry them for a while when they walked back by the cottages, so the cottagers would think Little Joe caught them. But Little Joe, seeing the barricade being built, ran ahead, dropping the trout into the dust on the side of the lane. Everyone began to throw things on the barricade – even tin pans. Mattresses and pillows, too.

One boy took off his Timex watch. "It takes a licking and keeps on ticking!" he said.

Little Joe went home, smelling of trout and worms, and was put into the bathtub. Mrs. Francis put some bubbles in and began to scrub his ears and his face. He had all of his trout sinkers and spinners lined up on the bathtub's side, three bobbins in the tub with him bobbing about, and a red devil lure Markus had given him lying on a facecloth – he was counting them, as if they were gold. He told Mrs. Francis he had almost caught a trout, and had seen four chipmunks and a skunk.

She continued to scrub, and then emptied his pockets of gum and liquorice and three small worms.

"Church tomorrow," she said. "We are still a family, no matter what."

Little Joe asked why people would put up the roadblock.

"I don't know – but stay away from them. It'll be over soon."

Mrs. Francis was old-fashioned – that is, she secretly distrusted the young men now saying they were working valiantly on her behalf, and so did two dozen other families who never once had any say about the blockade but were now obligated to say they approved of it.

These were things that couldn't be said. That is, that a terrible division had surfaced among some families. Everyone on the reserve knew this, and knew they had to keep this division out of the papers. Most of the families were sick and tired of it all. Half of them secretly supported Amos.

So Isaac was trying to keep everyone in order until such time as the demands they had made were discussed.

He told a general meeting of the band council that the phones could not be used to speak of anything about the crisis – for he had his reporter, yet he knew that other reporters, from as far away as Hamilton and Toronto, were trying to tap into the lines. This is what had happened in the Nathan Blacksnake case out West, he told them. Too many opinions. He needed to control what he could, for as long as possible. He wanted no television cameras on the reserve unless he said so. Isaac felt that if he did not regulate what was said or done, too many others would say and do things that would work against them all, and make them a laughingstock. He had seen this in too many other cases. And he was concerned again about Joel.

Also, the warriors had wanted to be paid, and Isaac had confiscated the pay from the recreation centre to give to them. He intended to give it back, but right now it was the

154

only measure he could take. He told his men he didn't want any of them to speak to the press unless he said so.

Mr. Doran could come and go with a special pass – the behind-the-curtain pass, as it came to be known.

"I am trying to keep you safe," Isaac told Joel when he complained. "We can control one reporter – we can't control fifty. And I want the marijuana gone. The last thing we need is to have that discovered. And," he said, "do not take one more salmon from other men's nets. If that comes out, the sympathy people have for us will go! They will tar us all with the same brush – just like they did my father!"

With all that said, he walked home as most men of influence and power did, alone.

4

At the cottages, things went along much the same. The cottagers began to arrive little by little, from as far away as New York.

Mary Cyr, Mr. Cyr's at times estranged granddaughter, was the sole resident of her large gabled cottage nearest the reserve, and drank most of the summer. She was in a kind of rarefied holiday state, where very often one would not think of her as drinking until they spoke to her. Then they would hear the disconnected phrases and see the suddenly slight stumble, which she would excuse by giggling. She would enter the windswept doors of summer cottages at midnight and sit with teenagers, some of whom had no idea who this woman was watching them play some board game like Monopoly or Trivial Pursuit. She would talk about love and astrology and tell them that her sign and Jesus Christ's was Capricorn. This kind of common quirkiness seemed special, not because it was special but because she was young and very wealthy and her grandfather owned one-sixth of the province. The trees would wave overhead on those oft lovely nights, and small cottage lights would interrupt the dark along the shore road, and teens would giggle and whisper, and the whole world had a charm.

And Mary Cyr talked of magic wands that would take all the sorrow of the world away. The cottagers soon relied upon her to find out what was happening on the reserve because her grandfather owned the paper and liked Chief Amos, so she became an extraordinary guest who was sought out and coveted while the wind blew smells of ash from shore fires on the beach.

Sometimes she would walk up to the barricade and speak to the natives.

"How are you guys now? You want a toke?" And she would reach out and hand them one, with her $3,000 gold bracelet falling back on her arm. "I agree with you guys!"

That her own huge cottage, its outbuildings, its motorboat shed, its croquet lawn, was not bothered by them was, she believed, ironically enough, because of her and her love for them and for all things.

Then she would turn and walk back and sit in the large country kitchen and watch the shenanigans through the bay window, and watch the little hummingbird wash that the gardener had placed outside her window. Or she would put in an order for scallops from Collette's father and he would arrive *tout de suite*.

Little Joe Barnaby, whom she did not know, would wander to the brink of the barricade and sit eating an apple and watch the goings-on, with his feet dangling down and his toes wiggling, until one of the warriors would tell him to go home. So she would invite Little Joe over, and in he would come, standing on the mat, looking at her with big, dark eyes and a smile on his face.

"You want an ice cream?"

"Sure, why not."

"And a Coke?"

"Sure, why not."

And since everyone was his friend and he was everyone's friend too, he would tell her all the stories of the reserve that Max Doran didn't seem to get. That his adopted mom was scared, and at night he heard an owl, and that some men tossed rocks at Amos's porch.

One day Little Joe saw a strange sight. Mary Cyr had driven the truck and trailer carrying her small sailboat to the barricade. There it sat like some kind of Trojan horse waiting to cross so it could be launched from the slip on the reserve,

157

something she had done every other summer. But now they would not let her cross.

"C'mon, guys, I'm Mary Cyr," she said, somewhat incredulous.

But the warriors would not let her or her boat pass. It sat in the shimmering afternoon heat on one side of the barricade, with the beach smelling of seaweed and sandstones and the slip on the other. Little Joe climbed a tree to watch, and wondered, sitting there and trying to blow a bubble, what he would do if he had a sailboat.

Finally, late in the day, they told her she would have to go back and take her boat up to the wharf.

So she drove the trailer back to her yard and let the sailboat sit.

Some days Mary Cyr would make a call to Halifax to see if someone might drive her Jaguar up to the beach for her. Sometimes she would telephone the stables in Toronto to find out about her horses. Sometimes she would sneeze because of allergies.

Sometimes on a very few occasions she would speak with her grandfather in Quebec, who owned the local paper and dozens of others. She did this when Max Doran, her sudden new friend, was there, to show him – well, that she was exactly who she was. To place his and her new friendship in the right context, and that right context was simply – that she was Mary Cyr.

That the very summer air that surrounded her was better than other summer air, and Max liked this air better than other air as well. And she made him realize that he should and must. He could smell lilac scents in the rooms, and fly-dope in the porch, and these scents were not only ordinary but wondrous. So he was influenced by her to write the best story, because after all she was Mary Cyr who had had dinner with Prime Minister Mulroney, and she liked to say, between small sips of sherry, that she could "influence you to the Max."

She was Mary Cyr. She had smoked marijuana in Amsterdam and bared her beautiful breasts on a beach in southern France. Her rebellion, her irreverence had an exclusive quality, and could only be done in a certain way.

She told him she was a woman with tricks up her sleeve. He asked her in what way, and she smiled, cracked open the tail of a lobster and winked. That wink was rather fatal for poor Doran, who had never had much luck with women, and was now head over heels in love. If she knew this or not, she did not seem to care. She spoke endlessly of her own dreams and her need for true love, and the fortune teller she went to, and he would sit in rapt attention unable to move his lips. In fact he found it hard to take his eyes off her, and all as he could do was swallow.

Then she would sway away from him, and look back over her shoulder and smile. "You get the story, and we'll be a team!"

And Doran could not help thinking about wanting to be a team. He even thought of marrying Mary and her grandfather giving her away. There would be some great joke told at the wedding, everyone would laugh – Isaac Snow would be best man. He was lovesick and he knew it, and he telephoned his mom about Mary Cyr and spoke about things going better. He wanted to visit his mother but he couldn't at the moment. "Yes, Mom, but right now I can't because I'm, well – indispensable, I guess. That's what Mary says. Mary – well she is someone you'd be proud that I know. And,' he whispered, "I think she likes me too!"

"Oh that's so lovely, Max," his mother said. "I am happy for you, dear!"

Tears flooded Doran's eyes, because of how weak her voice was now.

Then, a week later, after a call from Mr. Cyr, Mary was allowed to cross the barricade and place her little twenty-one-foot sailboat – which she almost never sailed – into the sea.

And after that phone call, Doran, who hadn't been allowed stories for a week because Isaac had told the band not to speak to him, and whose managing editor was worried lest he lose out on this whole summer, was fortunate enough to begin to file his reports from behind the native blockade and thus capture the attention of radio and television, who were being kept away by the warriors. So for a brief time he became indispensable to each and every other reporter, for they all had to rely upon him. He became the conscience of Canada – or so said Mary Cyr.

"Am I indispensable?" he asked.

"Yes, and I made you so," she said.

Doran went behind the barricade, with his special dispensation, and was filled with determination to tell the exact truth. Which is what he told Mary he was after, and to which Mary replied: "Ah yes, the truth. How vital that is. And so we have made you vital too," and she patted his cheek with a slim hand that smelled of soft fabric.

Still, the story that Doran was indispensable to tell was not really his idea anymore. In fact, the story was basically Isaac Snow's. And Isaac had played his cards right by sending Max away and then bringing him back. That made Max reliant upon him. Since Isaac was the only source, and since Max was the only link between Isaac and the outside world, Max slowly but surely became the voice of Isaac. And since Isaac wanted one slant on his voice and another on Roger's, the story was told that way too. Everyone was now singing Max's praises. And he told this to Mary Cyr, saying in a vulnerable moment, "Yes – they will probably even want to give me some award."

"Yes, an award – maybe even a humanitarian one," Mary said. "I discovered that Canada is like that at certain times."

And although he believed Mary Cyr was waiting on his reports and longed for information because she cared deeply for him (because she told him she did), in truth she cared for the story only insofar as people would like her better if she had more information. And though Doran was clumsy, inept and shy with women, Mary Cyr was not at all clumsy or inept with men. Neither here, nor in Spain, nor in Amsterdam, nor in Australia in 1983.

Doran bought her a present – a little pendant – and wrapped it, and wrote on the card, "Love." Then, tearing this up, he wrote on the second card, "With affection," and tore that one up as well. Then he decided not to give her a card when he gave her the present. He handed this present awkwardly to her one late afternoon. After an hour, he said, "Are you going to open it?"

"Oh – it's for me?"

She opened the box, removed the white cotton, and the poor pendant fell to the floor. But she did not notice and kept looking in the box in a rather mystified way.

"It's on the floor," he said.

"Oh, of course!" She picked it up and placed it on the table and looked at it with a fresh and serious gaze. "Yes, it is – gorgeous – wonderful – thank you."

She put her hand – her wonderful hand – to his cheek, and he blushed.

"They are taking your stories away," Isaac told Doran the next day, "and shelving them. Gordon Young has that story about the oil spill on the Bay of Fundy. Maybe you are spending too much time in love with Mary Cyr."

Doran blushed and blinked and didn't know what to say. How could anyone know this? But he was obviously deeply infatuated. And worse, he didn't want to be teased about it, and people could tell. And so Isaac began to tease him there and then.

The next story Doran wrote was one Mary Cyr told him to write. It was about day-to-day life on the reserve. It was published on page three while a story by Gordon Young took up the top half of page one.

Suddenly Doran felt he was failing.

"No no no," Mary said to him. "As for me – I loved the story."

"You did?"

"Well, of course I did. You are so particularly bright!"

"I am? I mean, you think I am?"

After a suitable pause she said: "Well, what do you think?" He noticed that she was wearing his little pendant on her blouse.

And poor Doran's heart leapt with joy.

People understood what was going on – that certain men were now running the reserve. Mrs. Francis at the moment was caught in the middle. She begged her two oldest boys to come home, especially Andy, but they did not listen. She was out half the night tramping the ground looking for them, and coming home tears in her eyes.

She wanted Little Joe, her foster child, to go to the Tim Hortons summer camp, as he had been approved, and had been waiting to go, and the night she gave him his bath he had packed his knapsack, taking the lure Markus had given him. But now she realized this was impossible, so she had to tell him it was impossible. So on the day he was to leave he sat on his bed, with his Mickey Mouse knapsack, and stared at the floor. He had waited half the year, and now he could not go.

"I don't care," he said, "it don't matter."

He spoke more English than Micmac, and so this is how they spoke to him.

"But we need you here," Mrs. Francis said and smiled, "so you have to be brave."

"I am brave," Little Joe said, matter-of-factly.

All of this time Amos remained chief, and remained positive. He told people the barricade would come down soon and things would get back to normal now that Roger was not going to be charged. And this is what most people wanted.

162

But without them being conscious of it, their every action created a counteraction and caused greater consternation. And this consternation caused more worry, and this worry made people more likely to say and do things they would not normally ever do. The barricade became the place where everything was most concentrated, and that is where Joel Ginnish most often was. Joel and Isaac had not spoken to each other in some time.

After trying to keep things on an even keel for two weeks, Amos received word that the funding for the recreation centre was cut off, and would probably never be re-established.

"Why – why do that to the children?"

Because the men had taken equipment to use at the barricade and used Recreation funds. Amos had to break the word at the council meeting that night. When he walked in, and sat down, and stared at his pen, he looked much older than he had before. Even Doran was surprised at how much he had aged. "The funding has been cut." Amos smiled apologetically and shrugged. He spoke only to a few people. He did not say the funding was cut because equipment was stolen or money had been taken to pay the warriors – but this was the reason.

Many asked him questions, but Amos went home, and closed the door, and opened a tin of peaches, and sat in the dark eating them, and rocking on the rocking chair.

Now Joel, who had wanted people to stay away from the recreation centre and not help build it, and had insisted the warriors confiscate the equipment, said he was outraged because funding had been cut. He called a meeting without Isaac Snow being present and said things were untenable. But he wanted Doran present.

"Yes," he said, smiling, "the ground is rocky and shaky, and I would even say volatile. That is what our leader Isaac won't admit. He is too interested in getting his name in the paper. But we don't see much of our names in the paper, do we? So," he said, frowning now, "it will be left up to me to turn this around!"

What happens when the situation men find themselves in becomes volatile? At first there is silence. And there was, for a week complete silence.

On the evening of July twenty-eighth, someone wearing a sweater and a hood climbed the bulldozer from the back, and taking his cattail torch, set the dozer ablaze. It had already been doused with gas – and the flame scorched the sleeves of the man who lit it. (It was reported ten years later that this was Andy Francis.)

The fire could be seen across the water for twenty miles. It could be seen far away along the road, where the RCMP were at that moment debating what action to take. Sparks and heat filled the air, and peeled the paint on Roger's front steps.

Roger, like everyone else, came out to stare at it. Some of the men backed away. Others decided to throw tires on the blaze, so it grew to cast an eerie light on all the cottages around it. The reserve's new pumper came, but the four firemen from the reserve couldn't get it to work. Finally they set the hose up, and though the men braced for a great rush of water only a dribble came out. All the women who were watching began to roar and laugh – one even fell on the ground laughing.

Sparks flew in the air and the fire trucks from Neguac were called but the pumper was kept away by the warriors. Some of the warriors, guided by this hooded man, twisted one of the hoses to cut off the flow of water, and torches were lit from the blaze and thrown at Roger's house. One shard of glass thrust toward him cut his arm. He ran back and forth collecting the torches and throwing them back toward the warriors. Then he disappeared, came out a moment later with his rifle, pulled down the lever and put in a shell. The firemen left them and began to wet down the cottages. There was great fear that the 100-year-old Cyr cottage, a landmark from the lumber baron years, would go up in flames. In fact sparks did catch a back eave, and had to be doused. So did Roger Savage's propane tank.

Little Joe sat far up in an elm tree, looking down on the great sight, his eyes staring at the world in wonder and alarm.

People said this fire signalled the end of Isaac's power over the warriors. That he had no more – and it was all a joke – everything was a joke – and Joel would soon be in charge.

The next morning Roger Savage came out of his house, in the twilight created by the still-hovering smoke, and with determined gestures seen only by the young, planted a sign in the middle of his yard. People said later it was written in his own blood from the cut on his arm the night before. The sign stood until the end of the affair:

I will not apologize for who I was or am
I won't be driven out
And I do not give a damn!!

5

If Isaac's power was over, then the reserve would reel into chaos. And Max Doran knew as much. He went to Isaac to get a statement – in fact to help Isaac put a better perspective on everything – but could not get an interview, and the whole reserve was the same. No one would tell him anything, about the fire, or who had set it or why, and some seemed to blame him for something. Many of the women and more than a few of the men seemed ashamed.

So after a few days, with no one speaking to him, he decided to go back out, after filing only four stories, including the one that was published on page three.

He was allowed to cross over the barricade at nine the next night.

"If you go, do not come back," Joel told him, "for if you come back, you might not get away so easily. For so far you are telling the wrong story. I have been in touch with a reporter from Halifax, and he says you are an amateur."

It was the closest Doran had ever come to swinging at someone, but he knew even if he managed to hit Joel he would never be able to hurt him. In fact he had seen Joel punched in the mouth by one of the warriors a few days before, and simply laugh.

"No one can do the story as good as me," he said instead.

But Joel just looked away and busied himself with other things.

Doran crossed to Mary's yard. Some of her grasses had been singed by the fire, and he could smell burned rubber that had melted right into the asphalt. There had been a camera crew from CTV there all day, and they had finally been told to pull back.

Doran had his bag packed and was ready to go down to Saint John. That was because no one would talk to him. He knew that to file another story about the reserve or Roger Savage and not mention the fire would be unprofessional. Yet here is what he felt secretly: to file a story about the fire Isaac did not approve of would be psychologically damaging and would work against him and his position at the paper. He sat in Mary Cyr's house, thinking he had done his level best, even if he had failed. She had a handyman there helping replace the eaves. But he walked back and forth looking at Max with distrust.

Max asked Mary for advice.

"What do you think you should do?" she replied.

And here he sensed for the first time that she was not as wise or beneficial as he had believed, or perhaps wisely beneficial to herself. But that made him love her even more. He then tried to make a joke about the pendant falling on the floor, but she looked at him for a long time, as if she didn't remember.

"Oh," she said finally. "Yes. The pendant. How nice that was of you."

Doran went to town the next day just to be away from things. The RCMP let him pass their monitoring station without a word – except they did check his licence and the car trunk.

When he got back from town at seven in the evening, Mary Cyr told him that all day her grandfather had been trying to reach him.

"Reach *me*?" Doran said, flabbergasted. "Your grand-father – my God – why reach me?"

Mary shrugged as if she had been the one to orchestrate this, and walked away from him with her beautiful hips moving in what could only be described as triumphant.

And so he spoke to her grandfather that night.

"That equipment was donated by me," her grandfather said, quite distinctly. "I was asked to donate it. I donated it to help the band. So what I want to know is this: why was it burned? And I also want to know this because my cottage was almost destroyed. But what you were writing never indicated this kind of situation might erupt. Your last piece was simply a human interest story – good enough but not enough." This was said without the least change of tone.

"But I had no idea this would happen," Doran said, "and I don't think, sir, that anyone could foresee it."

"I was told this would happen two weeks ago," Mr. Cyr said.

"Oh," Doran said. "Yes." He tried to think. "By whom?"

"By Gordon Young."

Mr. Cyr simply hung up. After this, the managing editor telephoned. Though obsequious and polite with Mary Cyr, he was furious with Doran.

"I vouched for you, damnit!" And he too hung up.

Doran had to go back into the reserve or lose the story. Yet Doran didn't know if they would allow him to cross, and if he did write, he would have to be 100 percent right in what he said – if not, his career would be over. If he lost it, he would never get another chance. But he could not really change his story or he would lose face. That too he knew.

So suddenly Doran was in another bind. How could he write the same thing and say nothing about the barricade being burned? He couldn't. How could he change the angle of his story? He couldn't.

He slept in the back bedroom of Mary Cyr's and had nightmares about trees and nets and big smiling fish. The next morning he learned that the handyman fixing the eaves was a private detective sent along by Mr. Cyr to keep an eye on the property and protect his rather impressionable grand-daughter. And this private detective did not seem fond of Doran and what he was implying about the whites in the area being backward and bigoted – though these words were never used exactly. And once the man stared at him with eyes of steel from the far side of the room when Max was trying to flirt with the woman under his protection.

"No, go on – go," Mary said, pushing him by the back after breakfast and waving goodbye. "You are our indispensable mole – and so do go and do the mole-like things!"

So Doran resolutely went to the barricade and asked to go back in. For two hours they did not let him. They just laughed at him.

Finally Isaac gave word that he was allowed to pass.

"He is not," Joel said. So two of the young men, Andy Francis being one, Gig Parrish being the other, told him he couldn't cross back over.

Then Joel went to see Isaac, while Doran waited, with his big notebook sticking up out of his back pocket and holding his portable typewriter in his hand.

"Hopefully they will not let me pass, and I will end this story," he thought. But at the same time, he thought of being mentioned by that famous person on the CBC. Another week or two – certainly he could last that long!

Another hour passed. He sat down in the dirt, hauled out a pack of cards – he always had one on him – and played solitaire on the road, with his straw hat pushed back on his head and First Nations cars passing around him. Sometimes their tires came very close to his knees.

He was wondering if being kept on this side of the line was not for the best when word came once again that Isaac had said he could pass. Joel came to the barricade with a .30-30 rifle, and shrugged, opened up the side gate of wire and waved him through.

And so reluctantly the warriors let him pass.

Doran went to Isaac that evening. Isaac was too smart not to know that Doran had come to ask permission to write about the conflict now emerging between him and Joel. If he dared write this, about his warriors being out of control, Isaac would be humiliated.

So unlike before, when it was easy for Doran to come in or out of the house, and even take a beer out of the fridge if he wanted, he now had to wait at the door before Isaac came to see him.

"I don't want to see that mooch," he heard Isaac saying, and then saying things in Micmac he did not understand, and then the word "mooch" once more.

Isaac finally came from the dark back room with the flickering shadows of trees on the wall. He had a blinding headache and the light hurt his eyes. Three houses were being targeted by Joel's men – the two Wissards who had tattled on him over the fish, and Amos Paul's. Isaac had been on the phone all day trying to bring this tension to a rest.

Now he stood at the door and reiterated his position. Yes, he said calmly, there is evidence that Roger Savage burned the "dozer.

"There is?" Max asked, dumbfounded.

"Yes," Isaac said, looking down at him sternly. "Yes, there is evidence that Roger burned it. Why do you think that is strange? Look at the sign he put out on his yard – doesn't that prove it? He wanted to stop the barricade so he can travel to and from his house. It's simple to see!"

"So you minded that the bulldozer was burned."

"Of course we minded – it was Roger who burned it! But you always miss the point. All summer you have missed the point – you mooch about missing the point. So if Roger lit the fire, tell that to your paper!"

"Is that what I should say?" Doran asked.

"You're the reporter, so tell the truth," Isaac said finally, and he turned away.

"Could I just ask – where you heard that Roger burned the bulldozer?"

"Tell him to go fuck himself and tell the truth," Isaac said to his wife as he went to the cupboard to get some aspirin. He

170

took four and went into the back room. Then he gave a big blast of Micmac.

Collette looked at Doran and shrugged as if she didn't know what to say.

Doran went away knowing he would not file that story about Roger – that he could not. He also knew that if he wrote any other story, Isaac would disown him. He sat down at his typewriter. He imagined everyone was looking at him as he poured out these words:

"It is not in my nature to cast blame, so I do not play favourites here. There is just no evidence to suggest it was the warriors. In fact – "

He tore the page away. What he was really thinking of was Mary Cyr and how he did not want to disappoint her – and how he longed in his heart and soul to see her once again. And the way to do that was to have everyone like him, and everyone on his side.

He sat up all night, without writing another word.

The next day Andy Francis came on behalf of Joel and told Doran he was no longer allowed to leave the reserve – that he had been invited to do a story and he must stay until the story was done, and they would give him a place to keep him safe. But his story about Roger burning the bulldozer should be done as soon as possible. In fact this was an order from Isaac himself, and Joel too wanted it written by the afternoon.

"It's not a bad thing to stay on the reserve, is it?" Andy added, to change the subject.

"What do you mean?" Doran asked.

"Oh, well . . . we've been staying on the reserve for two centuries," Andy said.

They could still smell the burned tires and the diesel. It wafted through the air and tainted everything so the mothers couldn't take their young children out without putting cloths over their mouths.

171

"Is this what Isaac thinks?" Doran asked. "I mean, do we have proof?"

Andy took Doran's head and turned it in the direction of the barricade, still singed by black soot and burned tires.

"There it is – proof," he said.

Isaac had managed to allow the women and children to pass up the road to Sobeys that day and shop. So to lessen antagonism the store was kept opened and hours extended just for them. Little Joe went shopping with his sister Sky. He had a big cart. He had some bananas, four bags of marshmallows, a bottle of ketchup, a can of tomato soup, two big bottles of Pepsi, seven Cadbury bars, a bar of soap (to be respectable), fifteen puddings and a pie mix.

They had put Doran in a shed, on Stone Street, with a sink and a small tub – but no hot water. If he wanted hot water he would have to go across the street to Mrs. Demers's house. He had a toilet and an old stove – it was a wood stove, but he had an electric burner. He had one main light, and could type at the metal kitchen table. He learned this was the shed where Markus" father, a Vietnam vet, had lived with his son and his daughter for almost three years. He learned that Roger Savage used to come over now and again to look in on him and the kids, and bring them groceries when he had the chance, for he was very close by.

"You mean *the* Roger Savage?" he asked when he went to Mrs. Demers's to have a shower.

"What other Roger would it be?" Mrs. Demers said, as if nothing was amiss, and shrugged.

Staying here, and seeing the great kindness of the band toward him by all but a few, made Doran feel deeply humble. And after he took his shower he sat on the edge of the tub with a white towel wrapped about him, his thin shoulders freckled, and listened to the waves beating monotonously out on the shore.

"What will I do," he thought suddenly, "to get myself out of this mess?"

But he felt the only way through was to keep going.

Two nights later, at about seven in the evening, Doran was listening to robins call from the trees. There was a knock on the door and Little Joe and Sky were there, bringing him a blueberry pie, from blueberries they had picked the day before.

They burst out laughing and left it, still warm from the oven, at the door, and turned and ran away.

Joel came to Doran the next day before noon. He said, "Did Andy treat you well?"

"Yes."

"That's good, for he's young and mighty impatient. He wants all the changes now," Joel said, and he laughed as if this was impossible.

Doran nodded and said he understood how that could happen, for in his life he also requested justice for all. "That's why I write my articles," he said. "I demand justice too!"

"Noble, noble," Joel said, looking around as if agitated, "noble for sure." He paused, lit a cigarette and added: "I will show you where Roger hayed our nets and washed our livelihood away. You can use that in your next submission. Come with me."

"Is Isaac mad at me?" Max asked.

"Why?"

"He seemed very angry at me."

"Don't worry about Isaac." Joel smiled his engaging smile. "I never do!"

This struck Doran as a strange comment, even a betrayal, but he said nothing. He went with Joel to see where this haying had occurred. After they looked at where the hay supposedly had been dropped, Doran was going to leave, but

173

Ginnish said, "No, stay with me. You don't need to tell Isaac's story – you need to tell mine."

"What do you mean? I thought – I mean, it's the band I'm dealing with."

"Not a bit. People are upset," Joel said emotionally. "Isaac wants all the publicity for himself. I said let it go, but many people are telling me Isaac's getting too much attention – that's what the men are saying, that there's too much about him in the paper. He is leading you in the wrong direction." Here Joel whispered, emotional still, "We think he and Roger might have made a deal about the pools. I don't want to believe it, but other bands are making deals with the Government and Isaac won't. Anyway, everyone is sick to death of Isaac. So you have to tell some other story – about my struggle for independence, even from Isaac himself! Isaac wanted you back on the reserve to control you, but I am going to put a stop to that. You come with me tonight, and I'll show you what to write about."

Doran waited for Joel near a laneway until nearly eight that evening. It was better than having Mrs. Demers tell him innocently that his managing editor was expecting to hear from him. So he stood in the laneway and chain-smoked. Twice he had written a story about the bulldozer burning being suspicious – perhaps even the result of "he who is being investigated." He wrote, "The whites wanted the barricade destroyed. Some whites said they wouldn't tolerate First Nations men in town." That was probably true. Yet twice he'd torn it in two.

Then an hour before dark, Ginnish appeared and took Doran to the back cove in a canoe to meet one of the people who had been in the hold. Doran, hoping for some firm proof of what had happened. To finally put the story to bed.

Part IV

Markus Paul's diary, September 11, 2006

I will take the canoe down tomorrow and put it in just below the Bailey Bridge, where I cut the juniper last fall for the keel, and I will put on a 6 lb test leader. If there is a mist, I will try bug or butterfly and drift down to Green Brook and wait until the sun hits the water over the back trees. This will be my last chance to fish before moose season, and I have yet to scope my rifle. I have yet to do all those things, and my wife – well, my ex-wife now – Samantha Dulse has asked me to come in for an X-ray, but what is an X-ray against this? So the day should be cool, and therefore the water, too, cool enough – and then when the sun splits the back trees the fish will be active enough. I will use the old heavy rod I like, with the hardy reel. The new one given to me, I never have used. I put it together once, and once I felt it for balance, and as fine as it is, it just doesn't seem like mine. I have not had a fish on the hook most of the summer, and do you know what – I will tell you a secret – most of the time, I hand tail them, take the hook out and let them go. They slide back into the great water of our river, and disappear.

1985

1

They hid the canoe between some maple saplings, for Joel
was suspicious, and lifted from the shallow water two broad
boxes that he had hidden too, and walked the windswept
barrens between two roads that cut down through the small
pines. Joel was not as big as Isaac but he was very powerful,
with longer than normal arms and big hands. He helped
Doran along, manoeuvring those heavy boxes between fir
and pine, and spoke to him quietly about his life. And it was a
life that Doran himself couldn't imagine. Physical violence –
the mere idea of which Doran had always shrunk from – was
as much a part of Joel's life as breathing. Being cheated, shot
at and thrown from a half-ton were part of a succession of
stories Joel told to impress this young white man who wanted
to please both him and Isaac, and was trying to do the best
story he could.

They were the first there, and waited in the evening with
bugs flicking and whining in their ears. Doran was filled with
a kind of unease. He realized now that he would have been
much better off if he had never heard of this story of his. He
thought at this moment that his safety depended on something other than his integrity, and he was confused about
what he should do. That is, the trail to the bottom of the
lobster trap was complete, and he could not for the life of him
back up and walk away.

After a while a man and a boy approached through the
darkness, and Max did not see them until they were less than
five feet away.

178

They met with Tanker Monk, who had brought the water boy with him. Tanker told Doran that he had almost died in the fourth hold of the *Lutheran* because the load was meant to drop on them all, because they had given the Indian a union card.

"It weren't just meant for the poor little Indian," he said.

But something else was important. And Joel seemed not only to flaunt this but to want to flaunt it. It was what he had promised Isaac he would not do.

It was the salmon that Ginnish had, and that Doran had unwittingly helped carry though those woods under the dark night sky. And Ginnish was selling them.

Ginnish took some ten salmon out of the two large cooler boxes and laid them out on the grass, and counted them. They were beautiful fish, the smell still wonderfully fresh. They had just entered the river pools from the sea a few nights before. Each fish was over eight pounds and under twenty.

Tanker complained about the two smaller fish, saying they were grilse – that is, the smaller two-year-old salmon, which almost never go over five pounds. But this argument was dispensed with on the other side, when Joel said the twenty-pound salmon weighed twenty-five. So finally after twenty minutes everything was arrived at. The wind came up slightly, which was a blessing because of the whine of the flies. They put the fish in cooler boxes Tanker had brought and covered them with grass and ice.

Then Tanker paid Joel two hundred dollars.

"This is how we make money for our struggle," Joel smiled at Doran, waving the money quickly for some reason before tucking it into his shirt. "So thanks for helping me." Joel was happy with Doran now and spoke to him like a brother. He took out a bag of marijuana and began to roll it in with tobacco.

"Pretty good stuff, this," he said. "I call it 'my reserve'," and he smiled at this and shrugged when Doran did not smile. "You take things too serious," he said.

179

"I do?"

"Sure – too serious. Have some fun – slap some pussy, get drunk, steal a car, go for a milkshake – do something! And stop wearing shorts!" And he laughed hilariously. "No one gives a fuck about this. Why do you write so much about it? I think you want to make a name for yourself with all those concerned fuckers in Upper Canada who always write about the Indians every summer, their faces all as pinched as weasels. They can't shit without their wives" permission."

"That's not the reason." Doran began. "I came here to do a story and to get it right."

"Well let me tell you a secret – you'll never get it right. Not with us. And you arrived here just to pretend. But Roger is in that house up there all alone . . . Sometimes, oh oh oh – sometimes I feel bad for Roger because of you. Because you have the big pretend going."

"Pretend?"

"Sure, the big pretend. You can smell any white man who has it. The big pretend – pretend to know Indians and to like us. You don't know us, and you certainly don't like us."

"Of course I do."

But here Joel just held up his finger over his lips and said, "Shh," and smiled sadly.

Then they were silent a moment. An owl fluttered by and scared Doran. Joel looked at him, smiling delightfully, and shrugged.

"Well then, do you like me?"

"Sure."

"Well then, tell my story," he said, "tell what I've been through – I have been the one who had to deal with this. Tell about me – how my brother was Hector. Take my picture for the paper!"

"Sure I will," Doran said, hoping that they would leave to go back.

But they did not go back. They sat on the bank and smoked some grass, and drank a little from a bottle, and Doran found himself becoming a part of the story he was writing. He suddenly blurted this out. It surprised even himself that he did.

But when he said this, Joel simply shrugged.

"Haven't you always been? I know exactly how Isaac thinks. Now you stay here until this is resolved – please, for my sake." And he put his arm around Doran and handed him the bottle of rum. "You said you like us, prove it. Later you can write a book about me. I'll give you all the information – about Amos and the whites – Isaac too – and how much he has against me. Now we'll do things my way. No more Isaac. Isaac is a dead man. And when the movie is made I can be a consultant – or play a small part!"

Of course he was drunk and falling sideways – but Doran was drunk too.

"Who's the only one willing to do something?" Joel said. "Wait and see, and it will be *me*!"

About an hour later the wind came up much stronger. There was the smell of the enclosed trees and the rushing water. Doran was unfamiliar with the woods. If Joel left him, he would never find his way out.

He went to the trees to relieve himself and there suddenly the young water boy, Brice Peel, tugged at his arm and whispered to him these words:

"Roger Savage didn't do nothing. The load didn't fall on anyone – tell them at the paper."

"What?" Doran said.

The boy said nothing else, because Tanker was coming toward them, and he moved away quickly, grabbing onto the grasses so as not to fall into the water. But he fell in anyway. Joel laughed and rushed down and helped him out.

"There you go, my little white poky-dot friend."

Tanker smiled and slapped at some flies, and asked Doran if he liked it here and was everyone nice to him? Doran nodded, listened to the wind rising. He tried to be comfortable and sit like Joel did. Joel, who seemed to be impervious to wind and flies, and simply stared into the dark.

There were real tears now in Joel's eyes. "You have not done enough to promote our cause," he said, "so maybe I'll have to kill you someday. How would that be?"

Doran now knew he had compromised himself, even though it was not intentional.

He decided to take his typewriter and leave the next day. He was surprised at how relieved he was to have come to this decision. Because if he did write a story, how much different would it now be from the one Joel wanted?

Tanker and Joel began to sing; then they had an argument. Then the talk filtered out into a diatribe in the drunken evening, about the marijuana and when Joel could get it to them, and how to get it off the reserve, and that Isaac wanted him to destroy the crop before the press found out about it. Joel said this and winked at Doran.

And how many girls Joel had had. It seemed to be many more than Tanker had had.

And how many barricades had ever worked? "The craziest thing an Indian ever did," Tanker said.

Doran said nothing to all of this.

Then Joel and Tanker shook hands. The white men moved off with the fish, and Joel and Doran walked back through the woods, every now and again Joel waiting for Doran to catch up, once or twice standing by a small opening and saying, "This way."

They came to the water, and Joel backed the canoe out, jumped into the stern and told Doran to get in. He stumbled as he did, and the Micmac patiently waited for him to straighten himself up.

"You like this canoe, Max?" he said.

"Sure."

"Yeah, well, it isn't mine."

"No?"

"No, Christ. You know who owns this canoe?"

"No."

"Markus Paul – you know him?"

"Not well."

"Yeah, he's a prick. He fishes salmon with a fly rod – in the summer, one at a time." Joel gave a short, low laugh, and then said, "Though his cast is perfect and he throws out a wonderful line!"

They started back down the river, in the dark under moonlight. The trees went swiftly by, and Doran felt sleepy and happy. But suddenly Joel jammed his paddle down and the canoe stopped dead.

"You get out here now," he said.

"Where?" Doran said, looking around.

"Here. If you cut through there two hundred yards you'll meet the old dividing marker. Just follow that out to the shore."

"But where is the reserve?"

"We're on the reserve – we just came on it. I have to see someone but you can't come."

"But where's this marker?"

"Just go south down that path," Joel said.

And so Doran, who had never known the woods and hated it, was left in the dark with the terrible insulting whine of mosquitoes, and the only other human figure slowly moving away in the moonlight.

He walked into the woods. The light of the moon was an easy lantern on the shore, but in here it cast out vaguely, and though Joel was essentially correct in that no one should lose their way walking to this marker, Doran within five minutes had come to a big tree fall he could not get around. At first, he didn't even know what it was. And by the time he realized, he had moved farther off the path and could not get back. So he continued on in the line afforded by the tree fall – which meant he was going northeast into the cedar swamp where Amos had once hunted moose as a boy.

Finally, being haunted by blackflies, with the air suddenly

still and muggy and in some places smelling putrid, he turned back toward the tree fall, hoping to retrace his steps, and tripping over undergrowth he fell into swamp water.

He stood quickly, feeling water rush under his pants and into his shoes. The only thing he could now hear was the sound of his heart.

He did not know whether to try again or wait in the bog. But he could not wait – he had to get away from the flies. But as he turned, hoping once again to find the river and retrace his steps (he would not have found it, for he was going deeper into the bog), he saw a man leaning on the end of another tree fall, watching him. At first he did not even know it was a man, it was so dark. But after a time he realized this. The man simply stared at him, an ornate lever-action rifle in his hand.

"Hi – I'm kinda turned around in here," Doran said.

For a few moments – painful moments they were – the man did not speak.

"Yer on my line side of the reserve," the man finally said.

"And the reserve is where" – he paused – "sir?"

"Five more yards your way," the man said. "Come, I'll take you back."

Doran followed him quietly. Now and again the man would wait for him to climb over some bush or stumps, and soon they were back on the pathway Joel had spoken about, and within minutes they were at the marker Joel had told him about – and then he saw the lane to the shore and could even hear the waves of the bay against the breakwater. He wanted to ask the man a question but when he turned around the man had gone.

And Doran realized (he had been unsure) that he had met Roger Savage, the man who had decided to take on the world. He felt suddenly ashamed that he had insinuated so much in the press about the man. And now he was worried he had not done what was just.

"But it is my job," he thought. "I am only doing what I

have been asked to do. Someone else would have done far worse."

And for now he left it at that, while having a sudden intense feeling that he wished Roger Savage was his friend.

When Doran got back to the shed, people were all over the road. Women were crying. He walked down to see what had happened. People were saying Isaac had been taken prisoner. Five police officers had come in from the woods in SWAT gear and had raided the old shed at the back of his house, and had taken him away. He had fought valiantly, thrown three of them over his back and knocked one cold, but he was alone.

Some of the women were talking to Doran in a mixture of English and Micmac, and he tried to understand. They threw broken bottles onto Roger's porch.

An hour later Joel arrived, having just heard the news himself. He walked up the road with everyone speaking to him, and while he moved through the throng he passed some grass around to the young men, and then sat on a tar pole near the breakwater. Then he passed around some uppers out of a huge bag to Andy and Tom. And he passed a hit of acid to one of the women. (Doran did not know that this woman was Amos' granddaughter Peggy Paul.)

But everyone felt as if there could be no reconciliation now. The dark was salty sweet, the wind was warm off the waves, and they could just make out each other's faces, like lovers on a lane.

"We'll fight now," Andy said happily, "so write that down in your fuckin paper. See what they say to that!" And he smiled and took another drink of beer.

To Little Joe it seemed as if a big war had come and he must do something to protect his mother Mrs. Francis and his big sister Sky. Sky of course was trying her best to protect him, and no matter that three or four of the young men were trying to impress her, hoping everything would go back to the way it was. But now they knew this had come to something none had really expected – all of them were vulnerable.

"I don't want to see you near the barricade anymore," she told Little Joe.

He was seen in his yard with a BB gun, but he did not have any BBs.

2

Yes, it was cold in the bar, and colder outside, and almost November, 1985. Doran had written his last article on the "disturbing" case weeks ago, and today he had just resigned from the paper. He had his hair cut above his ears, and he looked older. He had promised his mother for years he would get his hair cut, and had done so for her funeral yesterday.

He had heard that Chief Amos had tried on four occasions to get Roger to leave his house. Yet each time, Roger had come to the point: he stated that he was innocent and was finishing his room. It was a room, Doran knew, that Mary Cyr could see from her bath. She would sometimes stand in the light at the opened window, with a bath towel loose around her, her hair damp from the shower.

All during this time Roger's sign was still in place in the middle of his yard:

I will not apologize for who I was or am
I won't be driven out,
And I do not give a damn!

Doran wondered if he himself would be that courageous. Most men wouldn't be.

What had happened since that night he'd met Roger Savage? Well, for one thing, Doran had refused to write any more stories because of how he was being told what to write. And because of this, both Mr. Cyr and Joel Ginnish were furious

187

with him. But he had stood his ground. He reread all his copy, and decided he had said what he had said, and for better or worse he would say no more.

"Get someone else in here to write," he said. "Get that old Mr. Thompson – you know, the man who said he taught me all I know, and has never written a line in his life worth reading. And fuck it." His face was thin, and he couldn't eat for being worried, but he stuck to his decision.

Just when people were beginning to think things had gone as far as they would, that the bulldozers and the graders and the trucks sitting like battle-scarred portents was enough, the police had arrested Isaac.

They had arrested him not understanding that he was actually a moderate influence, but believing that he was the main broker of the unrest. They had arrested him because he had five big bales of marijuana in his shed.

But Isaac was not Joel's moral support; he was Joel's moral stabilizer. To arrest Isaac was far worse than arresting Joel – for Joel was like a man standing on a cliff and being swayed by his own preternatural desire to fall.

Isaac sat in his cell most of that first long hot afternoon after his arrest without moving a muscle. He did not speak to anyone, either. The same compressed rage that Amos had seen on his face reappeared. He had started out in the earlier part of the summer to get lobster licences for his poverty-stricken band, and to keep his men from revolting because of Hector. He had tried, and now he was in jail! No matter how you thought about it, it was a betrayal.

He stared straight ahead. A few of the local toughs yelled through the window at him.

"Hang him!" they yelled. Isaac did not even glance at them.

Nor, as the shadows lengthened at supper, did he react when they set his food down. Not that day nor, in the swell and smell of rain, the next.

After two days it became clear Isaac was on a hunger strike. He said nothing to the nurse Pamela Dulse when she came in to check his blood pressure and pulse on the third day. By this time he lay on his cot all day, with his face to the wall, and listened to the rain breaking down over the barrels outside, listened to the kids coming and going from the old volleyball court down the hill, listened now and again to a siren.

"You have to eat," she said.

He shrugged. So she left the cell.

Then he wrote a long letter to the editor of the paper, speaking about his trials since his father, an innocent man, had been hanged by a white court and an all-white jury in 1955. He spoke of having his mother die of cancer. He spoke of quitting school, and of being in jail for taking meat for himself one winter.

He spoke about how he fought injustice by picking up seaweed and by fishing with gill nets in a private pool. Arrested again, and again.

But he said that the bales of marijuana were planted. He did not use marijuana, nor did he encourage anyone to, and everyone on the reserve knew this. It must have been the police who planted it. So if he was not released, it would cause even more trouble.

This sparked outrage and pleas for his release around the province. These pleas and the publicity his hunger strike received did one thing only. They made those in power more inflexible, to prove he could not sway law, because to them he had disobeyed the law and had stored marijuana.

But his hunger strike did something else, and Isaac knew it would – it truly saved his reputation within the reserve. For Joel, ready to act on his own, in direct conflict with Isaac's orders, now more than ever seemed to be acting on Isaac's behalf, and in his honour. Further, it did this – it did not allow him to give up his hunger strike even unto death. And one reason he had the courage not to give up

189

was because of the police planting the marijuana in his shed.

The police officer Hanover believed Isaac was the one who had fired at the spotter plane, and Hanover believed keeping him in jail would defuse the situation, and that's what Hanover believed no matter what.

Isaac, as he began to grow weak, called his wife to see him. Collette came and sat outside the cell and was shocked to see how her husband had failed.

"You have to eat," she begged him. "Who cares about this anymore?"

"I care," he said. Then he paused and gave her a smile. "I have to care. You see, everything now is up to me. It is as if the load fell on our whole band – that now we must do something – if not now then never."

He smiled at her simply, showing the dimples on his face that were childlike and that she loved. And he said:

"Do not worry. For at this time next year you will walk to our wharf, to stand on our lobster boat – or to our graveyard, to stand by my grave."

The reserve became more tempestuous, anxious and depressed. No one knew what to do. Joel took control of the houses, of the recreation centre, of everything to do with money. This was done to keep Amos away from power – and it was done, in a certain way, as a reaction to Isaac's growing fame. Which meant that something else, something more dangerous and something better, would have to be done, and Joel knew this. To take power was to enact powerfully – and more powerfully than your predecessor. That, in fact, was what having power meant.

So Joel and his supporters held meetings each night from August 21 on, trying to decide what this something should be.

On that very day, Joel had asked Doran to write an article

about the police planting the marijuana. But Doran said he could not, because it could not be proved.

"Of course it can be proved."

"How?"

"Because I saw them."

"You saw them plant the marijuana?"

"Of course."

"Then why didn't you say something?"

Joel assumed a hysterical look and began to walk away. "Write the story," he said. "Tell the truth."

But Doran knew the truth, or suspected it, and could not write the story. Other than that, he did not know what to do. No one was going to get him to write another word unless he himself decided to.

On this day, too, young people from the university began to arrive at Mary Cyr's cottage to mount a protest against the police for complicity or cover-up in the death of Hector Penniac. That is, the idea of a cover-up was an active one in the university corridors, and many professors wanted to display their outrage over this. Students set up a human shield to protect the natives from the police and army. Mary set up her barbecue and ordered in sea crab and salad. But by the end of the day she was tired of it all, bored with the students and their inflamed mimicking talk, and so she dismissed them from her yard in a way only Mary Cyr could do, and sat in the back veranda and smoked.

On August 25, the warriors decided they would exact the same penalty on Roger that Isaac was suffering. Rain began to fall, the days became cooler. Doran was at that meeting, but he declined to take notes. It was very tense, and people were worried the army was going to invade. Joel too seemed erratic in what he said. He looked around the room with glittering eyes to pick someone to blame. At first he cursed at two young native men who he felt were not doing their jobs

191

at the barricade – for many now had grown tired of it. Then he spotted Doran.

"If Isaac dies, you'll pay the price too," he said to Doran, without the least emotion. He shrugged as if this wasn't terrible news, and pointed to Andy, as if Andy was the one who wanted to exact justice.

And Andy, who had not known he would be singled out simply said: "I told you I didn't want you back here. Well, you came back – so if anything goes wrong, it's your problem."

Doran went back to his shed and lay down and listened to the rain against the small roof. He had stated the warriors'' case and now they were against him. He had no alternative but to resign from the story. That did not mean he thought Penniac's death wasn't unjust. It did not mean the concerns of the First Nations band were wrong. It just meant he would hand the story over to someone else. That is all he was thinking. He would go back across the barricade in the morning.

But the next morning when he went to go, the warriors told him he couldn't. Isaac was too sick, so he must stay, for they had already decided Doran was the one who had betrayed Isaac to the police. They asked him for his passport and said he couldn't cross without it.

"If you did not betray Isaac, then write the story about the police planting the marijuana," Joel said, wagging his finger happily. But Doran said again that he would not, because it could not be proved.

"I saw it," Joel said.

"How did you see it? I was with you at the time," Doran said.

Joel shrugged and walked away.

All that day Doran heard students shouting insults at the police and at Roger Savage. Roger Savage couldn't be seen, but now and again the curtain in the upstairs window would move slightly, as if a hand had moved it. The police had decided to take Roger away for his own safety, but approaching his house was now too dangerous, not so much for them as for Roger and the warriors, and especially the students, who had locked arms and stretched from roadway to roadway. So they remained in consultations, trying to defuse the situation. They tried to talk to Roger on the phone but Roger unplugged it, and would not consult with anyone.

Then something else happened to Doran. He suddenly hated the chants of those students. All of them now calling for justice for natives that they could never provide. Doran hated them, but in a way he felt – well, he felt he had created them. And now the students became the main story, and other papers interviewed many of them. And many of them proved they too could be vandals and began throwing rocks. Their pictures appeared, and they would be happy their pictures appeared, until such time as they found themselves ashamed. Doran listened to them, and walked from the barricade like a forlorn creature and sat in his shed with half the pie the little girl and boy had made him sitting on the table.

After a while Joel sent two men, followed by one of the many stray dogs, to search Doran. The men said he had helped the RCMP plant the dope and Joel was deciding if they would put him on trial. After they searched him one of the men wanted to hit him, but the other said no. Then they decided to take his tape recorder. They left with the stray dog following them back across the dusty road.

After supper, Doran went to see Joel to get his tape recorder back.

Joel said that he could have the tape recorder back when he left, but there might be sensitive police information on it.

Doran replied that there were only the sounds of birds he'd recorded and he was ready to go because he wasn't doing stories anymore. Joel turned on the tape recorder, and smiled expectantly, waiting to hear the police, or pretending to want to hear this. Then he turned it off.

"Why in hell would anyone record birds?" he asked, mystified.

Max didn't answer.

"Tell the truth," Joel said, "in a story about them planting the marijuana. That's the big story. If you write about them planting it, I'll let you go."

But what Doran was hearing was something else. This is what his informers told him (yes, Doran had informers – three boys he paid): Joel and his boys were going to come and get him – the boys did not know when – and they were going to force him to help them get Roger out of the house.

"They think you can go up to the house because you are white – and Roger will open the door for you – and then they will rush him, with a gun."

"Roger won't trust me," Doran said.

"Joel says he will make you do it – that it's the only way to get Roger, and you were the one who started this."

"I was the one!" And Doran and the three boys laughed.

3

Old Amos knew that Isaac had started something he could not back down from. If he gave up his hunger strike he would be looked upon as a cheat. Worse, he had set out nobly to help his people and now he realized this was the only way to do so, even if he died. If he died they would have those lobster licences he so desperately sought. And so he lay with his back to the wall, staring at a small spot.

In that small distinct spot, a tiny green bulb of paint over a crack, he saw the entire world, and for days the entire history of the world, and at times the entire history of his people over the last three thousand years. When the jailer came into talk to him, to beg him to eat, he whispered:

"Let me die so my people will live the way people should."

On the night of the ninth day of the hunger strike, Isaac fell into fitful unconsciousness. They took Isaac from his cell to the hospital, but word came that he had pulled an intravenous from his arm, in order to deny the sustenance that might keep him alive.

They all had a meeting later that night at Mrs. Francis's.

It ended with a nine-to-two vote to take Roger out of his house and hold him.

Later that night, the RCMP turned the power off, and the entire reserve was left in darkness.

Just after this happened, Max Doran was sitting alone in his shed, staring at the book he was trying to read without being able to, when Joel and Andy came to see him. The room was in semi-darkness, as were their faces, while the air outside seemed wet and still, and the trees no longer blew.

They were filled with an excitement that Doran did not understand. But then he realized Joel was high, as he had been every day since Isaac was arrested. Andy was high also, and filled with an exuberance that only proving himself to others would contain. "Do you want to help us?" Andy said, pulling up a chair to sit beside him and looking at him intently. Doran could see only parts of their faces in the semi-darkness. The wind blew just as Joel moved his chair closer.

"C'mon, you have to help us now," Joel said.

"Of course," Doran said after a moment. He was sweating, and felt ill.

"You must help us – it's our last bargaining chip to get Isaac back."

"How? I can write only what I know – and I do not know about the marijuana, I do not know about the bulldozer being burned." He ended in a whisper: "I don't want to blame – anyone."

"No one has ever put the blame on us," Joel said simply, "have they?"

Doran said nothing.

Andy then took a .22 pistol from his pocket and put it on the blanket.

"Roger'll trust you. Go to the door and knock tomorrow – say you want to write his story. Then you pull this on him and we'll rush him – that's all it'll take. We take him to our jail until we get Isaac back. Do it for Isaac like we are! There's no one else here that can do it!"

"Roger will not trust me."

"Well, he will trust you more than he will trust me." Joel smiled.

Doran stared out at the small fence rails in the backyard,

until they had disappeared with nightfall, and he could hear an owl in the trees, the same owl Little Joe had told Mary Cyr about.

The next afternoon was quiet and dusty. Joel, sitting in his mother's house, could smell dust from the gravel lane and see dust on the small leaves and his windowpane. And suddenly it was as if everything, from the dust to the light coming in, was preordered. It was that strange a sensation, and Joel had not had this sensation for years. But he realized that this sensation was not at all trivial. For if not for Hector's death, he might still be in jail. Certainly without his half-brother's death he wouldn't have half the reserve doing his bidding and confiscating trucks and guns. He wouldn't have men from other reserves – men who would not have spoken to him at other times – now waiting to hear what he had to say. He looked at his mother and wondered if she knew what he was thinking – that all this sudden power had been thrust upon him by the death of a boy. That in a certain biblical sense all power, the preponderance of all men's desires, might be granted in just this way. That is why Saul must kill David. So a story from three thousand years ago was at this moment true.

And then, suddenly, everything changed again.

For just as the reserve had heard of Hector's death, now they heard of Isaac's.

He had died in the ambulance on the way to Moncton, people said. Two young men ran to tell Joel. One of them was Little Joe Barnaby.

"Mr. Joel!" Little Joe said, tugging at his arm, looking up at him with a strange kind of brave independence, goodness and love. "Mr. Joel – they say that Isaac has just died."

Joel's mother had made him a steak, for she worried he was not eating. And just as Amos had learned about the giant

197

taking over men in the room, the giant had taken over Joel. And he was suddenly frightened.

That is, he did not know what to do. He called a meeting of the warriors, but it was as if he could not speak. So Andy and Tommie told him that Doran must be arrested and Roger taken from his house.

"They will give us a bargaining chip," Andy said. And Joel nodded that they were right. Both of them cast their eyes away, as if he was now losing their respect – just as Saul had lost David's – and this is what he could not allow.

Joel went out just at dusk, in a cold wind, to Doran's shed, to hold him against the threat of the police, and discovered him gone. So he went searching and could not find him, carrying the .30-30 lazily under his arm. He walked the reserve shouting Doran's name.

"He's gone," someone said.

"How did he get away?"

"I don't know. But we have to get Roger now, or he too will go!"

All these young faces were now inordinately urgent as they looked to Joel for advice. The wind began to blow crazily in the trees.

"We should hear what Amos has to say," someone said. "He's still our chief."

Joel only laughed. But he felt terribly stung by this. "Come, then," Joel nodded. "Come with me."

He took the sixteen-foot canoe and stood and poled it upriver, against the rapids, and between the stones and rocks, without touching the bottom on anything. He put the canoe in some bushes by the back field and walked to the road that came out at the side of Roger's place. He had Andy and two others with him. He suddenly realized, just as so many other men of power had, that if he did not do something for his men, they would no longer follow him. This idea of being in charge did not make him look wise as

198

it had with Isaac, or kindly as it had with Amos. It only made him look afraid. The men saw this too, and reacted to it by not looking at him.

They came behind Roger's house and heard shouting from the street, shots being fired, and saw wild and burning cattails against the night sky.

Ginnish and Andy crouched down and hid near some bushes behind the house.

"What in hell's going on?" Joel said.

"Fire at him," Andy said.

"What?"

"He's firing at us!" someone else yelled. "Fire or give Andy the gun – if you're too gutless."

"But I don't know what to do."

"Then give me the gun," Andy said.

Joel pushed him back, took aim, his body shaking, put the rifle down, aimed again, and fired two shots at the propane tank. The second shot hit the lit lantern in the room – one of two lanterns attached to the propane tank.

In an instant a flame caught the curtains over the back porch door of Roger Savage's house, and spread to the propane tank itself. They saw Roger turning to look in their direction. It was the last thing he would do. Within five seconds everything blew, back and out as if in slow motion. Great pieces of plywood flipped high in the dark night air.

People said that the explosion killed Roger Savage in an instant.

That is all that young Andy Francis remembered when he spoke to the police. He remembered nothing else, for he was close enough to suffer a major concussion.

Joel had left his friends and tried to run away – something, people said, Isaac or Amos never would have done.

The RCMP, a dozen strong, came in directly after, along with two companies of soldiers from Gagetown. They had been held up on the road, near Cyr's cottage, by a couple of dozen students and their professors. The captain in charge of the second company was a Micmac, Freddy Ward, who had known Isaac for a number of years. Finally he talked the students into letting them pass without incident. He arrested five people, turned them over to the RCMP, restored order with fifteen soldiers, and returned the band to Amos Paul.

All this, briefly, was what happened after the police officer Hanover ordered Isaac taken to jail.

Over the next many weeks Amos Paul, wanting to know what had happened to Doran, wrote letters to the editor of Doran's paper, simply signing his name "Amos." October came and went, and now it was almost November.

Doran now drank his wine and stared out at the small flurries of snow. No one considered the stand-off would lead to death, he told people.

Especially the death of a little boy.

What was his name? Doran tried to forget it, but he never could – Little Joe Barnaby.

There had been a rumour going around that Isaac had died. Who had put that rumour out? Someone told Doran it had been one of the students, who had become hysterical the day before and started shouting, "You killed him!"

Others said it was Kellie Matchett who had told the students this as they gathered on the road near Mary Cyr's.

But no matter who it was, because of this rumour about Isaac that Joel and Andy Francis went to take Roger to jail on the reserve. Men came toward the house from the front, and Andy and Joel were at the back, and Roger Savage fired that beautiful ornate lever-action that Doran had seen that night in the woods.

Little Joe, who had run toward the house with his BB gun to arrest Roger and take him to jail, suddenly said, "Oooo, Markus," and fell face first into the mud.

It was pouring rain. The men then rushed the house. There

was no time for Roger to come out before the propane tank exploded.

And everything ended on August thirty-first.

Little Joe, with his cheeks painted with stickers and his small cowboy boots, and his coupons for free pizza he had gotten from the delivery man, was going to take Roger to jail and, he told Markus, give him a pizza.

He fell face first into the mud, the back of his navy blue jacket covered in blood, and blood spattered on the front of Markus Paul's shirt.

What was terrible for Markus was how Little Joe's eyelashes kept blinking those last few seconds of his life.

Two days later Isaac was released on bond.

A week later all the charges against him were dropped.

Yesterday, Doran had heard, Isaac had become chief of the reserve. There had been subdued fanfare and a realization that things between the government of Canada and the First Nations people would never be the same until certain issues were addressed. At least, that was part of the last story Doran filed before he resigned.

Part V

September 16, 2006

If not for an accident playing softball, RCMP officer Markus Paul might never have gone over the Hector Penniac case once again. That is, for the tenth or twentieth time.

A broken foot, which laid him up during the spring and summer of 2005, caused him to revisit it. Penniac's death had happened before computers and DNA. Many of the participants were dead. Many of the places they'd lived no longer existed. The particulars were stored in the basement of the old section of the RCMP headquarters in a filing cabinet, and in all there were seven files. (That was all he could find, anyway.) They had sat in file cabinets in one of the old cells that was ventilated in order to lessen the smell of drunks, but was still persistently hot and morbid all summer.

He remembered his grandfather Amos Paul had broken his ankle just the year before all of this had taken place in 1985 – so, with Markus having a broken ankle as well, it was a revisiting in almost a physical way. And perhaps the ghost of his grandfather was telling him that now was the time to get this done. Markus wanted to solve the case too, not only because he was an officer and determined to find the truth but because of his grandfather, who had tried to keep the peace that summer.

So, as he started going over it again that spring and into summer of 2005 while his ankle healed, dressed as it was in a great big bun with his toes sticking out, and him using crutches, he realized that the case had never left him, even for a second. As early autumn of 2005 came, his foot had healed enough that he could walk down to the local store with a cane to play his lotto or buy his cigarettes or go to Blockbuster and get a movie and come home and sit in the dark, going over in his mind how it had all happened.

He was trying to concentrate on finding Roger Savage's rifle – for that was, perhaps, in all of this, the most important missing part of the puzzle. But no matter how often he went over all the information, the rifle's whereabouts eluded him. Sometimes late at night he would sit in the dark talking out loud to the memory of his grandfather: "Well, Amos, as you see I am in quite a mess here – my wife is gone, my VCR is broke and I can't solve the case I promised you I would solve. Besides that, everyone is at me about my smoking."

Then, one bright last-of-summer day, Markus received notice that his divorce was final. The next day – that is, September 6, 2005 – he received a letter from his ex-wife, Dr. Samantha Dulse, asking his forgiveness.

But of course, so much of life had gone on. Where was everyone now?

He slipped into a depression of some sort, put all the Penniac files away, and yet would mull over the case, day in and day out, for another year. And in mid-September 2006, he thought he might take a trip – the one trip his grandfather had never managed to take – and try to remember the things his grandfather Amos Paul had told him never to forget.

1985

1

The night in August after the power had been shut off, the night after they had voted to take Roger out of his house, when the reserve was filled with noise and commotion, Markus made his way outside and looked here and there, and saw only darkness filtering down and the lights of cattail torches and candles.

That night, Sky was home with Little Joe. Mrs. Francis had told them to stay where they were until she got back. She had gone to find Andy and Tommie and bring them home. People were saying that Isaac had died. No one knew who started that rumour, and it probably didn't matter, but no one could get a message in or out to say it was or wasn't true.

There was a smell of fall in the air and smoke from the fires along the road, a smell of tin and tar. Everyone shouted at Markus, telling him they were on the way to the barricade. They had broken all the dead streetlights and had ruptured the fire hydrant.

Old Amos was sitting in his living room when Markus left.

"Be a man!" the crowd yelled at him when he stepped into the night air.

All the faces in the crowd were filled with an almost incomprehensible determination and alarm. Markus thought: One understands the fastidiousness of a mob when people begin to look and dress the same.

The army was supposed to come, and everyone thought Amos had sent for it. There was going to be a showdown,

and people – the boys and young men – had armed them-
selves, with rifles and rocks and sticks and bottles and
Molotov cocktails, and were now going to the barricade.
If Markus did not go he would be considered a traitor.
Markus walked to Little Joe and Sky's in great agitation,
and Little Joe ran to get his cowboy boots.

"I'm coming I'm coming I'm coming!" Little Joe yelled.

"I don't want Little Joe to go," Sky said. "You stay here
with us and we will make popcorn – I promise – I just have to
go to the store. I can cook it on the Coleman. Please – we can
have a few beers when he goes to bed – just you and me –
Grandma Francis is not here."

She was pleading with Markus and offering the only thing
she had: herself. She took his hand.

"I'll take care of him," Markus said. He suddenly liked the
idea that he would be seen by Joel and the others. He could
smell the ash from fires and it filled him with a kind of happy
rebellion. He would prove to them that his family was okay.

"Please!" She grabbed Markus" hand again. "You bring
him back."

"We'll just stand by the side and watch." And then he
laughed and lit a cigarette. "Why don't you trust me?"

Little Joe ran out the door, came flying back in, grabbed
his BB gun and raced out the door.

"Bring that back!" Sky called, tears running down her
face.

"Don't worry, I don't have any bullets!" Little Joe yelled,
rushing up the lane, jumping over puddles like a deer.

"Please, Markus – please," Sky begged.

Markus knew he had to go too, for his family's sake, for
Amos's sake. He did not want to wake in the morning and be
called a traitor by his own people.

Roger had dropped the load and then had fired to scare
people away. That was what everyone had decided by the
first real frost of the year. The inquests came to no other

conclusion. The reporters had finally all gone away. It was now November. But old Amos, sitting in his porch, with the sun on his legs, still wondered about it.

Markus would come and go from school in a kind of daze. But he had changed now – changed deeply. He felt sorrow for his doddering old grandfather and wanted to help.

Now, when people wanted to restart the recreation centre, Amos only sat and looked out the window. Now, when people told him he was still part of the band council, he didn't go. Now, when they told him he should still be chief because Isaac wasn't doing right, he only shrugged. Now people would see him walking beside Roger's burned-out house. There were no cherished mementoes there. Roger had had nothing. A father dead and a mother who had abandoned him for her vices. A girlfriend who had no courage to take his side. Yet who could blame her? Scared to death. And she had begun to realize Roger was a boy she hardly knew, that he was a boy who actually would put his life on the line – not in some romantic way, as she had dreamed of as a girl riding her bicycle in the wanton heat of bygone afternoons, but in some obstinate, deliberate manner where, just like Isaac on his hunger strike, he had no choice.

But sometimes Amos would walk through this burned-out house anyway. And when he got home his boots would be covered with soot, his ears would be cold and red and his wrinkled face would look even more sunburned.

Markus felt guilty for having disobeyed his grandfather and gone to the barricade because he had wanted to be seen to be doing something brave. He had since learned that Amos had told the police not to take Isaac off the reserve. But they didn't listen. They believed arresting Isaac would solve everything. But what a place was jail to put men? How could one think that doing this, incarcerating Isaac, was just? And what justice did they seek? And what would the men on the reserve do now? And who would say if the whites were taken and put on a reserve, at the edge of a forlorn bay, they would not burn a bulldozer too? In fact if you gave them a thousand bulldozers and kept them where they were, sooner or later people would burn them all, and who could blame them?

"Pretty foolish thing," Amos said.

But that was the harshest indictment he would come up with.

Amos had no reserve now. As the wind swept down over the bay, days in autumn walking alone along the shore, the wind at his face, Amos would remain alone. No, not even Markus could get him to eat his fish cakes. Markus was afraid that, like Amos's friend Simon Terri, his grandfather would walk into the woods one autumn day and disappear. How could this man, Amos Paul, not have been awarded his war medals, and not been made a part of Canada?

Markus was studying now, many things. He was reading all he could. He said he would do something great for his grandfather.

But then one afternoon, when the wind blew down on the house from all angles, Amos simply said: "Remember the pictures I took?"

"Yes," Markus said.

"I am not sure – but maybe right now would be a good time to look at them again."

Markus decided he would do this, just to have the old fellow do something. And so after supper, which Amos hardly touched, his old face looking puzzled, they climbed the stairs into the attic and sat down at the old desk, and Amos pulled out his pictures and carefully laid them down and sighed when he did so. And tears came to his eyes.

"They treated me with the utmost respect," he remembered saying to Isaac. "They treated me with the utmost respect."

"What are you seeing there?" he asked Markus finally, having spread his little pictures out on the desk.

Markus looked a long time at the picture of the fatal logs.

"The logs that dropped," he said.

But Amos was puzzled by this.

"Did they all drop? Can you tell me? They are so close together."

As promised, Amos, as chief during the crisis, had a complete copy of the files for the investigation. These had been handed to him by a mailman a week ago in a big manila envelope. And he had not had the heart to look at them.

So now he delicately pondered something and opened them up.

They were very orthodox and detailed – and somehow aggravating in their mundane specifics: the size of the *Lutheran*, the number of holds, the trips it made to Canada, the amount of wood it had taken (a lot more than what it took to build Roger Savage's little house).

Then the number of sailors – where most of them came from, their nationalities, their religion. Then the number of stevedores working the yard – the history of the yard work from 1954. The history of the settlement, and the reserve. There were two documents on the fishing disputes, both in the river, over the salmon pools, and on the bay, over the lobster, over the last twenty-nine years.

Except for the captain, no Dutch sailor had made a report. The men in the hold said only that it had happened too fast to save the boy. Roger Savage was called negligent in the first act, against Hector, but not criminally negligent. He was, though, held criminally responsible for the second incident, the death of Little Joe. But the initial inquest found that the reserve, too, bore some responsibility, for deciding to take Roger Savage from his house. The students were reprimanded for blocking the road. There would be a full inquest a year later and it would reach the same conclusion.

Amos read over the report about Roger.

He was considered a mean man, Roger Savage. And he could have been a mean man, but Amos never thought he was.

"That's not the Roger you or I knew," Amos said.

Markus remembered Roger Savage at a party with his girlfriend in the sunset over the tarred logs on the shore. Christ, everyone was happy then. Six days before the *Lutheran* had made berth at Millbank. The first poem by Yeats that Markus had ever picked up had this line: "And what rough beast, its hour come round at last, / Slouches towards Bethlehem to be born?"

Markus decided that same fall that someday he would become an RCMP constable. It was an evening when there was a snowfall, when he walked the streets of downtown Newcastle after school, all the shops lit by street lights, and snow falling over boarded-up alleys, the smell of roasted peanuts and perfume from drugstore vents. In a jewellery shop he saw a little Indian figurine called Miramichi Pete, a little boy who lived long ago, when the Indians ruled the land. When they would have fought the Inuit and Huron too. He stared at it a long moment – wanting to buy it for Sky. But Sky had not spoken to him since her brother had died. He had tried everything he could think of to ask forgiveness. Except it could not be asked.

He had a strange feeling for some time, however, and it came from his nausea at "the inner ring" that he had read about. Markus reflected much on this, and decided that the inner ring C. S. Lewis had written about was actually present in those awful days, from the busload of students who came with a professor, his goatee and bald head appearing as a tribute to the kinder man we were supposed to become. They all had a barbecue at Mary Cyr's and read poems over a loudspeaker against racism although nothing that approached William Yeats.

One young girl, in an army jacket that came down over her small wrists, yelled: "You killed Isaac like you killed his trees! You take our moose and our honey bees!"

And then began the Golgotha of Roger Savage, who had just got his grade twelve equivalency.

He telephoned his girlfriend, May, to ask her not to believe what the papers said, and to stay with him. She was the only person he had ever begged to do anything.

"Please – you are the only one I have!"

"Of course I don't believe them – of course I don't," she said.

But it was her tragedy too – this May Grant – to be caught up with people who wanted her to be free of him, to acknowledge her mistake and use that knowledge wisely. She was not so pretty and not so clever – and amid all of this, she seemed incapable of knowing what to do. So she vacillated, first one way and then the other, as if trying to find the side of the dory that would not tip over. Finally she decided in a way to be passive so as not to be imperilled, to sit in the middle and let others handle the oars. And went back to her mother's house in Doaktown where many did not know that the man she had been engaged to was Roger Savage. She entered a contest in August, and won second prize for blueberry muffins, and put Roger Savage behind her.

Two years later she would marry a Loman man from Howard who had been in the air force and liked things "just so" and said there was no use going into it, her blueberry muffins were the best.

If Roger had just left the house, many later said, no one would have bothered him. That very well might have been true. But then again he couldn't – in the flecking off of human guilt and shame, one sometimes had to make a stand.

Certainly it cost the life of Little Joe.

"Maybe you could do something to solve this, if I am unable to," Amos said when Markus told him he wanted to be a policeman. Then he asked: "What would you do about a standoff?"

"I don't know," Markus said. "I do not know. Any side I would be on would be the right side – and the wrong side."

Markus realized now, in 2006, that when Amos had said at a band meeting in late July 1985, "Beware of what you wish for," he was speaking to those who were hoping for the death of someone, anyone, really – though no one would say this. Why were they hoping for such a death? So they could say they had partaken in something that was dangerous without its being dangerous to themselves.

"I bet I'll catch a trout next year," Little Joe had told Markus when he carried the trout that August night, running along in the dust to keep up, his bare feet as tough as leather. "Maybe four – or even five!"

2

Amos started in late October of 1985 going over the autopsy report of Hector. Here, after about forty minutes, he found something unusual. He stared at the picture of the boy in the morgue. It was part of the files, along with everything else. The skull had suffered a severe fracture causing immense hemorrhaging into the frontal lobe. The death was registered first as undetermined and finally as an accident.

The police officer in charge was Sergeant Hanover. They had interviewed the crane operator, and George Morrissey, who had told them that first he had hooked and then two days later said he had not. The crane operator could not be sure how the load fell. At some point he lost it, but had no idea when exactly. The Monk brothers said the clamp had been left open, which would be extremely dangerous, and almost lethal.

Reading everyone's statements, from the boys in the hold to the crane operator, it did seem to Amos as if Roger had done something and someone was trying to cover for him.

But suddenly Amos said: "What if it was the opposite? What if Roger was covering for Morrissey, who was away from the site – and hooked in innocence?"

"Except for the fact that he wouldn't admit that he hooked," Markus said. "So that made it all seem deceitful."

"Well, his innocence is just as possible as anything else," Amos mused. Then he said, "If you become a policeman, please do not become one like Sergeant Hanover, who seems to always take the wrong man to jail."

215

Markus went to school the next day, and he saw the water boy, Brice Peel, with a lame pigeon he was trying to heal. He would not look at anyone, and for weeks and weeks did not speak, and rumour had it that he'd threatened one boy with a knife one day after class.

In the late fall, the apples shed from the trees and the side of the river made ice, and thin rivulets and streams went down, and the ground turned grey as an owl's back, and maples thrust naked and crooked to the sky. Nights were filled with the glorious scents of frost. The storm windows sat glassy and black in the houses along the roadway. Halloween was over, and then came Remembrance Day with its smell of gunpowder along the miles of uncovered tamarack trees.

People said, most good-heartedly, that what defined Amos Paul as Micmac was his procrastination. That he would start and stall, many times. And this was true of him, and everyone who knew him knew this. He was also absent-minded. Even his beloved school could have been finished sooner if he had not lost a list of government contracts and had to establish contact with all of them again, retrieving the quotes and estimates he had been given.

But in fact many great men did this, and had to be prodded forward. And Amos had other things to think about besides that terrible case that seemed to veer this way and that in his conscience. He had his grandchildren to look after, and many other things going on.

Still, Amos had discovered one thing. The case against Roger Savage rested on flimsy evidence. And he was becoming more certain that Roger had done little – and perhaps, just perhaps, nothing, not even to Little Joe.

The feeling did not leave him, and could not until he tended to it.

Amos sat in the attic and sifted among the papers for a number of days in this cool fall, and heard the trees wave outside, and listened to the bay water cry out in cold turbulent ways the cost of living beside it. He would be there when Markus came home from school and he would be there late at night when Markus went to bed.

In the corner of this attic was Amos's father's old hat, and the fishing spear he used up on the Tabusintac River as a boy, until he was told by the landowners up there that the river where his Micmac Nation had fished in peace for twenty-five hundred years did not now belong to them, and the old hunting grounds of caribou and moose were gone from the leaning barrens. This was when Amos himself was fourteen.

There were other things here as well. A letter from the premier of the province that was covered in plastic and placed in a binder when Amos became chief. So too was an article about his seventy-fifth birthday in the local paper.

But beyond this, in the old attic there was little else, the smell of burnt paper and a mannequin for dressmaking that Amos's mom once owned, where she would blister her hands working for the white choir and children getting First Communion.

Then there was a small grey stone placed on a table where the binder sat. It was in fact the stone that had come from Amos's shoe when he had walked up to see the RCMP officers that early-summer day after Hector Penniac died.

Amos and Mrs. Francis never got to take their trip. But this was Amos's decision. In the end, as Mrs. Francis packed to go away on that trip of discovery across the great wide North America, he simply stated, "I am too old."

"But don't you want to see where the Apaches were and the Sioux?"

"No, not anymore. They are where they are, and I am where I am, and we should leave it at that."

For a few days Mrs. Francis tried to make him change his mind, for she wanted to try to escape the memories of Little Joe.

How was it that tragedy happened so easily? It was not

that he had been too old. But the death of Little Joe Barnaby, which he blamed on himself, had broken his heart. It had broken Sky's heart as well. Both Markus and Amos knew this, and said nothing to one another about it.

Sky was drinking and went to dances, and dated white boys from up the road, all petulant and sure of themselves in their dull daddies" cars. Her beauty startling her eyes dark, she tried and tried and tried again to wrest the agony from her heart.

Amos was alone morally, and painfully aware of this fact. All as he had was the boy Markus, who was obligated to him in such a way it seared the old man's heart.

"I will solve it or I will die trying," Markus said, "no matter how long it takes – if it takes me to the year 2000," he said, believing that date was so far away it would never come.

Amos was as tragic as a king relying on his only son when the enemy had entered the castle and there was nowhere left to go. He no longer had his camp. It had been burned by some whites after the barricade went up, which had put many of them at a two-month-long inconvenience. Still, he would go hunting once more.

He planned to stay in a tent, which he would shore up with boughs, and if the snow was right he would use his snowshoes. He could track a deer quite easily this way. He loved more than anything to track deer in a snowstorm, and was known to have gone thirty miles on snowshoes in a day.

So here is what he had asked himself.

What did the protesters and screaming young warrior poets in their army jackets want? They wanted Roger to feel the full weight of their displeasure while taking pleasure in it as modern and conciliatory whites. This is what Amos, the odd little fellow, decided the real case was about. It is what he had known since last August but couldn't say. For he could not say to the whites, "You are just being conciliatory, but if I had to rely on anyone in a storm at sea, it would be

Roger Savage. I would rely upon him in the woods – and in fact all of you would, too – and be very thankful he was there."

The snow did not fall much that autumn, so Amos waited for a time to hunt. And he began to surmise what might have happened in the hold of the *Lutheran*.

Amos would lie on his back in the dark with his cigarette glowing in the room and he would try to think. Then he would speak to Markus, who was alone in his own bedroom.

"What happened to Hector down in the hold? Certainly he was way out of place – and if he was, then something happened to make him be out of place. Why was the water bucket so far away?"

Sooner or later all things would be understood. Everything came around in one way or the other to that truth.

Amos's mother had been able to look at a dress and see a flaw. The flaw might be an almost unseen thread, and when she pulled on it, the flaw became evident and the skirt unravelled. And now Amos worked from the thread he had found, and the case little by little began to unravel. The thread was the autopsy picture, and the fact that not a bit of pulp, as he remembered, had ever hit the upper sides of the hold. When the sailor Vanderhoof was sent to wash away the blood, he had concentrated on washing only in one place. But that would have been almost impossible if Hector had been hit by the full weight of the load.

The front of Hector's skull had been crushed, but not another bone in his body – not even a rib was cracked, though two were bruised. And under all that pulpwood too. That pulp that hit him was still in Amos's side shed.

"I can tell you one thing," old Amos said to Doran one day shortly after Isaac was arrested.

"What is that?" Doran asked.

The old man patted Doran's arm kindly.

"It is not the Conibear trap that kills the beaver, but the

drowning that follows," the old man said. "You will come to realize this with time, my son."

So Amos had his first lead. He did not particularly see it as being definitive, though. The Conibear and the beaver story was one he had told many times. He had first mentioned it to Markus when the boy's father was found dead that long-ago day. The drink was the Conibear trap, and the man slowly drowned.

But then Amos considered how tall Hector Penniac was – five foot ten – and he realized the drop would have to have been from that distance. And the Monk brothers said the load fell fifteen feet. If that was the case, a fifteen-foot drop of two tons of pulp would certainly have bruised some bones, and have landed helter-skelter, and might have injured more than one person. Unless it missed Hector, and he suffered only a glancing blow. But if it missed him, then why was the boy lying under the wood? He would have been thrown to the side.

Strangely enough, thought Amos, the fact Hector was under the pulp, which made it look like the pulpwood had killed him, meant that he had not been killed by the pulpwood at all. Which meant he had been placed underneath. This was not so difficult to comprehend now that Amos saw the autopsy photo and read the report. Why hadn't he seen this long ago? He should have figured it out. But others had not figured it out either.

This is what Amos took to Joel, when Isaac was incarcerated in August of 1985 – that is, the idea, though he hadn't completely proven it, that something else might have happened to Hector. Joel sat at the head table in the band council office, and liked the idea that he had two phones. He had a phone to the barricade, and one to the outside that the police had supplied in hopes that he would tell them if anything got out of hand. He liked to look at them as he spoke to people who came to see him. These phones made him weary of little Amos who now came with his claims while Joel sat exactly where Amos had two months before.

"What's this about, then?"

Joel had really too much to do to bother with Amos.

Amos said his surmising was about the fact that Roger had done nothing – but that perhaps the Monk brothers had.

Joel smiled while he listened, sardonically, because he knew the truth and did not want the truth impinged upon by the old fellow. Besides, there was another problem, perhaps the real problem. It was the fact that Joel had dealt with the Monk brothers over the last four years. He supplied them with amphetamines for the stevedores, and this would come to light if they were investigated.

But Joel allowed Amos to speak to him and explain his reasons. And then he said: "Couldn't have happened that way."

"Why?" Amos asked.

"Just didn't," Joel said, sniffing. And then he said, "Be gone with you."

Both Andy and Tommie were with him. They sat at either end of the table and stared at Amos as Joel spoke, wearing bandanas and camouflage pants. This was their standard now, how they observed decorum.

Amos picked up his pictures and went back out into the sun.

"Didn't happen that way!" Joel yelled as he left the building. "Remember I told you that."

3

The night before the catastrophe that led to Little Joe's death, Joel had called a meeting of the old council and the new. And they made their way over to Mrs. Francis's, where Andy had assured them safety from being arrested.

There they sat saying little to each other for the longest time. Amos came in, with his cowboy hat in his hand, and no one got up to give him a place at the table. So he sat on a heater at the end of the room – now out of favour with everyone who wanted action. And many there wanted action to prove that Amos was out of favour, and to prove they had done with the old days. And for Andy, who was the embodiment of this spirit, it was to prove to his former friend Markus that he had gone on in the world. The crux of his thinking was this: if you did not now take on the white man, you never would.

The two Francis brothers said they would take Roger to the small holding cell they had on the reserve, and keep him.

Amos said he could not allow it.

"What are you talking about?" Joel Ginnish said. "You cannot allow it. Who are you again? I didn't get your name."

Everyone began to laugh.

This was to be the last and crucial disagreement between Amos and Joel.

"We will hold him until the whites press charges against him and let Isaac go. Once they do, we will hand him over. If they don't we will keep him," Andy Francis said, looking over at Markus with grave pride.

But the little old man was neither frightened nor troubled by Joel Ginnish. He simply stared at his young grandson Markus and then looked back at Joel. He mentioned that if Joel was strengthened by anything, he was strengthened by the fact that Isaac was out of his hair, and he could act accordingly.

This was considered very bad to say. It did not matter if it was true.

Amos continued: "The police were silly to take Isaac, and I don't know why they did. But I cannot allow you to hold someone who is innocent in a cell for the guilty."

There was silence, and Amos set about rolling a cigarette. He took his tobacco out and put it on his knee, then his paper, and held it in his right hand, and pinched out some tobacco on it, rolled it and licked it. Then, seeing others looking at him, he attempted to pass the cigarette papers and tobacco around. But no one wanted any. He cracked a match with his finger and lit the smoke, and spit a bit of tobacco out. Then he was silent, and folded his arms.

The warriors, some in camouflage, with bandanas tied about their glowing black hair, looked from one to the other.

"Many know you're in cahoots with them," Joel finally said.

"No, son, I'm in cahoots with no one, and never have been – well, except for my wife, I was in cahoots with her for a bit, but not since she died have I been in cahoots."

Old Amos said this in a pleasant enough voice and was kind when he said it. When Markus looked at his grandfather, his grandfather sneezed and shrugged.

Not very much like a hero.

Amos sneezed again and took a big white handkerchief and wiped his nose.

"Look," Joel said. "He already has the white flag out."

Amos laughed when others did, his false teeth slipping.

Looking back, Amos remembered that Little Joe was all this time sitting on the counter, looking from one person to the other, preoccupied with eating peanut butter from the jar, with a spoon.

Just before they left the Francis house, what Joel had been warned about happened.

The power to the entire reserve was cut.

There were women and children on the reserve, and this was unconscionable. Joel pushed people aside and away from him as he walked outside. He pushed old Amos away too, and Markus was too young to stand up to him.

All up and down the road was blackness. Silence and just the sound of waves. People began to come out of their houses and stand in the streets.

"What are you going to do, Joel?" people said.

"What's going to happen?" Little Joe asked Markus.

"I don't know," Markus said. "We'll see."

And so whatever Amos wanted or hoped for was once again dashed by those outside. Beyond the reserve, the barricade, the lights flickered, and rain came down.

The evening before they heard Isaac had died, Doran knew he had to get off the reserve, for many were saying he was white and should be held too. But in fact, he was not concerned by this. The real reason he had to leave was that his own mother was now terribly ill. He had no one to take him past the barricade, however. He had gone there twice, but had been stopped. The Indians kept asking him to show his passport. So he turned and went back along the road. There he met Little Joe and Sky – and recognized them as the kids who had given him the pie.

"Can you help me?" he asked. "I have to go home."

Sky nodded, and she and little Joe took him to the old trailers beyond the ball field where the kids used to meet in secret. Then little Joe scampered up a tree, the better to see when everything was clear. Sky sat looking at this man for a long time, trying to think of what to do.

"Is what you said about Roger true?" she asked, point blank.

"I don't know – but I can't wait any longer to see."

She sighed and took Doran's chin in her hand, and studied him. Then she smiled. She told him to take his ponytail out and put on the ball cap that she wore and tuck his hair under it. Then she lighted a cigarette and looked at him, and handed him the smoke. "Put some dirt on your face and I will get you a jacket from home. Wait here – and then we will go."

"Where – where will we go?"

"Well, we will go to the only place we can go," Sky advised. "We will just go along to see Amos."

So later, after dark, and after Sky had come back with an old jean jacket stained with oil, Little Joe climbed down from the tree, and they snuck across the back field to Amos's house. There they left Doran, and he was overcome with emotion and wanted to hug them both goodbye. Little Joe gave him a thumbs up and then just disappeared.

Doran went onto the porch, and waited for the door to open. What if Amos wouldn't speak to him? But Amos came to the door, opened it, and smiled.

"Oh, how are you?" Amos said.

Doran asked if Amos could take him by the water up to the bridge. But the old man couldn't. He felt he had to stay where he was. For he was still chief, and he must be here. Markus stood behind the old man, listening patiently.

"Can you lead me back through, Markus?" Doran said.

Amos looked at his grandson. "Take him," he said, in Micmac. "It's our duty."

So Markus went and got his jacket and told Doran to follow him. And they started out, the boy of fifteen and the man of twenty-five with his hair up under an old ball cap. They got across the road and past the trailers, toward Stone Street where Markus's own father had died. When they came to the back field they saw Joel with the 30:30 walking along the upper lane with five or six men; two had shotguns, and

Andy had a .22 pistol. Markus had to tackle Doran and put his hand over his mouth as the men passed only ten feet away.

But Joel and his men moved away toward the south, holding torches made of cattails and gas, and speaking in Micmac.

"I'll never forget this," Doran said. "I'll do you a favour some day."

"Then someday I will come to you and get it."

"Okay, okay, you do that," Doran said.

It was hard to get across the river. Doran slipped many times on the rocks and in the swirling currents, and Markus had to hold him up. They were sitting ducks, too, in the middle of the water, where they could have been seen at any moment. And Markus was taking much more of a chance than Doran. Finally they made it to the slippery granite bank on the far side. There were three RCMP cars just at the turn.

Doran grabbed Markus's hand and shook it with a new resolve. "You come to me for that favour," he said, his white shirt soaking from the water and his loafers ruined.

Markus nodded quickly, slipped back, and returned in the dark to his own house by another way.

The next morning – that is, on the day of the confrontation – Amos went over to visit Roger to tell him to leave.

"Just leave the house until I figure this out. It might only be a month or so. I knew your grandfather – he was my friend," Amos said. "You have to get out now – you must – they think you are guilty, and they will think that until it is proven otherwise. They called you right wing," Amos said, trying to sound stern for effect.

"What does that mean?"

"I'm not sure," Amos said. "I don't know what it means – when I was in school I was left-handed, and they beat me with a ruler. It might have something to do with that."

"Well, I am not going anywhere. If they bring the barricade

down, I am not going. If the police come to get me, I will fire at them. I have done nothing to anyone – so, since I have done nothing, I am not going." Here Roger smiled a little self-contentedly. "Do you think I did something wrong?"

"Yes," Amos said. But he lied just to get Roger away.

Roger looked hurt, and said nothing for a moment.

"My father fished for thirty years," he said then. "He saved men in the Esuminac disaster – men who are now not saying anything. And we have university kids out here protesting who have never met me, and they have insulted my family. My girlfriend has left me – going out now with a pigeon" – by this he meant an air force man – "who tells her how sorry he is for her. So tell me, what have I done, and what good is it for me to go out? If I go I will be condemned by those students – they are yelling at me." Then he said, almost as if hurt, "They say I'm uneducated – well, I could tell them, I got my GED."

He spoke this with great dignity, though his lips trembled slightly.

"But you can go and clear your name," Amos said hopefully, his fingers twitching.

"But my name has done nothing it needs to be cleared of, so someday they will have to clear it for me. I will not try to clear my name for them. I will not. They will have to clear it – let them. They are the ones who say I am guilty and did it on purpose. What in hell did I do? I went to the ship, and I hooked a load because Morrissey went and had a piss. So let *him* clear my name. I will die here – and then we will wait and see." Roger seemed perfectly happy to say this.

"But if you could just tell them what you did."

There was a long, long, bitter silence.

"I will tell you what I did. I hooked."

"I know, boy. Ya hooked," Amos said.

On a weekend in November 1985, the day after Doran had resigned from his paper, there was snow coming down to

227

blur the edge of the fields, and Amos went hunting. He thought: If the body was lying underneath the pulp, and not hit by the pulp, Penniac was hit before the pulp came down. Yet if that was the case, then it was murder, or manslaughter or even an accident that had been covered up. So the outrage by the little Micmac band in the middle of nowhere was, in some ways, completely justified. But going in the wrong direction had caused the death not only of Roger Savage but also of Little Joe Barnaby. It had also ruined Amos's grandson's chances with Sky. She now dismissed Markus, and would not speak as he walked by her house in the snow that fell at night, or when he stood outside the house like, as Fitzgerald once wrote, "all the sad young men."

Amos was tracking a big buck – there were also two or three smaller bucks in this area of furious streams and birches that ran up the side of the hills and then went for two or three miles intermingled with spruce and fir. He had seen the big buck's tracks rounded at the front and deep in the twisted grass, and its weight had trampled the grass and left the snow beneath it bluish. But he lost any sign of it at the north end of Buckler Stream, and then he met another hunter walking toward him. It was the surveyor Kevin Dulse, with his daughter Samantha, out hunting partridge. They carried a small brace. So Amos stopped and talked a moment or two.

Mr. Dulse had been the man brought it to survey and re-jone the line between the reserve and the cottages after all the trouble was over the month before. His hair was prematurely white, and he walked with his shoulders hunched together. His eyes had become weak, and he wore heavy glasses. He was proud of his daughter – as life is proud of life. She was fourteen, thin as a rail, with big black eyes and jerking motions when she spoke. She was like her mother, high-strung and nervous, and her nervousness hid or showed an eclectic brilliance, whichever it might be. The zone had gone in the natives" favour, so the band had been completely in the right about Savage's house, and because of this Kevin was thought highly of. But now, after all of the tragic circumstances surrounding it, the band did not want the property to build on, and decided to make it into a softball field in honour of Little Joe.

Amos and Kevin spoke for a moment. The birds were no longer sunning themselves and had moved into the thickets, and after a while Sam and Kevin moved off.

Soon Amos was alone and prepared himself some tea, then sat on an old windfall, and realized that this area of the woods wouldn't have been much travelled by his ancestors, except perhaps the waterways below here. He stirred the tea with a stick and looked at its darkness, trying to entertain thoughts of the past and the future. Then he sat on the windfall so that his short legs didn't touch the ground, and he sighed. No, he wasn't a very impressive looking man, not like Isaac, or Joel Ginnish. There were the real men, he supposed.

And he thought about the dividing line. The new room Savage had wanted to build had been over it by four feet. But it was as modest as the house he himself lived in.

When Amos first went into the Cyr cottage as a boy to deliver a salmon, its hardwood floor and its huge stone fireplace, its caribou and moose racks had made him confused and he began to shake. They asked him if he was cold, and all he could do was shake his head, his teeth chattering.

He did not know which was the real New Brunswick or the real Canada. And that dividing line had always remained. At seventy-five years of age, he still did not know.

It was this chance meeting with Kevin Dulse that caused Amos trouble. He was suddenly seared by the thought of Roger being called a bigot. Because he knew Roger was not.

Amos stayed in the woods that night by himself and thought about the case. That is, he thought about the water boy Brice Peel, and the buckets Brice would have delivered to the hold.

Before dawn the next morning, Amos was making his pancake breakfast outside in the snow. After breakfast, he cleaned the frying pan, took the jam jar the pancake batter was in and placed it in his knapsack, rolled a cigarette and waited for dawn over the many trees.

Then he put his jacket and vest on, his snowshoes slung over them, and with his toes cold from being pinched inside his boots, he walked toward the hills above him, and the clouds remained light, with the sky a greyish blue.

His movement by afternoon had taken him far, far up the ridge, to look down toward the water of the North Church River where he had hunted pollywogs as a boy. He had flashes of that as he stood there. To his left a close cropping of small firs fed into the hardwood that spread down through the winterish floor, spiked by fallen branches and slivers of ice. The river below was as smooth as a floor but without ice, and he could smell deer in the wind.

About two-thirty in the afternoon he sensed the buck on the move again. He went farther along the ridge and found his tracks on the rut trail. The buck had gone to his left; its tracks were fresh and large. Most men would have followed it down. But resting his 30-06 against a crook in a poplar, Amos had no intention of doing so. He would go to the right – which was easier going. He would cross the river below the beaver dam where a spine of rocks allowed the best way, and he would move up the other side into the dark spruce to a rut scrape he had seen the day before, to wait the buck out.

He started down with the wind behind him, which would be good once he crossed the river. He reasoned the buck, if he could be quick, wouldn't know he was there. Soon, hanging on to branches to keep himself steady, he moved into the valley, spongy with snow and wet moss, and made his way to the water. He crossed it almost knee deep in his old work pants and moved halfway toward the upper slope on the south ridge. There, still feeling pain in his arthritic hands, he sat on a stump and waited. Every now and again he turned the rifle slightly sideways to check the screws, as one who knows hunting and rifles will do. The day was about to turn. It was about to snow, and his visibility would be almost zero. He had to keep his scope halfway clean, and keep it from fogging.

All the while, too, he was surmising.

There was only one thing to do, he decided, as he looked into the old growth of trees, and that was to drop some of the pulpwood load on someone or something and see what broke. If bones broke, he would have his answer. He thought of his ankle – which broke because of a slip on some moss the year before – and wondered what might have happened with thousands of pounds. Well, there was one way to find out. Yes. There was always a way.

People think deer are quiet in the woods. They are not. Not a buck in rut who believes it is alone. He heard the deer a long way, the deer who had gone to the river to drink, thirst compelling it to move and now, in late afternoon, desire and need for sex compelling it up the hill toward its rut marks, farther in toward Tabusintac.

Amos picked up his rifle, flipped off his scope covers. The snow had started. The wind was at his face, blowing this snow into his eyes.

The buck came into view at 4:35 that afternoon.

He hauled it by himself to the water. There he gutted it out. Its liver in a bag, he carried the nine-point buck on a litter of poplar poles and spruce boughs out to his truck.

It was dark and cold when he got back to his house, and late after he took the hide off the deer, and supper was the liver for him and Markus, and a glass of flat beer. He thought of the pain that would come by reopening the case. He felt it deep, deep in his soul. Like the pain in his hands and old, tortured feet. He spent the evening cutting the meat, and took some steaks over to Mrs. Francis. That night, he wrote in his little diary that Markus had given him in great celebration when he became chief: "I have lost everything in my life except my will to stay alive."

But, he thought, at times that wasn't a small thing to hold on to.

4

The water boy Brice Peel had had a deeply disturbing summer. All of this had been kept from everyone around him. How could it be that taking a job as a water boy when he was little – that is, a boy of fourteen, happily thinking that he would be able to buy a bicycle – how was it that because of this, everything good in his life had been dashed? That his whole life had been turned upside down, and his yearning and longing for goodness been eclipsed by his duty to protect a father who would not have protected him? And how was it that no one had come to check up on him? This, despite the fact that he lived in his little house near the old black station, that he lived near the grand old stage coach road where the Irish woman named Jessie Monk in 1864 had been ambushed and killed by a Scotsman and a Micmac hunter?

To say Brice was bad, though he stole and lied, was a mistake. Even to say he was wrong in not telling what he knew to the police was a mistake. For in so many ways he lived a life not only of fear but also of obligation to those who had given him and his father a job five months before.

Brice had grown up under the influence of the Monks, devoted to all they said. But he suddenly found out, on that one day in June 1985, that to them integrity was lack of integrity and character was lack of character; and once you lost these things, character and integrity, then to the Monks you were acceptable and superior.

So where was he to go and what was he to do?

Brice's father said, as they drove back from the *Lutheran*

233

and crossed the Bartibog, that it was a terrible thing that had happened.

At home, Brice sat for a long time wondering what to say, like someone stunned by being hit over the head with some pulpwood.

"Did Tanker hit him?" he finally asked.

"Don't be so foolish," his old man said. "They were nice enough to give us a job."

"But I just don't see – I mean, how is it – that Hector fell under?"

His father tried to explain in the mid-afternoon heat that he was upset as well. Then the telephone rang, and when his father came back from the other room he said, hauling up his suspenders, "The police will be coming – so you don't go yappin" or you'll get your mouth slapped. No boy of mine is a yapper."

This, then, was integrity. No one was a yapper. And Brice found this idea was to be enforced and reinforced.

But the boy kept asking about the water bucket. Ten times he asked about it. His father was shaking too, standing near the sink, with his hands blistered, and told him to shut up. Then his father left to find out what was going on.

In a while Brice's father came back. The sky was white and there were bugs filling the air, and the scent of evening dropping low, and cars passing down on the highway and the clucking of a chicken or two scratching for food, and a rooster half-blind and old that the hens would peck to death within a week. Behind the dark, blistering house was an old rabbit pen that the water boy had and his little rabbit pen was the only thing he lived for.

His father asked what the boy would say if the police came. He told the boy everyone down the hold was saying it was Roger Savage because he disliked the idea of the union turning on him and hiring an Indian.

The little fellow said nothing, tucking his thumbs up inside his fists and staring in a kind of silent agony.

234

His father said, "They were kind enough to take us on, and you cannot ever say they did anything wrong – first of all, they probably didn't, and second of all, they are the Monks."

Brice shrugged. Then he asked if he could lick the peanut butter jar, for it was almost empty and the welfare cheque had not come.

And so, the next day when the water boy was called upon to give a statement, when the police sat him in their car and asked him what had happened, he said that he had gone to get a bucket of water. The police officer wrote this down, but didn't seem to understand there was a glitch here, for he had never worked a boat before, and did not know that two buckets was the standard, and two buckets were already there.

"When I come up the load fell."

"So you saw the load fall."

"Certainly, like a ton of fuckin" bricks."

"Did you see who hooked?"

"No sir."

And that was it, in red pencil, written and laid away for four months, and now in the possession of Amos Paul – who had not got to the red-pencilled note yet. The boy's name was signed on that little note: Brice Peel, the water boy.

That night after Brice Peel gave his police statement, Tanker Monk came over to see the water boy's father, Angus. And Angus Peel went out on the doorstep and shook his head. He had a piece of straw in his mouth and he said, "Yes, I know it," and looked behind into the dark little window, where the paint was peeled. There was one highway light that shone down on the road, and now and again the sound of a car faint and tragic and longing.

Angus Peel came back in and glared at his son.

"What did you say to the police? Tanker is askin'."

"I never said nothing – I said the load fell."

"Tanker Monk has done a lot fer us."

235

The boy went into the living room with the glare of the television meandering out into the dull, drab furniture and the smell of sweat, and sat there, and looked guilty, as if he had done something wrong. He stared out at his rabbit pen. His knees shook. His father looked at him with compassion, his son's thin neck and the little bruise on his cheek.

"Tanker has done a lot fer us," he said kindly, "that's all I am saying. You know I've had a hard time – and I took that job even though they knew I couldn't handle it. It was the happiest day of my life – and you were water boy – and now I am sorry I got you into this."

"I know," the boy said. "I know, Dad. I know you're sorry – I know you always have been sorry."

Brice Peel woke up the next morning to the telephone ringing, and he listened as his father climbed the stairs.

"Tanker Monk wants to sees you," his father said. "So just mind."

"Mind what?"

"Mind what Tanker Monk is saying."

Brice got out of bed and put on his worn trousers over his skinny little legs, and an old red T-shirt that his mother gave him two years before so it made his arms hang out and came up on his belly, and his floppy hat that he liked to wear, and went out to his rabbit pen.

Tanker Monk did something very strange. He showed him the bicycle Brice had said he wanted to save for and placed it beside the cage, with the boy's mouth hanging open in the dry air, and the smell of dark manure coming out in whiffs as if from a dark tunnel.

"Now that's some bicycle," Tanker said.

And that bicycle allowed a preternatural silence for weeks and weeks, as the calamity grew over at the edge of the bay where Roger Savage was building a room onto his house. The boy hardly washed, and the bicycle was driven around the Peel yard in the desperate gloom. The boy drove around on the bicycle, his pants bobbing up and down on the black seat so it smelled of his own shit, for he was too scared or defiant to wash.

"Daddy," Brice said once.

"What?"

"Do you know Roger Savage?"

"Yeah, I knew of him. Can't say I know him completely, but I do know of him."

"They say he's the killer of that Indian boy."

"That's what they say," Angus Peel noted.

"But do you think so?" Brice asked, almost as a whisper.

"It's what I know," Angus said, and expressing himself as finely as some of the educated people, extended his grace to the band by saying, "I'm no Indian lover, but I will tell you, a death is a death and can't be celebrated."

Then there was silence for a moment.

"Son, I have to have dialysis, what am I supposed to do?" And Angus Peel looked at his son, who was born with such hope into such a world.

Later in the month Tanker Monk began to inquire whether Brice – little Brice Peel – wanted another job. One where the real money was.

"It's not so bad. Just go up to the end of Onion Brook and cut some sprags for the back of the barn. I'll give him six bucks an hour, which is not bad for a boy."

"But can he do it?" Angus asked, knowing if he was a father at all he would have to take up for his son.

"Oh God, yes, he can do it, Mr. Peel – he's not no idiot."

"I don't want to do it," Brice Peel said. "I don't want to go way up to the reaches of Onion Brook and stay there, for that's what they want me to do, and the flies will have a feast – I'll be bone soup for the bugs."

But his father could not get him out of it, and they both knew it.

Brice Peel went to Onion Brook. So if he was wanting to tell someone of what he thought had happened, that person would first have to travel the highway and then the upper stretches of the Tabusintac, then cross to Blueberry Barrens and from there walk toward Upper Onion where you would find in a place of nothing three small ruined buildings rotting against overgrowth – buildings that belonged to the Monk brothers" father's sister's father-in-law. A connection that had entrapped the father-in-law's siblings in a kind of hell. A Monks hell, as one them put it back in 1973.

There, someone looking for little Brice Peel was not done looking but would have to complete another three miles along a pathway ribboned out through a swamp and alder growth, toward the brook that could be heard now and then against a lost blue sky. Here, in among the smell of vetch and musk and the constant whine of bugs, one would hear the roar of Onion Falls sooner or later – and an old windfall over that deep gorge was the only way for the boy to get across to the other side.

In the entire universe, there was only one wee boy who could tell what had happened in the hold of the *Lutheran*. Worse, he was the boy the Monk brothers had taken on as a water boy because they genuinely felt sorry for him and his father. And George Morrissey was this boy's uncle.

"He's a problem," Tanker had said, sitting in the living-room dark the night before they decided to send Brice to Onion Brook. He heard of the commotion rising and falling on the reserve and knew things were pointed in one direction: away from them. The paper was open on the kitchen counter, with its story about the death of Micmac fur traders in 1839 – and all of this was true. But to the men sitting in that room, the story covered up a crime of gigantic proportions: the death of Hector Penniac in 1985.

Doran had interviewed them. And he had done them a favour. But Doran did not know this yet. That is, he was not irresponsible so much as doggedly sure of everything, just like Hanover was. He was a prim-ass, doggedly sure of himself, Tanker said, and yes that was true, Bill Monk said, and we made him more sure of himself.

"And he does not know it!" Monk said.

Yet that young boy, with his small frame, and the red T-shirt with the bumblebee on it that said "You bee my honey bee," did know it. Or he was certain of something.

Billy Monk was much thinner and smaller than Tanker. Billy's pale Irish skin and pale blue eyes looked out at the world of misery with resolute indifference. He had an absolute love of the gleeful torment, whether he was in school, on the bus or at home playing baseball. He had cultivated that torment into a pleasure that made life misery for certain others.

But he had liked the boy and he liked the boy's father, who was an old drinking comrade from the sixties, when they both grew their hair long in feral deference to the time and made sure they took their teeth out and wrapped them in Kleenex before they entered a bar.

"We'll take him to Onion till this blows over," Billy said, tapping on the newspaper's front page.

There was some strange loathing this newspaper reporter had for Roger Savage that they didn't understand.

Isaac would have to deal with that, they decided.

When Tanker brought him to the falls, Brice realized he had to cross a deadfall, and it was a thirty-foot drop to the low stream and boulders.

"Mark me words, you can do that, boy."

The boy shook. He did not know what to say. He stared at the falls and the rainbow it made, and felt the heat suffocate him. His father was supposed to have come with him. But his father was sick. Brice had never in his life been this alone.

He had to cross a log, and far beneath him he could see some sea trout. It will be so much fun, they had said. You will be able to catch trout.

"I can't go over alone," the youngster said.

"Here," Tanker Monk said. "Get up on my shoulders and I'll walk you across."

So Tanker grabbed the boy and put him on his shoulders and with his knapsack in one hand and the bucksaw in the other started out. By the time they were two feet out it was impossible to turn back, and sitting hunched up on Tanker's shoulders the boy was off balance and felt they'd fall.

"Keep straight up on me," Tanker warned.

The boy, with his red T-shirt black with sweat under the arms and with the bee on the front with its caption that read "you bee my honey bee," suddenly thought of the story his mother had told him about the fox and the gingerbread man. And he believed Monk was going to let him go.

"He won't be able to," the boy thought, "not when he has me – because if I go I'll latch onto his head until he goes too – I'm a pretty good latcher. In fights I can latch pretty good, no doubt about it. I'm a latcher!"

And he put both arms around Tanker's head.

"Hold 'er now there, Brice buddy, ya got yer fingers over my nose!"

So this is what the boy said when they were ten feet out over the thirty-foot drop to solid boulders: "If I go – you go."

"What are you talking about?" Tanker said. "Get yer hands off me head!"

But the man became aware that the farther he got out on the windfall the more dangerous it was with his top-heavy load – and here he was staring death in the face with a young boy because of an Indian man he had never seen before that terrible morning. And why did this happen to him? What law had made his life so certain to be this way, as it was from the time he was ten? And why now – when he himself had wanted to settle things and have his own house and back lot – why now did that Hector Penniac, a man he had never cared about one way or the other, come clamouring down the ladder into the hold with his fine features looking resolute and dignified and in some respects urban, and his kindness as he offered them gum and cigarettes? And what was in him and his brother to take to tormenting that man – for what sport did men do this, and for what reason did he think it was fine and noble to do that to the young Indian boy, and now that he realized that it was neither fine nor noble, what reason was it that he had to relive it every day, and could not rid himself of it?

Once they had reached the other side, Tanker crossed back and forth much more swiftly and left Brice's supplies in three boxes by the tamarack tree, near the cabin Brice was to sleep in, as the sun beat down on his red face. He took the boy and showed him that small one-roomed cabin with the two cots and the rusted stove, airless and sad with a poster from 1966 that said "Gunk, the Great Cleaner" and showed a girl in a half-unbuttoned top leaning over an engine.

"No one is going to leave you," Tanker said to the boy. "Your dad will be here tonight – everything will be fine."

He smiled then and patted the boy's head, and trod away, and crossed the log again, and went into the gloom on the other side of the brook and the child was alone.

His father did not come that night, nor until three days later, his face sheepish and his blood-red eyes downcast. The boy, bitten half to death by blackflies, was sitting near a pile of props from the tamarack he had cut, in obligation to his job. He had smashed his cans of beans on a rock and against a tree, trying to open them because they had forgotten to leave him an opener.

At night the temperature dropped so he was cold. He said he saw a bear. The camp smelled of urine because he had wet his pants.

The father talked of when he was a boy, and how he had done more, and how more was expected of him and he did not mind, for that was how to get ahead in life.

"And you've got so far," the boy said, for the first time in his life answering back. And for the first time in his life his father could not hit him.

Tanker Monk, who crossed the log again and went into the woods, realized the lie he was perpetrating. He was not pleased with it at all. The idea that it was a sin was beginning to inform him, too late. And now it was too late also to say anything about it.

He had almost not got to work that day himself, for he had been drunk the night before. But his wife got him up and out the door. And he arrived at the *Lutheran* at quarter past seven in the morning. The shed light was still on, and birds were singing. The *Lutheran* sat up in the black awful water like a hundred other ships of trade he had worked, and would work.

Strange, too, he had almost not worked in the same hold as his brother, but since they would move forward at the end of the day to the second hold, and because of seniority lay off two men, he was allocated to work the hold that would be done the swiftest. They had the boy's father Mr. Peel with them. And they were put in the fourth hold. And since they had taken Mr. Peel's son under wing, he would be water boy for them.

The other worker in the hold was Hector Penniac. He climbed down the ladder after the first load was stored.

The money they gave the boy for cutting his props out of the tamarack and spruce he saved for school. He would get new jeans and a new shirt and sneakers is what Brice Peel thought. He would leave Angus Peel and be someone special. He would go to dances and get hard-ons and talk to girls. Just as other boys his age who never had the benefit of parental care, he had no option but to buy clothes with any money he could get. But as the days bled away and the horizon became purple in the morning, and then nearing mid-August when the winds started, he was depressed and could not drive his bicycle anymore.

"What am I supposed to do?" Angus Peel said.

Each day the Monks would drive by, or drop in and look at him, and pat him twice on the shoulder. And sometimes he would stay up in his room so he wouldn't be patted on the shoulder, and they would call him down.

"Hey!" his father would call. "Brice – hey, Brice, come down here a moment, will you? Don't be so big-feelinged now, it's only Billy Monk."

And he would walk down and stand in the kitchen. Billy Monk would talk about almost dying in the hold. He would look at him with pale blue expressionless eyes, a small white mole under the left one, and he would speak almost without moving his lips, so you only saw one or two lower teeth, and Brice was so scared he could never take his eyes off of them.

Then Tanker arrived one Saturday with a whole bucket of chicken and a new fishing rod for the boy.

"I knew ya didn't have one, for ya got no fish this year – now you has a bike to take you fishin" and a rod to fish "em with."

Brice looked at his father and Tanker and nodded.

"Friends is what we are, right? Friends are what, now, Bricey?" Tanker asked.

"Friends," Brice whispered.

"Touch me pinky to make it true. C'mon now, touch me pinky."

So Brice touched his pinky.

"You gotta remember now, the only thing is, we don't want you to be blamed!"

What people did not know – or some did not know – was that the stevedores had a very good arrangement: they were able to work boats and get unemployment insurance at the same time, which gave many of them another four hundred dollars a month, while still collecting their unemployment for the winter. That this was arranged under the table at the dock, and the names shifted from one boat to another, and that Billy and Tanker Monk controlled it kept most people quiet about most things. So though no one knew what had happened in the hold, they closed ranks. It was a dangerous spot to work, and having someone do something careless was enough to have him expelled from the yard. That is why Roger did not work the *Liverpool Star*.

When Tanker came back the day he swore friendship on the pinky, he was still worried about the boy, so Billy Monk decided this: "Take him with you tomorrow night when you go to see Joel and help him bring back the fish. Give him some grass, and we'll show him we have nothing against those people, which we don't. An Indian is as good as us, and we were only foolin'. Then take a quart of the Captain, give it to him for his dad. You let him go with you tomorrow night to meet with Joel and it'll be fine."

"That might be a mistake," Tanker said, looking up quickly.

"I don't make mistakes," Billy Monk said.

But in fact, over the entire summer this was the one mistake he made. And no one would know that until it was long over.

And the boy Brice Peel went to school that long-ago year in a new pair of jeans and with lots of money given to him by Billy Monk. Some said they saw him drinking from a quart of Captain Morgan rum one night. And he got in fights, once for no reason, with the young Indian boy Markus Paul, because Markus refused to take twenty dollars he wanted to give away.

244

4

Doran kept going over things in his mind, as if some part of that mind had hidden something and he could not find it. No one knew why he had stopped filing stories. They thought he had been swayed by Joel into not saying anything. But he had refused to do what Joel wanted. But he did not tell them at work, for he knew no one would believe him.

"You were in Joel's pocket," one of the younger reporters said. When the managing editor passed him in the hall, he always looked away.

So many were against him now, at work and everywhere else. So he lived in his own world just as Roger Savage must have. He tried to contact Mary Cyr, but couldn't find her. And after a while he began to run – from everything that would remind him of who he was that summer, and of how silly and exploited he became.

Then, about the time Amos started to review the case, the Old Man, Mr. Blair Cyr himself, came down from Quebec. He stayed in a hotel in a windswept, frozen area, in a room where he would seem to be out of place, but very much like the hotel rooms in which he had started his newspaper empire forty years before. He ate shrimp in his room and thought of what had happened. He drank mineral water and stared at the bleak bay water, now sullen and deep. He walked though the lobby, passing racks upon racks of his own papers with brooding regret.

Then Doran and Mary Cyr were invited out to supper.

Doran believed he was to be told to rewrite the story, look

at it from another angle, and he would do so. He was nervous about it, but he understood he had to do it over. He believed that Mr. Cyr would ask him many questions dealing with all of this, and he would hand his notes and his tapes over (he had gotten them back) and Mr. Cyr would ask him to write more about it.

Mary picked him up in the Jaguar, and shifted the gears with insistency as she spoke to him of unrelated topics.

"Nice car," he said.

"You think?" she asked, shrugging. "It gets me where I'm going, I suppose." She no longer wore the pendant.

He still loved her, almost desperately. After he got his story going again, he hoped things would return between them.

"You chopped your hair off," Mary said.

"Yes," Doran said expectantly. But Mary said nothing more.

He knew he was meeting with a man who could make or break his life, and from the first moment of their encounter in the quiet lobby with its insistently noncommittal music he was aware of a certain taciturn demeanour in Mr. Cyr that meant much more than one might think shaking hands.

"I have the tapes back," Doran said for some reason. "I mean, of my conversations with Chief Amos – those might help us."

Mr. Cyr simply went around him, on the way to the restaurant.

Mr. Cyr did not ask for those tapes. Did not ask for anything, even a resignation. From the start he seemed to drive home another idea, and it was this: Cyr was not the enemy but the one who wanted change and a first-rate livelihood for the First Nations people. But even so, Doran's stories had permitted – or overlooked – a certain kind of situation. They were too one-sided. If the stories had been done better, at least with more insight, maybe the catastrophe would have been averted. For people were saying in fact the stories promoted the very catastrophe. This is what the paper was now facing. Competing papers were taking them on, and men who had grudges against Cyr were relishing this. The headlines in other papers said as much. Most of the province was sick of the story now, so when Doran mentioned re-investigating, Cyr just stared at him blankly. For Doran did not seem to realize that everyone wanted *him* investigated – no one else.

Cyr shrugged and looked at his menu for a bit. Then, after talking for ten minutes to his daughter about the sail-boat, the closing of the cottage, the covering over of certain hedges, and so on, he turned to Doran again, and as if just thinking of it, asked if anyone had wanted anyone else to be injured.

"Of course not," Max answered.

"Therefore we did not want Mr. Savage to be injured either. The idea that he was a "common enough journey-man," as one article stated, did not mean that he should be injured."

"Of course not."

"Well, this very strange – for the paper itself. This is what I have just spoken about today with my journalists," he said. "To be more circumspect. For it seems" – and here he took out Doran's articles – "that you hoped for someone to be injured. You seemed to delight in lessening Mr. Savage – well, him as a human being. Until it did not seem important that he wasn't protected."

That statement froze Doran. He could not believe Mr. Cyr had said this. It was not true – it wasn't true. All his life he would believe it wasn't true. But he was now in a position where the truth did not matter at all – for people were after him.

Mr. Cyr looked at Doran quietly, intently, and what is more, with a power Doran had never, ever felt before, except perhaps with Isaac Snow.

"What about the big hedge out front?" Mary asked.

"Wasn't that burned a little?"

"Yes, it was a bit," Doran answered for her, although suddenly it seemed inappropriate.

"What do you think of this circumspection, Max?" Mr. Cyr asked.

"I wanted to arrive at the truth," Doran said. "When I realized I couldn't, I stopped filing. But I'm willing to file again. I can travel up there next week. I was thinking – "

Mary looked at him a second and then glanced away, to the large plaque on the wall, as if suffering suddenly from some kind of personal injury.

Mr. Cyr picked up his glass of sparkling water to drink, still holding some articles crumpled in his left hand, a hand that in this light seemed large and blue. And it became evident – more so than anything else – that Mr. Cyr had been the one to allow every article Doran had written, and kept waiting for him to turn it about. That was what the phone call was about. And the managing editor who no longer looked his way had vouched for him.

"You had to continue to file," Mr. Cyr said, his eyes suddenly mirthful because he found it so incredulous. "You had to – that was the time to file – that was the *only time*! The *Globe* did not have the story. The *Star* did not have the story. No *Sun* had it. *We* had it!!"

"I don't think I could," Doran said, "and keep my respect at that moment."

"But you *had to file* – that was where your self-respect began and ended!" Mr. Cyr smiled. And one more time he held up the clipped articles in his large left hand – which now seemed so much like a part of the indictment.

"As I say, I do not think I could."

Mary said, quite suddenly, "I wish someone had been brave enough to get the real story. That's what I was waiting for all summer long – someone to come in and just get it right." She looked intently at her grandfather, as if this statement could be made as true as any of her others, as long as she said it suddenly and said it without losing her dreamy tone. To her, therefore, the summer, like so much else in her life, never really existed.

That is, truth and falseness had become distinctly insepar-able, and Doran felt exactly as Roger Savage must have. Mary Cyr had simply changed sides. Being the granddaugh-ter, she was allowed to do so.

As if feeling the weight of her own betrayal, she got up and left him sitting alone with her grandfather.

"I could redo the story – I mean look at it all again – get a different perspective. I could make sure of it – do one, no, two major pieces!"

Mr. Cyr looked at him with the same incredulity as before, and Doran did not know what else to say.

Doran had acted extremely decently in the end, but he could not say this now.

He saw the first snowflakes fall outside and blur the land, and sat in silence. He felt a sudden sweat over his body like a haze.

Mary came back to the table much later, after her plate of fries was cold. She spoke to her grandfather of leaving now, of going back to school, in Toronto.

"That will be fine," Mr. Cyr said.

She smiled.

Doran pretended it would be wonderful too.

What Doran did not know until that day was how exclusive this story was – how Mr. Cyr had gone along with the managing editor and chosen him personally for the story. Now Cyr felt he had been let down by them both.

That is, Doran had had to get it right, without knowing Mr. Cyr had chosen him personally or that he had to get it right.

So from this point on, just as Savage had been, just like a lawyer who botches a once-in-a-lifetime case, Doran was to be vilified. And the reason was Roger Savage's mother – penitent and justifiably angered by his death. The paper could be sued. She had hired a prominent lawyer from Toronto whose name Cyr feared. Everyone was running for cover, as people tend to. But much of the public was sick of them all.

"You are all whores!" someone shouted one night as Doran was leaving the office. Still, the policy and direction of the paper were ultimately Blair Cyr's. Cyr had made a drastic mistake that could easily have been hidden if it had not led to death. False reporting, and the wounds it creates, are often forgotten. Now, lawyers were looking over Mr. Doran's articles, and Cyr was trying to stop this. That is why, he decided, Doran could not write anything else for him – ever again.

Cyr had written two editorials that contradicted his own reporter. And he had secretly been behind the promotion of the young journalist Gordon Young, whom Doran so resented, to managing editor and fired the one who had recommended Doran. This had happened in the days before the dinner with Doran.

Then Cyr had telephoned his granddaughter.

"Let's have dinner with that Doran fellow – Yes, I have to meet him – You know I agreed to him in part because of you. By the way, no need for him to get dressed up."

Mary caught the inflection and said nothing more. But she knew getting dressed up was required of her.

For no matter how independent she was, no matter if she was able to smoke hash in Amsterdam or bare her breasts on a beach in southern France, eighty thousand dollars a year could be cut off with the snap of a finger.

In November, Doran was asked to go back to writing obits for seven months. He thought about it and declined. So he was let go by the new young managing editor. But this was not how it was stated. He was allowed to resign.

Doran stepped into the cold, silty evening, and went drinking in a bar, thinking of Little Joe.

He was getting up to go over to the jukebox when suddenly, looking over at the waiter running some water over dishes, he staggered a little. People thought he was drunk.

For the very first time he remembered what the water boy had said, what the water boy hoped he would write, come hell or high water. That Roger Savage, as simple and as troublesome and as redneck as he was, had done nothing. At all.

Doran would never be able to hold a steady writing job again.

5

The day after he came back from hunting, Amos went over to the house that had burned down, trying to find Roger's graduation ring – the one sent him because of his GED. This had been important to him, and Amos was going to send it to his mother. But in all the ruined things he could not find it. Only a few items remained, and the snow was covering them up. He put a few bullets in his pocket and decided not to mention them right away. He placed them upstairs in his desk drawer.

He told Markus after school that night that he might solve things all by himself. Except he was not completely sure what it was he was thinking. "Two things are wrong – but I am not sure what I am trying to remember," Amos said. He looked up from his tea, with an almost frightening expression, as if asking something so acutely painful it was hard not to look shocked. "Something is wrong at the boat, and with those water buckets, and something was wrong that night at Roger's house."

"In what way?" Markus asked.

"Well – it is like a dream you have where you almost grasp it. But what if we started in the hold, and stayed inside the hold, and did not go out of the hold until we saw what happened? The water boy is the key. Then later, after the hold, we can go for a walk to Roger's house and see what happened there."

"How could we ever do that?"

"I don't know. But since everyone else thinks they saw

what happened, why can't I see it too? Because perhaps we are seeing two different things."

People saw Amos and Markus outside on that late fall afternoon in 1985. They thought it was more than a little funny, that an old man would have a female mannequin out in the yard that had once belonged to his mother, and have constructed the moose tripod up against the old shed, and have the logs that had lain inside the small room hauled out and raised up on it. And they made fun of it, saying: "Well, he lost his wife and Mrs. Francis and he don't see each other no more, so I guess he's down to smooching with mannequins!"

A few here and there began to realize what he might be doing, and reacted with surprise. Trying to resurrect the bones of Hector by crushing a mannequin? Up on the highway, far away from the reserve, on those cold days, and into evenings with the stars glowing like cold, distant spikes, the stars that old Amos Paul could never finish counting Tanker Monk sat in his easy chair in the dark, curtained TV room and heard about Amos doing this. Tanker had a sore foot, and this gout would be with him forever. He whined too at times about his blood pressure, and often he went to see the doctor. He had taken a leave from working the boats, and in fact couldn't stand to see one in the channel. When he did he drew the drapes – and yet, as the saying goes, he could never draw the drapes on that.

Amos and Markus studied the marks on the mannequin for a good length of time. They dropped the logs seven times, for posterity, and placed the mannequin at different angles.

"You know what I think," Amos said, sitting on his haunches and spitting and smoking.

"What do you think?" Markus asked.

"There is no way my mom's dummy does not exhibit more trauma than poor Hector Penniac."

Markus said nothing. He picked up a stick and tossed it toward the black spruce below him. He had lost everyone now. No one spoke to him. When he walked up the street, kids he had known all his life would separate and veer around him. He did not want to tell his granddad this. Markus had found the yellow note, signed by Brice Peel, water boy, in the file the old man was given.

"If he was going back for a bucket – why?" Amos asked.

"Maybe one had a hole inside it or something."

"Maybe that's it. But if it is not the reason, then there is another reason that might tell us what happened."

Amos studied the mannequin. He knew one person who had taken care of his broken ankle, and had visited him, and maybe she would do so again. He talked to Markus and said, "Yes, she might visit me again, I am not sure – but she might, and help us decide what happened when the logs did fall."

So he called Kevin Dulse's wife Pamela, who was a head nurse at the Miramichi hospital.

"Are you sick, Amos? You know you can go to the hospital, and I will be in by nine tomorrow morning – "

"No, dear girl, this is about broken bones – "

There was a long pause.

"Okay, I'll be down," Pamela Dulse said.

"Thank you."

"But if it is your damn ankle and you were out hunting on it, I will chop it off!"

Pamela Dulse was, like many nurses, ambivalent not to the pain of others but to how much stock they put in it. For she had seen and dealt with it in trauma centres all of her adult life. She needed a healthy scepticism, a removal from what faced her each day, from the palliative care ward to the children she saw who would never get better, and this is exactly why old Amos had telephoned her. For she pretended an aloofness she did not have, but it made her the most professional of nurses. Besides, she liked scolding him about his cholesterol count, and he would put up with this for a while if she could tell him what he was seeing, both in the autopsy picture and in his re-enactment of the accident. She went to his house with her big wide eyes engaged in a kind of self-debate over whether she should be angry or not. Her face was milk white and thin; her chin, elbows and knees were sharp. Amos knew at a glance, as did Markus – just as they did with anyone – that she drank too much.

The first thing she looked at was the picture of Hector Penniac.

"He was hit with a blunt object," she said quickly, handing the picture back almost in accusation about such a frivolous inquiry. Amos nodded. He nodded not just at what she said but how she said it, hiding behind a professionalism that she never quite mastered, and so seemed more angry than she intended.

"Yes, but where?"

"On the head."

"Yes – but only there?"

She grabbed the picture back again and looked at it.

"Seems only there. Why?"

"Because that means for five months everything about this case has been all wrong, and a man and a little boy died for nothing – and the man was brave and the little boy was as brave as the man, and they both knew each other, since the little fellow was a baby and I might be old-fashioned but I do not think Roger had anything to do with it. I mean, it is not that he couldn't have hooked the load wrong. I am thinking, however, that if he did hook the load wrong he would have owned up to it. So everything is wrong."

"Everything about what? How it fell?"

"Come – I want to show you something."

Pamela followed him. It was the coming of winter and the reserve looked bleak, the shoal waters still and dark, and the sky seemed today to be perpetually at twilight, with swift-moving clouds, and all along the shore the boats had been lifted. The cottages, those great structures Markus once imagined never being in, were boarded up, their lawns stifled and stunted by salt. Ice clung to the ditches, and the Indian houses were closed up, some of the foundations banked with spruce boughs to keep off the wind.

It was to Pamela a strange sight. In behind the old house of Amos Paul, where the old man lived sitting out in his dooryard that looked out at a life that had betrayed him, a moose tripod had been fitted with great chains, and had four eight-foot logs pulled to the pinnacle, so they seemed like a brooding carcass in the autumn wind. They were not at the fifteen feet Amos had wanted, but the height would do. Pamela took a piece of gum and chewed on it, looking at Amos speculatively, her woollen hat pulled down over her ears, and every now and again rubbing her nose with her mitten.

Under these logs was a dressmaker's dummy that had been reconstructed a number of times, as if a child couldn't get enough of tormenting it. The sea outside the shoal water looked on with great dark waves, and the trees along the wood lane blew almost sideways, so she was freezing cold.

He left Pamela and walked toward the tripod. Then, looking back at her almost impishly, he pulled the chain from the spike on the shed wall, and the four logs came tumbling down upon the dummy, shattering the head and twisting all the arms and legs again, leaving gouges in the skull again. There was silence and a bit of cold dust, and a raven cawed out over them.

Amos was delighted when he looked at her. She went to the mannequin.

"Would that have broken a human bone?" he asked her.

"Oh yes – very many," she said.

He sighed, and coughed, and glanced away. It was as if a great weight had been finally lifted off of him, or perhaps off Hector Penniac.

He looked pleased with himself as he lit a cigarette.

"What is it?" she asked, taking the cigarette from his mouth and flicking it into the wind.

The little old man stared at the cigarette tumbling away, and then looked at her:

"It is proof, I think, that Hector Penniac wasn't hit by these logs, but that he was hit, as you say, by a blunt-force instrument."

"That's the case on the ship?"

"Yes, dear – the case on the ship. And I believe it will come down now like a ton of bricks."

But Amos felt he could not prove his case without the help of some eyewitness. So that night, in the cold, with little sleep, Amos made his way toward the highway, with the picture of the broken body in his pocket. They said that Hector was tormented on this highway when he would hike home after school, and now he was being carried along it in the pocket of an old man.

"I will show it to the water boy," he told Markus, who walked beside him.

"Then why not drive?"

"Oh, because it is better," he said, "because they will not see my truck parked at his house."

"Is that why you think he fought me – because he knows something?"

"I think this Brice is a good boy and is now in trouble. So it is better that we don't take the truck and better that we walk."

"And where do you think the *Lutheran* is now?"

"It is way over in Europe now – somewhere, and those sailors too, and the only thing they remember is this little old Indian staring up at them from the hold, so they will remember it for years, even though they could hardly see me in the darkness." He paused for a moment and then said, "You know, in 1944 I was on the bridge in Antwerp that we had to get over to enter their country. Roger's grandfather Lawrence was killed on that bridge. Do you think they would have all sailed off if they had known that?"

"It's as if they were the first ones who came here."

"Yes, that's the likes of it," Amos said, "that they were the first white men and I was the first Indian and there I was, and I told them to go back home and they turned around and left. But I gave them some lumber before they went, because I am a nice enough chief."

Markus giggled at this, in spite of all the terrible things that had happened, and they continued on.

And then they were quiet when they saw the lights in the distant houses. Small little lights that glowed out on an autumn night, against the trees, where ground fog rolled. The bear dens Amos had watched when he was a boy, with his silver Mauser from the Boer War, were now gone, the land they were burrowed in part of the long highway.

"You know, I was taught that to kill my enemies was the best thing," Amos said. "That was when I was little. But you have to find the enemy. And often when you do, you cannot bring yourself to kill him. And sometimes, like Roger Savage with his GED, it is the wrong enemy entirely."

In Markus's eyes, his grandfather seemed to be back to the same old Amos. He seemed again to be lively, even thinking of the recreation centre. Still, though the events of the summer and fall had given them a good amount of exposure, they were back in the same place, on the same reserve, and it all seemed futile, Amos told Markus. Once again the paper admitted many mistakes had been made regarding them, and once again they were told that things would soon get better.

But if one looked upon the world as being full of the minutiae of cause and effect, of balance and counterbalance, had they, the people on the reserve, done all of this, then, just to kill Little Joe? What would Glooscap, the God of the Micmac, think of them now? If they had just waited, buying some time, Roger would have come out of his house.

But they couldn't wait.

Joel had to act – he was as forced to do so as anyone else.

You see, not to act would have made him a disappointment to those children to whom he'd promised he would act. Such as Andy and Tom. Nothing could be done for him, for Joel Ginnish. In the end he was forced, like everyone.

"Someday you will understand and figure it all out," Amos told Markus.

Amos was supposed to be an old man. But years ago Amos had walked into a group of white men who were saying they were going to hang him one night, after his friend had been hanged, and he had beaten them all. And he now faced the labyrinth of his conscience because his band, when he was chief, may have acted in the same way, like those very white men.

This is why Amos went to Brice Peel's house with Markus. He appeared at the door like a child. Markus stood behind him.

At first there was no answer. Inside the door into the old porch, it was almost darker than midnight. They stood together, he and his grandson. And as Amos knocked, Markus whispered:

"Have you ever been in a white person's house?"

"Yes," Amos whispered, "when I delivered salmon to the cottages. But those are not houses, they are cottages – even though they are ten times the size of our house. But this house looks more like our house."

"Yes," Markus said, shaking slightly. "I've never been in a white man's house before."

"Well, I saw them up at Sobeys, and they buy Red Rose tea just as we do," Amos said.

Finally, after they spoke and knocked, and then knocked again, the door opened. And a light snapped on at the same moment, and out of that doorway a man stood looking at them, his face expressing a kind of bold and almost insane hilarity, as if he was waiting for them. And yet as if he was ambushed at the same time.

"Yes?" the man said, thrusting his face forward. "Yes – what?" His face gave away his fear-glazed merriment. His eyes were wide and ghastly.

"Yes – hello, Mr. Peel. How are you, sir?"

"I am just dandy – and I don't want no smelts."

"Ah well – I am not selling smelts. Besides, it is too early, the bay as you know has not made ice. I was wondering if young Peel was here."

"I am here. Is there anything I can do for you?"

"No," Amos said, "is young Mr. Peel here?"

"Who is young Mr. Peel?"

"Brice," Markus said.

"Oh, he's long in bed now – can't come out to play." And he gave the same look of inscrutable hilarity, with his head going back slightly into the kitchen.

"I see," Amos said.

"What do you want from him? Perhaps I can tell him when he wakes in the morning."

"No, thank you," Amos answered.

"Why – am I not good enough?"

"Oh, it is not a message anyone can deliver. In fact, it is something *he* might be able to tell *us*," Amos said.

Then he turned, and Markus turned with him. Markus did not know why he turned so suddenly, and in some respects did not know why they had come to this house. Very soon after they got to the gravel drive, Angus closed the door.

For a moment or two Amos stood still and clutched Markus's arm. When he saw the upstairs light go on above the porch, he pushed his grandson toward the trees.

"Wait here," he whispered.

"For what?"

"For him to leave."

He looked up at the stars, took his handkerchief out and wiped his nose, and looked up at his grandson – who was already taller than he was. There was one sound – a kind of muffled shout – and a door slammed. In two or three minutes, the door opened and Mr. Peel walked out, got into his own little Datsun and drove away.

After a while the sound of the car faded.

"He is gone far up the road," Amos said.

"Yes." Markus shrugged.

"Well, now we will go see Brice."

They walked into the room, and Brice was there, a scared little boy, with his T-shirt hanging off him, and eighty dollars on the windowsill, and a bicycle sitting in the corner of his room, and a fishing rod leaning against the back of the door.

Amos smiled. "Have you been working a shut-down?"

The boy looked at them scared to death, holding a bag of marbles in his hand. But he told them he had nothing to tell about Hector Penniac.

"What happened that day? Why did you go for another bucket? Why didn't you lift the other buckets and take them? That means those buckets were full, or partially so, so why did you go for another one?"

Then Amos took out the picture of Hector in the morgue and showed it to the youngster.

"You have to tell sooner or later," Amos said, not unkindly. "Then you won't be bothered anymore. Think of Roger Savage in his house all summer. He was a white boy, and he did nothing wrong – someone else must have."

The boy shrugged. "But Roger killed a little boy," he answered, "so what is so big about him?"

There were tears starting to his eyes, but he was brave enough to say nothing else.

"But just maybe he didn't kill the little boy," Amos whispered.

"Everyone knows he did!"

They left before the boy's father got back, and they walked along the battered old highway.

"Do you want me to try to hitchhike a car?" Markus said.

"No, it doesn't matter," Amos answered.

They were silent again. Sky and Little Joe's mother had no husband, and when she died they were taken care of by Mrs. Francis. Amos asked Markus if he knew who Sky's father was.

"Everyone says it's Isaac, the time his wife went away," Markus said.

They walked along for a moment without saying anything.

"And Little Joe's father?" Amos asked.

"I don't know."

"Joel Ginnish," Amos said.

Then he said he was tired, and wanted to know if Markus would like his rifle.

"Why?"

"I killed my last thing," Amos said.

Part VI

September 24, 2006

It is best to hunt moose in September when the wind has startled the branches and the nights get cool. Lately here in the Maritimes, as if the world is being reset, September has come in too warm, and the moose don't move in the rut as soon. And the rut is everything for a moose hunt.

Markus Paul was in his grandfather's attic thinking of these things, and cleaning the .306 that his grandfather had given him that night after they got home from Brice Peel's place twenty-one years before.

He thought about how in 1986 Joel had begun a lawsuit, charging the Canadian government with negligence because of his back problem. Joel became obsessed with the technicalities of it – dressed well in suit and tie and always punctual at court. His contention was simple: the soldiers came in to the reserve and wrestled him to the ground. He had been charged with arson and spent fourteen months in jail. When he came out, the reserve had changed – many men had their lobster licences and boats and many of them no longer wanted him around. Isaac had gotten all of this done when he was away, had weeded out the bad apples.

Joel got a settlement in 1994 and walked around the reserve telling people about it. He was going to buy a boat and get his own lobster licence. He walked into Markus's in a blustering way and showed him a letter from the minister of Indian affairs.

Joel had not spoken to Isaac in seven years, but he was going to go up to his house to show him too.

$34,354.27.

That's the amount on the cheque he showed to everyone.

Mrs. Francis told him she had won that much playing bingo.

He kept his suit and tie on, even though he was on the reserve. He bought drinks for people he didn't know.

"I was the guy who got our lobster licences," he said.

"You were?"

"Yep. Just ask Andy Francis – that was me!"

There was some dispute. Whatever it was, Markus couldn't remember now.

But Joel never got the licence for his boat. People wanted him off the reserve. He tried to open a small convenience store. He stood behind the counter waving at young people who no longer knew who he was.

Fifty-five hundred dollars. That's what Markus heard that Doran got: fifty-five hundred dollars as his severance, and not all at once. Doran tried to publish his own paper for a while, solicited articles from people he knew. He went back to journalism school, but felt out of place. He convinced a young woman taking the course that he was still a rising star in journalism. Everyone still knew who he was. He wrote for weeklies and spent time in bars. They married, that woman and he.

The woman told Doran to go to Newfoundland and investigate the terrible priests in the terrible Catholic Church. She told him to write about brutality in hockey. To both, he said no. Once when she thought he was on a story, she found out he had rented a room to hide in. There he was with a hotplate and a blanket over him, drinking a cup of tea.

Then Doran disappeared. The trouble was, and Markus knew this, that Doran's greatest moment as a journalist had occurred when he was on his own in a small shed at night, because he refused to do a story or help arrest Roger. That he was a journalist – and perhaps still a great journalist who could no longer write – had helped destroy him. It certainly destroyed his marriage. Doran's wife kept trying to encourage him to be the man she believed she had married. Finally she left, with a boyfriend from the *Telegraph*, to work on a paper in London, Ontario. Doran stalked her until he was arrested. He tried to give the severance money to Markus's band. They refused. So he gave it to the native band in Red Bank.

"It is not the Conibear trap that kills the beaver, but the drowning that follows."

When his grandfather died a few years later, Markus was nineteen.

"Everyone has been too kind to me," were Amos's last words.

Now Markus tested the scope on the .306 in the field beyond his grandfather's, just about where Doran had spoken to Amos on that first visit long ago.

It came in, at a hundred yards, high and to the right. He tweaked it a few degrees this way and that half the morning. But he didn't like firing shots. He fired only eight in all and realized he had it as well as he could. He fired from a fifty- and then a hundred-yard stop. Both would show the same trajectory and hit the same place.

"I can't hit anything, anyway," Markus said. That, of course, was not true. But it didn't matter anymore. He lit a cigarette, and sat on the porch steps and thought of something. The way the bullet went high and to the right. Strange, for he was sure the rifle had been centred – but there were so many variables. Anyway, most moose shots were not that far. It was warm, and the sky was light and the weeds in the garden were turning yellow. He would hit the moose below the shoulder. Best-case scenario. A car honked as it went by. He never knew if it was a derisive honk or not.

The neighbours would see his car or his truck in at his grandfather's, and they would think it was strange, and many would think he had come to prosecute them. Or perhaps, as Samantha once told him, he was being delusional and they did not think that at all.

"Ah yes – but you are white. And I can tell."

Markus would hunt the barrens, which would mean a longer shot. That was the thing. He took his shells out and lined them up, 180 grain. Many years he had loaded the bullets himself, but he didn't bother now, though he still tied his own flies for fishing and made his own rods. He had a ten-foot sage given to him by the department when he solved a crime last year that had been in the papers for months. But he had not used it. It seemed too special to use, and so he went back to his old heavy standard.

He lay down with the cartridges lined up on the coffee table, his truck loaded. He sipped on a beer. He thought of all kinds of bullets and shells and the different hunts he had been on, and what constituted a good hunt, and what were his happiest hunts – those with his grandfather, of course, when he had to borrow the old rifle from Roger Savage, a rifle he never fired, but just carried to make him look proud. The rifle had once belonged to David Paul, Markus's father. That is why Roger readily lent it back to him. But he was only a little boy and they never gave him shells.

He went to sleep thinking of Roger, and for some strange reason dreamed of his own mother, Conde, whom he had hardly known. The dream, like so many, was out of sequence. But his father, David Paul,came in and sat down, and patted his head, and Conde said: "You see, it's all right – and we will be with you forever – and you didn't even know."

"That people rise from the dead?" he asked.

"Yes – almost every day."

He travelled up to the great chop-down the next morning and made his way, with his tent and provisions, two miles south of the road, toward an old dead haphazard moss and blueberry ground. Here and there was bear scat, and the two front claws of a black bear digging away at something. Lonely was the sky, and the trees at dawn. Beyond him was the barrens. This is where he hoped for a sighting. Since he had no tree stand made, he would work the ground and wait for a bull to appear. Sometimes a cow would have a bull or two in tow as she came out in the evening, the bull or bulls following her, with their nose in her quiff if she was prime.

The first day of the hunt was warm. At noon on the first day, he sat in his small tent and peeled an apple, and looked out over the barrens. He had used his grandfather's old birch moose call; calling the short huffs of a mature bull, he got no answer. He followed this with the long moan of the cow.

"Unhhg," he would call, for the bull.

Then "Ohhhnnoooooooouuuuuoohhhhooouuu," he would trail off for the cow. And then a chipmunk would scold him. And he would shrug and go back and sit down. And wait. Of course, both calls were to attract a bull.

The first was the call of a bull moose challenging a bull, the second of a receptive cow. But the woods were silent and did not stir. In the late part of the afternoon it was warm enough to have a beer sitting in his shirtsleeves and playing solitaire on an upside-down box.

Later the wind picked up just a little. It was sharper, so perhaps it might cool. Far, far above him, planes travelling the route between Toronto and London, England made their way across the great blue sky.

"A sky-blue life," he thought, looking up, saying the name of a Maxim Gorky story.

He flipped the last card over and found he did not have a match.

He had gone into the woods with his father, too, years ago. And every time he did, his grandfather Amos would show up at eight or nine at night, no matter what Amos was doing. After supper at home, Amos would get his things together and make his way to the bog to see Markus and his own son,

269

David. For a few years Markus did not understand this, and then one night he woke with his father's knife at his throat.

"The bastards are coming," his father said. "Who are you?"

"David," came the sudden voice of his grandfather, who was sitting on his haunches in the corner. "That's your son, so you can go back to sleep, please."

After solitaire and the solitary meal he ate of beans and wieners, Markus heard the distinctive snap, snap down in the valley of a bull walking slowly toward him, and toward the smell of cow urine he had placed near an old bed a cow had dug up the year before. It was snapping the branches of birch and poplar with its great rack. Each snap had the reverberations of a .22 bullet. But he was no fool, this big bull. He came cautiously. Markus called twice more. Just at evening Markus heard the bleat of a young bull. Knowing the big bull was coming, he was choosing to back away.

Leaving Markus and the big bull alone.

As he lay down he thought of rifles and bullets and all kinds of things. He remembered that once his father David got so angry at his rifle that he was going to smash it against a tree. They were far away on the river hunting deer. Markus never knew what was wrong. But it was something to do with the shells a friend had given him. They were the wrong shells – though to Markus they looked the same as the shells his father had used before. But there was a mistake of some sort, and he had brought the wrong ones. He remembered this incident as one of the most important between him and his father – brooding, melancholy and holding the almost glittering brass shells in his hand. How could they be the wrong ones?

Then later David woke, and thinking Markus was someone else, took a knife and put it to his throat. That was the night Amos said: "That's your son."

So after that they took the rifle and gave it to Roger Savage.

Markus slept just in a tarp and sleeping bag. The fire died down, and the rain started about three in the morning. He pulled the tarp over his head and waited until dawn. Then he stood, had a leak and picked up his rifle to check it – see if it was wet or the scope fogged. He heard a sudden grunt, and turned. In the fallow dawn light a nineteen-point bull was staring at him, no more than seventy-five yards away. He had time to put one 180-grain bullet into the chamber, aim and fire before the bull ran over him. The bull stopped, turned slightly, staggered and fell over on the tarp Markus had just left.

Nothing in the woods was as dangerous as a bull moose in rut.

He usually quartered the animal himself – and he managed to do this now, after the animal was opened and staked out. Then he moved a pulley line to the hindquarters and got them lifted off the ground. It took him most of the day to get the hide off it, get it sawed and quartered. He removed the rack at the crown of the head and placed it in the back of the truck.

Late that night, some time way after dark, he was able to hang the four quarters down in the cold cellar in his grand-father's house.

Here were old *Saturday Night* and *Star Weekly* magazines – Canadian magazines that his own father had grown up with. In this house his grandfather had given him one thing, a love for reading. That is why Amos had tried to start the school, and had finally gotten it built. In one magazine, from August 1985, was a small article, on page 15. "A Reserve's Anguish," it said. It had a picture of Hector Penniac. When Markus looked at it, it seemed almost crisp and brand new – as if the article had been written the day before.

He was exhausted, and went upstairs. He sat in his room staring at a TV game show, *Wheel of Fortune*. It revolved.

Yes, he thought, there would be a time when he would kill no more, and perhaps this was the time.

He then emptied his pockets and lay out his cartridges on the table. Then he thought of how he used to hunt deer with a small .30-30.

No charging bull moose would have been stopped by a .30-30. Markus would have surely been injured, or dead. He shook slightly thinking of this. Amos had taken the rifle from his father David, after he had flashbacks of Vietnam, and given it to Roger.

So it was his father's rifle Roger had used that terrible night long ago.

"Fuck you," Roger had said at the last.

Markus went up to the back room to sleep. But he could not, so he got up, made himself a cup of tea and went back up to the attic and opened the gun cabinet. He took the two bullets Amos had found in the soot at the back of Roger's house and placed them on the table – looking at them as if he thought they might dance.

1985–2006

1

"You don't like people," Markus's Indian girlfriend had said to him once, just before they had broken up in 2005. "That's why Samantha left you – you don't like people."

"I do," he protested. "I do I do – I do like people."

Then he added: "On occasion."

But there was something he was trying to figure out. He got so angry over it that he threw a telephone against the wall. What's wrong? his Indian girlfriend asked.

"I know who is innocent and who is guilty and I can't for the life of me prove it," Markus answered.

She took the blankets away; she was naked except for small panties.

"Come back to bed. We are all guilty," she said.

After the final inquest into the deaths of Hector Penniac and Little Joe Barnaby, Amos had taken all his information to the police in three envelopes. But the case was not active then. It was July 1987.

Sergeant Hanover said: "Roger Savage killed Hector Penniac and Little Joe Barnaby, and you are here – bothering me – trying to clear his name to save your own reputation. You are a disgrace, even for an Indian. *Now go home!*"

So the old man took the envelopes and went home. And he never spoke of it again.

When he was a teenager, Brice Peel started to have seizures. Bill Monk gave him drugs. Brice began to like the drugs. He went to Bill to get more. He learned how to get the most out of them. He liked cocaine. He went to dances. He began to step-dance on a table, all by himself.

Most of the time he was "right out of her," as they say here. He lost his teeth in a fight. He was down to 122 pounds. He liked things that would give him adrenalin.

He quit school in grade eleven and worked at the carpet ranch but was caught robbing money. The Monks paid his bail. This was written down on a file that Markus now had. The Monks always paid.

Brice lived in town. He had no telephone numbers of girls. He had no happy memories of home. He kept some budgie birds and a rabbit, and picked up stray cats to feed. He had milk bowls outside his little apartment door.

He read Isaac Asimov and Arthur C. Clarke. The books allowed him to vanish into space gullies and dragons in the sky.

Though Markus tried to keep tabs on him, by 1996 Brice seemed to have disappeared.

Brice Peel worked at the pet store in Saint John for eight years. He never told anyone where he was from. The seizures continued, as long as he drank and took medication, and yet he drank and took medication because of the seizures. After a time no one paid any attention to him, so he was a lost soul, no longer a bother or a problem to anyone. Bill Monk told him he was a disgrace and not to come back.

In the autumn of 2004, he left the pet shop and walked out into the sterile parking lot with bread for the pigeons. Then, as always, he walked along the empty streets, the trees uniformly naked and the windows as dark and oppressive as a Sunday afternoon. He had been drunk for a week, and the owner of the pet store told him, for the last time, not to come back until he got help because he was upsetting the guppies.

His room was small, and he had two hamsters and a

guinea pig. He brought home their food in a big brown bag. Outside on the street he could hear children. He had newspaper over his window, so no one could see in.

His father was dead, so he would not have to go to jail. He turned the television on and sat down and wrote out his story.

Then, after he wrote his story, he wrote a letter to George Morrissey:

"Dear George – I am sending you over the story – I am telling you not to open it until my death – and then take it to Markus Paul who is now an RCMP – but not until I die – and am good and dead – as dead as a doornail – please – I have sent you along that new budgie food with the 3 kinds of vitamins for healthy beaks and polished feathers – Brice Peel."

He mailed the letter the next morning.

Then he lay down and sliced his wrists. He bled a lot, but unfortunately, it seemed to him, he did not die.

Doran worked at many odd jobs. He was, as he knew, provoking his own death, in subtle ways, mysterious to those who do not know. He drank, and used OxyContin to sleep, and Benadryl over the counter, was in his own way providing for a hatred of himself. He knew as much about journalism as anyone in the country, yet did not write a word, even when the young journalist Gordon Young switched papers and phoned him, asking him aboard.

"Of course – I'll think about it."

"Please, fly up to Ottawa tomorrow and see me."

"Sure – "

He did not go.

He sat alone at lunch and went alone to and from anyplace. Those who tried to get close to him were rebuffed. In some ways he spoke to them in the same gruff language that Roger Savage once had. The wounded always do that in the end.

275

There were moments when he would recharge like a battery and come together. But for the most part he kept going back to that summer – to those days when he might have acted differently.

"I blamed a man who maybe should not have been blamed" is all he thought about.

He tried to write for different papers throughout the Maritimes but was always let go. The last paper was the *Bugle*. His attention span would suffer – or he would refuse stories he was sent on. Or he would be sent on a story and not come back.

So after a time, left alone with a child that came from his failed marriage, he took odd jobs.

The worst job was cleaning septic tanks for Toyne and Toyne out in the small villages. He sometimes sat alone at lunch thinking that if he was wrong and the boy Brice was right, then he, who had gone to get the story, did not get it very well, and had to come forward. He still had a few connections with a few editors – one, of course, was Gordon Young. But was it now possible? Part of the problem was, no one listened to him anymore – and without evidence he would get nowhere now.

He took OxyContin to sleep, and sleep did come after he took enough. He grew thinner and shakier.

He took a job at the Saint John call centre in 2001, and he decided that it was for the best if he did not say anything again.

"There is much falsehood in the world," a young, sad-eyed blonde prostitute told him one night when he went to her for comfort he could find nowhere else. "And I figure all falsehood is much the same."

One day in 2003, as he passed a trash can near Loch Lomond Road, he spied an old paper and the picture of Markus Paul, who had accompanied Prince Edward on a five-day trip to the North. He picked the paper out, and sitting on a bench in the rain, read what had happened to that boy he had once so dismissed, and his lips, blue with cold, trembled.

"It is not the Conibear trap that kills the beaver, but the drowning that follows."

2

Markus gave most of his moose meat away. And in October of 2006 he packed his bag and got on a flight in Moncton on a clear day when you might be better off in the hills hunting partridge. He flew out to Toronto, and sat in a departures lounge, wanting a cigarette. He read over the brochures he had with him, telling him that his trip should be fun. He took a plane that night, late, into Arizona. Of course, he went to a hockey game the next day just to see Wayne Gretzky behind the bench. The arena was only half full, and the ice was wet.

Then he had a drink in a bar, alone; he was always alone.

"Someday you will meet someone," he remembered Mrs. Francis saying when he'd asked her about Sky Barnaby the year before.

He read promotional material the next morning in his hotel room, material about the Petrified Forest.

He had taken some time off. He wasn't expected back on duty for a month. He would use the time to do what his grandfather had never had the chance to do.

He smoked constantly, often rolled his own, like Amos had. It was what had killed Amos eventually. Markus had promised his ex-wife, Samantha Dulse, who was a doctor, that he would get in for an X-ray as soon as he came back.

"You had better," she said.

So he determined to buy her a present to make up to her his own lack of consistency.

The heat in Arizona, even in October, bothered him. He

needed the sound of the bay and the smell of pine. He had not realized how much that was in his blood.

Markus travelled everywhere he could, carrying brochures and a camera he never seemed able to work. He travelled to many places. He visited the land of the Apache. He walked where the Seminole and Cherokee walked. He did those things his grandfather wanted and never managed to. He visited the museum of the Texas Ranger, stared at the Colts and pistols, the hats and boots and badges.

Later in the month he went north by plane and bus and visited the land of the Lakota Sioux.

"A great people," a young Dutchman with an inquisitive, hopeful face said to him when they were on the bus together.

"Oh yes," Markus acknowledged. "Yes."

"They were so brave. They hunted the bison," the man informed him. "Did you know?"

"I heard as much," Markus admitted.

The Dutchman said that no one could do anything like that today. He carried a picture of Sitting Bull that he had bought at a craft store. And he said that his favourite movie was *Little Big Man*. He said he had seen it five times. The Dutchman said he, too, wrote about the Wild West and asked Markus if he knew about it.

"Not so much," Markus admitted.

The Dutchman studied the picture of Sitting Bull and said that if he was here at that time, he would have sided with the First Nations people. He asked Markus if he would have sided with the First Nations people too – did he think he would stand up for them? Markus said he hoped he might. The Dutchman said that he himself certainly would have – He would have been there. He would have fought to the death to protect all the Indians. Markus told him that was commendable. The Dutchman seemed pleased. He smiled and nodded to himself. Markus's eyes started to fill with tears. He kept looking out the window so no one would see. The day got dark – there was frost, and Markus was thinking of how the deer would be on the move, up the rut trails in the afternoon. He wanted to speak to the Dutchman about rifles and grains of bullets, and how the deer moved just at dark, with the smell of musk in the air, snow starting to fall, and the sound of water before it made ice, but realized there was no point at all.

He had bought in a gift shop in the Petrified Forest a wicker basket and a baked clay pot for Samantha Dulse, as a kind of token of their divorce maybe, and forgot them in the overhead bin on a bus. He only remembered them when sitting in the terminal in Chicago, ready to fly back to Canada. He looked around for them and they weren't there.

Like most of his life, he was always losing things. Wives and girlfriends too. It was raining and cold. And as they flew down into Moncton the blinding snow had started.

"We will have some chop coming in," the pilot said, and Markus remembered Roger Savage helping him and his grandfather take their boat out of the rough sea the year before Roger died. He remembered when they hit big chop, Roger had put his large hands over Markus's on the oar.

"Keep 'er on, boy," he had said, and then he smiled a rough smile.

Now, like magic, Markus' little Honda was still there in the airport lot, appearing as if it hadn't moved. Or as if it had gone on a trip itself around the entire world, and had just come back in time.

He had brought home a poncho for Sky Barnaby. Although, as always, he did not know where she was so as to give it to her.

And so it was, after all this time, that Markus would solve the case of Hector Penniac and Roger Savage because he saw at a museum in Texas a bullet fragment taken from Billy the Kid.

"Quien es?" were Billy's last words when he walked into

the adobe kitchen in the dark. "Who is there?" or "Who are you?"

"Who are you?" Markus said, four lifetimes and four time zones away.

Late at night, long after he'd eaten, Markus went into the RCMP office. The short blond constable at the front desk looked at him. "You back?"

Markus walked into the old room that was the command centre of Sergeant Hanover the night he had sent in the men to arrest Isaac Snow. Now it had drawers and filing cabinets of old cases. Once when he'd been busy in here, on a hot day last July – trying to figure out this case, the case of Roger Savage that consumed him – the commissioner from Fredericton had come to visit. As he walked past, this man glanced in and saw Markus, his holster against his back right hip, holding a sandwich in his teeth and reading over a file.

"Who is that?" the commissioner asked.

"Oh, that's Markus," the sergeant whispered, "our Indian."

Now Markus took the files again, all of them, out of the cabinets and took them home. He spent the next three days looking at them. Everything to do with Hector Penniac, Roger Savage and Little Joe – faded, yellowed and forgotten pages dealing with what most of humanity would think was nothing important at all. He knew what had happened, but without the rifle it would be impossible to prove. He went to bed, thinking it was useless – and then he suddenly realized he had seen an envelope in a file and had left it at the office. He had seen this envelope before and just assumed it was empty. But perhaps it wasn't.

But he was too tired. No, he wouldn't get up. He decided it was nothing. Just an old empty envelope stuffed away for years that no one bothered throwing out. It was nothing, he was sure. Besides, it was three in the morning.

Then he sat up in bed, coughed and lit a cigarette. He left his apartment and went back to the office. Some poor drunk hollered at him from one of the cells. He went to the filing cabinet, opened it angrily and found the envelope. Inside was a piece of yellowed RCMP paper, with nothing on one side. He turned it over.

"Rifle damaged in fire – .30-30 – owned by Roger Savage. 0-3-9."

He went to 0: the basement. He went to 3: room 3. He went to 9: an unlocked wooden cabinet he had never known existed that had two old toilets and a sink torn out of old cells placed in front of it. He put them aside.

He opened the door. There was a mop, a broom, a rifle.

While Markus was away in Arizona a letter had arrived from the hospital, signed by his ex wife Samantha Dulse, reminding him of an X-ray he had promised to get.

That evening, when he went to the hospital for his X-ray, Markus wandered into the east wing and found himself in the palliative care unit. He was hoping to see Samantha and say hello. But she was not on duty. She had scheduled the X-ray for him when she knew she would not be there. He heard there was a lawyer she was dating. They owned a little sloop called *Raison d'être*. "Good for her," he thought.

He went back along the naked corridor with its soft lights and the stifled sounds of people in agony. He glanced into a room and saw a man withered down to nothing, lying in bed with a blue monitor against the darkness, and the smell of urine.

Alone.

The man looked familiar. So Markus, just on the off chance he knew him, went to the nurses' desk and asked about him.

"Yes, dear, he has prostate," the nurse said, with a sweet Miramichi accent. "He may have two weeks – or a month."

Markus started to leave, then came back and asked the man's name.

The nurse looked at the chart. "George Morrissey."

It took him ten minutes to compose himself. He sat on the chair in the hallway outside the room and tried to breathe. Then he finished his coffee and went in to visit George. He sat for a long time beside him without saying much.

"You like some ice cream?" Markus went down to the cafeteria about ten that night, just before it closed, and bought some ice cream. When he got back George was awake, and as he fed him the ice cream with a plastic spoon, Markus asked, point blan, "Do you think Roger hooked good?"

George looked at him and nodded. He had a bib on like a child. There was a pause and Markus tried to breathe, but he found it difficult.

"Did you tell him to hook?"

George, a shadow of the man he once was, trembled. "Yes – I asked him to hook," he said, managing to wipe his mouth.

"Do you have anyone to visit you – anyone – any relative?"

George shook his head.

"Well then, I'll visit you," Markus said. "Okay, pal?"

"Okay." George managed a little smile.

Markus phoned Samantha that night. He asked her about her lawyer friend, although inside he felt heartbroken. He told her he thought he might solve the case now.

"Oh – the case," she said. It was, in fact, what had broken up their marriage. That and his love for Sky. He had never really been off the case. Even when he was attached to the governor general's office. Or when he was a bodyguard for Prince Edward of England on a trip to see the Inuit villages. Or when that author complained that they only sent one man to protect him while in England he had four. The author, very famous and wise, complained that his hamburger might be poisoned, and how would Markus tell? So Markus had picked it up and took a bite, chewed and swallowed. "No," Markus said. "I believe it's okay." Markus did not know he had done anything wrong, until the Author lodged a complaint through his embassy to the RCMP.

"I'm looking at your X-rays tomorrow," Sam scolded him, just as her mother Pamela had done years before to his own grandfather. "You take care of yourself, please!"

They had killed old Amos's dog. Sometimes Markus would go for days and not think of that. Then it would all come back. He would shiver and even now, so much later, tears would come to his eyes. He remembered running along the ditch in his bare feet and picking the dog up in his arms.

"It was your best friend Andy Francis who did it," he would whisper. "Long time ago."

In the ball field where Roger Savage's house had once been, there was a memorial to Little Joe Barnaby. There was a picture of him in his Braves uniform and the hat that made his ears turn down.

The next day – that is, the day after he saw George Morrissey – Markus went to the ball field to look at it. It was something he had never in his life managed to do before.

"Well, Little Joe," he said, "look how old and ugly I managed to get – while you remain the same."

Over the years, Markus had kept tabs on the Monk brothers. He had done this for over fifteen years. Their fights and arrests for poaching etc.

The anger of the stevedores over the pension fund had long passed – that is, the stevedores who were angry that Bill Monk cheated them when everything closed down. But nothing at all could be proved. It was just one more case, a little uproar with vague details.

"No sir, no one came out of it rich," was all Bill could say.

Tanker sold milk up and down the long roadway. Sometimes he came to Markus's apartment and left a quart at the door. Sometimes when he saw Markus he gave a hurt but understanding smile.

Bill was retired from everything but had a fishing camp where he took sports fishers. He owned a glider too, which was seen on occasion out over the bay. He was one of those angular tough men, still wiry at sixty-two and had never gained a pound, determined to keep himself solid and thin as a rail. His eyes stared out at you with a coldness he could not hide. Perhaps it was not his fault – compassion and everything associated with it had eluded him. Sometimes when he spoke or laughed, Markus caught in his inflection that he was trying to denote those things humanity had instructed us to have, but couldn't seem to.

Bill had spoken to Markus about his camp, how it was being broken into. Bill was going to set up a bear trap and mangle whoever it was.

"I think it's some Indians," he said.

"Yes, perhaps. But what if it's only a boy – say, like that Indian boy Hector Penniac a long, long time ago? Would you injure him too?" Markus asked.

There was a long pause. Sometimes Markus would have liked to say, "Swing at me," but he never did.

"You guys have to do something – can't you solve crimes?" Monk said, walking away.

"We are trying, sir," Markus said after him.

A week after he got back from the States, Markus went to the co-op and bought gun polish and cleanser. Then he went back to his apartment and spent the night cleaning and refitting the old rifle of Roger Savage that had lain away in a closet at the RCMP building for twenty-one years. He took off the stock and cleaned it out, and took gun polish to the barrel, took a scrub to the inside, re-tapped the screws and made it sound. Then he went outside walked a quarter mile to the gravel pit, adjusted the sights, and took a new bullet from a box of shells and tried to insert it.

He knew it wouldn't fit.

285

So he took another bullet from a different box and fired it at a pumpkin at a hundred yards.

He believed he knew exactly what had happened now, probably in both cases, both the death of Hector Penniac and that of Little Joe.

He had promised George Morrissey that Roger Savage had done nothing, not even accidentally, so if Morrissey had something to say, he should say it now.

"Clear your conscience," he had said quite simply.

He had not told the Monk brothers what he knew yet.

Markus polished the bullets Amos had picked up in the soot twenty-one years ago until they were pristine. He had found them in the desk drawer, after moose season. They had been in his mind all through Texas, right to the Little Big-horn. And now he knew why. Strange how easy it all was once you knew why.

Markus went to Morrissey's hospital room, and there among the neutral colours of death would read the sports pages to him, pages with the bylines of Stephen Brunt or the local boys. George would sit up in bed, sometimes shakily holding a cup of yogurt, listening to it all.

"How is the Leafs gonna do this year?" he would rasp. "I lost my shirt to friends on them – except," he said, "as you see, I have no friends."

"Well," Markus would smile, "here I am."

The only thing George had, over his life, was his sports pool. It was where he could, if he wanted, pick and choose multi-millionaire hockey players to work for him in the small room he lived in with his two yellow budgie birds. But he hadn't picked the right multimillion-dollar hockey players after all. He had lost his pension in the dispute among the stevedores and Bill Monk, and been forced into a room at the hotel.

The birds were a present from his nephew.

"Oh? Who's that?" Markus asked one afternoon. "I mean, your nephew?"

"Brice Peel," George said.

Markus nodded quickly and said nothing for a time. He gave a terse nod and his face flushed. He fed Morrissey some yogurt with a spoon.

George told Markus he had taken it upon himself to rewire his room for a computer last winter and had short-circuited the entire hotel and put everyone in the dark. People were banging on his door, he said. "George, you get out here, you crazy son of a bitch!"

"They were some upset about that," George said. So he was worried about his funeral, and whether those at the hotel would go. It made him very anxious to think they might not attend because they were still angry at him.

"I'll see that they do," Markus promised.

"I'll need six pallbearers too, and I don't know where they'll come from."

"I'll see to it."

"Would you mind being one?"

"Honoured!"

"And I wouldn't mind someone buying a toast and drinking to me."

"I'll do that too."

"That's about all I'd want." George smiled lamely at this. He had come and gone like a shadow the last fifteen years. The ships and their livelihood had gone from the river for good. All that internecine play in the holds and at water level, over who worked or did not work, the rows over who got on and who didn't, did not matter one bit now.

After a time, George gave Markus the key to his hotel room.

Markus would go to this room, on the second floor of the hotel, and feed George's budgies. There was no light. The place was dank and musty. A plaque on the mirror was for a softball team George once had been part of, as assistant manager or coach. His discoloured window looked over a gravel lot with an oil barrel and a shed. Ice had by now crept into the puddles. There were two pornographic tapes, *Pumping Irene* and *Little Oral Annie*, on the windowsill.

"Quien es?" Markus thought. When he went back to the hospital he told Morrissey that everyone was somehow in the same position over the miscarriage of justice that had happened so long ago. Then he quoted William James: "Acceptance of what has happened is the first step to overcoming the consequences of any misfortune."

Whether George understood this, Markus did not know.

"When Joel died I had to go and identify the body," Markus said. "Not one of the warriors or anyone else went to his funeral. By then, at the end, they even stopped him from going to see Isaac. He got thirty-four thousand or something from the lawsuit, and two months later he was walking along the highway, not enough for a taxi."

Then he said: "I can solve the second case – if you help me solve the first, Mr. Morrissey."

"If you solve the second case, I will tell you about the envelope I got from Brice," George whispered.

"Oh – the envelope. Well, in point of fact you have just told me."

3

One afternoon, twenty-one years after the deaths of Hector Penniac and Roger Savage and Little Joe Barnaby, the smell of cold salt and tar coming from the shore, Isaac Snow sat in his comfortable chair in the living room of his house, with the door opened and evening coming on. He had a Jacuzzi and a swimming pool. He had a corkboard on which articles that had been written about him, and tributes given him, were posted. Behind his house there was a huge lawn that ran back to a large hardwood ridge, where many an outbuilding sat. There was a smell of newness and lime on the land, even in the side lane. All of this suggested Isaac's status now.

He saw Markus Paul coming to the door.

"Hello!" he yelled out as the younger man entered. "Hide the drugs – the cops are here!" he shouted. "Come in and see me." His voice was that of a man used to having his way.

Isaac half stood and reached out his hand in a laboured way, while holding his body up with his other hand clutching the armrest. That very movement, impeded as it was, showed him to have been once strong and resilient, and of his own mind, since the death of his father to win back for the natives their identity. Markus shook his hand quickly and sat down when the hand beckoned him to do so.

"What's the honour?" Isaac asked with sudden mock gravity.

"Nothing – come to see how you were," Markus said. "You've given up your band meetings."

"Just until I get back on my feet," Isaac said.

He asked Markus if he would like a beer.

"No, not today," Markus said.

"Diet?"

"Diet." Markus smiled. In fact, he was thinking that this was the first thing he remembered Isaac saying to him – "Beer?" – the night he had visited Isaac's house after Hector's funeral. Then Isaac had said: "Come on, yer grandfather won't mind." It was the first beer Markus had ever drunk.

"Do you ever think of Joel?" Markus asked now.

Isaac looked at him a second.

"Ah, poor Joel . . . The booze, eh – you think?"

That summer was never mentioned anymore. There had been numerous investigations, and they had all been closed for lack of witnesses.

But now that it had all quieted down – now that the world had gone on by twenty-one years, and so much was forgotten – perhaps it was time to revisit these things. Yet why him, why Markus Paul? Why not someone else? It was as if in the entire world of comfort and relative ease a man suddenly chooses to go away and protect a bit of jungle from criminals, or to take on the mob.

Perhaps he would be called a traitor.

Still, Markus reasoned, he had known many traitors in his life, some of them white and some of them First Nation, and he was not about to pick one kind over the other.

Isaac was loved and honoured now.

He had addressed convocations and been honoured by the premier, just the year before, with the Order of New Brunswick. He had been given an honorary doctorate by Saint Michael's. All the academics tried to get their picture taken with him, for their proxy fight for justice. Isaac was to receive the Order of Canada. He told Markus this and smiled. "I'm a bona fide saint!"

Markus smiled.

Markus had not come to talk about the lumber boat and the death of Hector Penniac. That was another matter. This visit was about Roger. "Do you mind if I smoke?" he said.

"Go ahead!"

He lit a cigarette and looked out the window.

It was about the rifle that had killed Little Joe Barnaby. There was something he had been trying to remember – and he remembered it when he looked at the bullet fragment taken from Billy the Kid.

"Quien es?"

All of a sudden Markus had realized what he had witnessed when he was eight years old.

He remembered his father David, that night deer hunting, angry because he had picked up the wrong bullets and had tried for over an hour to fit them into his rifle.

David had .30-30 bullets that night – and a .32 Winchester rifle. That is, two rifles, two bullets, almost identical – almost.

It was on the tip of Markus's tongue to bring up Hector Penniac, but Isaac looked at him as if to say, *I know*.

Or at least this is what Markus thought. He shrugged and smiled slightly.

Isaac said: "It is something I still think about – all of them." He said it softly, as if he had mellowed into his situation now. "Even poor Roger – holding out over something so insane. Losing his girl, and his life – over a drop of logs that might well have been an accident."

He was silent a moment, took his feet out of his slippers and then slipped them back in again. Then he said, while staring at his slippers:

"Little Joe – you know when he played peewee hockey he was never able to score a goal? So I went to the players one day when he wasn't there and I said, in a big speech, Boys, now you know Little Joe is out with an injury to his big toe and won't be back for two games, but he has never scored a goal – so wouldn't it be nice if you guys could try to set him up, get the puck to him, so he could score one goal – so he could look back and say after his career is over, I scored a goal when I played hockey? And Markus, they all looked at me for a long time and said, Mr. Snow, we have been trying to do that since the start of the year – we have been doing all we can! Every game, we say: let's set up Little Joe, let's get Little Joe the puck. Even the goalie is in on it and says, 'I will stand out of the way to let him score – if you allow us an even up.' But it just doesn't happen. It's an impossibility, Mr. Snow. He misses the passes or shoots wide and falls down." Isaac said, "The little fellow never did get a goal. He always said he would next year, remember?"

Markus nodded. His eyes welled. His lungs ached as he took a drag, and so he dragged deeper. Snow had started to fall. Snow would clear everything up. The bay would make ice, and in a sudden, incomprehensible reverie he trembled as he remembered his father and him in happy times. They were going to build a smelt shed on the ice. They never did. His father had four medals from Vietnam, and left the Bronze Star to him.

"Do you ever think of how it happened – I mean, if it could have happened in some other way?"

"Not too much anymore," Isaac said now. "It was a bad thing – it got out of hand, but nothing can be done about it now."

"I suppose not," Markus said.

His father David had gone to Vietnam because he wanted to prove himself to Amos. It was easy to do. A First Nations man just went across the border to Maine. A different David had come home.

"It's all forgot now – no one much remembers."

Markus shrugged. He looked at Isaac and said, "So many things have remained unanswered about all of this."

Isaac shrugged too, and then looked out the window as if contemplating something.

After a pause, Markus, without knowing he would bring it up so soon, said, "Can I see the .30-30?"

"What, my old .30-30? Why?"

"I just want to show you something. I have a rifle in the car I want to show you too. And we will compare both rifles for a moment."

"Ah, I knew it – come to shoot me!" Isaac laughed.

"No. I would be ashamed to lay a hand on a great man," Markus said.

Isaac shrugged as if he didn't believe him or was embarrassed. He spoke to his wife in Micmac: "Bring out the old rifle in my closet – not the one in the case, the little one without the scope."

And as she went and got the rifle, Markus went outside and brought in the rifle that had belonged once to his father and then to Roger Savage. He held it lightly in his fingers like a man who knows rifles does.

"This has been damaged," he said. "But I polished it over and over, and cleaned it, and stroked it up. You see, it belonged to my dad – "

"Amos?"

"No, no – David. He used to take me hunting deer. Then it was given to Roger Savage. It was his weapon that night. I kept trying to think of something about it – but you see, it was all damaged, and they never took the time to even consider it wasn't the weapon."

Markus took the .30-30 from Isaac's wife, a dour, small woman who had never interfered with anything her husband did and whose reluctance to speak or be a party to life Markus had never understood.

"Here," he said. He took out two cartridges from his jacket pocket and stood them on the coffee table. "What do you see, Isaac?"

"I see two bullets."

"The same calibre?"

"Sure," Isaac said.

Markus handed the shells to him, and Isaac studied them. "Almost identical – .30-30?" he asked.

293

"Yeah – almost identical," Markus said. "Almost."

He took Isaac's rifle. He fit the first shell into the chamber, and then the second. Both fit into the chamber.

"You won't believe why I became a police officer."

"To protect the nation," Isaac said, partly as a question, partly as an answer.

"Yes. But the reason – well, someone killed our dog when I was a boy. They did it because they disliked my family during the barricade. Old thing, lame and blind, had never done anything to anyone except wag its tail."

"Someone killed your dog," Isaac said. He gave a slight start, and blushed.

Markus nodded. He didn't say anything else but kept almost mirthful eyes on Isaac, half-ashamed of having to mention such a thing in front of a person he considered a brave man. He took the second shell out of the rifle, and holding both of them in his hand, he handed the .30-30 back to Isaac, and picked up Roger Savage's rifle.

"So that's why you became RCMP," Isaac said, his left hand trembling involuntarily.

"That's it," Markus said. "In some ways I'm still looking for the man who killed my poor old dog because he disliked my poor old grandfather's stand during the barricade. Anyway, both those bullets fit into the .30-30."

"Yes, they do," Isaac said.

Markus then picked up Roger Savage's rifle and pulled the lever down.

"This rifle, the one Roger had that night, lay away for twenty years, in the cellar of the RCMP office. And for twenty years I was sure something was amiss, but I was too stupid. Then I went down to Texas, and I saw some bullet fragments taken from Billy the Kid."

"Really – "

"Yes."

"You saw bullets out of Billy the Kid."

"Yes – and suddenly it all made sense. Pat Garrett's bullets

294

made sense of a case a hundred years later. It made so much sense that I started to shake. I couldn't stop shaking for three days. I was like a big baby. Well, that's what Samantha called me anyways – a big baby – so I guess I am."

Markus took the two shells that both fit into Isaac's .30-30. He put the first one in the chamber of Roger's rifle, still with a cigarette in his mouth, and his eyes half closed because of the smoke, cradling the rifle in his arm, resting against his thighs.

"This bullet fits?"

"Yes, it does," Isaac's wife said suddenly, and quite convinced of something.

There was another silence. Isaac and his wife watched Markus intently.

Markus removed the shell, and very carefully took the second one, the one that had also fit into Isaac's rifle, and attempted to put it in the chamber of Roger's rifle.

It did not fit. He lifted it out, showed it to them, holding it up as if he were a magician, and then tried to put it in again.

It did not fit.

"What's wrong with it?" Collette Snow asked, as if the magician's trick was about to be revealed. She smiled suddenly, and in the flash of her smile was tension, as if this was a moment twenty-one years in the making. She looked at her husband, who glanced over at her.

"Nothing is wrong," Markus said. "But this second bullet is a .30-30 calibre, and it will not fit into the chamber of Roger's beautiful little rifle because Roger's rifle is a .32 Winchester. A .32 Winchester is almost identical to a .30-30, but it is not one. That was the difference between Dad's rifle, this beautiful rifle which was given to Roger, and the other rifles around here. Roger had a .32, but almost everyone assumed it to be a .30-30."

He said this slowly, and looked about. In the corner was the article written by Mr. Max Doran: "Isaac Snow: Profile in Courage."

295

"What we need to know is that both a .30-30 shell and a .32 shell will fit into the chamber of a .30-30 rifle," Markus said. "But the .30-30 shell will not fit into a .32 chamber. That is because the .30-30 shell is ever so slightly larger. Otherwise, both rifles are identical. Roger's Winchester was damaged, and no one was smart enough to check it. But I have to ask, how could Roger Savage have fired a .30-30 bullet from a .32 Winchester into the stomach of poor Little Joe Barnaby when I have just shown it cannot fit?"

"What does that mean, though?" Mrs. Snow asked.

"Little Joe was killed with a .30-30. bullet." Markus put his cigarette into the ashtray. "That bullet couldn't have been fired from Roger Savage's .32. It had to come from a .30-30," he said. "It had to come from the back of the house at the same time Roger was firing from the front of the house – Roger was firing into the air, because he wanted to hurt no one. Joel must have fired your rifle. He was really only trying to scare Roger, I am sure of it. He certainly was not trying to hit Little Joe – and didn't realize he did. Maybe not for a year or two. Then it came to him suddenly like a revelation. Though he couldn't admit it – and within ten years he was dead of misery and shame. For Little Joe was his son."

He put down the Winchester on the hardwood floor as carefully as he could and picked up the .30-30. He took out a bullet fragment that he had taken from the evidence locker.

"This is the .30-30 rifle that Joel had. Your rifle, Isaac. It killed Joe Barnaby," he said, looking over at the man. "This is the rifle that killed my little friend – yes sir! This is the .30:30 bullet that killed him."

"Why didn't the dumb-as-dirt RCMP ever figure that out!" Isaac said.

Markus looked at the rifle with a peculiar sense of self-affirmation.

"Well, sir – well, sir – yes, sir, they just have," Markus answered.

Markus took Roger's Winchester and went back to his car. He sat for a long time.

Then suddenly he decided to go and visit Roger Savage's grave because no one ever did.

The grave was overgrown, at the edge of the trees. It didn't have a tombstone, only a small marker, with the initials and dates: R.F.S October 5, 1962–August 31, 1985. He stared at it for 10 minutes or more.

Soon there would be whiteouts and a blizzard. The bay would be making ice.

Milton, Markus Paul remembered from *Paradise Lost*, suggested that politics had started in hell – hell is where it became fashionable. In this hell, such as it was, people cozied up to ideas they didn't even believe in – wrote columns about things they knew were false to promote an idea of justice they themselves didn't share.

He didn't know why that mattered anymore.

Samantha and he maybe even got married because of that – because of it all – because they wanted to prove to each other they could love each other. And they did, but at least for them, not in the way they needed to.

He went back to his car. He took out his makings and put them on his lap, took out a paper and rolled himself a cigarette carefully, so the tobacco wouldn't be too tight. Then he snapped a match and lit it, and sat there and smoked, listening to Hank Williams sing about a cheatin' heart.

Yes, he thought, we all have one.

A few days later, Samantha called Markus back about the X-rays.

"It is not good, Markus, love," she said. "It is not at all good. You have spots on both lungs. I want you back here tonight. I want to schedule biopsies in Saint John."

"I cannot do it yet," he said. "I will be in – I promise."

"Why the hell did you smoke?" she said, suddenly starting to cry. "Why in Christ did you smoke – ?"

"I don't know, Sam. Why be Irish if you can't be stupid?"

"You stop – you stop what you are doing and get in here – now – or I'll have you arrested!"

"Sure, love, sure."

He hung up. Then his cell phone rang. It was her, but when he went to answer it he accidentally pushed the wrong something or other, something he had never figured out, and cut her off.

"Christ she'll be angry at me now."

He went in three days later, sheepish for having hung up on her. It was a cold day, and he sat in the small examination room off the outpatient ward, shivering, and she asked how his trip was.

"Fine," he said. "I bought you a present."

"Good. Where is it?"

"I left it on the bus at Little Bighorn."

She looked at him a second.

"I want you to have your left lung looked at in Saint John," Sam said to him. She had the stethoscope on his chest, just above the tattooed *Sky*. She was looking above his forehead to somewhere. "I want you to see a Dr. Moses – he is a cancer specialist." She took the stethoscope away, and folding it, said: "There are things we can do now. I think your right lung is okay – it's the left lung I'm worried about."

"When?"

"Today."

"Today?"

"Do you want to live?"

He put his T-shirt back on and picked up his jacket.

"I can't go today. I have budgies to feed."

"Cancer rates here are higher than anywhere in the province," Sam told him. "They are twice as high here as a lot of places in Canada."

He told her he would quit smoking, but lit one in the parking lot, it was the urge.

The trouble was that Markus knew police officers. They were as susceptible to rumour and ego as everyone else. They would get a lead in a case, and each new piece of information they would try to fit together, like the puzzles Amos used to do, so it would form into what they already believed to be true. Rumours in the office helped as well.

So suddenly the man who was too scared to come out of his house was the man they wanted. But the trouble was, the prosecution couldn't charge Roger and the police begged off – and finally, in 1987, allowed the case to die. So when Amos went to them with all his information, they did not want to look at it again.

The case had been dead now twenty years.

He went back to his apartment and lay down. He listened to "Unchain My Heart" by Joe Cocker. He liked milkshakes and so he had bought himself a strawberry on the way home. Sometimes he would buy vanilla. He had bought them in Texas too, and Arizona, but liked the ones he got at the Kingsway restaurant on the King George Highway in Newcastle best of all. One day long ago he and Sky had gone to a sock hop and shared a milkshake from the Kingsway and he had been going there ever since, thinking that she would come there just once more to get a milkshake too. She was so innocent then, and so was he, and in love, too, he supposed, for that moment in time.

Today he had no choice. He had to go take care of George Morrissey's budgies. So he would take care of the budgies.

"What are the names of those birds?" Markus had asked George during the last visit in his quiet Micmac voice.

"They are called Number One and Number Two."

"Good. Are they easy to tell apart?"

"No, pretty confusing. And you have to clean the cage."

"Good."

"And they like their heads patted."

"Good."

"But they aren't half the budgies I had before."

"I see."

"Those were good budgies ... You take care of the budgies and I will give you the envelope."

Markus looked at him. "Thank you."

"I was going to burn it . . . but – that might not be right."

4

Markus went down to Saint John and rented a room near the hospital, and for the next while he came and went through the lanes without meeting many people. He went to the malls, and sat alone in the big common below the library, or wandered through the streets looking at the buildings, or sat near the wharf entertained by seagulls.

This is where his own ancestors came from, those before the Micmac some 3,500 years ago – the Paint. And he thought of this, too.

He had brought the budgies with him, in the big pockets of his coat. Dr. Moses, who was an Iraqi, gave him a series of tests and scheduled a biopsy.

"We will find out how long you have."

"Good. There is no expiration date stamped on my big toe," Markus said.

"When did you start smoking?" Dr. Moses asked.

Strange that this question had become incessantly bothersome to Markus now. That is, here he was trying to quit and this Iraqi was trying to remind him when he had started.

"I was three," he said.

"Pardon me – you were thirty?"

"No sir, I was not 30 – I was smart enough by 30 to try to quit. I was three."

"How could you smoke at three?"

"I didn't inhale until I was eight," Markus said, as a compromise of some sort.

A blizzard had come in from the bay.

He walked back to his room, with his jean jacket on. No one would ever know by looking at him that he was an RCMP officer who had been a bodyguard to Prince Edward, or that he could stifle the attack of five men in fifteen seconds. In fact he rarely thought of that himself.

He lay down in the dark, in the half grey of a Saint John Blizzard. He didn't feel sick. He felt stronger now then ever. He wanted to get back to work and solve it all. But he had to go for the biopsy, and that wouldn't be for a while.

Markus was now very sorry he had once knocked Joel Ginnish out. Ginnish had wanted to prove something after he lost all his money. He had said he was going to turn pro.

He remembered how Ginnish had slapped some boys around when they were trying to be brave. Perhaps this is what he remembered most. And Markus had finally stepped into the ring with him.

"You're in my office now," Ginnish said.

Markus moved his head and hit him once and knocked him out. And now he was sorry he had done this.

Ginnish had started saying he was going to murder every-one on the reserve after the money was gone. Markus couldn't bring himself to arrest him and sent a white officer instead.

Ginnish had smiled and shrugged,

"They all betrayed me," he had said. "That Markus especially – he betrays everyone."

Markus had looked at the pictures of Roger's old house, and he knew what had happened. Joel Ginnish had wanted to hit the propane tank, or the sign Roger had planted in defiance. He couldn't fire straight. Markus knew that. Joel Ginnish never hit a thing on the first shot. And he had fired high and to the right just as Little Joe was running toward the house.

This is what Markus had suspected since September, when he had sighted in his .306.

"Someday you will figure it all out," Amos had said. For he himself, as an old man, had already done so.

Both had sighted enough rifles to know.

Old George had not opened the envelope. He was too frightened. But he did not destroy it either. He was too frightened.

Brice still sent George free birdseed for his budgies.

"Why?" asked Markus.

"Well, first of all he likes budgies, and second, I am his mother's brother – and was the one who cared for him."

George Morrissey could not bring himself to turn this envelope over to the police. But since both Brice and Morrissey always believed that Roger had killed Little Joe Barnaby, why open this letter and put others in trouble? So the letter, which was never supposed to be in Markus's possession when Brice was alive, came into his possession now.

In his room in Saint John, Markus had nine hours without a cigarette, and began to pace the floor. He paced the floor for a long time, until his cell phone rang. It was Sam Dulse, who had promised to phone him every night to see if he was smoking, and to come down to visit him on the weekend.

He didn't pick it up.

"One more cigarette more or less won't kill me," he said instead.

He lit a cigarette and lay back on the couch and watched the hockey game on the small black-and-white TV provided. He knew poor Sam had been having an affair long before he and she had broken up. He was never home, he supposed – and the Savage case had consumed most of his life without his knowing. He had heard from friends about this fellow doctor that she drove back and forth to work with. This self-aggrandizing doctor who believed those in his care were in his control.

303

Markus shrugged and said to himself, forget it.

It had taken him six months to mention it to her. They were in the living room, and she had just come home from work. He remembered it was raining, in July, just before they were to go on vacation. He stared at the flowers out in the box as rain came and laced the window.

He simply mentioned the man's name. She jumped up from the couch and ran to the bathroom and locked the door. It was as if he had hit her – although he never would.

He left the next day, with a little suitcase, and found the apartment near his reserve. She tried to make it up.

"It was over long ago," she kept saying. "He never mattered to me. You do. It was a mistake!"

"Mistakes happen, for sure," Markus said. At any rate he did not go home.

Everyone goes away.

He was supposed to go to a support group about his smoking. Samantha had registered him. It was held in the palliative care unit in Saint John Regional Hospital. He didn't get around to it.

George had given him the letter – if he promised to feed the budgies. So what else could he do?

For the last year Markus had known where Doran lived, in a small house in a hardscrabble part of lower Saint John.

Markus had brought a book from his own bookshelf down to Saint John for Doran to read. He had searched for the book for a long while, and discovered it at the very end of the third row on one of his bookshelves just before leaving for the hospital.

And so in November of 2006 he brought the little odd book down to give to Doran, along with Brice's envelope, of course.

But after he had arrived in Saint John, Markus discovered something else about Doran. Doran had a disabled daughter and lived with her alone. His wife had left him and the child some years ago, though she would come back to visit with great excitement and concern every year or so.

Each day Doran worked at a call centre. Then he would go home at night by bus from Union Street, through the gloom of the city, and pick his child up from a caregiver on Manawagonish Road.

Years ago, Little Joe and Sky had spent all day making a blueberry pie for Max Doran, the man who had come to help them, they believed. Little Joe was the taster and walked about the kitchen wearing big yellow oven mitts. It was Sky's first pie. Then they left it at Doran's door.

If this envelope was opened, thought Markus, what would become of Doran now?

But if Markus did not open this letter – minding that the letter actually said something – what would that mean for Amos, or more importantly, for Roger? Could Markus change that – could he even attempt to?

And Brice Peel: What would become of that thin, harmless man with the stooped gait who worked in a pet store in Saint John, in one of those terrible malls, endless in Canada, that have no light or mercy or freedom from anything; Brice with his beloved rabbits and hares? These were the things – the rabbits and hares – that had cured his seizures. Would opening this letter bring attention to him as a person who had said nothing, who had helped hide a crime? Even his age at that time would be no guarantee of immunity from blame. Would this letter he wanted opened only when he was dead put him into the glare again? Yes, it would. And would that bring the seizures back?

Markus took time to find Brice. And when he found him, he saw that Brice was obsequious and adrift – a vagabond who showered kids with stories about the rabbits and turtles in his care, and had hauled his sleeves down over wrists that he had cut, the stitches leaving a grey, obtrusive gash.

More than anything, watching Brice, Markus wondered what would be the use.

Brice had used an envelope with the address of the pet store on it. It was not the brightest thing to do, but it was in some way comforting to Markus to know Brice was still that gullible – which probably meant he never in his life intended harm to anyone at all. His attempted suicide had not worked, and he had asked George for the letter back. But George could neither send it back nor destroy it.

Markus bought a birdcage from Brice, but Brice did not know who he was.

It was as if in the struggle for Markus's own life, the places where the answers would be given about his past life would soon be made available.

For he was now being told what to do by everyone.

Don't smoke; don't drink; eat vegetables.

But just when they thought he was in his bed for the night – just when Sam said she would drive down in the morning and be with him – Markus disappeared.

He went to the oldest part of the west side of Saint John, through small, broken-up streets, past little shabby houses, carrying a birdcage, and two budgies in his pockets.

Doran was surprised to see him – or maybe not.

"I have a present for your daughter," Markus said, "budgie birds – "

He thought: "What a thing to bring after twenty-one years. Yes, he just might take me to be completely insane."

But he stood at the door with the cage and the birds in his hand, and Number One hopped back and forth and Number Two sat silent. Doran after all these years was hard to recognize, and he didn't recognize Markus instantly either. Then he said: "Oh my god – good to see you!"

It was as if the gulf of years had suddenly been closed, like the closing of a time warp in some exaggerated story of the universe.

Max Doran, too, was very ill, with his heart. His little girl did not know. But Markus did. He smiled at the man, and stepped in with his little birds.

When he went in, a little girl looked at him. There was a smell of enclosed space, and the rooms were very small – smaller than any Markus had grown up in. There were a few mementoes on the wall. There was a bundle of laundry in the hall, an old vacuum cleaner. Doran had been cleaning the house.

Markus had brought the girl a milkshake and the budgies. Her name was Heidi. When he entered the house, she was sitting in the middle of the hallway in her wheelchair watching him intently. She wheeled forward slightly, then stopped, her little face one of mysterious charm. Then came forward again. Markus saw that, to her, her wheelchair seemed as natural as his walk did to him. She knew who he was – her daddy had spoken of him, as being from that reserve up north and having become famous. Markus followed her to her room, and he put the cage up and placed some bird food in the dish.

There were pictures in the room of the girl and her daddy at the Atlantic Exhibition. Doran was holding her up on the merry-go-round. They were both waving at the camera. Yes, Markus told her, he knew her dad.

Heidi's favourite hockey player was Sydney Crosby. She had his picture in a scrapbook. She showed Markus her goldfish and guppies and let him feed them as well. The water was cloudy. But Markus told her that he knew someone who knew all about fish and turtles and birds and filters for tanks and had healed pigeons when he was young. "Do you want him to come here and help you set up the tanks, and teach you about the budgies?"

"Yes – sure!" the girl said with an open gaze.

Doran listened to this at the door to Heidi's room, and watched Markus without comment. In the long corridor were the photos he had taken that long-ago day – the eagle, the two Parrish girls hugging, Little Joe making a face at the camera, the stop sign at the end of the road.

Doran had lost weight. Gone was the straw hat. Like

Markus, he still smoked. Those little cigarillos that he'd always liked. He offered Markus one.

"Well, it can't hurt," Markus said.

"You've become famous – travelling with the Governor General, Prince Edward and all of that. I keep up with you." Doran smiled. "I keep up with Gordon Young, too – a real journalist. That story with the navy he did – nothing in Canada better last year – and now reporting from Afghanistan!"

Quien es? Markus thought. Doran could have been as great a journalist as any. "Mary Cyr is on her third husband," he commented. "I think one – that cabinet minister – used to beat her up."

"Yes, I know too many ghosts," Doran said.

Then Markus began to talk of things seemingly inconsequential. Of the little adobe village in Chile, of raw blubber he had eaten at a ceremony in the North, of the site of Custer's last stand. He stayed for a long time, talking of this and that. He learned that Doran was on three kinds of medication, that he was worried about the child. "We should quit smoking, you and I," Markus said.

"Sure, if I take my meds and do my exercise, I will be okay." Doran smiled. "But then, what cures a broken heart?"

Suddenly Markus wasn't even sure why he had come, or why he was saying what he was. Doran tried to play host, offered him an Alpine, and tried to remember pleasant things about everyone, even about Joel and Andy. Sometimes he breathed heavily for no reason.

Doran asked about everyone, and hoped everyone was fine. But he knew the whole time that this visit had to do with the favour he'd promised Markus the night long ago when Markus had delivered him across the river. If he was here to collect, whatever he might want, Max was hoping to oblige him.

Yet Markus hesitated, because he knew that if Doran opened this envelope and then wrote a book – and told the truth – he would be sued and held in contempt by others. But, he decided, that was the chance he would have to take. So, after a length of time, Markus decided to talk about what Doran might or might not want to acknowledge. It was a strange topic: the condition of their souls.

"What? The condition of our souls?" Max Doran said. "What do you mean?"

Yes, thought Markus, you go into a man's house you have not seen in twenty-one years, carrying budgie birds, and suddenly begin to talk about the condition of the soul, when both of you look like you should be in hospital beds. He would take you for a lay preacher, a Pentecostal enabler, gone insane.

"Do you write anymore?" Markus asked. "What if I have come to collect the favor you promised at the rivers edge and ask you to write something fully and completely? Make you a great writer once again – "

"Oh no," Doran said, "I just work at a call centre. I have a little girl to take care of – so here I am." He smiled. "I can't afford to write – who would take care of Heidi?" he asked, almost incredulous at the suggestion. But then he said, "I still have a book in me – if I could get it out. But it always seems to falter somehow." He smiled wistfully, perhaps having said it in so many places and so many times, he did not believe it anymore himself. Perhaps he said it not to comfort himself but in some way to comfort Markus, just as he had comforted his little girl with the idea that he would someday write the book he spoke about (and had even, haltingly, started).

Markus wished the case he had spent so many years on could be over. And but for the idea of – well, it was strange one, but except for the idea of *sin*, it would be over. This is what Markus said now.

For if something else had happened then hat people think happened, Markus said, then the case was not yet solved. The bigot of the Bartibog did not really ever exist, just like old Mallory or those monsters of our youth on long walks home, and we must say he did not exist, for the memory not only of Roger but of gentle Hector Penniac and Little Joe. Other bigots might exist, and they are the ones that must be held accountable and come out from the shade of our youth to stand in the light and be recognized for who they are.

Doran simply said: "I'm getting a cold – I get one every fall."

"I know," Markus said, "but maybe you would like to do a real book – a book that you could really write. What do they call it – a blockbuster!"

They sat in silence for a couple of minutes, Markus trying to think of something else to say and rubbing his face. He lit a cigarette. "I probably have cancer," he said, "so I shouldn't be smoking – find it hard to quit. So you with your heart and me with my lungs should quit together."

Doran looked at him, startled. Markus winked. Then he took a book from his big pocket and put it on the table, his large hand almost covering the soft cover.

It was the Oxford University Press's 1985 edition of Joseph Conrad's *The Shadow Line*. Markus had sometimes thought about the fact that perhaps it was being printed at the time the struggle over Roger Savage was happening on the river. But what he said to Doran was that it was a novel about the sea in the nineteenth century. "Have you read Conrad?" he asked.

"Too gloomy."

"Well let me say something about *The Shadow Line*."

He spoke about this book for a while, for about a half-hour. He had read it in his youth just after Amos died. And it was about youth who are for the first time confronted with the harsh reality of the world – events that will turn idealism around, like a becalmed ship. It is a very funny book too, in an absurdist way, Markus said, and he trusted people more who understood that, and thought of people less who did not. He paused for a while, not knowing what else to say.

Then he said, "This is what happened – in our case. The

310

contest was not between Roger Savage and us. That was the secondary show, the secondary battle. The primary war was between you and you, or me and me, or my grandfather and my grandfather. Isaac against Isaac. Joel against Joel." He was almost whispering now. "That is a strange thing. It was *The Shadow Line* – and suddenly truth became untruth, and we encountered sin. If we even believe in sin."

"Believe in what?"

"In sin – believe in sin. Do you believe in sin?"

"I – I – don't know. I suppose I have to in some way."

"Oh, well – I do, too," Markus said. "Now more than ever."

He continued: "Joel Ginnish is dead. He was killed in 1997. Amos is dead. Mrs. Francis is dead. Andy, my friend who killed my old dog, is dead." Then he whispered, choking up: "If we waited until everyone died, would that be better?"

Doran shrugged. "I do not know, Markus," he said quietly. But he was saying "I do not know" because he had been running from wanting to know for many years.

"It is up to you," Markus said, "to find out. I can give you the start of the book, but you have to collaborate with someone, and you have to say, even to your daughter – even to her – that you made a mistake and that may have caused a life to be taken, and that is a terrible duty for us to get right. Me and you, we have to get it right – to get rid of the sin. We will be partners, okay?" He smiled. His lips trembled slightly, and his voice faltered. "White man and red – partners, okay?" Then he took the envelope, placed it down beside the Conrad book. He took out a pen and his little notebook.

"I am going to give you his address. He won't know you are going to phone him or want see him – if you do – if you decide to do so. He won't want to talk to you, maybe. But I'm going to leave it up to you and him. Then you have to decide to finish the story the way it should have been done years ago. I am putting my confidence in you that you will decide to finish this story now – for me and for you. To keep the promise you made to me years ago."

He put the piece of paper in Doran's hand. "Not in spite of your child but for her sake – and not in spite of my reserve but for its sake. It will be very hard on you if you do this. I of course will need the envelope back, no matter what you decide."

Markus stood, and went toward the door. He was tired, and his ribs and his lungs hurt. The little girl came out to say goodbye. He saw her energetic bright face and thought of Little Joe Barnaby – and a dozen other little boys and girls in that adobe village in Chile. He patted her head with his large hand and bent and kissed her cheek, and placed an American silver dollar in her hand.

5

It was before Markus left Saint John Regional that they came to see him.

He was in a sitting room looking out over the hills in the distance, beyond where the Bay of Fundy must have been. It was cold and he could feel this cold through the window. He wore a hospital gown and huge slippers and was drinking a bottle of iced tea. He had a nicotine patch on his upper right arm. He had had the biopsy. He had not had a cigarette in a week (well one). He heard the elevator door open. Behind him, as always in hospitals in mid-afternoon, it was still dark, and the corridors were filled with pushcarts, filled with levels of things, and somewhere there was the sound of a telephone ringing, and somewhere else some man speaking.

He turned, and Max Doran and Brice Peel were standing there, Brice with the letter in his hand.

For some reason Max had his hand on Brice's neck, as if to guide him forward, an action that may have been required more for Max Doran than for Brice – a kind of civil mentoring that he was now obligated and determined to fulfill. They had brought back the envelope.

"You have to read this," Doran said. "You are the one he wanted to bring it to. I don't know how to prove it, that's all. But I will do nothing until you do prove it, and then I will write what I have to – that's my pledge. I will file the damn story!" Here his lips trembled slightly with determination and dignity.

Then Brice handed the envelope to Markus, with his arm

pushed straight out. Brice looked at him like a scared bird might. He was still little Brice with the big ears and thin, knobby knees, a rural boy caught up in a world no longer rural. Just like the First Nations world, too.

Markus suddenly remembered a pathetic old dog licking his hand one night – and looked down at his wrist, to see the scar from the rabbit snare he had got when he was thirteen. They'd killed that dog with rocks. Even when they were throwing the rocks, it had tried to wag its burr-covered tail.

He said he would read the letter, and act upon it, but not that day. He would go back home before he did. He would wait for the right moment.

Markus did not get back home for another week. The spot on his left lung was benign. The one on his right lung was not a spot in the lung, but blood outside the lung itself that had coagulated after he had been hit in the ribs in a brawl one night.

The unopened letter was in his possession and the weather had turned cold. Snow was falling and the world was white and even, the roads to and from long and almost forgotten. This little place, this little reserve, was at the end of nowhere at all.

He snared a rabbit, skinned it off and left it hanging over the sink. He was chopping onions and carrots to make a stew when he decided to phone Isaac.

"When do you get your Order of Canada?" he said.

"Next week."

Markus didn't speak.

"Why?" Isaac asked.

"I would like you to get it," he said. "I think you deserve it."

"Thank you."

"Have you ever visited your father's grave?" Markus asked.

"No – I never did."

314

"I suggest you find time to visit it, and request the body be brought home. I seriously suggest you visit Roger Savage's grave – and say a prayer."

There was a pause on the other end. Markus hung up without saying goodbye.

All the goodbyes save one had been said.

That night, alone in his apartment, Markus opened the letter, sitting on the couch in the living room with a beer on the table and his arms on his knees. He realized as he opened the letter that he was unfolding an event from ago that had caused everything since. That had caused Amos's heartbreak, and his own – and Sky's. He stared at it a long time, looked at the number of pages, and then found his reading glasses.

Then he took a drink of beer. He finished the beer and went to the kitchen and opened another. Then he went back to the couch and sat in the exact same position.

It was written in Brice's hand, and filled with spelling mistakes. This is what it said:

The first thing Brice wrote was that he remembered Roger coming into the yard ten minutes late, just as Hector Penniac was climbing the gangplank. Roger ran down to the yard and was out of breath when he got there. It was Hector's first boat. No one was sure if he could handle it. So they put him in the fourth hold with Bill Monk and his brother Tanker. Brice's father was the other man in the hold – he was in the cubby below. The other two, Bill and Tanker, would move forward at the end of the day to the middle hold. That is why Roger hung around. He was hoping when the fourth hold was full his seniority would give him another day and a half. (And that is why he had sent the extra load to the fourth hold instead of hooking to the third – to fill the fourth hold faster.)

Hector had fine hands and delicate features, but he was willing to work, and he offered gum to everyone just after he had climbed down the ladder. The name *Lutheran* was written on the inside of that hold for some reason, and Brice

315

remembered it years later. He remembered the bulwark was painted brown instead of green as it was along the other holds. He remembered too how insufferably hot the day became – which made people only wonder why Roger was hanging around, and then allowed an accusation when he hooked to the fourth hold. Tanker was hungover as well, and Bill Monk was in a hurry to get the fourth hold done and move on, and so he took some amphetamines that he had on him, to work at a faster pace. There were two water buckets in the hold, one on the left, the other on the right nearer the cubby where his father, Angus Peel, worked.

Brice remembered that some of the men were talking about the stag film *Little Oral Annie* that George Morrissey had, and how she sucked good cock. Bill Monk said he had problems with his stomach the last week. That is when Brice remembered Hector said he was going to be a doctor and maybe Bill Monk shouldn't take so many amphetamines. They didn't like this comment, especially Bill Monk, and felt it a presumption to have an Indian talk to them about being a doctor. But Hector with his refined manners did not know he had made a mistake, crossing the line talking about civil matters to uncivil men. What was more troubling is the conversation had started because Bill Monk was worried about his own doctor telling him he had to take a certain kind of pill for his stomach. It was in some way an intrusion on his own limited knowledge.

So when Hector moved too soon to pulp hook a log and it dropped near Tanker's boot, Tanker gave him a shove, a small, unpleasant but un-noteworthy one.

"Watch that, sweetie pie," he said, "or you'll need a doctor before you become one."

"A medicine man," Angus Peel erupted from down in the cubby. They all laughed.

Hector smiled and offered an apology, but when Bill Monk asked why he said 'sweetie pie', Tanker answered, "Everyone knows he's a fruity boy – that's what Joel Ginnish tells us."

"That's not true," Hector said.

"But it is – it's what a dozen of yer Indians told me," Tanker said. "Yer a fruitie pie! – trying to fruit them all the time."

Tanker wished to make no more of this, except Bill Monk said, "Then he can drink no water of mine out of my bucket."

And Tanker shrugged and said, "Why is that?"

"Well, Hector is the big doctor – big medicine man – telling us all what to do! Ridiculing me for what I do! So I want no AIDS-ridden Indian slobbering over my water – not with that AIDS. I ain't drinkin' from the same bucket as a foul-mouth Indian," Bill said, his eyes mirthfully cold. He looked to the others and nodded, and they did too. Hector smiled clumsily and said only that none of that was true.

"That's right," Angus Peel said, in order to show his complicity, because he himself had never belonged to any- thing – and so it started. What was at first a joke became by 9:50 a matter of civic responsibility for these three wonderful men, and they kept taking turns to guard the buckets. Hector tried to go without, and tried to suck the liquid out of his gum, but by 10:30 he was unable to open his mouth.

As the morning wore on, and as the work increased, Bill took off his shirt and worked in a T-shirt, which showed his arms to be as taut as iron and his eyes as blue as steel. The smell of wood and human sweat permeated the hold.

"No man who sucks dick will get a drink out of my bucket," Brice heard above after Hector asked for water. Hector again said that was not true.

Brice Peel was ordered then to lower buckets only to one of the two Monk brothers.

"Maybe then youse the fruit," Hector said to Bill Monk, and this enraged him. Hector kept working, and kept trying to get to a bucket to get water, at first playfully, but as the morning became hotter his quest became more and more urgent. He said he would go up the ladder, but they told him climbing out was a dangerous thing when loads were coming

317

and he would never be allowed on another boat. And he needed to work them.

"Not only that, but no other Indian will get a union card – I'll see to it!" Bill Monk said.

So Brice, watching this, and trembling because his own father was caught up in this, said, "Just a minute, Hector."

He ran down the gangplank and searched in the yard near the scales for another bucket. There he heard his uncle George Morrissey say he had to take a piss, and for Roger to snap the next load after the backhoe came by. And there seemed to be no worry about it.

By now, the men believed their unjust behavior was somehow commendable and hilarious – and the three of them in the hold swore than Hector would not be allowed to drink if he had aids, and he as a "doctor" should understand that.

"You of all people should know," Bill Monk kept saying, "a medicine man like you is!"

By eleven that morning Hector could not spit, his mouth was so dry.

It was about eleven fifteen in the morning when Roger hooked, and it was then, as the load was lifted into the hold, that Hector realized his chance, because the men had all gone to the same side. He ran under the load to take a drink.

"Don't you let him, Tanker!" Bill said.

So Tanker determined he would not drink from his bucket tried to knock it from his mouth when he lifted it. He ran to that side, and in a careless moment swung the pry bar in his hand. His wide overhand swing missed the bucket entirely and hit Hector in the forehead, and the boy was dead before he hit the ground. Cigarettes he had offered everyone, and the gum, too, fell from his shirt pocket. He lay still as the load came down.

There was only a bit of blood and bruising on his forehead, and a bit of missing scalp.

It had all started as a joke, just an hour or two before.

The men ran to the load, unhooked the cable at about five

feet from the ground, and put the load over Hector. When they looked up into the sunlight above, they saw little Brice Peel with the third water bucket that he had gotten out of kindness looking down in resolute terror.

They yelled up that the load had dropped and the clamp was unhooked – they yelled there was a man under it, and for someone to come and help.

To their surprise and consternation they learned later that it was Roger Savage, denied a job that very morning, who was lurking around.

The pry bar was hidden in the bulwark under the cubby and, along with the *Lutheran*, was returned to the sea.

Markus sat for an hour, staring into nothing. Once in a while he would begin to shake, so terribly that the muscles in his legs would tremble. Then he would be very calm.

He looked again at the front of the envelope: *To be opened on my death. Brice Peel, water boy of the fourth hold in the* Lutheran *on June 19, 1985.*

2007

Sometimes during that long last winter, Markus would take Brice's envelope out and look at it. But he did not open it again.

At times when he went to his grandfather's house he would look at the pictures Amos had taken. Then it all became clear – the bucket damaged by the swing that Tanker had taken, the logs lying in one place, everything in order, and the gum from Hector's shirt, that he had so offered about, lying up against the bulwark almost unseen. The same gum Hector had offered him in the truck cab that morning.

There was a story he heard when he was a little boy, one his father David had told him. It was about a boy years ago working alone in the woods. He had got turned around, and had not eaten or drank in two days. And he stopped at an old Indian house near the barrens, and knocked on the door, and he asked for something, and the woman in the house said, "I am sorry – but I only have a glass of water."

Now, years later the woman was in hospital, and was unable to pay for her care. Her doctor happened to be Dr. Hennessey, who had paid his way through school by working in the woods years ago. He went to her chart late one night and he wrote across her bill: "Paid in full, with one glass of water."

Markus thought of that story, now and again, as the days got shorter, and colder, and the snow scattered between the buildings at the edge of this nowhere. Sometimes he would sit in the window to catch the sun.

Markus once again borrowed money – that was his problem – and bought a snowmobile, though he couldn't afford it. Sometimes he hunted coyotes up on the barrens as they came out just at dark. He could bring one down at 250 yards with a 22.250 that he had also borrowed the money to buy.

He went to a skidoo party and began to date a French girl from Neguac. They would go for pizza and have a beer or two. Twice in bed, he wanted to tell her what had happened so long ago. He had a duty to, he knew – and he would – soon. He would. He inquired about exhuming Hector's body and was told it was best to wait until the spring.

He went to Bill Monk's late one morning as Bill sat there entertaining one of his friends.

"Yes – what do you want?"

"Nothing much," Markus said, and he walked over to the sink and poured himself a nice cold glass of water, turning around to face Bill as he drank.

He listened to Bob Dylan a lot that winter.

He listened to Hank Williams.

He saw Roger's old girlfriend May in at the Kmart one evening. She worked there now, and was a rotund, greying-haired woman. He wanted to tell her about Roger's complete and heroic innocence, but did not. There would be no point.

One cold day in February of 2007 he went to the co-op and bought and wrapped a pry bar, and sent it to Tanker Monk.

The phone would ring and he would not answer it.

Heidi Doran sent him a Valentine's Day card.

Once he saw Sam Dulse in town and didn't even say hello.

Sometimes in the dark he would listen and listen, to nothing at all.

He decided he would get a court order to have Hector Penniac's body exhumed as soon as the weather got warm. They told him April 26 would be the best day. So he decided that was the day the case would be reopened, and he would hand the evidence over.

He inquired by email about the *Lutheran*, and a week later word came back, not from the Netherlands but from the retired captain who had been forwarded the message in Brisbane, Australia where he had retired. From him, who seemed a nice enough gentleman, Markus discovered the *Lutheran* had been dry-docked, not scuttled, and at last report was blocked and rudderless in a yard in Rotterdam.

If the pry bar had been hidden well enough, it just might still be there.

He decided he would go to the Netherlands in the spring before the body was exhumed. He told his commanding officer this one day, out of the blue.

He thought how truth had now snapped those chains that had once seemed impossible to break.

He visited his father's grave, for the first time.

Then one morning, in a freezing March snowstorm, Markus woke to a call from the office. "Get over here. Someone's in the cell," the boyish constable said.

Markus got up and dressed. He knew from experience that it was probably an Indian in the cell. And it was his duty to go. Well, it was his duty to go anyway, First Nation or not. He put the pistol toward the back of his right hip, by habit.

He arrived at ten and went in through the side door. There was loud talk when he entered and then a kind of mirthful silence. Back behind the front office, a corridor led to the metal stairs where the footfall sounded heavy, and beyond the grey-coloured heavy metal door were the six cells, which were more often than not occupied by drunks and small-time thieves.

He walked right past her. He thought the constable had pointed to the fifth cell. She was in the fourth. She was handcuffed to the bed – but was lying on the cement floor, almost naked. Her long, greying hair fell down her back. They had taken her false teeth out, and her bra was lying in the far corner.

He stared at her a brief moment. She was still beautiful.

"Why is she only in panties?"

"Didn't want her to injure herself," the young constable said, chewing gum.

"You had to take her bra?"

"Didn't want her to injure – "

"Where did you arrest her?"

"Neguac – in a fight at the bar. It's always something with her. This time she said it was her brother's birthday. Who knows? She was pumped full of ecstasy."

She was shivering and had pissed the floor.

"Do you know her father is a member of the Assembly of First Nations and a recent recipient of the Order of Canada – Isaac Snow – and one of the great men on this river?"

"Well," the young constable said, snapping gum and frowning, "just goes to show. Do you want to go in?"

"Sky," Markus whispered, not staring at her nakedness. "Sky."

Sky turned, made a lunge at the air – her brilliant eyes flashing.

"Fuck you," she said.

Acknowledgements

Thanks to Philip Lee; my first reader, Liz Lemon-Mitchell; my agent, Anne McDermid; my editors, Maya Mavjee and Lynn Henry; my wife, Peg, and my children, John and Anton.